RESTITUTION

RESTITUTION

BOOK TWO IN THE RECUSAL SERIES

Donald Catalano

coffeetownpress

Kenmore, WA

A Coffeetown Press book published by Epicenter Press

Epicenter Press
6524 NE 181st St.
Suite 2
Kenmore, WA 98028

For more information go to:
www.Camelpress.com
www.Coffeetownpress.com
www.Epicenterpress.com
www.donaldcatalano-author.com

This is a work of fiction. Names, characters, places, brands, media, and incidents are either the product of the author's imagination or are used fictitiously.

Cover design by Scott Book
Design by Melissa Vail Coffman

Restitution
Copyright © 2021 by Donald Catalano

ISBN: 978-1-94207-848-7 (Trade Paper)
ISBN: 978-1-94207-849-4 (eBook)

Printed in the United States of America

*To those who continually strive
for social justice and equality.*

ACKNOWLEDGMENTS

MANY THANKS TO MY LITERARY AGENT, Barbara Hogenson. Much appreciation to my publishers, Phil Garrett and Jennifer McCord. Thank you for your support and faith in me. Love and gratitude to my friend, Wendy Kachingwe, whose laughter and joy allows me to always see the light even in the darkest moments.

CHAPTER 1

THE WARM EARLY SUMMER BREEZE SWEPT the distinctive fragrance of the Southern Magnolia tree blossoms through the open doors of the old church. The parishioners seemed to sigh in contented unison from the olfactory delight. Nature's perfumed essence swirled from the front door to the flag draped alter of Citadel Square Baptist Church in Charleston, South Carolina on that early Sunday afternoon in late June.

"Do you smell that fragrance?" Senator Perry Douglas asked the assemblage. "That sweet pungent aroma wafting from the large creamy white magnolia blossoms? Henry would talk for hours about that smell. About those trees. But then again, Henry would talk for hours about pretty much anything and everything. Those of us who were fortunate enough to call Henry our friend, knew that when Henry was not in Washington tending to and protecting the nation's delicate garden of freedom and equality, he was here in Charleston, planting and tending to his beloved trees and garden. You see, Henry was an arborist by desire, and a United States Senator by devotion. He would have been perfectly contented to place his spade deep into the rich soil and plant a tree. But had Henry chosen to stay in South Carolina and tend to his oak, palmetto, and magnolia trees, this nation would have been deprived of the true artistry of one of its most prominent and exceptionally talented gardeners." Senator Douglas paused for a moment as the hushed congregation listened intently for his next words.

"There is an enormous Angel Oak tree not far from here on Johns Island. The Angel Oak is well over 400 years old. Henry took me to see it several years ago. I was amazed by its size and majesty. Henry loved that tree. It was older than our Constitution, and much like our democracy, it has survived some very hard and trying times. But its roots run deep and it is anchored in rich soil. My friend Henry, through his many decades in the United States Senate, has done a magnificent job in making sure that our democracy will endure and thrive as long and as well as that large Angel Oak. So, today is not a day of mourning. It is a day of celebration. As most of you know, besides his love of trees and his lust for the fight for equality, Henry also enjoyed an excellent glass of bourbon, from time to time. Therefore, there is a bottle of aged Elijah Craig bourbon and a crystal whiskey glass that sits atop Henry's flag draped casket. Henry would not want to leave this world without it. So, later today, after we say our final goodbyes to Senator Henry Fitzsimmons, please raise a glass and celebrate Henry's life. The last thing a man of that much joy would want is to see his friends in sorrow. So please join me in saluting a damn good arborist, a truly unique and exceptional United States Senator, and a wonderful and joyful friend. Cheers Henry, we love you."

The crowd began to filter out of the church into the bright light of the warm day. Katherine Douglas took her husband by the arm as they waited for the casket to be loaded into the hearse. Joining Perry and Katherine Douglas on the sidewalk in front of the church were Aaron Rose and Clay Grover. Perry vigorously and warmly shook Clay's hand. Clay had served Henry Fitzsimmons very well for two years as a Senate aide and then for five years as his Chief of Staff. Perry took his own Senate aide, Aaron Rose, into his arms and hugged him firmly and deeply.

"Did you see Justice Winchester attending the funeral services for Henry?" Perry Douglas asked Clay and Aaron. "It's hard to believe that it's been two years since Stanford Winchester withdrew his name from nomination for the Supreme Court. So much has happened since then."

"Yes," Clay replied. "Prior to the service, Justice Winchester sought me out and personally offered me his sincere condolences. Though it was but a brief meeting on the day Senator Fitzsimmons suffered his fall during the Senate Judiciary Committee hearings vetting his nomination, Justice Winchester remembered that I was the Senator's Chief of Staff. He could not have been more polite and earnest. He told me that he considered Senator Fitzsimmons a true American hero and someone he had endless admiration for over the past decades. I have to admit, I was a bit taken aback by the authenticity and kindness of his words and manner."

"Stanford Winchester is a gentleman in every sense of the word," Perry Douglas added. "I may not agree with his political philosophy but it is difficult not to respect the way the man carries himself and acts the way he does."

"Indeed," Aaron quietly intoned.

"THE PRESIDENT WILL SEE YOU NOW," President Andrew Cochran's secretary, Nancy stated to FBI Director James Turner as he patiently waited to see the President. Director Turner took a deep breath and slowly exhaled as he entered the Oval Office.

"Jim, good to see you," the President greeted, as he stood and walked to the front of the Resolute Desk, in order to shake hands with the Director. "Please have a seat, make yourself comfortable."

"Thank you, Mr. President," James Turner responded as he extended his hand to the leader of the free world.

"My Chief of Staff informed me that you wanted to have a word with me. What can I do for you?" Andrew Cochran pleasantly asked.

"Well sir, I wanted to personally inform you about something that we've been monitoring at the FBI. I thought you should know, now that we have confirmed the origins of some messaging."

"Sure, what is it?"

"For several months, not long after your nomination and appointment of our new Supreme Court Justice, there has been a substantial uptick in activity across several Internet websites and social media," Director Turner began. "At first it appeared to be just your normal grousing about politics that is always present. But then the messaging turned much darker and threatening. The usual political discourse was pretty much contained to the common social media outlets, but this disturbing messaging was becoming more apparent on 4chan."

"Did you say Fortran? Isn't that just computer programming language?" The President inquired.

"Yes, it is, sir. I mentioned 4chan. It is an anonymous English-language image board website. It is a hub for the Internet subculture. Various groups participate on the website, including radical groups, leftists, the far-right, anarchists, white supremacists, and religious extremists and alike," James Turner explained. "There has been one group, one thread of dialogue that has become particularly disturbing. Unfortunately, sir, it concerns you and your Supreme Court choice."

"OK, you've got my attention," Andrew Cochran replied.

"There is a far-right group that attempts to cloak itself in righteous religious fervor. They call themselves the 'Killers for Christ.' They believe that they are called by God to bring physical violence and death to those who aid and abet abortion. In the past, they have been linked to the bombing of abortion clinics and the murder of abortion providers. Since your nomination of Justice Carruthers to the Court, the vitriol and threats on 4chan have substantially increased, including calls for your assassination. There are no specific threats that appear plausible or actionable, yet I thought I should bring this to your attention," FBI Director Turner stated.

"I appreciate that Jim. Justice Carruthers is hardly pro-abortion. He is a moderate jurist who intends to keep an open mind on all matters before the Court. Have you informed him of these threats?"

"With your permission, that is my next step, sir. I wanted to speak with you first."

"Yes, thank you," the President responded. "Let's make sure we ensure Justice Carruthers safety. I've got a fairly robust Secret Service detail, so I'm not concerned about my well-being. I appreciate you taking time out of your duties to stop by and discuss this with me, Jim."

"Of course, Mr. President."

"Mama, it's time I start a new life and make a career for myself. I can't just sit here in Savannah feelin' sorry for myself," Posy Whitaker stated to her mother, Charlotte Branch.

"Well, if you want a job, your Uncle Delmar said he'd make you an assistant manager down at his Dollar Store," Charlotte replied to her daughter.

"No, mama, I need to make a fresh start, in a new city with a business of my own. And I need to get rid of Nathan's name and go back to my maiden name. I always liked Posy Branch, got a nice ring to it," Posy stated with a wry smile.

"Well, I certainly agree about getting rid of Nathan's name. I ain't sure why you didn't change your name right away when you divorced that no account scoundrel last year," Charlotte responded.

"Heck, I don't know. Everything was changing so quickly I wasn't ready to give up all of my past at once. But I sure am ready now," Posy declared.

"Well, that's fine to hear. You should have your proper name back. The name you was born with, that I wholly agree. But what's the rush to move out of your hometown? You're a lovely woman Posy. There's plenty of eligible bachelors in Savannah that would fall all over themselves to be with such an attractive woman in her prime," Charlotte pronounced with pride.

"I just feel like I need a fresh start somewhere new, Mama. I need to prove that I can stand on my own. After almost fourteen years with Nathan, I want to be my own person. Start something different. Here in Savannah, I'd always be pretty little Posy, Charlotte Branch's beauty-queen daughter. In a new city, I can be who I make myself to be. When I was living in Washington, I was seen as the pretty, but stupid gal on Nathan Whitaker's arm. I wasn't allowed to express my own ideas. And instead of working to change that impression, I let people believe that I was just a pretty airhead. Nathan would parade me around like some show horse, but I wasn't allowed to speak to the important folk. I could have stood up to them and Nathan, but I didn't. As a result, it made me mean. It made me resentful. Sometimes I'd act up just to be spiteful. That wasn't me, you know that in your heart. I allowed my husband to define who I was and who I wasn't. I'm done with all of that now. I want to show folks the real Posy Branch. I need to demonstrate what I'm capable of being professionally and personally. In a new city, there will be no man that charts my future. No one to tell me how to act and what to say or not say. I get the opportunity to write my story on a blank slate. Fortunately, there was a pretty nice hunk of cash that I got from my divorce from Nathan, that the prosecutor didn't freeze, so I got a good cushion to start a new life with wherever I go," Posy explained.

"Well, think it through Sugar, don't make no rash decisions," Charlotte Branch cautioned her daughter.

"Mama, I've been living here with you in Savannah for over a year, I think we can count out me doing something rash at this point," Posy kidded her mother with a smile.

"Do you have a place in mind that you want to make this new start in?" Charlotte questioned.

"I need to think on it a tad more, but yeah, I think so," Posy replied.

"And where would that be?" Charlotte inquired.

"I think I want to move to New Orleans," Posy declared. "I think I'd fit in real nice in the Big Easy."

PRESIDENT ANDREW COCHRAN SAT AT HIS DESK in his private office in the White House residence. The late afternoon light illuminated the room, as the President sipped at a glass of bourbon while he wrote in long hand.

"It's Sunday, Andy. I hope that is not work that you've brought upstairs," Sue Lynn Cochran admonished her husband.

"No, it's not work," Andrew replied to his wife. "I'm writing a condolence letter to Corrine Fitzsimmons, the widow of Senator Henry Fitzsimmons. After five decades of service to his country, I felt that Mrs. Fitzsimmons deserved a hand-written letter of condolence from her President. I must admit watching Corrine Fitzsimmons standing at the side of her husband's casket as he lay in state in the Capitol rotunda for all those long hours truly touched me. Speaking with her, reminded me so much of my Grandma Blanche. A strong, devoted Southern woman who would not leave the side of her husband. I was proud to participate in the tributes and ceremonies here in Washington, but thought it best to let the Senator's family and friends have their private moments at the funeral in Charleston. Today was Senator Fitzsimmons burial, so I was moved to write his widow a letter."

"That's lovely Andy, what a thoughtful gesture," Sue Lynn stated as she began to gently rub the back of her husband's neck with her open hands.

"Well, things won't be this friendly and collegial for very long. We are entering yet another election season, and by this fall, the inflamed rhetoric and rancor are sure to elevate. No doubt my right-wing challengers in next year's primaries will view my writing a condolence letter to the widow of a revered Democratic Senator as aiding and abetting the enemy. They already are portraying my appointment of a moderate justice to the Supreme Court, and my occasional compromises with the Democratic Senate to actually get things accomplished for the American people as high crimes and misdemeanors," Andrew Cochran stated with a smirk.

"For one, I think it is a kind and generous gesture and only shows what a compassionate and caring man inhabits the White House," Sue Lynn replied.

"Thank you darling, there's one vote for re-election. Now if we can convince about 68 million of your fellow citizens of that fact, we might have a chance," Andrew laughed as he took a long slow sip of bourbon from his crystal glass.

Stanford Winchester stood silently as he watched the pallbearers remove Henry Fitzsimmons casket from the hearse and slowly walk in unison to the Senator's final resting place under a large shady oak tree. Attired in a black suit with white shirt and black and gray bow tie, he gently patted his left suit coat pocket which contained a small photograph of his deceased wife LeeAnn. It had been almost seven years to the day when he grieved at a cemetery in New Orleans. Stanford Winchester was all too familiar with devastating loss and bone-deep grief and sorrow. He attentively watched as Corrine Fitzsimmons stoically stood at the graveside of her devoted husband, whom she had spent over fifty-five years of her life committed and married to. The memories of his own long and loving marriage brought a tear to Stanford's eyes.

Stanford Winchester was not a close friend of Senator Henry Fitzsimmons. In fact, the only times he had much interaction with the Senator was when he was being vetted by the Senate Judiciary Committee for appointments to the Federal bench and the Supreme Court. However, so deep and unfailing was his respect and admiration for Senator Fitzsimmons that he felt compelled to travel from New Orleans to Charleston to attend his funeral.

After the internment ceremonies had completed, Stanford Winchester patiently waited his turn to offer his personal condolences to the widow of Henry Fitzsimmons.

"Mrs. Fitzsimmons, my name is Stanford Winchester," he quietly began. "I am a great admirer of Senator Fitzsimmons. I am also a humbled man, who your husband was able to teach some valuable lessons to at my advanced age. Senator Fitzsimmons gave me a much-needed perspective on judicial conduct. As he has given greatly to the people of his state and this nation. I have devoted my career to justice and equality, and those two American principles had no greater defender and protector than Senator Fitzsimmons. His career and service to his country are in a word, remarkable. A true American patriot. I am so very sorry for your loss, but eternally grateful for the countless contributions of a great American Senator."

"Thank you very much for your kind words, Justice Winchester," Corrine Fitzsimmons replied. "I know who you are. Henry told me much about your generosity of spirit and your dignity and grace, sir, upon the conclusion of the Senate Judiciary Committee proceedings. Henry had very high regard for you, for the way that you acquitted yourself during very trying times. It's a pity that the two of you never had the opportunity to develop a friendship with one another."

"Oh, but we did, in our own way, Mrs. Fitzsimmons," Stanford stated with a slight smile. "We surely did."

A day later, Stanford Winchester sat on the balcony of his home overlooking Royal Street in New Orleans' French Quarter. He gently rocked back and forth as he thought about the funeral for Senator Henry Fitzsimmons that he had just attended in Charleston. What a fine send off, he thought to himself. Stanford felt a true kinship with Henry Fitzsimmons even though they weren't more than passing acquaintances on opposite sides of the political fence. He admired the way Henry Fitzsimmons handled himself publicly. He was a Southern gentleman, who seldom raised his voice or showed his ire in public discourse. Stanford was pleased that he had taken the time and made the effort to attend the small private burial in Charleston, instead of attending the far more planned and far less personal public ceremonies in Washington. Besides, Stanford had had enough of Washington. It was not a place he chose to be situated in. He delighted in the easy pace and carefree attitude of New Orleans.

CLAY GROVER STARED OUT THE WINDOW of the commercial jet headed to Washington, D.C. from Charleston. Aaron Rose quietly thumbed through a magazine as the flight reached cruising altitude. Aaron knew that he needed to give Clay his space and time. The death of his mentor, protector and friend had taken a toll on Clay's psyche. Gone temporarily was that Southern wit and charm and Clay's infectious zeal for life. Instead a dour and confused Clay had a short temper and a sullen disposition. Clay continued to vacantly stare out the window while barely moving a muscle or saying a word.

"You OK?" Aaron asked softly while gently nudging Clay's shoulder.

"Yeah, sure," Clay replied. "Just lost in my thoughts."

"You'll feel better once we get back home," Aaron offered.

"Washington is not my home," Clay stated matter-of-factly. "It's cold and isolating. It's a hostile place where politics has become a blood sport and compromise is viewed as an evil concept. If you are not in government or a lawyer or lobbyist, you don't exist in that city. I'm no longer anyone's Chief of Staff, and frankly I don't think that I have the desire to be one again. There will never be another Henry Fitzsimmons. No one that would make you proud and happy to go to work every morning. It's time to get out of Washington while I still have a modicum of conscience and morality left in me."

"The shock of Senator Fitzsimmons death is still so fresh to you. You need some time to recover emotionally," Aaron stated.

"No, that's not it. I've been done with that town for the past two years. Pretty much since the Winchester Judiciary Committee hearings and everything that transpired afterwards. The last couple of years I've just been going through the motions, but my heart hasn't been in it. And as Senator Fitzsimmons' health began to fail and he spent far less time in the office, I lost my joy for that job. Now, that he is gone, what is left?" Clay asked, his voice full of melancholy and sadness.

"Give it a few days. There's no need to make any decisions now," Aaron sympathetically advised.

"True. But my mind is made up. I need to do something that I will be proud of again. Without Senator Fitzsimmons, there is nothing left for me in that city. Time to move on. Time to move on," Clay softly repeated as the plane began its descent towards Reagan International Airport.

"I KNOW BESSIE, I KNOW," Lucius softly said to his wife as she violently woke up for yet another night from yet another vivid dream. "It ain't easy trying to make any kind of sense of it. But you can't live your life based on some dream about your aunties' death."

"Her suicide haunts me to this day. It was two years ago," Bessie confessed. "Sometimes in the dreams I see myself working in her shop, providing people comfort for the loving souls that they have lost. I ain't sure what to make of it. I don't know what I should do."

"I don't understand why you'd give up your job at the dress shop that you enjoy, to go run that rickety old voodoo shop that your Auntie Rita owned? You was never into spirits and such," Lucius responded to his wife.

"That was before the spirits began coming to me and talking to me every night in my dreams," Bessie replied forcefully. "They tell me that I can help people by easing their pain. That shop and my auntie gave comfort and hope to folks seeking answers."

"And that shop and what went on there also lent itself to some dark magic that caused a lot of harm to folks," Lucius countered.

"I know my Auntie Rita talked about serving with both hands and practiced both the light and dark magic of Haitian voodoo, but that ain't what I would do," Bessie offered. "First off, I don't know nothin' about it. I would just sell the books, and amulets, and charms that give people some hope and happiness. I'd learn up about doing some spiritual readings and the such. I'd only bring positive energy to folks. Auntie Rita left that shop to me. I ain't done nothing with it for two years. And for goin' on two years I've had dreams telling me about the good I could do for folks by re-opening that shop. Maybe, iffin' I do this, the dreams will finally end."

"Bessie, you is my wife, and I will love you until my last breath, you know this to be true. But I don't understand what good can come from getting involved in that voodoo world. It ain't fittin' for a proper church-goin' woman like yourself," Lucius replied.

"I don't know, Lucius. I feel like I'm being pushed in a direction and being convinced by these dreams that I can make a positive difference in the lives of folks. Ain't nothing more Christian than that," Bessie said as she gently rubbed the crucifix hanging around her graceful neck.

A SMALL GROUP OF THREE PEOPLE strode through the large open commercial space located on East Randolph Street in Chicago.

"Steps from City Hall to the west and Michigan Avenue to the east," Molly said as she gave her client a tour of the vacant ground floor space. "For a property of this size and location, the rental price is pretty reasonable."

"Yes, a few private offices against the back wall and all of this open space for staffers and volunteers, I think this could work rather nicely," Carolyn Barnes confirmed to the realtor. "Let's put in a two-year offer, Molly. This space should be just fine. As you said, you can't beat the location."

"Great, I'll give the landlord a quick call," Molly replied as she glanced down at her smartphone and wandered towards the back of the commercial space.

Carolyn also scanned the text messages and emails on her phone. Twenty-six un-responded-to messages in just the last thirty minutes. Such is the life of the campaign manager for one of the most prominent Democratic Senators in Washington, and one of the leading candidates for the Democratic nomination for President of the United States.

Four years prior, she had joined Perry Douglas' Senate campaign staff as communications director. Born in the Hyde Park neighborhood of Chicago, a graduate from the University of Chicago Law School, with a master's degree in Political Science from Loyola University, Carolyn Barnes had cut her teeth on presidential politics as a local campaign staffer working ten years ago to elect the first African-American to the White House. On a mild early November election night in Grant Park, she sobbed with joy as her passionate dream came to fruition. The daughter of one of former Chicago Mayor Harold Washington's top staff aides, Carolyn grew up in the world of politics. Now, an attractive, forty-five-year-old African-American woman, she prepared herself for an even larger role in the presidential campaign of Senator Perry Douglas. She had risen in four short years from communications director for the Douglas Senate campaign to campaign manager and chief strategist for the Senator's presidential bid, and she was ready to accept this greater challenge.

"All set," Molly stated. "The landlord is emailing the rental agreement for signature. The space will be yours."

"Excellent," Carolyn replied. "This place is perfect for the national headquarters of the Douglas Presidential Campaign."

AARON ROSE AND CLAY GROVER sat in Clay's D.C. apartment recounting the events of the last several days.

"As I mentioned to you the other day, I'm through with this city," Clay forcefully reminded Aaron.

"Yeah, I guess I get it," Aaron responded. "Now, that Senator Douglas is running for President, I barely see him in Washington. He offered me a position on his campaign staff, but I just don't have the stomach for two years of presidential politics. Not after everything that has transpired since the Winchester nomination hearings."

"So, let's get out of Dodge. Let's start something different," Clay announced.

"Doing what?" Aaron questioned.

"I've got an old friend from Duke Law that is running a public service legal practice in New Orleans. They assist lower income folks from the Ninth Ward in processing claims from Katrina and other civil rights work as well. He's looking for a couple of young attorneys to help build his practice. How about we go do some good deeds, help the underserved in New Orleans, and actually put our law degrees to work?" Clay asked energetically.

"Really?" Aaron replied with a smile on his attractive face.

"Let's talk to my friend on the phone, and you can ask him some questions and see what you think," Clay responded.

"Hmm, you and me practicing law in New Orleans, that could be interesting, and more rewarding than remaining in Washington politics," Aaron stated affirmatively.

"You've said before that we make a good team," Clay replied.

"We sure do," Aaron confirmed.

"Which is why I want to marry you, Aaron Rose," Clay said quietly, his voice low and full of conviction.

"Truly, Clay?" Aaron questioned, his eyes filled with tears as his voice trembled.

"Truly, Aaron," Clay stated as he took his love into his arms and gave him a deep passionate kiss.

Sunset and sunrise passed before the two friends, the two colleagues, the two lovers ended their joyous, devoted, and rapturous embrace.

CHAPTER 2

ALMOST THREE MONTHS TO THE DAY that Clay Grover proposed marriage to Aaron Rose, the two stood under a large maple tree on Promontory Point in the Hyde Park neighborhood of Chicago. The mid-September sun bathed Lake Michigan as the skyline of downtown Chicago shimmered in the far distance across the tranquil waters. About fifty assembled guests took their seats as the commitment ceremony was about to commence. Both Clay and Aaron were nattily attired in light colored tan suits. Both smiled ear-to-ear as they surveyed the beautiful surroundings and the gathering of their friends and family to celebrate their life-long commitment to one another in the state of marriage. It was not lost on either of them the vast number of years that the LGBTQ community fought for the right to marry. Now, they were prepared to share the same legal status, benefits, and obligations of their fellow citizens.

Perry and Katherine Douglas held hands as they patiently waited for the wedding ceremony to commence.

"I wonder if we will ever experience this with Robert?" Katherine Douglas inquired of her husband referring to their twenty-eight-year-old son.

"Don't you think that Robert will ever get married?" Perry asked with some surprise.

"I'm not sure," Katherine replied. "I don't think that all gay men feel the need for a formal commitment ceremony. I'm not so sure that Robert is the marrying kind."

"Well, firstly, we are not even sure that Robert is gay? He's never officially come out to either of us," Perry whispered to his wife.

"Oh, Perry, please," Katherine stated with an askance glance. "Robert doesn't need to tell us he's gay in order for us to figure it out. He's twenty-eight years old, he has never brought a girl home to meet us, let alone even mentioned the name of a girl he's dating. He lives with a male 'friend' in Chicago's Boystown neighborhood, whom he brings to our home for Christmas. Robert attended art school at the Art Institute of Chicago and he is now the art curator for a fashionable art gallery in the River North neighborhood. Other than wearing a large sign that reads, 'Mom and Dad, I'm gay!,' I'm not sure what else you need for proof."

"Then why doesn't he just say so? Why not tell your loving and supportive parents?" Perry queried.

"Do you expect black people to tell you that they're black?" Katherine sarcastically questioned. "Robert knows that we love him and support him. He is living his life openly in front of us, which is how comfortable he feels in himself and in his relationship with us and with his sister Eleanore. If you asked him if he was gay, I have no doubt he would not hesitate for a minute and tell you 'yes.' So, very possibly he doesn't feel the need to vocally state what should be and is obvious to those who know him best."

"I must admit that a couple of years ago when I was playing Cupid to Aaron and Clay by sending them on a trip to New Orleans together, in the back of my mind, I was thinking about Robert and his happiness. And, of course, wise old Henry, called me on it. He saw what I was doing. Now, I couldn't be happier to be sitting here at their wedding ceremony," Perry confessed to his wife.

"You're a good man, Perry Douglas. You treat people equally and your only measure is the goodness of their hearts and their acts of kindness and respect. You are a wonderful husband, a loving and devoted father, and you will make for an excellent President of the United States," Katherine stated as she squeezed Perry's hand with her own.

"Henry always said I married far above my rank. He was a smart man," Perry offered.

The branches of the large maple tree swayed with celebratory joy in the fall breeze as the wedding ceremony began on the grassy shore of Lake Michigan.

POSY BRANCH ENTERED HER MOTHER'S HOUSE in Savannah with a big smile on her face and a bounce in her step.

"Mama, it's official. I'm done with being Posy Whitaker, I'm now back to being Posy Branch, and I could not be happier!" Posy exclaimed like a young school girl.

"Well, it's about time," Charlotte Branch replied. "You don't want to carry that murderous liar's name around like some scarlet letter for all time."

"No ma'am, I surely don't. Now that I've taken my name back, it's time to move on with my life. I'm going to a new city to start a new career," Posy stated confidently.

"I reckon you got to do what you think is best for yourself, but I'm gonna miss you girl. It was nice having you around for the last year," Charlotte said with a hint of melancholy in her voice.

"I know, Mama, I'm going to miss you too. But I got some divorce money to make a new start of things, and to put Nathan and the last fourteen years behind me. I'm headed to New Orleans and I'm just gonna let the good times roll," Posy stated grinning and giggling.

STANFORD WINCHESTER BECKONED TO HIS SECRETARY Naomi Cutler from his office in the Federal Courthouse in New Orleans.

"Yes sir," Naomi responded as she entered the Chief Judge's office.

"Naomi, thank you for coming in on a Saturday. It's been so busy around here lately, it's hard to find enough time to deal with all of the organizational details," Stanford Winchester stated.

"My pleasure, sir. With Virgil laid up for a while, I'm grateful for the overtime," Naomi replied.

"Well, thank you all the same," Stanford reiterated. "What I wanted to get organized were some upcoming dates for the court. Earlier this month, we had the lottery for assigning cases to the Fifth Circuit judges for the last quarter of this year. There are a couple of matters we need to add to my calendar," Stanford Winchester continued. "As you know from the news, the Federal trial court issued its ruling in the Hurricane Katrina victims class action lawsuit against FEMA, the Bush administration, and the local government authorities a couple of months ago. Hundreds of the New Orleans flood victims sued the Federal and State authorities for restitution and damages. After several years of litigation they won their suit. Well, that case has now landed in the Fifth Circuit on appeal. By a blind lottery, I've been assigned to that case. Judge Charles Sewell and Judge Whitlee Hammond will round out the panel. This is going to be a very high-profile case, so we need to make sure we get it on my calendar and move some things aside if need be."

"Yes sir, I'll get it docketed on your calendar and I'll speak with the clerks first thing Monday morning," Naomi replied.

"Excellent, thank you kindly. You're the one that keeps this courthouse in order, Naomi. Beside every good man is a great woman," Stanford stated.

"Well, I appreciate the kind words, but it simply ain't true. The Fifth Circuit ain't nothing' without Stanford Winchester," Naomi countered.

"Alright Naomi, I'm gonna let you have the last word. My mama didn't raise no fool," Stanford said with a hearty laugh and a big smile.

PRESIDENT COCHRAN'S CHIEF OF STAFF, SAMUEL Brainard entered the Oval Office in the White House carrying a small stack of files.

"Good afternoon Mr. President," Samuel stated.

"Oh hell, Sam, you don't need to be so formal on a weekend. You can call me Andy, it's just you and me," Andrew Cochran replied.

"Yes sir, I mean Andy," Sam responded.

"Did you see Cletus Sawyer on CNN this morning calling me a traitor to the Republican Party?" Andrew Cochran asked his Chief of Staff.

"Yes sir, it was disgraceful. Senator Sawyer is the traitor for referring to a sitting President and the leader of his party in those despicable terms," Sam replied.

"After the whole ordeal and scandal involving Nathan, there were still some in the party who thought I went too far to accommodate the Democrats in the Senate. After Winchester withdrew his name from nomination to the Supreme Court, and with scandal about to upend my administration, I had little choice but to put forth a moderate jurist for the Supreme Court. Someone who would get some support from the Democrats. My nominee was not vehemently pro-life, which has led many of my former Evangelical supporters to claim I was doing Satan's bidding. And, of course, there are the party firebrands, like Cletus, who thought that I had wholly capitulated to the Democrats. Compromise, reason and practicality are lost on them," Andrew Cochran stated while shaking his head.

"The Tea Party caucus wasn't exactly thrilled that you selected me as Chief of Staff to replace Nathan Whitaker either. I've been called a squish and a Republican in name only more times than I can keep track of," Sam added with a smile.

"They're coming after me in the primaries. They refuse to have a President who considers compromising with the Democrats from time to time to get things accomplished for the betterment of the American people.

This party is at a crossroads, and we will let the Republican primary voters determine what direction we are going in," Andrew Cochran defiantly said.

"I'm ready for a battle," Sam added with emphasis.

"And what about Howard, does he really have our backs?" The President asked.

"Yes, I think the Vice-President is with us. After all, it's his re-election as well," Sam offered.

"Howard Mason doesn't give one flip about being Vice-President. He is merely waiting his turn. Face it, Sam, with Howard and I, it was always a marriage of political convenience and nothing more," Andrew Cochran confessed. "A shotgun marriage of electoral college expediency at that, mostly arranged by Nathan Whitaker and Howard's people. We were never friends and we still aren't to any great degree. Howard was a popular Republican Senator from Ohio. I needed to win Ohio in order to become President. It was simple math. When the shit hit the fan right after the indictment of my former Chief-of-Staff, where was Howard? Defending the Presidency to the media? Lending moral support to me? No, he was off on an economic summit in Europe, followed by a week in Thailand for God knows what reason, other than to remove himself from the stench of scandal."

"There is certainly truth to that, sir, but Howard Mason is not a firebrand like Cletus Sawyer. There is no love between the two of them either," Sam pointed out.

"Perhaps not, but Howard is a political opportunist. He would be very happy to see Cletus and I tear each other apart and then surface from the shadows as the party's compromise candidate after the blood and guts are removed from the political battlefield. The simple truth Sam, is that I am the only thing that stands in the way of Howard Mason becoming President of the United States. That doesn't make me an ally, that makes me an impediment."

"Point well taken, sir."

"What's on the agenda this week, Sam, where can I make some political points with what's left of my Republican support?"

"There's the National Prayer Breakfast, sir. A few remarks about your zealous position protecting faith and religious freedoms might smooth over some of the ruffled feathers," Sam responded.

"Excellent! That's the perfect forum. I've got a few comments I've been drafting for an opportunity to try to quell the Evangelical uprising against me for not putting a strict anti-abortionist up for the Court."

"I'M READY FOR A DRINK," Clay Grover stated as he stood near a bar in the Ratner Reception Gallery of the Smart Museum of Art located on the campus of the University of Chicago.

"Well then, by all means," Ben Carroll said as he accompanied his friend to the bar.

"I'm so glad you were able to come to our wedding," Clay said as he raised his glass to Ben.

"Wouldn't miss it for the world," Ben replied.

"I must admit I feel a little like an orphan here in the midst of all of Aaron's family and friends," Clay confided to Ben. "My mom died last year, and my father and brother refused to come to Chicago to acknowledge my marriage to a bi-racial man. Conversely, there's Aaron's Jewish mother Sarah fawning all over her gorgeous boy, and Aaron's four siblings who couldn't be more loving and accepting of their gay brother. And over in the corner," Clay said while gesturing to a corner of the room, "Aaron's proud African-American father Richard is chatting with Senator Douglas, Aaron's devoted mentor. It is inspiring and so heartwarming to see how my amazing husband is surrounded by such a welcoming and loving family and group of friends."

"They're all your family and friends now," Ben pointed out between sips of his cocktail. "I saw how lovingly Aaron's mom brushed your blonde hair out of your eyes and straightened your tie before the ceremony. She adores you and sees you as just another one of her sons now."

"Truly, and I am blessed," Clay professed. "It just would have been nice to have a few members of my family here to be a part of this."

"We're brothers. Have been for seven years now," Ben reminded Clay.

"Yes, we are, and I love you for reminding me of that fact," Clay said as he put his arm around his friend's shoulder. Moments later, Perry Douglas walked over to the bar where Ben and Clay were speaking.

"Congratulations Clay," Senator Perry said as he extended his hand to shake Clay's.

"Thank you Senator," Clay replied.

"I am going to miss having Aaron around to keep me organized and on time, but I couldn't be happier for the two of you. It's wonderful that the two of you will be doing public aid work in New Orleans."

"Well, thank you, sir. I can tell you that Aaron will miss you very much as well. He came home and cried the day he told you he was leaving your staff. He has such high regard and affection for you, Senator."

"As I do for him, and for you as well, Clay. Senator Fitzsimmons would be so very proud of you today. There was not a day when Henry would not praise your work, your loyalty to him, and your attentive support. He thought the world of you, and I only wish that he could have been here, at your wedding to Aaron, to tell you that himself. But know this, Clay, Henry greatly admired the man he watched you become working with him for all those years. He loved and respected you, and he considered you as part of his family," Perry Douglas said with full conviction in his voice.

"Thank you Senator," Clay replied softly, his head bowed and a tear rolling down his cheek.

From across the room, Clay could hear Aaron calling, "Where's my husband?"

"I'm right here, my love, I'm right here."

CHAPTER 3

BESSIE COLLINS UNLOCKED THE DOOR of the small voodoo shop located on North Rampart Street in the French Quarter of New Orleans. It had been well over a year since Bessie had set foot inside the store. Dust and cobwebs greeted her entrance back into the space where she had spent a good portion of her adult life visiting with her Auntie Rita. Bessie turned on the lights as she began to take mental inventory of the shop that was now hers. She turned as she heard a gentle knock on the front door.

"You in there, Miss Bessie?" the voice called from beyond the doorway.

"Yes, please come in," Bessie beckoned.

"It's so nice to see you again," Bessie greeted her Auntie Rita's long standing and devoted friend Papa Levi.

"Been too long," Papa Levi responded as he slowly ambled towards Bessie and took her into his weather-worn arms for a long squeeze.

"Almost two years now," Bessie confirmed. "The last time I saw you and Auntie Rita's friends was not long after her burial. It was such a sad time."

"Surely, it was. But time moves on and eventually comes for all of us," Papa Levi replied. "I was so surprised and delighted when you called me to tell me that you was thinkin' of reopening this here shop."

"Well, I've been thinking on it for a good spell now. I keep having these dreams that seem to be moving me in this direction. I can't rightly explain it, it just seems like the proper thing to do," Bessie explained.

"But I can't do it by myself. I don't know nothin' about running a voodoo shop. I need your help, Papa Levi."

"Queen Rita always would tell me that the spirits would come to you. You was always her favorite Bessie. And I devoted myself to her. So, iffin' you need help, I'm here to do what I can," Papa Levi solemnly stated.

"Thank you so much," Bessie replied with a warm smile and a nod.

"Well, if we's gonna open this old shop, first thing to do is give this place a good sweepin'," Papa Levi stated as he grasped the broomstick that sat in the corner of the back room. "It surely needs a good cleaning."

Posy Branch and her realtor Miriam Sanchez walked down Decatur Street in the area adjacent to the French Market.

"Thanks for agreeing to take me around on such short notice," Posy said to her realtor. "I flew down here from Savannah this weekend to find a place to live and see if I could locate a good spot for a business I'd like to start."

"This is a good location for a business with plenty of foot traffic and tourists," Miriam offered. "The owner of the nail salon on the other side of the street, ain't looking to sell yet, but she is open to taking on a business partner and may sell eventually. Otherwise, this small commercial space over here to the left is available for sale."

"Can we take a look at the nail salon?" Posy asked.

"Sure thing. It's an enormous space for a nail salon. Kind of a waste of all that space if you ask me," Miriam replied.

Miriam opened the door and Posy walked into the nail salon.

"Heck yeah," Posy exclaimed. "You could put a bar in here with a dance floor with all this space, and still have room for a good half dozen or more workstations for the nail beauticians. Is this area zoned for a bar?"

"Yes, Ma'am. They're all over this area. You'd have to apply for a liquor license, but you could put pretty much any commercial endeavor in this space," Miriam responded.

"Well, that there is food for thought, Miriam," Posy stated with a smile. "You done given me something to chew on."

Carolyn Barnes' long black braids gently swayed in the warm breeze coming off of Lake Michigan as she waited outside of the new campaign headquarters she had just leased for Senator Douglas' presidential campaign headquarters. Her fashionable Ray-Ban sunglasses shielded her beautiful hazel eyes from the glare of the mid-afternoon sun.

At a statuesque five feet eight inches tall, with a shapely figure, Carolyn was a striking woman. Her mocha-colored skin practically gleamed in the bright sunlight. She smiled broadly as she noticed a small entourage walking down Randolph Street in her direction.

"Good afternoon Senator Douglas," Carolyn greeted her boss.

"Thank you for agreeing to meet me here on a Sunday afternoon," Perry Douglas said as he approached his campaign manager. "I was in Hyde Park yesterday attending the wedding of my aide Aaron and thought I would take the opportunity to stop by and see my new national campaign headquarters before I fly back to Washington this evening."

"I think that this space will do nicely," Carolyn stated as she opened the door to the commercial rental property located in the heart of Chicago's downtown area.

"Yes, yes, this will do nicely," Perry said as he walked around in the empty space. This is a good launching pad from which to build our fifty-state campaign plan. We're just a little over two years and a month from Election Day, are you ready for this?" Perry asked Carolyn.

"I've been working for the chance to run a Presidential campaign for years now, yes, I'm ready," Carolyn affirmatively responded.

"Excellent, good work," Perry stated. "Let's go!"

NATHAN WHITAKER SLUMPED INTO HIS LIVING ROOM SOFA with a legal pad on his lap and a pen in his hand. Ostracized from the White House after resigning in scandal, and without any personal contact with his old college friend, Andrew Cochran, Nathan was no longer White House Chief of Staff. However, that didn't keep him from playing one while watching TV. As he watched the daily White House press conference on cable television, Nathan couldn't help himself but to scribble notes while taking in every word from the White House Press Secretary. He jotted down facts that could have been utilized to make an argument clearer and more persuasively. His criminal indictment had sidelined him from his official job, but that didn't mean that he didn't continue to do it from the solitary confines of his sofa.

Nathan often dreamt that he was still occupying his position of power and prestige. That he was sitting in the Oval Office with the President, sharing his sharp insights and political acumen. Oft times, he awoke with a startle, realizing that it was only a dream, and that his reality of possible life in prison was staring him in the face. He was more focused on paying attention to the minute details of Cochran administration policy stands, than on preparing for his own defense against murder charges. So, Nathan hung on every word uttered from the White House Press Office and ferociously took copious notes of strategy points he would never be able to share with anyone else.

His best friend, Andrew Cochran, was clinging on to an administration that had been rocked by scandal. Nathan understood that he was the cause of that scandal. Still, he longed to call his friend, and give helpful advice, as he always had done throughout Andrew's political career. But, that was just a dream. Even though he had placed phone calls and sent letters, they went unanswered. He was seen as the cancer on the Presidency that had to be cut out with precision and finality. That had become Nathan's uncomfortable reality. Exiled to his sofa, jotting down thoughts that only he would know. Old habits die hard.

STANFORD WINCHESTER SAT ON A BAR STOOL at Fritzel's jazz club on a late Sunday afternoon. Stanford often enjoyed listening to Dixieland swing music while partaking of a well-made cocktail on a weekend afternoon. He tapped his toe along to the rhythmic beat of "Mack the Knife." Stanford turned slowly when he felt a hand gently landing on his left shoulder.

"Well look who the cat dragged in," Stanford offered as he greeted his longtime friend, Calvin Putnam.

"Been a while Stanford, what have you been up to?" Calvin asked as he sidled up on the bar stool to Stanford's left.

"Not too much, Calvin, not too much," Stanford responded. "Working and enjoying life, nothing of any note."

"Did I hear correctly that you're on the Fifth Circuit panel taking up the appeal of the Katrina victims' class action suit?" Calvin inquired.

"Yup. It's going to be me, Charles Sewell, and Whitlee Hammond," Stanford replied before taking a long slow sip of his Sazerac.

"Whitlee Hammond is the only woman on the Fifth Circuit, ain't she?" Calvin asked.

"Yup."

"She's about fifty-six-years-old, if I remember correctly. Nice looking woman, ain't that right?" Calvin slyly questioned his old friend.

"You're about as subtle as getting hit in the head by a bag of nails, Calvin," Stanford responded as he grinned. "Whitlee and I are colleagues, end of story."

"Well, some stories have very intricate subplots that don't readily appear until you're far along in the book," Calvin knowingly smiled.

"Smart, good looking, mature women don't just grow on trees. And a Federal Appellate court judge to boot!"

"And friends who know better than to meddle in the affairs of other friends, don't grow on trees either," Stanford sarcastically stated in return.

"Perhaps, you ain't wandering through the right orchards, Stanford," Calvin countered.

"Alright truce, you old fool," Stanford laughed in reply. "I can't sit here and pretend that I haven't noticed what a lovely and intelligent woman Whitlee Hammond is. There is no disputing those facts, counselor. But, Whitlee was appointed to the Fifth Circuit about a year ago. I am the Chief Judge of the court. Discretion and proper Southern etiquette and decorum must prevail. After all, it is a court of law not a dating service for tired old lonely jurists," Stanford summed up.

"Do you know how many people meet and marry their husband or wife at work?" Calvin asked.

"Probably quite a few, but they are not named Stanford Winchester. So, though I appreciate your Cupid-esque escapades, drop it old friend," Stanford responded.

"We just passed the seventh anniversary of LeeAnn's very sad departure. You shouldn't wall yourself off from ever getting involved in another loving relationship," Calvin counseled.

"Oh, I am very aware of that anniversary, trust me. And, perhaps, Calvin, I will once again find a woman to spend my life with. And perhaps not. But I will not use my position nor my proximity to curry favor with a woman I work with. So, you can read that as end of story, old chum," Stanford replied.

"If that's the case, all I have to say to that is, "Eddie, another round, please," Calvin called to the bartender as he smiled at his old friend.

SAM BRAINARD SAT ON THE EDGE OF HIS SEAT on the couch in the Oval Office as he waited as President Cochran wrapped up a telephone call.

"Sam, what's the good news?" Andrew Cochran cheerfully asked while placing the telephone in its cradle.

"You are going to be the keynote speaker at the National Prayer Breakfast on Thursday," Sam responded.

"Who else will be speaking from the dais?"

"Reverend Archibald Burrows will be giving the invocation. Senator Hellen Raymond, and the guy who wrote the book, 'Love Your Enemies,' will be speaking. You will be introduced by Bishop O'Malley."

"How long do I get?" Andrew Cochran asked.

"About 20-30 minutes, I've been told."

"Sort of a hoot that the author of 'Love Your Enemies' is speaking before me. My Republican colleagues believe that I am already doing that. And frankly, these days I get along far better with Hellen Raymond than I do with Cletus Sawyer," Andrew snickered. "I'd like the draft speech given to me early on Wednesday, so that I have some time to add my own touches and ideas, ok?" President Cochran requested.

"Of course, sir."

"This is my opportunity to explain some of my recent decisions to compromise with the Democrats in Congress, as well as score some points with the Evangelical community that supported me in my quest for the White House almost three years ago. I know that's going to be tough, but we've got to at least try. Frankly Sam, I still don't understand the animosity from my religious supporters. I didn't appoint a pro-abortion jurist to the Supreme Court, the man just said that he would go into any case with an open mind and without pre-existing conceptions," Andrew Cochran related to his Chief of Staff.

"Evangelical leaders wanted a strict pro-life appointee. Period. They viewed your compromise choice as a slap in the face to all they hold sacred. It's their one issue, they really don't care about anything else. Well, homosexuality is an abomination is right up there as well, of course."

"I can tell you honestly, Sam, that personally, both of those issues are so far down my priority list. I don't care who people sleep with, as long as they are consenting adults. And, I'm not thrilled about dictating what a grown woman can or cannot do with her own body. But Nathan correctly identified those as being vital issues to my chances of winning the Party's nomination. So, I tacked hard to the right, and well, here we are in the Oval Office. We still have some Evangelical supporters left, don't we?"

"Of course, sir, but not too many vocal leaders. Reverend Burrows is an exception. He was quite adamant about inviting you to be the keynote speaker this year. He knows you could use a hand during these tough times," Sam replied.

"Do you know when the National Prayer Breakfast began as a Presidential event?"

"No sir," Sam answered.

"It was 1953, Billy Graham invited President Eisenhower to address a group of about 400 people."

"Well, there will be significantly more people in attendance, not to mention that several cable news networks will be taking it live," Sam stated. "It's a good opportunity to let the religious communities in this country know that you are still a man of faith and an advocate for their religious freedoms."

"Indeed," Andrew Cochran responded.

CHAPTER 4

Posy Branch and her realtor walked towards the nail salon that Miriam had shown to Posy one day earlier. They had a 10:00am meeting with the owner of the store.

"Posy, Chantale Calypso is from Haiti. Her English is a little broken, and she can be hard to understand at times," Miriam cautioned Posy as they approached the nail salon.

"Shoot, my ex-husband Nathan use to say the same thing about my English being broken and me being hard to understand at times," Posy said with a snort and a short laugh. "Me and Chantale goin' to get along just fine."

"Oh, I'm sure that's true," Miriam replied as they approached the doorway to the shop.

"Hey, ain't Calypso that music that Harry Belafonte use to sing? He sure was a nice-looking man. Ain't that the God's honest truth, Miriam?" Posy asked energetically. Miriam just smiled politely and opened the door for Posy. Chantale, Posy, and Miriam all sat in the back room of the large nail salon.

"I no look to sell now, want partner for nail shop," Chantale said in her lilting Haitian accent.

"Yes, Ms. Branch is aware that you are looking for a business partner, and that you are not selling at this time. She may be agreeable to those terms under the appropriate conditions," Miriam Sanchez related to Chantale Calypso.

"Look, Chantale, can I call you that?" Posy asked. "You got a great shop here, but I see a lot of unused space and lost potential. If we moved the six nail work stations over to the left with just a divider between the stations, we'd have all this extra space. I was thinkin' we could build a bar against this far wall. We could hire a couple of cute boys to serve the gals drinks while they get their nails done. I love me some juleps, especially mint. We could get us a liquor license and serve the women clients a nice mint julep with one of them long twisty straws, while they is getting their nails done. Then, we could get us a little jazz quartet, like the ones that is playing all over the street corners here in the French Quarter. A gal can come in get her nails done, enjoy a well-made julep served to her by a good-looking young man, and listen to some sweet jazz. Don't that sound good Chantale?"

Chantale sat motionless for several moments. She then slowly turned towards Posy.

"I think you are a crazy woman. But I like your idea. I will have my lawyer draw up agreement. You look over and we talk again," Chantale stated.

"Well, that sounds just fine. And believe you me, Chantale, you just one in a long line of folks who has called me crazy," Posy replied. "I even got us a new name. French Tips, Juleps & Jazz. We gonna make us some money, girlfriend!"

AFTER SEVERAL DAYS OF INTENSIVE CLEANING, the small shop on North Rampart began to look more like an operating voodoo store and less like a cobweb- filled museum. As they cleaned, Papa Levi carefully explained to Bessie the history and purpose of each item. At times, Bessie stopped to take some short notes. Each amulet, every gris, all the potions were explained by Papa Levi and noted by Bessie. He explained the role of every loa or spirit and their accompanying role in the realm of the living. Day by day, Bessie became more aware of the items and practices of the spiritual world. Papa Levi proved to be a patient and thorough tutor.

"What is this again?" Bessie asked while holding up the small object.

"It is the bone from a raccoon penis," Papa Levi stated. "It has been boiled clean with a red string tied around it to hang around one's neck. It is a love amulet. It is also lucky for gamblers."

"Guess it wasn't so lucky for the raccoon," Bessie replied with a short giggle.

"Bessie, this is not child's play," Papa Levi gently scolded. "People take the spiritual world seriously. If you are not serious about what you do and what you sell, people not come back."

"I understand, I'm sorry," Bessie said her head bowed.

"What is this?" Papa Levi asked quizzing Bessie about an amulet.

"It's a Mamuli fertility amulet from Sumba," Bessie correctly answered.

"And this?" Papa Levi challenged.

"Oh wait," Bessie hesitated. "It's a Tibetan Khadga curved fire sword."

"And it's use?" Papa Levi questioned Bessie.

"It is a symbol of enlightenment. It is used to destroy ignorance from the bonds of worldly attachments," Bessie proudly proclaimed.

"That is good, Bessie, but remember the more you think you know the less you actually know," Papa Levi counseled.

"I got a lot to learn, I understand. But I have a wonderful teacher, who is patient and kind with me, so I have no worries about learning what I need to know to run this shop successfully," Bessie replied.

"With help from the spirits, we will do what needs to be done," Papa Levi quietly offered as he sat on the hard, wooden stool his dearly departed friend often occupied.

WHITE HOUSE CHIEF OF STAFF SAMUEL Brainard and President Cochran's Campaign Manager Landon Hamilton sat patiently in the Oval Office waiting for the arrival of the President.

"I found a good-sized store front in downtown Savannah for the President's national re-election campaign headquarters," Landon Hamilton offered.

"What about the one we used for the last election?" Sam asked.

"It was owned by one of Nathan Whitaker's political cronies. The President wants to make sure that nothing we do this time around has any connection with Whitaker. He's worked so hard over the last two years to put that scandal behind him," Landon related to Sam.

"I'm not so sure about that, Sam responded. "Of course, he wants to put the scandal behind his administration, but he still talks lovingly about his old friend. From time to time, occasionally the President slips up and calls me Nathan. After all, they spent forty years of their lives in constant contact with one another. They were best friends."

"The name of Nathan Whitaker is a blot on this administration. The less he is spoken about the better. We need to navigate around him becoming an issue when he goes on trial," Landon replied bitterly.

"What is going on with the trial, do you know?" Sam inquired.

"Last I heard, Nathan's murder trial is set to begin in January. It's been over two years since his arrest. A few delays were from the prosecution, but most of the delay has been on behalf of Nathan's defense team," Landon responded.

"It's going to be odd around here when the trial begins. The President, at times, attempts to play it off as if he is not interested. But, he has forty years of his life invested in his relationship with Nathan Whitaker, he can't just shrug it off like it means nothing to him."

"True, but perhaps the re-election campaign will take some of his focus off of the trial," Landon stated. "Whitaker can't be an issue or a distraction for the good of the President and the campaign."

"Easier said than done," Sam answered.

Ten days later, Clay Grover drove his car down Elysian Fields Avenue in the Marigny neighborhood of New Orleans. The Marigny is located on the north east border of the French Quarter. Following closely behind Clay's car was Aaron Rose driving a rented U-Haul truck. Clay pulled his Audi over to the curb and exited the car walking towards Aaron in the truck.

"I think our house should be right around here," Clay said while looking at a sheet of paper containing the address of the rental home.

"One can only hope," Aaron wearily replied while staring down at Clay from the truck cabin.

"Hey, are you Clay Grover?" A woman waiving a clipboard shouted as she approached Aaron in the truck and Clay standing next to the truck.

"Yup, that's me," Clay responded cheerfully.

"Hi, I'm Ellen. My partner Karen rented you the yellow shotgun house across the street. She said you'd be showing up about now, I just wanted to give you a set of keys and show you around."

"That's great, thank you. This is my husband Aaron, we pulled up about three minutes ago, so it's perfect timing," Clay replied.

"Pleased to meet you, Aaron," Ellen stated while shaking Aaron's outstretched hand as he climbed down from the truck. "Let me show you guys around."

"Excellent," Aaron said with a big grin.

"It's a typical New Orleans shotgun house. It was completely remodeled in 2007, it had sustained some minor damage after Katrina. Yellow paint job is two years old. The porch slants a little towards the street, but nothing in New Orleans is straight, including most of your neighbors. We are very friendly LGBTQ folks mostly, interspersed with musicians and artists. The little table and two rocking chairs on the porch come with the house. There's some very interesting people watching in this neighborhood. The wrought iron fence that spans the front of the house was also put up two years ago. Here's the keys, give it a whirl," Ellen said to Clay as she handed him the set of house keys. Clay unlocked the door as they all walked into the house.

"These tall ceilings are wonderful," Aaron exclaimed. "The floor to ceiling shuttered windows along the front of the house provide so much light, it's great!"

"As you can see there's exposed brick walls in the front living room and a working fireplace. The master bedroom is off the living room and also has a working fireplace. Plenty of cabinet space in the kitchen and the spare bedroom also has a fireplace but it doesn't function. Plenty of original molding and the wall sconces in the long hallway are antiques," Ellen proclaimed.

"Wow, this is even better than the photos that Karen emailed to us," Clay said.

"Well, I'm glad you're pleased with it. We've got your deposit and first month's rent, thanks for that, so if you can just sign the rental agreement, we're all set," Ellen stated.

"Perfect. Welcome to the Big Easy, guys. Enjoy! Karen and I live in a very similar two-bedroom pink shotgun on Frenchmen Street. I'm sure that we will be seeing you around the neighborhood. But if you need anything, please don't hesitate to give us a call. Y'all take care now," Ellen said as she shook the guys' hands and walked off into the distance.

"How cute is this?" Aaron asked with great satisfaction as he surveyed their new home.

"Cute, but not as cute as you," Clay gushed while kissing Aaron on the cheek with his arms locked around his waist. "Let's get the bed down from the truck."

"Sounds like an outstanding plan," Aaron smirked in response.

PRESIDENT COCHRAN HAD COMPLETED HIS COMMENTS before a crowded ballroom at a local hotel in Washington to a rousing ovation. His speech hit the right notes of faith, social justice, respect, and love for one another. He encouraged cooperation and compromise in all facets of life, but he clearly was speaking directly to his Republican colleagues who were choosing division and political advantage over-extending a supportive hand across the aisle.

At the conclusion of the National Prayer Breakfast, the President was escorted through the kitchen area of the hotel by his Secret

Service detail to his waiting limousine. Billy James, the head of the President's personal detail led the way. As they exited the hotel, the entourage walked the fifty yards from the kitchen door to the street corner where the President's car waited. A group of admirers cheered the President, as he slowly walked, waiving to the crowd. Suddenly, there was an unexpected surge by one man through the assembled gathering of supporters. The jostling and pushing of the individual quickly drew attention. People began to panic. A Secret Service agent quickly moved to intervene.

"Gun!" The agent shouted loudly.

Billy James forcefully pushed Andrew Cochran into the limousine and covered the President with his body. Moments later, the car sped off as chaos ensued on the sidewalk outside of the hotel.

THE NEWS COVERAGE OF THE ARMED ALTERCATION outside of the site of the National Prayer Breakfast was fast and furious. Fortunately, no shots were fired. It was reported that the President, at no time, was in serious harm. The Secret Service and local D.C. police were lauded for their rapid response. The initial report was that the armed man was Robert Gooding. A Georgia Evangelical minister, who two-years prior had led the prayerful invocation at one of the Presidential balls on Inauguration Day. Gooding had been an avid supporter of President Cochran and a contributor to his campaign. His motives for what appeared to be an assassination attempt against the President of the United States were unknown.

Back at the White House, after a thorough examination of President Cochran by the White House medical team, the President sat in the Oval Office with his Chief of Staff.

"Are you sure that you don't want to go up to the residence and rest, sir?" Sam Brainard asked his boss.

"I'm fine, Sam. Just a little bruised from being forced into the car by Billy James, and having the weight of his substantial muscular body crushed against me. By the way, perhaps tomorrow, I'd like to personally thank each member of my Secret Service detail and the local police officers who were responsible for making sure that I was never in any harm. Let's do it here in the Oval Office. No press. I just want to thank them all and shake their hands," Andrew Cochran requested.

"Will do, Mr. President. We'll put something together fairly quickly."

"Any word yet on the man wielding the gun?"

"Yes sir. His name is Robert Gooding. He is a forty-seven-year old Evangelical minister from Savannah," Sam replied.

"That name sounds familiar. I think I might have met him personally."

"I believe you have, sir. He was a contributor to your campaign and gave an invocation address at one of the minor Inaugural balls. Undoubtedly, you probably met him at a campaign event, and may have shaken hands with him at a rope line event during your Inauguration."

"Any reports on his possible motive?"

"Not at this time," Sam answered. "But we will keep you apprised as information becomes available."

"It used to be that I only had to be concerned about the actions of my political enemies," Andrew sighed.

"Unfortunately, sir, some of your prior supporters now consider you their enemy following your Supreme Court nomination."

"I suppose that's right," President Cochran lamented with a shake of his head.

CHAPTER 5

Wednesday night and Stanford Winchester was seated at his regular table in the main dining room at Arnaud's restaurant.

"A gracious good evening to you, Justice Winchester," a beaming Lucius Collins politely greeted his friend of seventeen years.

"Tell me, Lucius, is it ever going to be just Stanford?" Stanford asked with a peevish smile.

"As long as you are my customer and I am your server in this here establishment, no sir, it surely ain't," Lucius replied with a hearty laugh.

"You are as stubborn as the day is long, my friend," Stanford said in return.

"Folks are too ready to throw off old and honored customs these days. There ain't no respect for tradition and decorum. Time was a gentleman and his lady came here dressed to the nines and stayed for three hours casually enjoying the fine food and the jazz music. Now they is dressed in t-shirts and shorts and want to be in and out in less than an hour. It's a sorry state of affairs, iffin' you ask me," Lucius sighed while shaking his head.

"You're preaching to the choir, Reverend Lucius, you surely are," Stanford said with his left hand raised up to the heavens. "And your fine preaching has me thirsty for redemption, so can I get a Sazerac and an amen, brother Lucius?" Stanford nearly laughed out in response.

"Most certainly," Lucius chortled and smiled. "Yes sir, you most certainly can."

A few minutes later, Lucius returned with Stanford's cocktail, "Here you go, sir, made just the way you like it with that extra splash of bitters."

"Lucius, my friend, you are the best," Stanford replied, whilst taking a protracted sip from his glass. "Now, do tell me, how is your lovely wife Bessie?"

"Oh, Bessie is fine, Justice Winchester. I know she been tellin' you 'bout them dreams she been having for quite some time now. She finally decided to open up her Auntie Rita's old shop and run it. Though, I got to say, I ain't sure I can see what good can come from it," Lucius solemnly explained.

"A woman running her own business is an admirable pursuit," Stanford responded encouragingly to Lucius.

"Yes sir, I do understand that. But nothing good come out of that shop the last few years. Problems and no good trouble were the last things that came from that shop before it was shuttered down," Lucius firmly stated.

"Well, Lucius, you know better than I what a kind and wonderful woman Bessie is," Stanford replied. "In her loving hands, I can't imagine that any trouble could come from Bessie running her own business."

"From your lips to God's ear, sir. From your lips," Lucius softly intoned.

ANDREW COCHRAN AND SAM BRAINARD WATCHED TELEVISION in the West Wing together as Senator Cletus Sawyer of Alabama was being interviewed on Fox News.

"That was about as newsworthy as the sun coming up in the morning," President Cochran sarcastically said to his Chief of Staff. "Cletus Sawyer has been threatening to launch an exploratory committee to look into a possible Presidential bid ever since I nominated a moderate to the Supreme Court."

"He is a disgrace to this party, sir," Sam responded.

"As you well know, he's no fan of yours either," the President said with a sly grin. "I believe he said that I was appointing a lifelong Democratic sympathizer as my Chief of Staff after I selected you to replace Nathan. A rather odd statement when you take into account that Nathan thought that Cletus was dumb as a rock and afraid of his own shadow."

"Well, the petrified rock appears to be running for President," Sam laughed in return.

"He won't be the only one. The Tea Party Caucus boys are tripping all over themselves to unseat me and save America from villainous compromise. Cletus is only the first, he won't be the last. I'm guessing that right now Howard is regretting accepting the Vice-Presidency last election. If he was still the darling Senator from Ohio, he'd be first in line to challenge me. But instead, at the moment, he is politically obliged as my Vice-President to lend me his tepid support," Andrew Cochran surmised.

"Landon is opening your national re-election campaign headquarters in Savannah this week. And no one else has the Presidential bully pulpit," Sam added with emphasis.

"I just think that the American people are tired of decades of viperous acrimony and social and economic stagnation. Legislative compromise is not a mortal sin that threatens the soul of its citizens," the President said with a shrug and a sigh.

"Try explaining that to the petrified rock," Sam replied.

"I will Sam. They're called debates," Andrew Cochran responded with a nod of his head. "I will."

"Yes sir."

"Changing topics, anything further about the gunman? Any word on his motive? President Cochran inquired.

"Yes, we received word from the Justice Department an hour ago. Gooding admitted that he came to the National Prayer Breakfast with a gun with the intent of assassinating you.

He confessed that he was distraught over your choice for the Supreme Court nomination for several months. He informed the agents that he believed he was receiving instructions from God in his dreams, to kill you to prevent you from nominating any additional baby-killing judges on the Federal bench."

"Does the FBI think that he was a lone shooter?"

"They haven't closed that out yet. He made a statement that others would rise up to smite the disciple of Satan," Sam responded.

"I take that to be me, huh?"

"I believe so, sir."

"Jesus, Sam. In over two years' time, this man, this Evangelical minister went from contributing to my campaign, and even speaking at one of my Inaugural events to driving up from Georgia and attempting to kill me after a speech at the National Prayer Breakfast. All because I nominated a well-respected moderate judge to the Supreme Court after the failed nomination of Stanford Winchester. That type of transformation should scare the crap out of all of us," Andrew Cochran replied with concern.

"The fragility of the human mind," Sam responded. "Billy James will be adding another few agents to your detail, sir. Also, additional precautions will be added as you begin to actively campaign."

"OK, anything else I should know about?" The President asked.

"One more thing, sir," Sam answered hesitantly. "Nathan Whitaker has made several calls to the White House and sent a few messages after he heard the news about the attempt on your life."

"Yes, I know. Nathan called my personal phone and left a message shortly after the news story broke in the media."

"If you allow me, sir, we can have his calls blocked on your smart phone," Sam suggested.

"No! No!" Andrew Cochran responded vehemently. "Nathan's only concern was for my well-being. Despite what my wife and Landon think of Nathan, he was my best friend for forty years. You don't just block that out of your life."

"Very good, sir."

"So, I suppose I can dissuade myself from the notion of receiving a presidential pardon, eh?" Nathan Whitaker facetiously questioned his attorney.

"I'm told that the President still can't say your name out loud without trembling in anger," Rupert Grassmonk definitively lied to his client with a smirk. "Yes, I think it's fair to accept that analysis."

Nathan sunk a little deeper in his chair. None of the consequences of his actions had truly registered fully, until he was told unequivocally that the person who he had loved the most in this world could not bear to even say his name. Of course, none of that was true. Rupert Grassmonk, in his three thousand dollar suits, with his nationally acclaimed reputation, was preparing his client. He was making sure that Nathan was fully committed to his defense. That any hope of a gateway to freedom other than through a successful criminal trial was not even a slight fantasy in the mind of his client. And if he had to force that commitment by lying about how Nathan's friend of forty years, the President, felt about his client, it was a very small price to pay.

Rupert Grassmonk lived in a different world than Nathan Whitaker. Nathan was born and raised in Tennessee. He went to Vanderbilt on a full scholarship. He met and befriended a shy, kind, and naive young man from Savannah, Georgia, whom was raised in a middle-class home by his grandmother after his parents had died in a horrible home fire. That man, in great part due to the devotion and steely-eyed determination of Nathan, became Governor of the State of Georgia, and eventually President of the United States. Nathan Whitaker was not born and raised in privilege, yet he achieved it working hand-in-hand with his best friend, Andrew Cochran.

Conversely, Rupert Grassmonk was born into one of the wealthiest families in Connecticut. Educated European nannies, an outrageously exclusive prep school, Yale University, and Harvard Law School all resided on Rupert's life-long resume. He wanted for nothing. After graduating in the top five of his law school class, Rupert immediately started his own criminal defense law practice. In twenty years of practicing law, Rupert went from the ultra-privileged child of enormous wealth and advantage to being considered one of the top five criminal defense attorneys in the country.

At forty-seven years of age, the slightly pudgy and slightly balding Rupert Grassmonk, with his piercing blue eyes and deep and commanding voice, was ready to enhance his already sterling reputation by defending the former Chief of Staff to the President of a murder charge in a District of Columbia courthouse.

A TALL FIGURE STOOD IN THE CORNER of the dimly lit office staring out of the window. A cellphone cradled next to his right ear as he paced back and forth in front of the window.

"There is only one outcome. Failure is not an option, are we understood?" The tall figure stated firmly in a deep Southern accent.

"Yes sir," the voice on the other side of the phone replied.

"It can be by election. It can be by resignation. It can be by impeachment. It can be by an arranged accident. But one way or another, two years from January 20th, Andrew Cochran will not be President of the United States. Do you get my meaning?" The tall figure pointedly asked his companion on the phone.

"Understood," was the only acceptable answer.

"One more thing, the caller asked. "Have you looked into the adventurous predilections of our Buckeye colleague?"

"It is in the works. Preliminary indications are that he could be open to adventure," was the response.

CHAPTER 6

THE TWO STEPS OF THE OLD STOREFRONT on Chartres Street creaked as Aaron Rose and Clay Grover took the first two noisy steps into their new legal careers. The Bywater neighborhood was directly east of the French Quarter and their home in the Marigny along the Mississippi River. The lower Ninth ward, which was completely devastated during the aftermath of Hurricane Katrina was directly to the east of the Bywater. Aaron glanced at his surroundings and the door of the old storefront. The new signage outside of the building read, "Law Offices of Caleb Butler & Associates, LLC."

"Not quite what I expected," Aaron whispered to Clay.

"What were you expecting, Jones Walker in a brand new high-rise building in the heart of the Central Business District? We're public service and civil rights attorneys now. Our clients to a great degree will be the people who live in the Ninth ward. You practice where your clients are located," Clay stated with a touch of exasperation in his voice.

"You're right. You're right," Aaron quickly acknowledged. "It's just a little bit of culture shock, going from climbing the stairs of the United States Capitol Building, to squeaking into the weather worn wood planks leading up to a pronouncedly left-leaning storefront."

"Then lean on me, I'll help straighten you out," Clay offered as he affectionately smiled at his husband.

"Oh geez, I hope not for both our sakes!" Aaron exclaimed with a sarcastic laugh.

"Get in there you, here we go," Clay said as he playfully shoved Aaron through the open doorway to their new career.

"This could very well be the last major case of my judicial career," Stanford Winchester said to his secretary Naomi Cutler.

"Oh go on now, Justice Winchester, you know that ain't true," Naomi replied.

"No, I'm telling you the God's honest truth, Naomi. I'm already past retirement age, and I've got no inclination to be one of these federal appointed judges that they got to pry his cold dead gripping hands off the bench. There's more to life than just one's career. And lord knows, I've had a lengthy career that many of my colleagues would envy," Stanford wistfully relayed to his secretary.

"I just get sad thinking that there will be a day when I ain't helping you get your arm through the sleeve of that old black robe and looking at your grinning face while I straighten out your bowtie," Naomi said with a touch of melancholy.

"Hold on girl, I ain't dead yet," Stanford chortled in response. "I said I was thinking of retiring, not dying."

"Yeah, Chief, you're right as rain. You know me, I just get all sentimental thinking about not seeing you every day. But, right now I need you to approve this order setting, the briefing schedule and oral argument for the Hurricane Katrina victims class action appeal," Naomi said as she slid the document across the judge's desk. Stanford visibly started to count days with the fingers of his hand as he carefully reviewed what would be his scheduling order for the large appellate matter he would preside over.

"Looks good to me," Stanford acknowledged, as he affixed his signature to the last page of the scheduling order.

"I'll get this over to the clerk's office," Naomi stated as she reached down to grab the multi-page document.

"Well, alright then," Stanford said slowly and clearly. "It's on, here we go."

"Here we go," Posy Branch announced to her business partner, Chantale Calypso, as she handed her a sketch of the new signage for their nail salon, bar, music venue. "'French Tips, Juleps & Jazz', pretty cute, ain't it?" Posy asked with pride.

"What wrong with Calypso Nail Salon?" Chantale bluntly queried Posy.

"There's no jazz to that name," Posy replied. "You got to grab people's attention. As the song goes, 'It don't mean a thing if ain't got that swing,'" Posy sang/said to Chantale.

"I must be magnet for crazy. And in this city, that is much to say," Chantale stated while looking deadpan at Posy and shaking her head.

"Nah, you're just lucky you met me. You got a lucky horseshoe up your butt 'cuz we gonna make some money, partner o' mine," Posy giggled.

"Boy-girl waiting for you in back," Chantale informed Posy.

"Oh heck yeah. That's my 10:00am interview for the hostess position. I best sashay my behind back there and see if we got us any hiring material," Posy said as she turned and walked into the backroom office of the nail salon.

"Good mornin'," Posy cheerfully greeted her interview prospect. Rising out of the chair by the old desk was six foot four inches of a slightly odd-looking and somewhat pretty but very statuesque African-American drag queen in five inch stiletto heels and a bright yellow, green and pink sun dress adorned by an orange feather boa.

"Good morning, Ms. Branch, I'm Chiffon LaBelle," a fairly low and a bit masculine voice stated.

"Oh no!" Posy exclaimed. "My mama is Mrs. Branch, heck you can just call me Posy. Ain't you a tall drink of water?"

"Here's my resume," the job applicant said as she handed the paper to Posy.

"I'm not much for reading unless I got to. I don't read much, I just wait for them to make the good books into movies," Posy laughed and snorted in response. "Them courtroom dramas, the who did it kind of deal is right up my alley, what about you Chiffon?"

"I suppose I enjoy a nice romantic comedy," Chiffon replied to her interviewer.

"Oh, shoot yeah, I love a nice romance. Give me a bottle of wine, some of that Godiva chocolate, a fine-looking George Clooney movie, and a couple of AA batteries and I'm set for the night," Posy howled in laughter. Chiffon shifted uncomfortably in her chair, crossing and re-crossing her long, well-shaped legs.

"So, tell me about your work experience and why you want to be a hostess for our nail salon?" Posy asked.

"I've worked as a bartender at Bourbon Pub, I was a waitress at a small restaurant in the Marigny, and I've been a hostess at a music venue on Bourbon Street as well as a hostess for a strip club," Chiffon replied.

"I see your real name is Ernest Johnson?" Posy inquired while glancing down at the resume.

"Yes, I have not had my name legally changed yet. I am a pre-op transsexual on hormone therapy, but I am wholly committed to living my life as a woman," Chiffon stated.

"Heck, I just had my name changed not so long ago as well. But in my case, it was a matter of just jettisoning my ex-husband's noose around my neck," Posy allowed with a smile. "So, what would you say are your best attributes with respect to working with the public?"

Chiffon hesitated for a moment before answering Posy's question. "I guess I'd have to say that I am polite and courteous to everyone. I have infinite patience with people. I'm very organized and a bit of a clean freak. But mostly, I just enjoy the company of others. I love to talk and I like to have a good time."

"Well, me too, girlfriend!" Posy exclaimed. "You got to have fun in life, right? My ex-husband Nathan, use to always say that I was a good time Charlene. You know, like a 'good time Charlie', but for a girl. Always up for a couple of cocktails and some energetic conversation. I love to dance as well."

"I use to be a dancer at a club," Chiffon added.

"You been around. I like that," Posy said loudly. "I like fun people, and Chiffon, you sure seem like you enjoy life, ain't that right sugar?"

"Yes, ma'am. I'm generally a cheerful person and I like to share my joy for life with others," Chiffon responded.

"Alright then, I think we've found our hostess. We're gonna open in about a month, but we will start training the staff in a couple of weeks. That going to work for you?" Posy asked.

"Yes ma'am, that will work just fine," Chiffon stated as she rose out of her chair.

"It's gonna take me a minute gettin' use to looking up at you," Posy said while staring up at Chiffon and shaking her hand. "But we are going to make some money and have some fun. Oh, I forgot to ask you, do you like juleps?"

"I love a good mint julep made with fine crushed ice," Chiffon replied.

"Well, if that don't seal the deal," Posy laughed. "Here we go!"

Senator Perry Douglas was back in Washington and slowly strolled down the hallway of the Hart Senate Office Building. He passed by the office of his friend Henry Fitzsimmons on his way to his own office. Henry's seat on the Senate had not yet been filled. A special election in South Carolina in November would determine Henry's successor. Perry entered the office space, and asked Henry's secretary if she would allow him to sit in Henry's office for a few minutes. Of course, she gladly obliged the Senator's request.

Perry sat in his accustomed chair on the opposite side of Henry's large ornate desk. He glanced at the crystal whiskey glasses that were on a shelf behind Henry's desk. Nothing had been changed, at least, not yet. Perry sat deep in the chair, crossed his legs, and began to softly have one last conversation with his dear friend in his old Senate office.

"My God, I miss you so much, Henry," Perry quietly began, his voice low and solemn. "I've been traveling a lot recently, partly because I didn't want to confront this moment. I didn't want to experience life in the Senate without the distinguished gentleman from South Carolina. I've sat in this chair for twenty years having conversations that shaped my life. I learned how to be a better husband, father, friend, and Senator sitting in this chair and chatting with you. But more importantly, I was just smart enough to listen. The wisdom, kindness, and unique perspective that you imparted to me was one hundredfold more important than anything I learned in college or law school. Life with you Henry was exactly that, learning about how to live."

Perry hesitated. A tear formed in the corner of his eye, as he could feel his body slightly tremble with emotion. Perry swallowed hard as his lips curled into a slight smile.

"Oh, you would have been so proud, Henry," Perry announced, his voice more cheerful in tenor. "Katherine and I attended Clay and Aaron's marriage in Chicago a few short weeks ago. Yes, Clay and Aaron were married! It was a lovely ceremony against the backdrop of Chicago's gorgeous skyline on the shore of Lake Michigan. It was so heartwarming to see Clay happy again. When you passed, Clay was crushed. I've never seen a man so despondent. So utterly lost. But with the comforting support of Aaron's love, he was able to regain his footing, his zeal for life. They're living in New Orleans. They're practicing civil rights law near the Ninth ward. Clay has devoted his life to following your shining example. You championed civil rights for your entire career. It seems more than appropriate that your Chief of Staff would take up the cause of equality and justice in your honor." Perry hesitated once again, looking all around his dear friend's office as if taking a mental photograph.

"Alright, my friend, it's time for me to go. As you know, I'm running for President, so there never seems to be enough hours in the day. I've got a new national campaign headquarters in Chicago, and we are almost fully staffed. I'm not sure how I will get through the next two years without your wise counsel, your uplifting spirit, and most importantly your genuine and loving friendship. I'll try to do my best to honor your legacy. So, goodbye, Henry. I will always miss you. But as you would so aptly put it when it was time to go vote on a piece of legislation in the Senate, 'Let's get our butts out of these chairs, Perry. It's time we go do the people's business.' And that we will, Henry. That we will. Here we go."

CHAPTER 7

"**I**T'S A PLEASURE TO FINALLY MEET YOU IN PERSON," Caleb Butler said to Aaron Rose as he warmly shook his hand. "I must admit it was a bit weird interviewing you over Skype, but after everything that Clay had said about you and your amazing resume, the interview was nothing more than a superfluous bow to tradition. Southern men waste a great deal of time bowing to obsolete traditions."

"Wonderful to meet you as well, Caleb, and thank you so much for the opportunity to be a part of your successful law practice," Aaron cordially replied.

"C'mon, let me show you guys around," Caleb said as he led Aaron and Clay through the law office. "There's four small offices in the back. One for each of us and my other associate, Emily DuBois. We all share one secretary, Anna Havens, and one paralegal, Elliot Archer. Our tech person, mailroom guy, filing clerk, jack of all trades is Cooper Fischer. It's a good group, you'll meet them all tomorrow morning."

"Did you say the other associate was named Emily DuBois?" Aaron asked, a bit taken aback.

"Yes, do you know her?" Caleb inquired.

"Possibly," Aaron allowed. "Did she clerk for Stanford Winchester on the Fifth Circuit?"

"That's Emily," Caleb replied with a smile. "Clerked for Winchester for a couple of years, and then worked for a large corporate law firm downtown for almost three years. Turned out that wasn't her thing. She wanted to do civil rights and public aid work. I hired her about seven months ago when things were getting out of control and I couldn't handle the client workload alone. She's been a great addition since day one."

"Wow!" Aaron pronounced. "Clay and I interviewed her over lunch a little over two years ago when we were talking to witnesses in New Orleans in preparation for Winchester's Senate Judiciary Committee hearings on his Supreme Court nomination. We were both very impressed with her."

"Ha! It's a small world," Caleb laughed out loud. "That is hilarious. She's a wonderful attorney, the clients absolutely love her. I can't wait to see the expression on her face when she sees you two guys again."

"Excellent," Clay said. "Lunch is on Aaron and me tomorrow. We're going to have lunch delivered from Cochon Butcher. That is where Aaron and I interviewed Emily two years ago. She said it was her favorite place for lunch."

"Nice touch, guys, nice touch. Y'all are gonna fit in just fine." Caleb offered while nodding.

SAM BRAINARD AND HIS BOSS, PRESIDENT Cochran, watched television together in the family residence in the White House.

"Well, another Tea Party extremist is getting ready to challenge me in the primaries," the President stated with a smirk. "I don't know how you can get to the right of Cletus Sawyer, but hell if Lamar Clarkson hasn't managed it. And the Governor of Mississippi has all but claimed that I am a Republican socialist. I remember a time when political rhetoric had to at least have a whiff of truth to it. Now, it's nothing but complete fabrications."

"Well, we knew this was coming," Sam acknowledged with a sigh. "After Winchester withdrew his name from nomination, the party crazies wanted you to go even further to the right in your pick. They could care less that your administration was embroiled in scandal brought on by Nathan Whitaker's actions. When you compromised with the Senate Democrats, they went ballistic."

"For Christ's sake, just look where all of my competitors come from. Cletus Sawyer is a Senator from Alabama, Lamar Clarkson is Governor of Mississippi, Carlton Smith is a Senator from Utah, and Jebediah Wilson is an evangelical pastor of a super church in Arkansas. All solid red right-wing conservative states. In comparison, I'm the pinko from the purple state of Georgia. Hell Sam, the primary race for the Republican Presidential nomination is turning into a contest of who hates abortion and homosexuals more. That's one race I have no intent on participating in," Andrew Cochran stated firmly. "There is a big difference between the American people at large and the Republican base that votes in primaries," Andrew responded.

"True, the trick is to be President of the United States, not just President of a handful of southern states and a few western states where the number of mountain goats dwarfs the human population of those states, right?" Sam queried.

"Oh, I have no doubt that none of my announced competitors for the nomination would come remotely close to winning a general election. If your family didn't come over on the Mayflower, they basically want to deport you. If you have an abortion, you belong in prison, and if you're homosexual they want you stoned. That is not a recipe for electoral success," Andrew Cochran sarcastically spat out to his Chief of Staff. "But the Republican base who votes in primary elections, that's a different story. I told Landon just yesterday that I will not pander to the far right. If it means losing the nomination, so be it. In retrospect, in the last election I allowed Nathan to take me further to the right politically than I would have gone myself. I'm not going to do that again. I will run as a sitting President who does not find political compromise with the Democrats as being the mortal sin that Jebediah Wilson has already proclaimed it to be. I serve all of the American people, Sam," President Cochran declared.

"As you should," Sam acknowledged. "On that point, there was an interesting development the other day in some national polling. It appears that your overall approval rating rose by 4 points immediately after the attempt on your life at the Prayer Breakfast. Mind you, most of that improvement was from Independent voters and some Democrats. Though even Republican voters looked at you a bit more favorably. People tend to support their leader in times of crisis."

"That is interesting. Perhaps assassination attempts by disgruntled Republicans is the way to go for raising my popularity and poll numbers," Andrew Cochran joked and laughed. "Of course, the downside is that it needs to be an attempt and not actually succeed. Though that would make Howard Mason a very happy man."

SAM BRAINARD WAS NOT THE ONLY WHITE HOUSE Chief of Staff who noticed President Cochran's jump in the political polls in the immediate aftermath of the unsuccessful attempt on his life. Nathan Whitaker, as always, was taking notes. He was an avid political polling junkie, who followed the various candidates positioning in the polls very carefully, always looking for what might make an incremental difference in popularity. The CNN poll taken days after the unsuccessful assassination attempt on the President drew his attention, as it had with Sam Brainard. Nathan wanted to share some thoughts with his old college roommate about how to take advantage of the bump in the poll numbers, but of course, he could not, and that proved immensely frustrating.

"That would be a very dicey move," Vice-President Howard Mason stated as he listened to his longtime political advisor, Mark Backus over dinner at a prominent Washington restaurant.

"We're just talking now, exchanging ideas, nothing more," Mark stated with a nod. "Presidents have shed their incumbent Vice-Presidents before seeking re-election for various reasons. Jefferson replaced Burr in 1804, after the duel with Hamilton. Lincoln replaced Hannibal Hamlin when he ran for re-election in 1864 with Andrew Johnson to appease the South and offer an olive branch. Hamlin was a Maine abolitionist who Southerners abhorred. Gerald Ford replaced Nelson Rockefeller in 1976 with Bob Dole. Rockefeller was far too liberal for the party base. But there have also been instances in which an incumbent Vice-President has challenged a sitting President for nomination."

"Vice-President Thomas Jefferson challenging and defeating President John Adams in 1800 doesn't count. It occurred when the party nominees were not tied together prior to the passage of the 12th Amendment," Howard Mason replied.

"Very true," Mark responded, "but that was not the only instance. After completing McKinley's term after his assassination and then winning his own term in 1904, Theodore Roosevelt decided to retire leading into the 1908 election. His Vice-President William Howard Taft won that election, and in 1912 when Taft ran for re-election, Roosevelt decided to come out of retirement and challenge Taft for the Republican nomination. The party preferred Taft on the ticket and Teddy Roosevelt ran as a Progressive third-party candidate fronting the Bull Moose Party."

"And in doing so, he handed Woodrow Wilson a landslide victory," Howard added, while running his hands through his graying blonde hair and sighing deeply. "Besides, that is apples and oranges. It was not an incumbent Vice-President challenging his party's President."

"Perhaps not, but there is one instance that is demonstrably on point,"

Mark acknowledged. "In 1939, Franklin Roosevelt's then Vice-President, John Nance Garner, had become disillusioned and disagreed with some of FDR's policies and political maneuvering. Garner was opposed to the Judiciary Reorganization Bill of 1937, where Roosevelt attempted to stack the Supreme Court with his judges. Garner believed that the bill enshrined far too much power in the President. Garner also believed in a balanced Federal budget which was being challenged by FDR's New Deal deficit spending. They no longer were aligned on several key issues, and Garner sought the Democratic nomination for President."

"Yes, but if memory serves, at the time Cactus Jack Garner declared for the party's nomination, FDR had not yet decided if he would run for a third term. Which of course he did, which further embittered Garner who thought that FDR should not pursue a third term. He did not believe that President's should be allowed to serve three terms," Howard Mason interjected.

"True," Mark Backus conceded. "But the point is that there is your precedent. An incumbent Vice-President who had become disillusioned with the policies and political machinations of the sitting President had had enough. For principled reasons, Garner challenged the incumbent who he no longer agreed with on many salient and important issues. Andrew Cochran has changed his stance on most of the Conservative values that he ran on during his election. He has abandoned many of the party platforms in an effort to appease the Democrats. And that appeasement, is a direct result of scandal and impropriety in his White House and among his highest-ranking staff. The practical, moral, and ethical grounds for a challenge have been well laid."

"And how does history remember President Garner?" Howard asked with a twinkle in his deep-set blue eyes. "I understand and appreciate your point Mark, I do. But the terms traitor and renegade are not something I care to be associated with."

"On the contrary, I firmly believe that many in the party would hail you as a champion. Someone to deliver them and the country from the liberal Cochran bombast and issue bastardization of the past three years," Mark firmly stated.

"I've given speeches in defense of some of those issues," Howard quickly added. "I've defended the President's positions because that is the role of a Vice-President. Doesn't that make me an accomplice to his policies?"

"It makes you a loyal soldier. But there is always that last straw, the line that should not be crossed. You will be applauded for your loyalty, but then when one cannot any longer accept the scandal, the corruption, and the destructive liberal policy positions, you rise up and righteously challenge the man you once faithfully served for you can no longer hold your tongue when truth and an ethical imperative dictate a need for action."

"I should have made you my speechwriter," Howard replied with a wink and an affectionate smile.

"There are many people of great power and influence who are waiting to get behind you, but they can only wait for so long," Mark cautioned.

"Understood. But truly the only decision that I plan to make tonight, my friend, is what to have for dessert."

"GOOD MORNING SENATOR," Carolyn greeted her nominee for President as she entered his Senate office. "I have it on good word that the field for the Democratic Party nomination for President just trebled."

"Salutations, Carolyn. And who pray tell is joining me in this contest of the absurd?" Perry Douglas asked with a sly smile.

"Your Senate colleague on the Judiciary Committee, Hellen Raymond, will be announcing later today just before the six o'clock news. And Governor Keith Stolts of Oregon is slated to make his announcement next Monday. I received that news as I was making my way through Senate building security a few minutes ago," Carolyn explained.

"So, I'm being challenged by the political right of our party by a female Senator from North Carolina, who is a fifty-four-year-old grandmother of two. Her husband is a Baptist minister and she has two adult sons who both serve as Naval officers. A woman born and raised in a rural farm community, who went on to graduate first in her class at Duke Law. A woman of great faith and family. OK, so there's that," Perry Douglas said while shaking his head. "Then at the political left of our party, Governor Keith Stolts, single, possibly bisexual, and who graduated first in his class from UC Berkeley School of Law. He describes himself as a Democratic socialist and an agnostic, and he wants to expand domestic spending by 40 percent and decrease military spending by 50 percent. Where does that leave us?"

"Senator, to quote from a song my older brother used to listen to, 'Clowns to the left of me, jokers to the right. Here I am, stuck in the middle with you,'" Carolyn sang/said to Perry.

"Well, you started off with nothing and you're proud that you're a self-made man. And your friends all come crawling, slap you on the back and say, please, please", Perry sang and laughed back to his campaign manager. "Stealers Wheel, 1972, written by Gerry Rafferty and Joe Egan. I love that song," Perry exclaimed.

"I never knew who did it. My brother played that song around the house all the time. I couldn't help but memorize the lyrics," Carolyn laughed.

"That should be our campaign song in the primaries, 'Stuck In The Middle With You.' It's perfect!" Perry exclaimed.

"Let's sleep on that decision, shall we?" Carolyn smiled, as she chortled with her boss.

NATHAN WHITAKER LOOKED AT THE SCREEN of his iPhone, the caller's name and number had been blocked. Intrigued, Nathan decided to answer.

"Is this Nathan Whitaker?" The low distorted male voice on the call asked.

"Yes, who is this?" Nathan responded.

"Someone who wants to give you some advice for your own good. Stay away from him. Stop reaching out, it's going to get you into some serious trouble."

"Stay away from who?" Nathan questioned.

"Oh Nathan, I truly wish you were as stupid and naïve as you pretend to be. If that were the case, there would be no need for this call. He's dead to you. Stay the fuck away!" The man insisted emphatically.

"Who are you to call and threaten me?" Nathan responded vehemently.

"I'm someone who can see to it that you spend the rest of your life in prison, regardless of your fancy lawyer and wealthy benefactor. This is a warning, Nathan. And in this game, you only get one strike and you're out."

"I'm not interested in playing any game," Nathan replied, but at that point he was speaking to a dial tone.

CHAPTER 8

Six weeks had passed, and it was the week before Thanksgiving. Posy Branch, Chantale Calypso, and Chiffon LaBelle stood in the center of the newly remodeled nail salon/bar/music club. The large room was filled with balloons, streamers and signs heralding the grand opening of French Tips, Juleps & Jazz. The long mahogany bar along the far wall gleamed under the bright lights.

The six nail stations were separated by colorful and tasteful six-foot-high dividers. Each nail station was meticulously clean and regimentally organized. Alongside the back wall near the bar, a four-piece jazz quartet set up their instruments on a slightly raised platform. The floor to ceiling hurricane shutters at the front of the store were open exposing the salon and bar to the casual passerby.

"A gal can walk in, get a fine pedicure, enjoy a tasty julep or two, and dance to the jazz band iffin' she's of a mind," Posy announced to no one in particular. "I can already smell the money walking through them doors, windows, shutters or whatever y'all call 'em."

Chantale looked directly at Chiffon and stated, "You can't fix crazy. Crazy is forever."

"What she say?" Posy asked Chiffon, who was between Posy and Chantale.

"She said she loves your energy," Chiffon lied.

Posy moved over to face Chantale and said, "Thanks, Sugar. It sure is fun, ain't it?" Chantale just shook her head in disbelief.

"Well, I wanted to be open by Halloween to cater to that freak show crowd, but that lying contractor screwed us on the schedule," Posy stated.

"We've still got the major holidays, we should do just fine," Chantale said encouragingly.

"I'm thinking after the first week, I'm gonna have the bar boys lose their shirts. Just a bowtie and suspenders over their bare chests. You know sexy but classy. What do you think?" Posy asked Chiffon.

"Can't hurt with bringing in the girls and even some of the boys," Chiffon replied with a wink and a smile.

"I like the way you think, girl," Posy laughed out while slapping Chiffon on the back. "Money is money, whether it comes from some gal's kids college fund or from just being pushed next to the sweaty balls of some shaved-down gay stripper. It's all money. Ain't that right?" Posy yelled over to her business partner, Chantale Calypso.

Chantale looked toward the heavens and muttered, "Crazy."

PRESIDENT COCHRAN MADE THE TIME during his short trip back to his home state to make a brief tour of his new national campaign office located in downtown Savannah. The First Lady, Sue Lynn Cochran, accompanied her husband as they surveyed the large space.

"I like this one better," Sue Lynn said to her husband as they walked arm in arm through the campaign headquarters.

"You like this space more than the one we ran the presidential campaign from over three years ago?" Andrew Cochran asked.

"Yes, it's got more of an optimistic feel to it. I can't really put it in words," Sue Lynn replied.

"Could it be the absence of Nathan and Posy Whitaker?" The President asked.

"Well, I wasn't going to put names to it, but since you mentioned it, yes," Sue Lynn confirmed. "You know I never cared for that woman, so I am happy to have her out of our lives."

"And Nathan?" Andrew questioned, his tone becoming accusatory.

"Nathan through his notorious actions made a bed for himself and for us that we are still dealing with. If not for what he did, there would be no primary challengers to a sitting president and the leader of the party," Sue Lynn stated sharply.

"You know I can't pretend like forty years of my life didn't happen," Andrew Cochran said slowly, his tone full of melancholy. "I abhor what he is alleged to have done, but two years since seeing him, I can't say that I don't still care about Nathan. That I don't miss him."

"Andy you've moved on. We have moved on. The country has moved on. The past is the past, and in this instance, must be relegated to a closet of old memories. That closet door needs to be sparingly opened, if it need be opened at all," Sue Lynn counseled her husband.

"It's just not that easy, Sue Lynn, it just isn't."

Bessie Collins stood smiling behind the counter of the voodoo shop on North Rampart. The shop had never been cleaner and more meticulously organized. For years, there was minimal signage outside of the shop. Only a small sign which read, "Voodoo Shop & Museum" had been outside the store for most of its existence under the ownership of Bessie's aunt. That small sign was now replaced by a larger new sign which read, "Queen Rita's House of Voodoo." Like similar shops in New Orleans, such as Marie Laveau's, Bessie wanted to make sure that the name of Queen Rita was remembered. It was very difficult for Bessie to allow her aunt's actions to color her affection and respect for the woman she grew up admiring. Despite her past transgressions and crimes, Bessie still wanted the shop to bear the name of her beloved auntie.

The well-worn small bell that hung over the shop's doorway gave forth its tintinnabulation as the first customer in over two years' time, entered the shop on the first day of its reopening.

"Welcome," Bessie cheerfully greeted her first customer. "If there is anything that I can be of help with, please let me know." Bessie wore an African dress of black, orange, and green colors. She had her hair pulled back and tied in a similarly colored head wrap. This was not how Bessie normally dressed, but she thought it important to assume a role in her new business, even in her attire. The tourist walked around the shop, selecting certain amulets and ceremonial tokens to closely examine. After several minutes, the customer selected a few items to purchase. Bessie rang the items up on the old cash register that her aunt used.

"Thank you, come again soon," Bessie stated as the customer left the store. Moments after the customer left, Papa Levi emerged from the back room of the shop.

"First sale of $32.59," Bessie beamed with pride.

"The spirits shine on you, Bessie," Papa Levi responded. "They surely do."

Aaron Rose and Clay Grover sat in Caleb Butler's small office as they discussed the law practices clients and the distribution of workload among the four attorneys.

"Until you guys take and pass the Louisiana Bar exam in February, Emily and I will cover all of the court appearances," Caleb stated. "But that leaves you with drafting the filing papers, motions, and briefs. As well as getting to know our clients." Caleb slid a printed-out list of his clients across the desk to Aaron and Clay.

"Each of the client names that bears an asterisk are part of the Hurricane Katrina class action that goes on appeal in the Fifth Circuit. There are two hundred and eighty-four members of the class; I represent thirty-eight of them," Caleb informed his new colleagues. "As you know the Fifth Circuit panel hearing the appeal will be Stanford Winchester, Charles Sewell, and Whitlee Hammond. That is where you guys become invaluable. You interviewed Sewell during Winchester's judiciary committee vetting. And after months of research leading up to the committee hearings, Aaron probably knows more about Winchester than most people on this planet. Your insights will be instrumental as the class appellee team prepares for the oral argument before Winchester's panel."

"It's been over two years since I handled the Winchester research," Aaron professed.

"Stanford Winchester doesn't change. He is a creature of habit, convention, and tradition. What you knew about him through your research from thirty years ago still holds true today," Caleb responded. "But the scheduling order just came down the other day. We have months to prepare for oral argument. In the meantime, I'd like for the two of you to get to know and work with some of my clients who are part of the appeal."

"There's a name here followed by another name in parentheses," Aaron pointed out as he scanned the asterisked names on the list. "Is that a husband and wife with two different last names?" Aaron inquired.

Caleb smiled as he ran his hand through his short dark hair. His blue eyes sparkled as he prepared to explain his client to Aaron and Clay.

"My client's legal name, as of now, is Ernest Johnson, however she doesn't use that name except in legal documents. You see Ernest is a pre-op transsexual who goes by the name of Chiffon LaBelle. She plans on having her name legally changed shortly. But for the time being, as it applies to this lawsuit, her name is officially Ernest Johnson. Her case is one of the more tragic that I handle. Like most of my clients, she owned a small home in the lower Ninth ward and lived with her lover, Baron Coleman. Katrina and the levee break completely destroyed her home, and Baron, who could not swim, tragically drowned as he attempted to save their dog. It's only been fairly recently that she's been able to get her life back together. Chiffon is full of life. A sweet and loving person with a great outlook on life considering everything that she's been through. She is a delight to be with, and she's going to absolutely adore you Aaron," Caleb stated with a knowing smile.

"Why is that?" Aaron curiously asked.

"Nice looking African-American man with handsome features and a strong athletic body. You are right up her alley," Caleb grinned.

"He's spoken for," Clay quickly interjected.

"I'll let you explain that to Chiffon yourself," Caleb said laughing. "She can be very persuasive."

LANDON HAMILTON AND SAM BRAINARD WERE sitting in a restaurant booth at a hotel nearby the White House.

"How goes the new campaign office and logistics?" Sam asked.

"Very well, I've got everything under control," Landon bragged.

"Cool, but no one has everything under control in a political campaign, it's just not the nature of the beast," Sam responded with a smile. "If you're lucky, the well run campaigns are organized mayhem."

"I told you, I've got everything under control," Landon snapped back.

"Look man, I didn't mean to offend you. It's just that this is not my first campaign. I've been around politics for almost two decades. Nothing comes easy. As White House Chief of Staff, I watch the clock hoping that I can make it through one day without screwing up too badly. I usually fail at that endeavor because things you don't expect or have planned for come flying at you all the time," Sam explained. "I sleep better at night if I can keep the damage to a minimal degree. When Nathan Whitaker was in my position and I was in the role of Senior Presidential Advisor, I was in awe of his political acumen and ability to control situations. Nathan was a pro's pro."

"Nathan Whitaker is indicted for murder. There is nothing special about him. He is the reason that the President is being challenged for nomination by members of his own party," Landon replied.

"OK, that's mostly true, but a bit harsh. Nathan hasn't been convicted of anything yet, and up until the scandal, he was the person closest to Andrew Cochran other than the First Lady," Sam responded. "They had a wonderful bond with each other."

"Nathan is a cancer on the Presidency. He cannot be allowed to ever be associated with our President again. Not if we intend to win re-election," Landon stated angrily.

"Chill, Landon. Maybe we should start with a cocktail."

CHAPTER 9

CHIEF JUDGE STANFORD WINCHESTER PRESIDED OVER an administrative meeting with the other seventeen active judges on the Fifth Circuit as well as three of the senior judges. He glanced around the room, taking in his colleagues as they conversed with one another. It was a good group he thought to himself. He got along with most of them.

Whitlee Hammond was a late arrival to the meeting. She took a seat in the empty chair to Stanford's left as he began to call the meeting to order. Stanford discussed the court's docket for the remainder of the year. Several matters had concluded briefing and had oral argument dates scheduled on the calendar. However, the case that occupied most of the discussion was the high-profile Katrina victims class action appeal.

Amos Trebold, a Democratic appointee to the court mentioned a rumor that he had heard.

"I've been told by reliable sources that counsel for the appellants, which includes the Solicitor General, are not pleased with Chief Judge Winchester being selected to sit on the panel," Amos posited in front of the entire group.

"And why may that be?" Stanford asked.

"Well, I've heard that they don't think that they will get a fair shake with the Chief Judge," Amos responded. "I hear tell that there's still a lot of skepticism and hard feelings after the Justice's withdrawal from the Supreme Court nomination."

"Firstly, the only reason I am assigned to that case is because my name was drawn by a blind lottery, as you well know, Amos. Secondly, that unfortunate predicament was over two years ago. I did what I thought was in the best interest of the country and the President, given all of the details that became amply evident. Finally, I harbor no ill will towards anyone. I will be fair and impartial and I will weigh all of the evidence, as will my colleagues Judge Hammond and Judge Sewell," Stanford professed to his assembled colleagues as he turned and smiled at Judge Hammond.

"From what I've heard," Amos continued, "Appellants counsel is considering adding Leland Calhoun to their team."

"Leland Calhoun has not practiced as an attorney in probably close to 20 years. He retired from the Louisiana Supreme Court over four years ago. He hasn't been in a court room for years; why would they do that?" Stanford asked perplexed and somewhat irritated.

"Mostly to force your hand to recuse yourself from the matter, given your previous antagonistic relationship with Calhoun when you served on the Louisiana bench together," Amos responded.

"No, I'm sorry. Parties appearing before this court are not permitted to pick and choose their judicial panel. Schoolyard bullying tactics and ridiculous parlor games will not interfere with even handed fairness and justice," Stanford stated confidently and with great equanimity. "If the appellants choose to waste their money by retaining a former judicial colleague of mine that is their prerogative. But if they believe for one moment that they can force my hand with such a transparent and ill-conceived ruse, well, my esteemed friends, I am here to tell you that that dog won't hunt."

"I am pleased to hear that," Judge Hammond added. "The whole scheme sounds far-fetched, and frankly, juvenile. Unless they plan to have an unpracticed litigator like Leland Calhoun present oral argument, there is no point to it."

"Alright, unless there are any other rumors that need to be shared or debunked, we are adjourned. Thanks y'all for making time for these administrative matters," Stanford stated as his colleagues began to filter out of the conference room. Stanford leaned over to Judge Hammond and hesitated for a moment.

"Whitlee, I'd like to thank you for that," Stanford slowly drawled as he unconsciously straightened his bow tie.

"It's all preposterous drivel. I'm not sure why Amos brought it up," Whitlee replied.

"Who knows why folks act and say the things they do. Perhaps he was trying to get my goat, or perhaps he's naive enough to believe in such things. I make no never mind of it. I am just grateful to have a colleague who is willing to speak on my behalf," Stanford graciously acknowledged.

"I admire the way you run this court. It is a pleasure to call myself a colleague of yours," Whitlee replied.

"Thank you, Whitlee. Thank you." Stanford felt a slight blush across his cheeks. "I'll see you tomorrow. Have a wonderful evening."

Stanford walked down Royal Street on his way home with an extra bounce in his step. The hibiscus tree blossoms smelled especially sweet that night.

Andrew Cochran sat down for dinner with his Chief of Staff and his campaign manager at a restaurant not far from the White House.

"I hate doing this to the restaurant staff and the other patrons but if I don't get out of that building from time to time, I will lose my mind," the President said over after dinner cocktails.

"Well sir, Cletus Sawyer is trying his best to make sure that in two years you will be spending all of your time outside of the White House," Sam Brainard offered.

"Yes, I heard that he had another press conference this afternoon," Andrew Cochran mentioned. "Has he accused me of kicking and beating my dogs yet?"

"No sir, not yet, but it's coming," Landon Hamilton chuckled.

"Jebediah Wilson made an off the cuff remark within the earshot of reporters after a recent prayer service that there are some factors that lead to the possibility that you and Nathan Whitaker were homosexual lovers. So, there's that," Sam said with a chuckle.

"Oh, is that one based on the college fraternity party photo when we were juniors at Vanderbilt?" the President asked.

"Not sure I know about that one," Sam hesitantly stated.

"It's been circulating for years. Even came up when I ran for Governor of Georgia," Andrew Cochran said with a smile. "Junior year of college, our fraternity was having a toga party. It was all the rage back in the day. Someone took a photo of Nathan and I dressed in togas, basically naked from the waist up, sitting on a couch in our frat house, and Nathan is leaning over and kissing me on the cheek. From that came the obvious inference that we were homosexual lovers. Of course, with the scandal surrounding Nathan, it was just a matter of time before someone seized on that tired old story again."

"In this case, one who is running for the Republican nomination for President," Sam clarified.

"Jebediah Wilson is the least of my worries. Frankly, I don't see any of my Republican opponents putting up much of a fight," Andrew Cochran surmised. "It's the general election that causes me greater concern. I can't allow the primary battles to take me too far to the right on policy. The Democrats have Hellen Raymond and Perry Douglas as two very formidable candidates. Raymond is as middle of the road as you can get in American politics. And Douglas is smart and aggressive. He's a progressive on social issues, but pragmatic on national security and taxes. It should be interesting, to say the least. But enough about that, this is my evening to escape. Let's have dessert."

"OOH, MICHAEL, THAT'S PERFECT!" Posy nearly moaned as she took a large sip of the Mint Julep that Michael had just made for her. Her fingertips caressed the long straw that accompanied the drink. "Last one had just a touch too much simple syrup. It was a little sweet. A gal wants to be able to taste the liquor."

Michael was the stunningly attractive and well-built bartender that Posy had hired for her business. At six foot two inches of solid rippling muscle, with long blond hair and dazzling blue eyes, he was the eye candy Adonis that she wanted for her new business enterprise–something for the women customers to look at, while they were enjoying a cocktail, having their nails done, and listening to Dixieland jazz and swing.

"Thanks Posy, I think I've got the right proportions figured out," Michael stated. "In bartending school, they overemphasize the use of simple syrup. So, it's just a matter of trial and error."

"Well, Sugar, this here julep is making my toes curl," Posy laughed. "I'm glad that you done figured it out and that you are applying your trade here with me."

"I'm thankful for the opportunity. It's tough to get a bartending job in New Orleans without spending months if not years as a bar back. I'm much happier being behind the bar instead of dancing on it," Michael stated with gratitude.

"Well, Sugar, you looked mighty fine dancing on the bar top at Oz when I was walking by and spotted you. I knew that I had to have you serving drinks to my clients. But it ain't all a picnic, I'm here to tell you. If you thought it was difficult having gay men rubbing on you and whispering in your ear, wait until a few of these middle-aged gals with one too many juleps in them and a nice new French tip manicure get their claws into you," Posy advised with a chortle. "Oh, and, Sugar, don't mention to the women clients that you is gay. If the fantasy seems more realistic, the tips will be much bigger. I learned that trick during my beauty pageant days back in Georgia."

"Sure thing, will do," Michael replied through his stunning white smile.

"Now, let's try an Apple Julep," Posy said while leaning up against the bar.

LUCIUS COLLINS SNUCK UP BEHIND HIS WIFE Bessie and wrapped his arms around her waist as she was washing the dinner plates in the kitchen sink.

"Quit that now, Lucius, you getting water everywhere," Bessie scolded her husband.

"Ain't nothing wrong with a husband giving his pretty wife a good squeeze," Lucius chuckled.

"They is, when the wife got to fetch the mop to take up all the water that done splashed all over," Bessie responded with a playful scowl. "Go sit yourself down in the parlor and I'll bring you some ice cream when I finish these here dishes."

"Bessie, it been forever since we had one of your fine pies in this house," Lucius stated. "You gonna make a sweet potato and pecan pie for Thanksgiving?"

"We'll see," Bessie replied. "Things been picking up at the voodoo shop. I been real busy lately with readings and ordering new merchandise and the such. Folks been snatching up most of my inventory what with the holidays and all. Everyone looking for a little extra good fortune."

"Yeah, well, I been thinking that you been spending too much of your time over at that shop," Lucius stated firmly, his brow furrowed.

"Lucius, it's a business. They don't be runnin' themselves. And it is my business. I can't rightly afford to hire someone else, at least not now. Papa Levi is old. He come and go. I can't always rely on him," Bessie explained.

"That shop is interfering with our lives," Lucius responded.

"That shop is part of our lives," Bessie countered. "It's my business now. I own it and I run it. And I am enjoying myself. I'm getting new customers every day. And folk seem to like me and what I can provide to them. Plus, since I opened that shop have I been awoke once in my sleep? Not a single time. Them dreams are gone now, and I'm happy again. You gots to see that?"

"I don't know Bessie. I surely don't know."

"Jedediah Wilson has planted the seeds, now we need to dust the crops," the deep Southern voice said into his cellphone. "And where are we on getting a commitment from a suitable replacement for Cochran prior to the general election?"

"There is no commitment, but I've been told there is also no firm denial," the second person on the phone call stated. "There may be some interest. It is a work in progress."

"That's not good enough. The clock is ticking," the Southern voice challenged.

"The first debate is still several months away. There is plenty of time for others to throw their hats into the ring for the party's nomination," the second person affirmed.

"Perhaps, and of course, there are other remedies as well, including the voters. Primary voters are nothing more than stupid cattle. They need to be corralled and moved in a certain direction. Make sure that we are ready to rustle 'em up and move them where we want them to go."

"Of course."

"I told you before, it is unacceptable for Cochran to be re-elected, and even worse if some liberal socialist Democrat is in charge of things. We need a good ol' boy that we can control, that we own."

CHAPTER 10

O NE MONTH LATER WAS THE WEEK BEFORE CHRISTMAS and Aaron Rose completed his and Clay's travel plans to spend three days in Chicago over the holidays with Aaron's family.

"My mom wants to know what you want for Christmas?" Aaron asked Clay from across the living room of their modest rental home.

"You can tell her that she has already given me everything that I could possibly want in you," Clay sweetly replied.

"Yeah, she's not gonna buy that. How about a new shirt or a sweater?" Aaron persisted.

"How about we skip presents and just donate money to a food shelter?" Clay replied.

"You do understand that my mother is a small Jewish woman whose favorite holiday is Christmas, right?" Aaron questioned with a smile. "If you don't accept and love what she buys you, you will ruin her holidays, possibly forever."

"Light blue V-neck wool pullover sweater in extra-large," Clay replied with a heavy sigh.

"Excellent, I'll let her know," Aaron stated with glee.

"And what about you. What do you want for Christmas?" Clay asked Aaron.

"I want to pass the bar exam in February and get in a courtroom," Aaron replied. "I love meeting the clients and working with them, but I don't feel like we're pulling our weight yet."

"We will, it's only been three months," Clay responded. "And Caleb already thinks you're great."

"He's such a smart guy and has built a very substantial law practice in his late-thirties. What was he like in law school?" Aaron inquired.

"Smart, energetic, out-going, much like he is now," Clay replied. "I was the shy one. The gay guy who was still somewhat closeted. Even after meeting Sebastian in law school, around everyone else, I pretty much hid my homosexuality."

"Did Caleb know?" Aaron asked.

"Eventually. But he was busy courting his wife Carol in law school. Between studying for classes and chasing after Carol he didn't have much time to pay attention to what I was doing," Clay stated.

"Did you bring guys back to your apartment when you were living with Caleb?" Aaron pressed his line of questioning.

"Only when I was sure he wouldn't be there. As I mentioned, I was still pretty closeted in law school," Clay responded.

"Who got better grades, you or Caleb?" Aaron asked.

"Pretty much a tie, you could say. I had a 3.8 GPA, and Caleb was a 3.6. Why are you asking all of these questions?" Clay inquired.

"Just curious about my husband's law school career, I guess," Aaron responded.

"OK, class is over," Clay stated. "Time to go to bed."

"Yes, Professor Grover," Aaron said seductively.

"Let's see if you can get an A, Mr. Rose," Clay replied with a big smile.

Posy Branch had just placed the closed sign on the door of French Tips, Juleps & Jazz. She turned around and broadly smiled at her partner Chantale Calypso and their staff.

"Let's get this Christmas shindig going," Posy shouted as she walked to the bar. She sat next to Chantale on a bar stool as Michael was busy preparing Mint Juleps for everyone. The jazz band played a swing version of "Santa Claus Is Coming To Town" as the nail beauticians began to dance with the attractive male servers.

"Been a real good first month, partner of mine," Posy stated to Chantale. "We made as much money in the last forty days as you had made in the three months before we closed for renovations."

"Yes, but it is holidays, they always make more," Chantale challenged.

"Did you make nearly this much last year during the holidays?" Posy questioned.

"No," Chantale admitted.

"Then lighten up, Girlfriend, and just admit that we make a real good team, and that adding a bar and serving liquor was a damn fine idea," Posy said grinning at Chantale.

"What you want, me kiss your feet?" Chantale replied.

"Not until one of the gals gives me a fine pedicure," Posy heartily laughed and snorted.

"Here you go, Posy," Michael said as he slid a julep across the bar to Posy. Posy took a long sip of her drink through her straw and audibly moaned.

"Michael, darlin'," Posy declared, "You make me as happy as a dead pig in the sunshine."

Michael stared back at Posy. His bright blue eyes looked lost as he attempted to search for a possible meaning. Eventually, he confessed, "I have no idea what that means."

"Oh, come on now, you never heard that sayin' before?" Posy questioned, unable to believe that Michael didn't know the meaning of her statement.

"I have no idea what that means," Michael reiterated.

"Ain't you never been on a pig farm?" Posy queried Michael.

"Posy, I'm from Cleveland," Michael replied.

"Ok, then," Posy began. "When a pig dies outside in the sty, the sun dries out its skin. This effect pulls the pigs lips back to reveal a toothy grin. So, the pig looks real happy even though it's dead. Get it?"

"I guess so," Michael responded though still looking rather confused.

"Simple as pie," Posy stated to Michael. "No one makes a better julep than you, Sugar. I'm gonna go mingle with the nail gals for a bit, but I'll be back for another round." Posy walked over towards the beauticians who were doing shots. Chantale turned on her bar stool and looked directly at Michael.

"No worries. No one understands crazy," Chantale slowly declared.

The snow gently fell from the dark Chicago skies as Carolyn Barnes briskly walked down Michigan Avenue. The small white lights on the trees along the boulevard glimmered as they reflected the glistening new fallen flakes. It was days before Christmas Eve and Carolyn needed to get to North Face to buy a fleece jacket and a couple of sweaters for her son Cameron. Cam had turned eighteen years old a month ago and was six foot two and growing. Juggling the responsibilities of being the campaign manager for a presidential candidate and being a single mom to a teenage son was not easy. But Carolyn refused to fail at either. Failure was not an option. She had failed once in her marriage. That was enough for one lifetime.

As she scurried through the new-fallen snow on Michigan Avenue, Carolyn's cellphone rang.

"Yes," she answered. "You've got the preliminary preference polling on Democratic leaning voters?" She asked. Carolyn listened intently to the voice on the other end of the line. She vigorously shook her head as she continued her snow-filled trudge.

"Well, it's early," Carolyn replied after hearing the results. "We need to work on name recognition and further develop the narrative. None of that is a surprise. Plus, we knew there would be a lot of support for a female candidate. All this tells me is that we have a good deal of work to do. The Iowa caucus is still a little over a year away. We've got plenty of time to tell our story. Alright, I'll talk to you later," Carolyn stated as she ended her phone call.

Carolyn had finally reached her destination for her Christmas shopping. She and her candidate, Senator Perry Douglas, as she had just found out, had a much longer road ahead of them.

ANDREW COCHRAN SAT IN A COMFORTABLE CHAIR in the residence at the White House and admired the family Christmas tree. The presents for their adult children and grandchildren surrounded the bottom of the lovely decorated tree.

"I truly prefer this tree to the public White House tree downstairs," Andrew confided to his wife Sue Lynn.

"Don't let Toni Green hear you say that," Sue Lynn replied with a smile. "She and her staff spent six months planning every detail of that tree."

"Precisely," Andrew stated. "It's too perfect, too planned. There is no home-spun authenticity to it."

"You mean it doesn't have the gold spray painted macaroni star that our daughter Claire made in Girl Scouts when she was nine, or our son Ben's Atlanta Braves team ornaments clashing with everything else on the tree?" Sue Lynn asked with a smile.

"Yes, this tree speaks of our family. The twenty-foot tree in the Blue Room is a tree for the country, not for us," Andrew affirmed. "Look at that ratty, well-worn upside down elf ornament. Grandma Blanche gave that to Nathan and me for our small dorm room Christmas tree that first year of college. That ornament is forty-two years old."

"And it looks like it," Sue Lynn stated. "I guess I never knew where that one came from. It was just always in the box with the other family ornaments."

"Yup, the first ornament that I was given as an adult. Grandma Blanche gave it to the two of us, so that we wouldn't feel so homesick that first semester away from home. She always tried to jolly up her boys," Andrew said with a touch of sadness in his tone.

"After everything that he did and even though he nearly took down your Presidency before it actually had a chance to get going, you still miss him, don't you?" Sue Lynn questioned her husband.

"You can't just erase all those years," Andrew confided as he looked directly at his wife. "Other than you and our children, I was never closer to another person," Andrew said as his voice began to crack. "I can't lie, I miss Nathan. I absolutely do. But I know that I cannot see him or talk to him. Yet, I look at that old ornament and I remember the autographed Hank Aaron baseball that he gave me as a gift on the first Christmas we spent together. I still cherish it to this day. Nathan is not the monster that the press has portrayed him as. Of that I am sure. I only wish . . ." Andrew began to say as his voice trailed off.

"I ONLY WISH THAT YOU COULD spend more than a couple days over the holidays with our family," Katherine Douglas said to her husband as they sat together at their kitchen table in Chicago wrapping Christmas presents.

"I know, I wish that I could as well, but with so little time before the new Congress begins its session, I've got to use some of that time off to get out there and make a few appearances," Perry acknowledged. "Running for President is a twenty-four-hour job that just happens to go along with my real job representing the people of Illinois. We made some nice inroads in the House, and even picked up a couple of additional Democratic seats in the Senate in the midterm elections. The American people have been shown the corruption of a Republican administration and they are ready for a change. I've got to be out there pressing the flesh to gain some momentum."

"Oh, I get it," Katherine admitted. "I'm just not thrilled that you are only allowed to spend two days with our children and our one grandchild."

"Are you complaining more about my lack of family time over the holidays or that we have only one grandchild?" Perry asked. "Should

I have a chat with Ellie and her husband John about being more productive? Would you like me to discuss the birds and the bees with our twenty-something year old son Robert?"

"Yeah, good luck with that!" Katherine chuckled. "Ellie and John might stop at one child, which is of course their prerogative. And well, Robert, that will need to be a bees and bees conversation. There are no birds in that boy's life."

"Are you really sure?"

"Robert asked me if he can bring his roommate Jason home for Christmas. This is the third year in a row. Do you actually think that they are only roommates?"

"Then why doesn't he just announce it to his old mom and dad?" Perry asked.

"Probably because he thinks that old mom and dad are sophisticated enough to figure it out on their own. How many times do we need to have this same conversation until it finally sinks in with you? He isn't hiding anything from us, he just isn't sitting us down to tell us something he assumes we already know," Katherine countered.

"Well, he's giving me too much credit," Perry replied.

"Oh, there's no doubt on that score!" Katherine laughed out loud and continuously.

"Merry Christmas to you too, dear," Perry mock scowled at his wife as she doubled over in laughter.

VICE-PRESIDENT HOWARD MASON SAT IN HIS RESIDENCE at the United States Naval Observatory staring out the window at the new-fallen winter snow.

"Come to bed," his wife Maureen encouraged.

"Momentarily, my dear, momentarily."

"Is something wrong? You've seemed preoccupied the last few weeks," the Vice-President's wife asked with concern.

"Every school child is taught about and remembers the name of Benedict Arnold, don't they?' Howard questioned his wife.

"Why yes, I assume so," Maureen responded with a quizzical expression on her face. "Truly, Howard, what is this all about?"

"Nothing, I think," Howard softly replied. "Yet, opportunity is a fickle mistress. She may come to call only once in a lifetime, and if you don't resoundingly reply 'yes' to opportunity, it may never visit you again."

"Howard, I have no idea what you're talking about," Maureen said, her voice becoming slightly agitated by the perplexing language being used by her husband.

"No worries, my love. Merely the ramblings of a tired and disconcerted mind. Pay no attention. You are absolutely right, it is time for bed," Howard Mason confirmed.

CHAPTER 11

A MILD BREEZE CHURNED THROUGH THE OPEN WINDOWS of Aaron and Clay's home in New Orleans. It was New Year's Eve and Ben Carroll was on his way to their house in a cab from the airport to spend a couple of days with his friends. Clay had made reservations for New Year's Eve dinner at Arnaud's, with Emily Dubois joining the three friends and rounding out their foursome. Aaron busied himself carefully ironing his tuxedo shirt as Clay rinsed out champagne flutes over the kitchen sink.

Seven hours later, it was eight o'clock and the foursome were being shown to their table by the tuxedoed Maître D' at Arnaud's.

"What a wonderful, elegant room," Ben stated as they pulled their chairs up to the well-appointed table.

"First time that we've been here," Clay said. "We wanted to go somewhere very nice and very traditional for our first New Year's Eve in New Orleans."

Moments later the waiter approached their table.

"A gracious good evening to the lady and gentlemen. My name is Lucius and I have the great honor to serve you this evening. Welcome to Arnaud's," Lucius Collins stated to the guests at his table.

"Mr. Collins?" Aaron questioned, recognizing that their waiter was the same man that he and Clay had interviewed over two years ago for the Winchester Judiciary Committee hearings.

"Why yes!" Lucius exclaimed. "You two," he said nodding towards Clay and Aaron, "are the fine young gentlemen who spoke with my wife Bessie and myself about Justice Winchester a couple of years ago. Ain't this a very small world," Lucius proclaimed while vigorously shaking both Aaron and Clay's hands. What are y'all doing back in New Orleans, if I may ask?"

"We live here now," Clay responded. "We no longer work for the Senate. In fact, we are both civil rights attorneys working here in New Orleans. We work out of a small office in the Bywater."

"Well, ain't that a kick in the head," Lucius laughed. "Now that y'all living in New Orleans, you should stop by the house and have some pie. I know Bessie be tickled pink to see you fine gentlemen again."

"That is so very kind of you. We would be delighted to see Mrs. Collins again," Clay replied, his southern accent becoming more pronounced the longer he spoke with Lucius.

"Well then, we surely will arrange something, we surely will," Lucius beamed. "It was a pleasure talking with ya back them years ago, just such a shame about Justice Winchester not being on the Supreme Court. Such a shame. But he's happy as a pig in slop being back here in New Orleans."

"Do you see him much?" Aaron inquired.

"Surely, I do. Every Wednesday night around 7 p.m. right here at Arnaud's. And Bessie and I do some social things with him as well. In fact, you see that empty table right over there," Lucius stated while pointing to a table less than forty feet away, "that's the Justice's table. He should be arriving in less than an hour for dinner with his friends, the Putnams. For years, Justice Winchester and his wife LeeAnn would come here for New Year's Eve with Calvin and Lucille Putnam. They still come, the Justice loves keeping up with traditions don't ya know. Well, enough gossip, I should do my job and wait on this fine table of gentlemen and one lovely lady."

"Thank you, Lucius, thank you," Clay said as he thumbed through the extensive wine list.

POSY BRANCH SMILED WITH SATISFACTION as she stared at the large crowd that was lined up waiting to get inside her establishment on New Year's Eve. The Dixieland band was in full swing as the bare-chested bow-tied waiters went from table to table getting drink orders. Chiffon LaBelle bedecked in a floor length gold lamé gown, smiled from ear-to-ear, as she led customers to their reserved tables. Michael busily prepared an assortment of juleps from behind the mahogany bar as his shaved chest glistened in the pin spotlights that illuminated the bar area. The room was a festive buzz of activity and Posy stood in the center of it all as its accomplished and successful ringleader.

The Christmas edition of *Time Out New Orleans* had heralded the nail salon, bar, music venue that Posy had named French Tips, Juleps & Jazz as one of the most innovative and fun-filled establishments in all of New Orleans. The magazine lauded Posy Branch's new business as a "fresh and entertaining must-see destination on the New Orleans scene." And the daily crowds that came in the daytime for manis and pedis, and the nightly crowds that came for the perfectly made juleps, the handsome male servers, and the killer jazz were a testament to the fact that Posy and Chantale had hit on the right touch for the Big Easy. Customers were the key indicator of success, and success was wrapped around the corner waiting to get into the new "it" spot.

Posy stood between Chantale and Chiffon admiring the huge holiday crowd.

"Look what *Time Out* did?" Posy exclaimed to Chantale.

"I am not a child. I do not need time out," Chantale stated with an irritated tone to her voice.

"No, Sugar," Posy laughed. "I meant the review in the magazine *Time Out*. They gave us a great review, and that's partly why we have these huge crowds. C'mon girlfriend, have some fun. We making money like nobody's business."

"It is my business, with you crazy woman," Chantale exclaimed. "It is not nobody."

"I think we've got a language problem," Chiffon whispered to Posy.

"The only language that matters is green and has them cute pictures of the Presidents on it," Posy stated with a wink of an eye and a hearty snort of laughter.

A FEW MILES AWAY IN THE GARDEN DISTRICT, Jim Bob McCallum and his wife Mabel sat at the large oak table in their ornate and posh dining room. A tuxedo jacketed server leaned over to cut the filet mignon into small pieces that sat on Mabel McCallum's china plate.

"Be careful there, don't get any of the bloody juice on her dress," Jim Bob instructed.

"Yes sir," the server acknowledged.

"That's fine, leave us," Jim Bob further instructed.

Mabel's head bowed as she looked at the plate. She tenuously grasped her fork with her shaking hand, speared a small piece of meat and with some unsteady movement was able to place the meat into her mouth.

"Ain't that a fine piece of meat?" Jim Bob asked his wife with a slight smile.

Mabel chewed the food slowly without acknowledging her husband's question.

Full comprehension and communication had become extremely difficult for Mabel McCallum over the past year. Despite her husband and the doctor's substantial efforts, her Alzheimer's disease was progressing. She had her good, lucid days, of course. But several days were a confused muddle where she had problems recognizing people and putting the correct words together in a sentence. And as much as she was suffering, Jim Bob was suffering as he watched his wife slip away further from him. His anger and resentment towards the world at large grew exponentially as his wife's hold on reality began to wane. The Happy New Years for the McCallum's had certainly ended.

The jazz quartet playing at Arnaud's was in full swing when Stanford Winchester, along with Calvin and Lucille Putnam, took their places at the Justice's accustomed table. Stanford surveyed the room prior to taking his seat. A large smile crossed his lips as he recognized a familiar face.

"Please forgive me, Lucille and Calvin, but I just spied my former law clerk Emily DuBois, and it would be highly unchivalrous of me, if I didn't go over and say hello," Stanford announced to his friends.

"Why of course, we'll be fine, please do so," Lucille courteously offered. Stanford nodded and walked over to the table where Emily was seated with Clay, Aaron, and Ben.

"Emily, what an enormous pleasure to see you," Stanford enthusiastically stated as Emily DuBois rose to greet her former mentor. She gave Stanford a big hug.

"It is so nice to see you Justice Winchester," Emily effused.

"Please, please, I insist that you call me Stanford," Winchester said as he looked at the other guests at Emily's table.

"Mr. Grover, is that you?" Stanford said with surprise. Clay rose to his feet to shake Stanford's hand heartily.

"Yes sir, what a great pleasure it is to see you," Clay exclaimed.

"Oh my word, what a genuine and wholly pleasant surprise," Stanford stated with a smile. "Unfortunately, the last time I saw you was earlier this year at the funeral of Senator Henry Fitzsimmons, may God rest his soul. Such a great man, and a true American patriot."

"Yes sir, Senator Fitzsimmons' death was a great loss to this country, and a very personal loss for me," Clay replied with a bit of sadness to his tone.

"Indeed, indeed," Stanford solemnly replied. "So, please tell me if you will, what brings you to our fair city at the beginning of a new year?"

"I, I mean, we live here in New Orleans now," Clay began. "May I introduce you to my husband, Aaron Rose, and my friend Ben Carroll," Clay stated, as both Aaron and Ben rose to shake hands with Stanford Winchester.

"Mr. Rose, have we met before?" Stanford asked while clasping Aaron's hand and shaking it vigorously.

"I used to work with Senator Douglas, perhaps you recognize me from the Senate Judiciary Committee hearings," Aaron responded.

"Yes, that's it!" Stanford exclaimed. "My old feeble mind is not what it used to be, but I must admit I seldom forget a face. It is a great pleasure to meet you, sir. You and Mr. Grover are married and living here now?"

"Yes sir. We are both practicing law with Caleb Butler, sir, and we live in the Marigny," Aaron replied.

"Well, if that's not the bee's knees. Excellent. Simply excellent," Stanford said with a good deal of enthusiasm and pleasure. "Caleb Butler is an excellent attorney and making quite a reputation for himself down in the Ninth ward."

"I now work with Caleb and Aaron and Clay as well," Emily cheerfully added.

"Gracious me, how outstanding is that!" Stanford stated, while placing his hand to the side of his head. "Well, then we must celebrate this astounding news." At that very moment, Lucius came to the table to check on his guests.

"Lucius, my dear friend, we need a very fine bottle of wine. New and re-kindled old friendships abound and must be nurtured with an excellent French champagne," Stanford proclaimed.

"Oh yes sir, yes sir!" Lucius repeated with excitement.

"Now, if this isn't the perfect start to a wonderful new year," Stanford joyously announced as he placed one arm around Emily's shoulders and the other around Clay's as he smiled and laughed.

"WHAT A PERFECT START TO A NEW YEAR," Posy Branch announced from the center of her establishment while toasting with a well-crafted Mint Julep in her hand.

"You have certainly brought a breath of fresh air to our fair city," Chiffon stated as she joined her boss in a toast.

"I wasted too many years of my life in Washington, D.C. married to a no-account liar, it's just so good to be in a city where I'm finally appreciated," Posy replied. "It's time to get on with my life and celebrate."

The jazz band in the corner of the room started to play "Lady Marmalade" as Posy, Chiffon, and Michael all began to sashay across the dance floor in the packed bar. Posy and Chiffon danced over to the band and began to sing into a microphone to each other.

"Hey Sister, Go Sister, Soul Sister, Go Sister. He met Marmalade down in old New Orleans, struttin' her stuff on the street. She said, Hello, Hey Joe wanna give it a go? Mmm Hmm, gitchi ya ya da da, gitchi gitchi ya ya here. Mocca chocolata ya ya. Creole Lady Marmalade."

Michael turned to one of the bare-chested male servers and shouted over the raucous din, "There goes our Lady Marmalade!"

CHAPTER 12

PRESIDENT COCHRAN WAS MEETING WITH HIS HIGH-LEVEL Presidential campaign staff and strategic team in a conference room in a Washington D.C. hotel not far from the White House. He rolled up his shirt sleeves as he paced back and forth listening to his campaign advisors.

"I've got to disagree," the President stated after a prolonged pause in the conversation. "I cannot see how Cletus Sawyer can possibly be considered our primary foe for the nomination. Sounds sorta funny, don't it? Cletus is hardly the sharpest knife in the drawer," Andrew Cochran stated with a wry smile.

"Sir, with all due respect, a high degree of intelligence is not an absolute requirement for becoming President of the United States. Our own party proved that point in the not so distant past," Landon Hamilton, the Re-elect Cochran for President campaign manager, stated to his boss with a touch of trepidation to his voice.

"Oh, come on now, Landon, you don't have to be shy about voicing your opinion around me. I know that you mean to imply that I'm a couple quarters short of a dollar in the accounting of cerebral currency," Andrew Cochran laughed in response.

"No sir, I certainly did not mean you, I meant that with respect to President . . ." Landon stammered before being interrupted by President Cochran.

"I'm just messin' with y'all. Boys, relax," Andrew pronounced to his assembled campaign advisors. "We're over a year away from Iowa, it's far too early to be getting our undies in a bunch over the likes of Cletus Sawyer."

"Sawyer's ultra-conservative super Pac 'Take Back America' is raising an enormous amount of money, Mr. President," Landon countered.

"And that is all well and good," Andrew Cochran replied. "But no amount of money will be able to persuade the American public to turn back the clock to 1958 on virtually all social and domestic issues. It's only conservative dinosaurs like Cletus Sawyer who remain stuck in time. If he was a better public speaker or younger and more charismatic, I might be worried. But Cletus is none of those things. He and the Tea Party cranks are challenging me because I don't find shameless moral decay in compromising with the Democrats, and I'm not calling for the severe persecution of gays and abortion providers."

"Well, that and they see your administration as scared and weak from the scandal involving your former Chief of Staff," Landon added.

"I think we've recovered sufficiently from those rocky times and have set a strategic moderate course for the country that many Americans can appreciate and support," the President surmised.

"Yes sir, indeed, we will take the fight to them with everything we've got," Landon interjected.

"Tell me Landon, does everything we've got include the enthusiastic support of my Vice-President?" The President asked.

After a lengthy delay, Landon finally stated, "I think so, sir."

"That response is not terribly reassuring," Andrew Cochran replied while shaking his head. "It sounds like Howard Mason is in the process of plotting a palace coup."

"I don't think that it's progressed to that point, sir. However, I've heard some rumblings coming out of the Vice-President's office that are a bit disconcerting," Landon offered with some hesitation.

"Well, I can't say that I'm terribly surprised. Howard has been attempting to put some distance between himself and the rest of the administration for some time now. He's a smart, articulate man with all the ambition in the world. Clearly, Cletus Sawyer and his ilk are not the only ones who smell blood in the water. The sharks are out, Gentlemen. We must not stray too far from shore for the next several months."

Nathan Whitaker sat in the opulent office of his criminal defense attorney, Rupert Grassmonk. Rupert took a long sip of his green tea from the exquisite china tea cup firmly pinched in his right hand.

"The prosecution has hearsay, innuendo and circumstantial evidence at best. There is no there, there, and they know it," Rupert unequivocally announced. "They're beginning to sweat on the eve of trial. They are willing to make a very reasonable deal."

"No deals," Nathan stated bluntly. "If they have no case, why should I accept any plea offer?"

"Because juries are unpredictable. You were savaged in the press. The press found you guilty far before a jury will have an opportunity to hear all of the facts," Rupert counseled his client.

"The Winchester statement to the police about Jim Bob McCallum's alleged conversation with him about our relationship and supposed plans will not get introduced at my trial will it?" Nathan asked pointedly.

"Well, as you know, we've got a motion *in limine* striking it, but we haven't received a ruling from our trial court judge as of yet," Rupert responded.

"If that statement is out, they've got nothing at all on me," Nathan stated with a sense of confidence.

"Juries are fickle beasts, be warned. A reduced plea to conspiracy is not a horrible compromise," Rupert offered to his client.

"No," Nathan stated without a moment of hesitation.

CHIFFON LABELLE SAT IN THE SMALL OFFICE of Aaron Rose directly across from him, separated only by his blond wood desk. She stared intently at Aaron as he spoke to her. Her long legs uncomfortably crossed due to the lack of space in the cramped quarters.

"Ms. LaBelle," Aaron began, prior to being interrupted by Chiffon.

"Please, Mr. Rose, call me Chiffon. I detest needless formality," Chiffon asked.

"Certainly, and of course, please feel free to call me Aaron," he replied.

"Oh, yes, my pleasure Aaron," Chiffon responded while leaning closer to the small and simple desk.

"We're currently assisting with preparation of the response brief in the Katrina victims class action appeal. I would like to confirm some information with you so that we can adequately respond to the appellants opening brief. Is that alright with you?" Aaron asked.

"Anything you want is alright with me, Aaron," Chiffon said with a smile.

"Could you please read the highlighted portions of these three pages of their brief? After you finish, I'd like to ask you a few follow-up questions, if I may?" Aaron asked, as he nervously fidgeted in his chair.

"My utmost pleasure to do so," Chiffon responded softly, as her hand brushed against Aaron's as she reached across the desk to grasp the document. Chiffon opened her large purse and extricated a pair of crystal embedded reading glasses. She placed them on the bridge of her nose.

"Do you like them?" Chiffon cooed at Aaron.

"Yes, they look very nice," Aaron hesitantly replied.

"Why thank you kind sir," Chiffon said sweetly as she lowered her gaze to the papers she would read. Moments later, Clay Grover walked past Aaron's open office door and peeked his head through the doorway.

"Do you mind if I join you?" Clay asked Aaron and Chiffon.

"Absolutely not, please come in," Aaron nearly shouted. Chiffon offered only a very disconsolate shrug.

Sam Brainard sat behind his large and ornate desk in his West Wing office. In a guest chair in front of his desk sat FBI Agent Joshua Schukas.

"So Josh, what can I do for you today?" Sam inquired.

"As you know Sam, a while ago FBI Director Turner met personally with the President regarding some alarming content posted on 4chan about plots involving the assassination of the President."

"Yes, the President mentioned the conversation to me not long after it occurred," Sam confirmed.

"And, of course since that conversation, there was the incident at the National Prayer Breakfast with Robert Gooding," Josh continued.

"Yes, but I didn't think that the two were at all related. Gooding was a former supporter of the President, who he had actually met, and who participated in an Inaugural event. According to the report we received from the FBI after the attempt on the President's life, we believed that Gooding was alone in his attempt to kill the President, that he was not part of any organized group involved in his deranged plot," Sam responded.

"We still believe that to be true. However, this far-right group of religious provocateurs that call themselves, Killers for Christ, have taken to championing the cause of Robert Gooding on 4chan and a number of other social media sites. They have declared that they are the righteous followers of Gooding. That the job he started must and shall be finished. The Internet traffic on this topic is becoming more prolific and more disturbing," Josh stated.

"Is there something that you would like the White House to do? Have you spoken with the Secret Service or Billy James directly?" Sam questioned.

"Yes, the Secret Service is well aware of these developments. We understand that the President is about to embark on campaigning for his re-election."

"True, but there are no scheduled campaign events at this time, though there will be debates in the not too distant future," Sam confirmed.

"The Director wanted me to speak with you so that the White House is aware of these ongoing threats. Perhaps keep these threats in mind when you schedule events to minimize the President's exposure to the public," Josh suggested. "Of course, there will be additional FBI presence as well."

"I don't have much to do with the campaign event side of things, but I will certainly pass this information on to Landon Hamilton who is the President's campaign manager. We will endeavor to do whatever the FBI thinks is in the best interest for protecting the President from harm," Sam acknowledged. "Thanks for the heads-up, Josh, much appreciated."

CHAPTER 13

POSY BRANCH AND HER BUSINESS PARTNER, Chantale Calypso were quickly becoming the toast of New Orleans social life. Lauded in the social columns of New Orleans newspapers and magazines, French Tips, Juleps & Jazz had become a destination hot spot. And that fact became more apparent during the two weeks leading up to Mardi Gras. Crowds packed the establishment as women got their nails done in a party atmosphere with shirtless young men serving juleps and other cocktails over the deep grooves of a talented jazz and funk band. The Mardi Gras season only made things that much more festive as lines formed down the block, waiting to get into the fairly new and very popular business.

Posy and Chiffon mingled with the crowds as Chantale manned the cash register. Smiles abounded. Posy Branch had once again become a queen. Though this time not a beauty pageant queen, but a social-ite queen who was giving interviews and posing for photographs on nearly a daily basis. In fact, for her first Mardi Gras in New Orleans, Posy was invited to be a parade queen riding on a float through the French Quarter.

"I am having more fun than I've had in years. And we as busy as a two-dollar whore on nickel night," Posy laughed to Chiffon.

"Posy girl, Chantale is right, you is crazy as a loon, but in such a good way," Chiffon hollered back to Posy as they worked the crowds that waited in line to get into their establishment.

"I love this city," Posy crowed at the top of her lungs.

THE INFLUX OF TOURISTS INTO THE CITY during Mardi Gras was keeping the cash register at Bessie's voodoo shop ringing a lucrative tune. Papa Levi struggled to keep the shelves stocked with amulets, voodoo kits, books about the occult, and pretty much anything else that Bessie had to offer in her store. Bessie had begun to take appointments for readings. The demands on her time grew exponentially as the days leading up to Fat Tuesday dwindled. But, Bessie and Papa Levi did their best to keep up with customer demands.

"I had no idea we would be this busy leading up to Carnival," Bessie stated with some exasperation to Papa Levi.

"Well now, Miss Bessie, it use to be busy when Queen Rita ran this here shop, but t'aint nothin' like this," Papa Levi professed. "Word spread about your kind and thoughtful ways and people come and bring their friends."

"But we's a bit off of Bourbon Street, I didn't think the tourists would find us," Bessie responded.

"During Mardi Gras there ain't no place in the Quarter that ain't busy," Papa Levi said.

"Business never been better. And I surely ain't complaining," Bessie said with a smile as the old bell over the entrance door to the shop kept ringing and ringing.

STANFORD WINCHESTER EXITED THE FEDERAL COURT building in the Central Business District to find his fellow jurist Whitlee Hammond paused to wait for the crowds from a parade to thin before venturing out onto the streets. Stanford sidled up next to Whitlee and nodded politely.

"I've lived in this city all of my life, yet every year the crowds for Mardi Gras just seem to get bigger and bigger. The population of our fair city almost triples as we enter the weekend before Fat Tuesday," Stanford stated to Whitlee as they watched the packed crowds shuffle down the sidewalk.

"Yes, that seems to be true. And if you live and work here, it can be a nuisance at times, but it's great for the city's economy," Whitlee responded.

"There's no arguing that fact. Even all of the hotels and motels in Kenner and Metairie are sold out this time of year," Stanford added. "Are you headed home?" Stanford asked.

"Actually no," Whitlee replied as she used her right hand to pull back her blonde hair from her pretty face. "I'm meeting a friend at a new establishment near the French Market. So, it's a walk through the crowds in the Quarter for me."

"Well now, I don't live far from there, would you mind if I accompany you on your traverse through the celebrating throngs?" Stanford asked.

"That would be lovely," Whitlee replied. "I questioned my own sanity when I agreed to meet my friend in the Quarter on the Friday evening of Mardi Gras weekend. But with the aid of a strong gentleman at my side, the walk may be much easier to navigate."

"Strong left me decades ago, but I surely can be a useful roadblock to the masses at times," Stanford chuckled with the wink of an eye. "Let's walk down Royal, it will be less congested than Bourbon Street."

Whitlee and Stanford slowly made their way through the French Quarter chatting and laughing as they paused to take in some of the remarkable sights that make up NOLA at Carnival time. Once they reached Dumaine Street they crossed Royal Street and strolled over to Decatur Street heading towards the French Market.

"What is the name of the establishment where you are meeting your friend?" Stanford asked as they ambled down Decatur.

"It's called French Tips, Juleps, and Jazz," Whitlee replied. "It's fairly new. It offers manicures and pedicures as well as fresh made Juleps and I understand they have an excellent jazz band that plays there. It is all the rage right now," Whitlee offered with a slightly embarrassed blush of her face.

"Why yes, I've been reading about it in the papers. And my secretary Naomi has already been a few times. I can always tell when she's been with her brightly colored nails," Stanford chuckled.

"You don't need to walk me all the way there," Whitlee stated. "You have already been such wonderful company. I appreciate you helping get me through some of the crowds."

"Nonsense, what kind of gentleman would I be if I did not escort a lovely lady all of the way to her intended destination," Stanford said quite sincerely. "And besides, I must admit I am a bit curious to see what this establishment is all about."

"How kind," Whitlee replied with a gentle smile, as the two colleagues continued their excursion. Once they arrived, Stanford assisted Whitlee as they fought through the crowds in an effort to locate Whitlee's friend. Stanford accidentally bumped into an attractive blonde woman as he attempted to clear a path for Whitlee. The woman turned on her heels and stared at Stanford for a long moment.

"Your judgeship, is that you?" Posy Branch yelped as she recognized Stanford Winchester.

"Mrs. Whitaker?" Stanford queried as he continued to study the woman's lovely face. Posy immediately threw her arms around Stanford as he slightly reeled back unsure of how to react to the extensive hug he was receiving, while at the same time glancing over at Whitlee with a look of embarrassment.

"Well, if this don't just beat all," Posy shouted in return. "My name is Posy Branch now, I'm through with my no-account ex-husband Nathan. Ain't it a small world, ain't it a small world," Posy repeated as she shouted loudly. Stanford's face mirrored stunned disbelief as he fumbled for words—something that he never did.

"What brings you to New Orleans?" Stanford asked. "Are you here for Mardi Gras?"

"Oh, shoot no!" Posy yelled. "I live here now. I'm part owner of this here establishment."

"My word! Isn't that astonishing news," Stanford responded. Then realizing that he was ignoring Whitlee, he quickly pivoted so that Whitlee was now part of the conversation with Posy.

"Mrs. Whitaker, I'm sorry, I mean Ms. Branch, may I please introduce you to my colleague and friend, Judge Whitlee Hammond," Stanford announced.

"Oh, Honey, just call me Posy," Posy responded as she took and vigorously shook Whitlee's hand. "I met the judge here at a party at the White House a couple of years ago. He spun me around like a top. He's such a marvelous dancer. You know he can really cut a rug, don't ya?" Posy questioned Whitlee.

"I'm pleased to meet you, Posy. And no, I wasn't aware that Stanford was an excellent dancer," Whitlee stated as she glanced over at a now blushing Justice Winchester.

"Well, we got a dance floor and a fine band right here," Posy said with a big grin. "They's on break right now," Posy continued, before she interrupted herself and began yelling in the direction of Chiffon LaBelle. "Hey Chiffon, Chiffon sugar, when's the band coming back from their break?" Posy shouted. Chiffon shrugged in response.

"Perhaps another time," Stanford said attempting to change the topic. "Whitlee, Ms. Branch, uh, Posy informed me that she is one of the proprietors of this business," Stanford proclaimed.

"Congratulations, you are making quite a mark on our city," Whitlee said. "In fact, I came here to meet a friend who raves about what a wonderful time she's had when she has visited your establishment."

"Don't that just dill my pickle," Posy laughed. "I've been so happy during my time down here in New Orleans. Y'all is my kind of people."

"Welcome. You are clearly demonstrating how successful a clever businesswoman can be in New Orleans," Whitlee stated with a gracious smile.

"Bless your heart," Posy replied as she swept a surprised Whitlee into her arms and into a full embrace. "This is a fine woman. She's a keeper, Stanford," Posy stated to a now fully blushing Stanford Winchester.

"Indeed," a somewhat discombobulated Stanford said in response.

"Look y'all," Posy began. "Unfortunately, I can't flap my jaws with ya right now, I got some things I need to take care of in back. But promise me you'll come back and we can have a proper visit when it ain't so crowded."

"Of course, we would be delighted to return," Stanford replied without hesitation.

"Excellent! It was a pleasure meeting you, Whitlee. And Stanford, such a surprise seeing you again. Whatever you want, it's on me. Michael, Michael," Posy shouted at the top of her lungs. "Make two of your finest Mint Juleps for my friends here on the house." Michael nodded affirmatively and with that Posy infiltrated the crowd and was soon out of sight.

Stanford turned towards Whitlee and simply uttered, "Remarkable."

Meanwhile, a few hours later and a few blocks away at the corner of St. Ann and Bourbon Street, Clay and Aaron were watching as several men were dropping their pants and exposing their penises. Cheering throngs of gay men were pressed up against the wrought iron railings on the second story balconies of the two large gay clubs on that corner. They were yelling their appreciation of the street level exhibitionism while they threw strings of beads down to the exposed participants below. Aaron dumbstruck at the public sight turned towards Clay.

"We're not in Washington anymore, that's for sure," Aaron laughed.

"Mardi Gras in New Orleans, my dear. Mardi Gras in New Orleans," Clay repeated with a devilish smile.

A tall gentleman with a deep Southern accent and a low voice, sat in a posh and darkened office conversing with his companion sitting across from him.

"I received an intelligence report from our boys doing surveillance in Washington this morning. Did you see it?" The man drawled with his heavy accent.

"I did, nothing terribly remarkable," his colleague responded.

"Apparently the FBI is concerned about threats against Andrew Cochran that are popping up on the Internet. Seems like since that Evangelical minister tried to take Cochran out at the National Prayer Breakfast, some group calling themselves Killers for Christ have pledged to finish the job that he so badly bungled."

"Yeah, I read that, so what? Regardless of who the President is, there are always death threats from moronic cranks pretty much every day. And nobody can ever get through the security surrounding the President anymore. The days of Lee Harvey Oswald, Squeaky Fromme, Sara Jane Moore, and David Hinckley are long gone. Lord knows, there are still those who try, but no one can get close enough these days," the colleague replied.

"Gooding got pretty close, he just couldn't get a shot off."

"OK, so? Where are you going with this?" The colleague questioned.

"Have our boys look into this group, Killers for Christ. See what they're about. Is there a leader? Does he have a brain in his head, or is it some loser who couldn't get laid in high school that still lives in his mother's basement at the age of thirty-eight? I'm not saying that we do anything with it at this time. But just in case, we can't convince our Buckeye buddy to play ball, it doesn't hurt to have a back-up plan," the man with the deep voice stated with a chuckle.

CHAPTER 14

ONE MONTH LATER AND APPROXIMATELY 925 MILES to the north, the City of Chicago was coloring their river green in preparation for the largest St. Patrick's Day celebration outside of Dublin. At his Lincoln Park home, Senator Perry Douglas was searching his closet for the greenest of green ties that he owned. The Saturday before St. Patrick's Day in Chicago is the day that the city celebrates with a large parade that winds its way through downtown Chicago. Local politicians usually are at the head of the parade, and especially so when elections are right around the corner. This certainly wasn't Perry's first St. Patrick's Day parade, but it was his first as an announced candidate for President. Thus, the search for the best green tie took on greater importance to him, silly as that seemed to his wife Katherine, who looked on in total amusement as she sat on the corner of their bed.

"You're kidding right?" Katherine questioned with a Cheshire cat smile etched across her face.

"No, I'm not," Perry insisted. "I don't think that any of these three ties are green enough."

"And of course, the Presidency of the United States rests on this sartorial selection," she smirked.

"You've lived in Chicago all your life, you know how important this parade is to the people of this city," Perry admonished his wife, not all together joking.

"My unsophisticated judgment, though not at all based on serving twenty years in the United States Senate, is that, for the most part, when people go to the polls to vote, that they may be more concerned about your stances on foreign trade deficits, job creation, and healthcare provisions than on how green your parade tie was. Of course, I'm not a political professional, so it's only my wildly uninformed guess," Katherine offered with tongue firmly planted in cheek.

"You're not helping," Perry stated, wholly unamused by his wife's sarcastic remarks.

"Dear Lord, Perry," Katherine sighed. "The Walgreens down the street is selling iridescent Kelly green ties with blinking shamrock lights on it."

"Really?" Perry questioned as his tone became uplifted.

"I'm voting for Hellen Raymond," Katherine pronounced as she got up from the bed and walked out of the room.

"Are you going to Walgreens?" Perry asked hopefully.

SEVERAL HOURS LATER, CAROLYN BARNES was at a Chicago Police station on the north side of Chicago. Her teenaged son Cameron had been taken into custody for resisting arrest.

"Where's my son?" Carolyn questioned the police desk sergeant.

"He's in the back in a detention cell," the police officer replied.

"What happened?" she asked.

"Well, Ma'am," the officer began, "he was pulled over on a routine traffic stop for not adequately breaking at a stop sign."

"So, he drove through a stop sign?" Carolyn asked.

"Not exactly. The officer at the scene did not think that your son had stopped for a sufficiently long enough time."

"Let me get this straight," Carolyn replied, her voice raised in tone as her face began to flush. "My son had applied his brakes and brought the car to a full stop. Just not long enough to satisfy the officer at the scene. Is that correct?"

"Basically, yes," the desk sergeant responded.

"Why is he now in custody?" Carolyn inquired.

"When the officer asked your son to exit the vehicle, he did not immediately follow the officer's instructions. Instead he was insistent that he had not done anything wrong."

"If I am fully understanding the facts. I don't understand what he did wrong," Carolyn insisted, as she began to slightly tremble with anger. "Of course, this has nothing to do with the fact that my African-American teenaged son was behind the wheel of a new Lexus and driving through an affluent white neighborhood does it?"

The police officer shrugged. Carolyn tried mightily to control her anger. She visualized the potential newspaper headlines in her head as she bit her lip. Righteous indignation would have to wait for another day. She had lived in Chicago for most of her life. She had been racially profiled by the police several times during her youth. This was nothing new.

"May I please take my son home now?" Carolyn asked as calmly as she could manage.

"Sure," was the response, which was not nearly enough.

SEVERAL BLOCKS AWAY, ROBERT DOUGLAS, THE SON of Senator Perry Douglas and his boyfriend Jason were on their way home to their apartment. They slowly sauntered down the street holding each other's hand. A group of young, clearly drunk and disorderly, college-aged boys approached in their direction. As they passed by, Robert heard one of the boys call Robert and Jason, "disgusting cock-sucking faggots." Robert was never one to look for confrontation. He was generally very affable and accommodating to most people. But he was also not one to hold his tongue when being confronted or challenged.

"Let it go," Jason softly urged his companion. And Robert heeded his advice, as the two silently walked on past the boys. That is, until one of the boys shoved Robert in the back while yelling, "Get the fuck out of here you queer fucks!"

Robert regained his balance from the shove. He slowly turned around and faced the boy who had shoved him. He had overheard one of the other boys say, "Let them go, Jeff." Robert slyly smiled and with a touch of flair said, "My goodness, Jeff, you didn't tell me that you wanted to play this rough when I was fucking your ass the other day. Oh wait, that's right, you couldn't with that ball gag in your mouth. You just wantonly thrusted your hips back for more cock." The other college boys laughed out loud at the comment and at their companion. Robert turned to walk away with Jason and then everything went dark.

APPROXIMATELY 925 MILES SOUTH OF CHICAGO down the Mississippi River, Aaron Rose was conducting a follow-up meeting with his client Chiffon LaBelle. They sat at a table in the back of French Tips, Juleps & Jazz.

"Thank you for meeting me here, Aaron, it makes it so much easier for me to speak to you for a few minutes during my break. We've been so busy with the new business, that it's been hard to find time off," Chiffon related to Aaron as she reached up to fix her hair.

"No problem at all. I'm happy to meet you here. I've been reading so much about this place in the papers that I was curious to check it out myself," Aaron replied with a smile. "I think we're good with the additional details that you've been able to give me. It helps clarify a paragraph that we might be adding to the draft response brief. There was some ambiguity in the transcript from the lower court trial that I wanted to pin down."

"Whatever I can do to help the cause," Chiffon stated. "There are a lot of members of the class action suit, so I know I'm helping them as well."

"Yes, you are, you're helping every plaintiff that filed," Aaron affirmed.

Chiffon looked away for a few seconds, she became sullen, as her accustomed upbeat demeanor momentarily became lost in her remembrances from the horrible days following the flood. She glanced back at Aaron, a world weariness etched across her face and a pronounced sadness in her voice.

"They let us drown. They let us starve. They left us to die. Our government, both state, but especially the federal government and all of the agencies like FEMA that are supposedly there to protect and help us, simply turned their backs on us. Days upon days of utter neglect as thousands of black people in the Ninth ward were left to fend for ourselves. I remember it like it was yesterday, Baron and I climbing up to the roof of our house with our dog Drew, to attempt to escape the rising flood waters after the levee was breached. We waited and waited for help. We slept on that roof. And when our dog Drew wandered off the roof and Baron tried to save him, well . . ." Chiffon stated as her voice trailed off and a tear formed in the corner of her eye."

"I'm so sorry," Aaron quietly responded as Chiffon attempted to regain her composure.

"Two days later after I was finally rescued from my rooftop, I was taken to the Superdome so that I could get some food and water. My God, Aaron, the stench, the suffering of those poor people stranded in that building, it was unbelievable. It was utterly inhumane. And still the government did virtually nothing to assist us. The images from those days in that building haunt me to this day."

Chiffon hesitated. Once again, she looked away from Aaron unable to continue for a few moments. She sighed heavily as she wiped the tears away from her eyes.

"Nothing is going to bring Baron back to me. Our beloved dog Drew is gone. My house is gone forever. I live in an apartment in the Bywater now. I'm learning each day how to move on with my life. All I'm looking for in this lawsuit and through this appeal process is to have an acknowledgment from the government that they should have done more to help us. That the response to thousands of black people suffering in New Orleans was too little and too late. Acknowledge that I am a worthy citizen of this country, and that I deserved a little more respect and assistance than I was afforded by my own government. Truly, that is all I want from all of this. Some respect and a little restitution for my losses."

Aaron nodded his head affirmatively as he reached over and gently squeezed Chiffon's trembling hand. Any words would have been meaningless.

A COUPLE OF DAYS LATER, SENATOR DOUGLAS and Carolyn Barnes sat together in the Senator's Chicago office. The Senator had cancelled his campaign appearances, as he stayed in Chicago so that he could be close to his son Robert. Fortunately, Robert was slowly recovering from his concussion and other injuries. He would be released from the hospital very soon. Yet, the Senator was still having a difficult time suppressing his anger.

"Carolyn, I'm not sure that I want to be President of a country where your son is stopped and taken into custody by the police simply because he is an African-American teenaged boy driving a nice car in a wealthy white neighborhood, and my son is assaulted by a drunken homophobe for the act of walking down the street and holding hands with his companion," Perry Douglas exclaimed to his campaign manager.

"These are the situations where we have to turn anger into action," Carolyn responded.

"Hellen Raymond is a fine woman, and frankly she would probably make a very good President," Perry wearily stated.

"There is no arguing that Senator Raymond is a good person, who follows her own moral convictions. However, her campaign is virtually silent on all issues of social equality. We won't be. How many times have you told me that you want to follow in the footsteps of Senator Fitzsimmons when it comes to social justice? You, Senator, are the strongest voice for my son Cameron and your son Robert and everyone else in this country who is oppressed or ostracized, not Hellen Raymond," Carolyn stated with steely-eyed conviction.

"You're absolutely right. Social attitudes and injustice won't change if you don't fight to change them in the hearts and minds of the American people," Perry Douglas confirmed to Carolyn. "Our campaign will be modeled after the wisdom and kindness of spirit of Henry Fitzsimmons. Economic fairness and social equality will be the cornerstones to our platform. It's time for our government to afford the economically and socially downtrodden members of our society the respect and restitution that they so amply deserve."

"Yes sir, and on those issues we will forge a winning campaign, of that I have no doubt," Carolyn replied.

"Thank God, I'm just smart and lucky enough to surround myself in my personal and professional life with highly intelligent, strong-minded, and forthright women, who don't allow me to wallow in self-pity," Perry stated with great appreciation.

"Yes sir."

CHAPTER 15

J IM BOB MCCALLUM'S ATTORNEY WAS SEATED in a large overstuffed leather chair in Jim Bob's corporate office. He gulped down the remainder of his bourbon from the crystal glass.

"We have received the final responses from the LSU board of directors and the governor's office about our petition," the attorney began. "They will not allow the new medical research facility in Baton Rouge, which is currently under construction, to bear the name of Mabel McCallum."

"Do you have any idea how many of my millions not to mention my political glad-handing went into receiving assurances that that facility would bear Mabel's name?" Jim Bob shouted in return.

"Yes, Jim Bob, I do, but all that changed when you were indicted for murder."

"Trumped up charges that will never stand up in a jury trial," Jim Bob shot back with anger.

"Perhaps, for the most part. But the prosecution's key witness is the current presiding Chief Judge of the United States Fifth Circuit Court of Appeals. Stanford Winchester was portrayed in the press as a highly honorable moral hero, who eschewed a seat on the Supreme Court because he believed that it was tainted by the actions of Nathan Whitaker and yourself. His word will have vast ethical currency with a jury," the attorney surmised for Jim Bob.

"Traitorous liar, who knew that he could not withstand the intense probing of the Senate Judiciary Committee and would ultimately fail to win confirmation from the Democratic Senate. Instead of suffering the humiliation of wholesale rejection, like Robert Bork did, he fabricated a far-fetched story in a craven attempt to preserve his own precious Southern honor," Jim Bob venomously spat back at his attorney. "That man has no honor. He is a viperous snake and should be portrayed as such."

"I'm only saying, Jim Bob, that a jury may see it quite differently. No other office holders in all of government enjoy the gravitas and public respect that is routinely given to judges."

"Ain't that what I'm paying you a shit-load of money to do? To convince a jury that Stanford Winchester is an opportunistic, self-important, treacherous, no account liar!" Jim Bob exclaimed in rebuttal. "If Stanford Winchester's lips is movin', he's lyin'. You can take that to the bank. And in Louisiana, we know how to pick a jury, if you get my meaning."

"But the trial is not in Louisiana, it's in Washington, D.C.," Jim Bob's attorney countered.

"That's right, the trial is in D.C., better known as the District of Criminals," Jim Bob huffed in response. "Washington is the only city in the world that has an established area on K Street devoted to nothing more than influence peddling. What does that tell you?"

IN WASHINGTON, D.C., PRESIDENT ANDREW COCHRAN intently listened to his Chief of Staff, Sam Brainard explain the reasoning for increasing his Secret Service detail once the President began campaigning for his re-election.

"Mr. President, the FBI believed, and I agreed that after a month following the attempt on your life at the National Prayer Breakfast, that the death threats would have subsided. They have only increased, unfortunately. Some are the usual suspects, anarchists, far-left activists, and similar groups. However, it appears that the assassination attempt has only emboldened the religious right zealots as well. That is the group that has predominated in the increase of threatening communications, especially on the Internet," Sam explained.

"So, the threat from one disgruntled Evangelical minister is not the end of it?" The President queried.

"Apparently not, sir," Sam responded. "Of course, it doesn't help that Cletus Sawyer and Jebediah Wilson are out there in the media daily portraying you as being in favor of abortion and homosexuality."

"Doesn't the truth matter anymore in this country, Sam?"

"It does, but misinformation and propaganda are also alive and well."

"How many additional agents are being added to the detail?" Andrew Cochran asked.

"I'm not sure sir, that number wasn't shared with me. They just feel that the extra presence is warranted," Sam responded. "A few voters and supporters that helped you win the White House are now perceived as potential threats to your life. We must take every necessary precaution."

"I get it, Sam, and I appreciate the concern. I just never thought that it would come to this."

Rupert Grassmonk stared at the letter sized envelope that Nathan Whitaker had handed to him.

"This will never get to him," Rupert stated with a sigh. "None of the other letters have, so neither will this one. He doesn't want to see it, Nathan."

"Please just have it personally delivered to the White House, will you?" Nathan pleaded.

"Look, I get it. I understand the cathartic release that it affords you to write these letters. And if this is nothing more than a necessary exercise of psychological purging that you need to indulge in, so be it. But don't delude yourself into believing that the President of the United States is receiving and reading your letters. I have it on very good word that he is not. Put yourself in Sam Brainard's position. Sorry, that's right, you were. So, you should know better than anyone else that he can't allow the President to even touch your letters. When it comes to the White House, you are a political cancer, Nathan, that they have and will continue to cut out. Sue Lynn Cochran is probably even more vehement about that than Sam. There is no love lost between you and the First Lady. She blames you for the fact that the President has to suffer through the indignity of a primary challenge by Cletus Sawyer and the other renegades of right-wing unreason. So, all I'm saying is that if it does you good to write these letters of regret, fine. But they are not being received by the addressed recipient. That I can assure you of," Rupert firmly stated.

"You don't understand," Nathan countered. "For forty years we were brothers. Neither of us had anyone else in the world that we were closer to than each other. There was a never-ending bond that cannot be broken."

"No, Nathan, you broke it. The President and everyone around him believe that you betrayed that trust with your words and deeds. That violation of trust is seen as eternal. Besides, you're looking at this the wrong way. You are working under the erroneous belief that the President will receive your letters. That upon reading the letters, that he will appreciate your apologies and contrition. That your words will rekindle the spirit of your forty years of shared camaraderie and love. And, I'm telling you, that none of your letters will ever make it to his desk. Between the sentinel protection of the First Lady, the Chief of Staff, and even the President's secretary, Nancy, your letters will never reach him," Rupert assured his client.

"Please deliver the letter," Nathan insisted.

"Alright," Rupert acquiesced. "On another note, I'm attempting to determine when Justice Winchester is testifying in the concurrent McCallum criminal trial. The last thing we need is for his testimony to surface before our case goes to the jury. Motions *in limine* in our trial are one thing, the press reporting on another public trial is something that we cannot control. Get some rest, it's going to be a grueling few weeks, " Rupert advised.

"Sure, sure," Nathan half-heartedly replied. "Don't forget to deliver the letter, please."

"I promise, I will," Rupert responded. "Anything else?"

"I received a call not long ago from someone I assume is with the administration. The voice was intentionally distorted with some sort of device," Nathan recalled. "The call was brief, but threatening. I was told to stop attempting the reach out to the President, that there would be consequences involving my trial if I didn't quit."

"When was this?" Rupert queried.

"Not long after the National Prayer Breakfast incident. I called the White House and the President's personal phone in an effort to make sure that he was alright. It was more a reflexive action on my part and concern for my old friend."

"Does the President still have the same personal telephone number that he did two years ago when you were still his Chief of Staff?" Rupert pressed.

"I believe so, why?"

"I would have thought that someone in his inner circle would have changed the telephone number after the scandal involving you surfaced. Or at the least, blocked your ability to reach the number. That is perplexing on a number of levels," Rupert admitted. "Keep me advised if you receive any additional threatening calls. This is definitely something to follow-up on."

THE POLICE DETECTIVE SHOOK HIS HEAD in disbelief, as he closed his note pad.

"I don't understand. Why don't you want to assist us with the prosecution of your assailant?" The detective asked Robert Douglas as they sat in the front room of Robert and Jason's spacious apartment.

"I'm recovering nicely. I'm going to be fine. I'd rather just drop the whole thing," Robert stated.

"We have Jason and other eyewitnesses. We know the name of your assailant and the address of his home. This will be a simple prosecution. In fact, his attorney will probably accept a plea deal," the detective assured Robert.

"I'm not interested in going forward with pressing charges," Robert reiterated, his left eye still swollen and a visible scrape on his otherwise unblemished cheekbone.

"Is your father aware of your decision?" The detective inquired.

"Leave my father out of this. I am an adult, this is my decision, not his," Robert stated with force.

"If you're worried about the publicity that this case would get given that your father is running for President of the United States . . ." the detective said before being cut-off by Robert.

"No!" Robert interjected. "I'm not interested in pursuing this matter legally. It's as simple as that. Now, if you don't mind, I'm getting a headache and I probably should get some rest."

"Sure, of course," the detective said as Robert led him to the door. "If you reconsider your decision, please give me a call," he stated while handing Robert his card.

"Thank you, good day," Robert responded as he slowly closed the door on the detective and the prosecution for his assault.

Robert walked back into the front room and plopped himself onto the couch.

"I don't understand. What was that all about? Why wouldn't you want to prosecute that Neanderthal homophobe who assaulted you?" Jason asked his lover incredulously.

"Just drop it!" Robert snapped at Jason, while reclining his head onto the couch and closing his eyes.

"Mom, really? I don't understand," Cameron Barnes said to his mother Carolyn as they stood in the kitchen of their Chicago home.

"Look son, I understand your anger. You were stopped by a police officer and taken into custody for the crime of being a young black man driving an expensive car in an affluent white neighborhood. It wasn't right and it certainly wasn't fair. You did nothing wrong. I understand that. But we are not in a position to be filing a civil rights law suit against the Chicago police," Carolyn attempted to explain to her son.

"I was humiliated. I was as polite and accommodating to that police officer as I could be given the circumstances, yet he was having none of it. He treated me like a thug. He wouldn't listen to a word that I had to say. I was racially profiled, pure and simple. Are we just going to turn our heads and allow that to happen?" Cameron asked, his voice rising as his temper flared.

"Honey, I know you're angry. I'm angry. And we will fight this, but not in a court of law, not now," Carolyn responded attempting to appease her son.

"Why? Just tell me why?" Cameron insisted. "It's your job, isn't it? You believe that you need to protect your boss from the potential adverse publicity more than you believe in supporting your son's civil rights, isn't it?"

"Cam, no, that's not true. I will always support you, you know that. But what you said about the adverse publicity is not completely off base. As campaign manager for the Senator, I have certain responsibilities to him and the campaign. Primary among those is to make sure that nothing can reflect badly on the candidate or the campaign. Surely you can see that?" Carolyn cajoled her son.

"Sure, I understand. I understand that I come second to your job and your career. I understand that you have taught me to stand up for my rights and then when I do, if it conflicts with the priorities of your job, it's, never mind Cam, this is not a good time for you to fight for your rights. To be a proud African-American man in America. That's what I understand, mom," Cameron said defiantly to his mother as he walked out of the kitchen.

"Cam, Cam," Carolyn called out, as she could hear the slamming of her son's bedroom door. She stood in the kitchen and shook her head and quietly mumbled to herself, "He's right, he's right."

BESSIE COLLINS STOOD IN THE KITCHEN of her New Orleans home and glared at her husband, Lucius.

"I surely don't understand what you's sayin', Lucius. Why on God's green earth would I give up my business?" Bessie questioned her husband with a perplexed look on her face. "That shop never been as successful as it is right now with me running things. We been making some good money. I'm bringing home nearly twice every month what I was earning working at the dress shop. We can afford to do some things, fix up the house, and even put some money in our rainy day fund. So, when you stand there and tell me that I should quit my business, I got to tell you Lucius, I'm looking at you, and I can see that the porch light is on, but clearly there ain't nobody home."

"It just ain't a fittin' way for a church-goin' woman to be carrying on," Lucius stoically responded. "I seen when I come to visit, and you is doin' one of them there séances, how you shaken' and carrying on. Moanin' and pretending that the spirits is in your body. I seen."

"Lucius, I done swear, sometimes you can't find your behind when you got both of your hands in your back pockets!" Bessie exclaimed. "People come to me cuz they be missin' their dearly departed. They want to have a conversation because it makes them feel better. I listen to them, and they get something out of it. Sometimes, I may moan a little or gyrate, but they is nothing wrong with it. I don't tell them that I is speaking for their loved ones from the beyond. I let them talk. And once they do, they feel a whole lot better. And they thank me. I don't see nothing wrong with that."

"Bessie, you is my wife, and I love you. But if you can't see what is wrong with you leading people on with such nonsense and then taking their money, I just ain't so sure I know who you is anymore," Lucius said as he turned and walked out of the kitchen.

Bessie pulled one of the kitchen chairs out from the table and sat to ponder what Lucius had said. After a few moments of reflection, she raised her hand up to her forehead and slowly stroked her brow.

"He may be right," she whispered to herself. "He may be right."

CHAPTER 16

Another month had passed and it was the end of April in New Orleans. The temperature was rising and the air began to hang a little heavier with the increase in humidity. Aaron Rose and Clay Grover had both successfully passed the Louisiana bar exam and were now able to fully participate in the practice of law with their colleagues, Caleb Butler and Emily DuBois. Aaron and Clay were both involved with the Fifth Circuit appellate case, but now they were also representing clients in lower court civil rights matters. Both were increasingly happy and satisfied with their decision to leave Washington politics for New Orleans civil rights and public aid litigation.

"This is the right place for us," Aaron said to Clay over lunch. "It feels so natural now to live here and help people who may not otherwise have viable representation in the court system."

"It is wonderful," Clay responded with a smile, "as is this bowl of seafood gumbo."

"Everything comes down to food with you, doesn't it?" Aaron scoffed with a grin.

"Not everything. Sex is pretty great as well," Clay offered.

"Speaking of, at first, I've got to admit that Chiffon scared the crap out of me. I thought she was coming on so strong," Aaron confessed.

"That's her thing, she likes to play. Especially with a cute young thing like you," Clay replied.

"But the more I deal with her, the more I talk to her, man, she's been through so much. I really feel for her. Her life has not been easy," Aaron added.

"Which is why, this work, what we do, is so important," Clay said. "Caleb is remarkable. He has built an amazing practice. After Senator Fitzsimmons died, he took a little bit of me with him. For a while, there was a hole in me that I couldn't fill. But, this work with these people has made me whole again. And working with Emily, it's like it all was destined to happen. It's all such a perfect fit."

Posy Branch was humming to herself as she was tidying up the nail stations in her salon. Moments later from across the room she heard Chiffon LaBelle join her by singing the words to Gloria Gaynor's hit song, "I Will Survive." Before long, they were both singing at the top of their lungs and shaking their hips.

"Damn girl, you can sang," Posy said to Chiffon as they finished the song and were breathing heavily after a spirited rendition.

"I always use to sing around the house when I was a kid. Well, until my daddy would come home. He didn't think that young boys should sing. Especially since I was always singing the girl singers' songs," Chiffon related to Posy. "My mama would sing with me, but when daddy came home we would stop."

"You got a fine voice, and you can hit some of them high notes," Posy noted. "I think that we should have a karaoke night once a week. But we'll do it up right with a live band."

"That could be a fine idea," Chiffon agreed. "A number of the bars on Bourbon do a karaoke night but it's all with canned music. No one does it with a live band."

"And that's why our karaoke night will be the best in town," Posy said with a laugh.

"What about Chantale, you think she'll go for it?" Chiffon asked.

"Oh, Sugar, please, old Chantale will be so busy counting the money, she won't care what we do," Posy declared. "Chantale never gonna say it out loud, but she knows I'm the best thing that's come her way in a long time. Business is great, we turning people away. She can call me crazy all she wants, but you see the big smile on that gal's face when the cash register is ringing like church bells on Easter Sunday."

"True dat," Chiffon confirmed.

President Andrew Cochran sat behind his desk in the Oval Office as he hummed and sang, "Georgia On My Mind" to himself while he was reviewing his morning briefing report. Sue Lynn

Cochran entered the office and listened to her husband before announcing herself.

"Andy, I haven't heard you sing in years," Sue Lynn said with a smile on her face.

"I use to sing a lot with Grandma Blanche when I was a kid. We'd sing some gospel songs and Irving Berlin, and some of the old jazz standards," Andrew related to his wife. "Then when I went to college, old Nathan and I both loved Southern rock music. We would get drunk and just wail to Marshall Tucker, or the Allman Brothers, or Charlie Daniels Band. Just singing up a storm and acting like fools. In fact, the last time I really sang was when Nathan and I spent a weekend at Camp David, not too long after my inauguration. We got sloppy drunk and smoked some weed and scared the crap out of the Secret Service boys we were carrying on so."

"I didn't know about that, you never told me," Sue Lynn replied with an irritated pique to her tone.

"Well, there are some things that I don't tell you," Andrew curtly responded. "Why is it that every time I even mention his name, you get this tone in your voice?"

"Because I don't understand why you keep bringing up these fond memories of that man. He was involved in the murder of two people, and he nearly brought your administration to an end before it even began," Sue Lynn replied forcefully.

"There's not much evidence of that that isn't hearsay or circumstantial. So far, he's not guilty of anything," Andrew said as his voice raised. "His trial begins in a few weeks, then we'll see what the prosecutor can truly present at trial."

"I don't get you, Andy," Sue Lynn responded, now clearly annoyed. "You've been making excuses for Nathan Whitaker for forty years. You are blindly loyal to that man, and that loyalty almost destroyed you once. I'm not going to allow it to happen again."

"And since the day he married Posy, you have never cut him one inch of slack. You've been quick to criticize him at every turn. It would be nice to see a modicum of empathy from you once in a while. You can be so damn judgmental, Sue Lynn," Andrew said as his voice became louder and his face was flushed with anger.

"He's gone now. Move on Andy," Sue Lynn shouted in return.

"That's not going to happen, so you better get used to it. Now, I have work to do. Please leave."

Stanford Winchester sat in his office at the Federal Court Building in New Orleans whistling a tune. The blue covered appellant's opening brief in the Katrina victims class action matter sat on the corner of his desk, with pages flagged and highlighted by one of his law clerks. Stanford was waiting to attend a meeting with his fellow judges on the appellate panel, Charles Sewell and Whitlee Hammond.

After the meeting concluded, Whitlee Hammond asked Stanford if he would like to walk with her, as she was going to French Tips, Juleps & Jazz to get a manicure.

"It would be a true delight and a great honor," Stanford responded to Whitlee's impromptu invitation.

"Well, I don't know about all that, but I'll try not to bore you on the walk," Whitlee replied.

"You couldn't bore me, that is an impossibility," Stanford stated as the two colleagues began their excursion through the French Quarter. With far less crowds to navigate through than their Mardi Gras venture, Stanford pointed out shops on Royal Street that were owned by his friends. He explained the history of some of the buildings in the Quarter. Whitlee was not born and raised in New Orleans, as Stanford was. She was originally from Austin, Texas, and moved to New Orleans after she was appointed to the Fifth Circuit Court of Appeals during the end of the first year of Andrew Cochran's Presidency. She had been a resident of the Crescent City for a little over a year, but still unaware of some of the deep history of the city. Stanford was only too happy to be Whitlee's travel guide and civic historian.

"You see that building," Stanford stated while pointing across the street. "That's the Pedesclaux-Lemonnier House at 640 Royal. It has a colonial origin. It was originally built by the grand Spanish notary Pedro Pedesclaux. In 1811 it was sold to Dr. Yves Lemonnier, who had the building enlarged and added his initials to the balcony. The curved-wall salon on the second floor is one of the finest in the Quarter. After the Civil War, a later owner added the fourth floor, which made it a skyscraper for its day. In later decades, the building was identified with George Washington Cable's romance 'Sier George'. Today, as you can see, it is home to a t-shirt shop. Some call that progress, I find it rather tear-wrenching."

"That's fascinating," Whitlee stated, "though I do see your point regarding progress. Speaking of history though, what is the oldest building in New Orleans?"

"Ah, that would be the Convent of the Ursulines at 1100 Chartres," Stanford replied, as his eyes lit up like a young boy on Christmas morning. "It is not only the oldest building in New Orleans, it is the oldest building in Louisiana and the Mississippi Valley. It was designed by a French-trained military engineer in 1745, though it wasn't completed until 1753. It resembles the Continental French buildings of the Louis XV period."

"Truly amazing how much you know about this city," Whitlee responded.

"I was born and raised here. This is my home," Stanford said with a shrug as if to indicate that knowledge of one's hometown is no great feat.

"There are people who live in one place all their life and couldn't tell you how old the home they live in is, let alone its history," Whitlee countered.

"Well, history and I are very close friends," Stanford responded with a grin. "If you don't know history, you are clueless to the future."

"I couldn't agree more," Whitlee said as she took Stanford by the arm and they continued their slow saunter through the streets and history of the French Quarter.

Several minutes later, Stanford and Whitlee arrived at the front of French Tips, Juleps & Jazz.

"Well, here we are," Stanford stated.

"Will you please allow me to buy you a drink?" Whitlee asked sweetly. "You've been such a wonderful tour guide, it's the least I can do to repay your kindness."

"It would be unchivalrous to rebuff such a generous offer. However, I would feel like such a cad, if I were to allow a lovely woman to waste her money on the likes on me. Please allow me to purchase the libations for the two of us," Stanford said firmly and sincerely.

"Well alright, if you insist," Whitlee replied.

"Thank you for indulging me. I'm a creature of times past, who cannot abide by some of these modern ways," Stanford explained.

No sooner had the words passed from between his lips when Posy Branch approached Stanford and Whitlee, yelping, "If this don't beat all! If this don't just beat all! It's so good to see you Stanford and Whitlee. I don't need to call you judges outside of a courthouse, do I?"

"No, of course not," Whitlee quickly responded. "It's so nice to see you as well, Posy. I've come for a manicure. My friend Gail raves about what a wonderful job your beauticians do."

"Yeah, the nail gals are pretty good, if I do say so myself. Just had my nails done this morning with a real nice peach color polish," Posy stated as she displayed her nails to Whitlee.

"That's a lovely shade on you, it goes so well with your skin tones," Whitlee complimented Posy.

"Oh, this one's a keeper, Stanford, she got a lot of class," Posy said to a rather uncomfortably flustered Stanford Winchester.

"Well now, what can I get you to drink?" Stanford asked Whitlee, attempting to change the topic.

"A peach julep would be lovely," Whitlee responded.

Stanford sidled up to the bar and attempted not to look at Michael's glistening shaved muscular chest while he ordered a peach julep and a Sazerac. Posy walked over to one of the beauticians to have a word, while Stanford and Whitlee sat at the bar and Michael prepared the cocktails.

"Oh, this is delicious," Whitlee stated after taking a sip of her julep. Likewise, Stanford nodded his approval and proclaimed to Michael, "Nicely done, nicely done, indeed," after taking a long slow sip of his Sazerac.

Posy returned to the bar and informed Whitlee, "Song Ye can do your nails whenever you're ready. She's our best beautician, but don't tell the other nail gals I said so," Posy laughed and snorted. While Stanford and Whitlee sipped their cocktails, the jazz band began playing the Gershwin song "Embraceable You."

"I adore this song," Whitlee said with a serene smile.

"It's one of my favorites as well," Stanford added.

"Well, land's sake Stanford, you gonna ask Whitlee to dance with you?" Posy loudly inquired.

"Uh, well," Stanford stumbled with his words as he began to blush.

"Go on now, you got the dance floor all to yourselves," Posy prodded. "Show Whitlee what a marvelous dancer you is." After a few hesitant moments, Stanford asked Whitlee, "Would you honor me with this dance?"

"It would be my pleasure," she replied with a smile. Stanford took Whitlee by the hand and led her to the dance floor. There he took her into his arms and demonstrated his thirty-plus years of dancing expertise that he had honed with his late wife LeeAnn. It felt right to have Whitlee in his arms as they moved across the dance floor, Stanford thought to himself. As the song concluded, Stanford twirled and deeply dipped Whitlee, who was giggling like a school girl. They returned to the bar where Posy was seated with a huge smile on her face.

"Ain't he the cat's pajamas when it comes to dancing? He's a regular Fred Astaire," Posy said to Whitlee as she took a long sip of her julep.

"Oh my word, yes," Whitlee breathlessly replied while looking over and beaming at Stanford. Stanford attempted to look nonchalant, but it was the happiest moment in Stanford's life in over seven years. Of that, there was no doubt.

CHAPTER 17

Rupert Grassmonk gently rocked back and forth in his leather office chair. He stared across his large ornate desk at his client, Nathan Whitaker.

"Just a little over three weeks until jury selection," he stated. "It's been a long haul with all of the delays, but judgment day is upon us."

"I'm looking forward to having my name cleared and my reputation restored," Nathan responded.

"C'mon Nathan, I want you to be optimistic but you've got to temper that with being realistic as well. When it comes to public perception, your reputation will never be fully restored. You've already been tried and convicted in the court of public opinion. Even with a not guilty verdict from the jury you will always be considered guilty by some of the American public," Rupert said to his client.

"So, I'm the O.J. Simpson of the new millennium," Nathan said with a shrug.

"Well, perhaps not that bad, but there will always be people who will view you as a murderer, even after acquittal through a trial and jury verdict," Rupert stated. "That is precisely why *voir dire* will be so important to our case. We need to weed out the potential jurors who already have too much knowledge of the case and preconceived notions about your guilt."

"What were the results from the jury consultants' research?" Nathan asked.

"Mixed, but you do better with younger white male jurors who don't get their news from more conventional media. Oddly, you also don't do too badly with older black men and women," Rupert stated.

"Well, that's something I guess," Nathan replied.

"Speaking of somethings, the prosecutor is realizing that his case is pretty circumstantial, and is making one last pass on a plea," Rupert offered.

"What do they have?" Nathan asked. "They speculate that I used a syringe to inject poison into a water bottle. Did they ever find the syringe or the vial containing the poison? No. The only witness that they have placing me anywhere near the victim is a law clerk who said he saw me at night from across the street enter a hotel not long after the victim entered the hotel. There are no records of any phone calls made to my home, office or cell phone by the victim. If she allegedly called me repeatedly on the phone, where is that phone? They didn't find it on me or on my property. Kate Wilson, through the testimony of their own witness, had often espoused hatred for the political views of Justice Martin. She had her own motivation for murder, she certainly didn't need me. And since I never met the women, there is no true link in the prosecution's case."

"What about the statements that she made to co-workers about having high ranking connections in the White House?" Rupert countered.

"What young man or woman hasn't exaggerated about their own connections or clout to self-aggrandize themselves in the eyes of their colleagues?" Nathan responded.

"You still cannot predict what juries will do," Rupert cautioned.

"They will acquit an innocent man, that's what they will do," Nathan replied with confidence.

"Hopefully you are right," Rupert answered. "By the way, any more threatening calls about you reaching out to the President?"

"No, nothing as of late. Though I keep my head on a swivel when I'm walking down the street late at night," Nathan added.

JIM BOB MCCALLUM LEANED BACK IN HIS CHAIR with his alligator cowboy boots propped up on the edge of his desk. He took a large swig of bourbon from his glass as he stared directly at his attorney.

"Oh hell no!" Jim Bob exclaimed. "I'm not cutting a deal with that lame ass government prosecutor. Do I look like Monty Hall to you? No deals!"

"Rupert Grassmonk informed me that the prosecutor also offered Nathan Whitaker a plea deal," the attorney stated.

"That's cuz he's finally come to the realization that he don't have jack-shit on either Nathan or me," Jim Bob ranted. "Hell, he's hopping around from one place to the other like he's the Easter Bunny. Problem is, he ain't got no eggs in his basket. He ain't nothing but the paid for mouthpiece of the Democratic liberal extremists."

"They do have Stanford Winchester's testimony in your case. Rupert filed a motion *in limine* to have that testimony stricken from Whitaker's case. There's a good chance the motion will be granted."

"I've told you once, I've told you a thousand times, Stanford Winchester is a no-good liar. The Democrats on the Senate Judiciary Committee knew it and were going to prove it," Jim Bob stated. "Look, all they've got is me having a conversation over a few drinks with Winchester. At one time, I considered the man a friend. If he testifies at trial that I told him that me and Nathan Whitaker plotted and arranged for the murder of Albert Martin he is just plain lyin'. I never said those words to him. We talked about Martin being in poor health and not long for this world, but that's it. I told Stanford that he would make a fine Supreme Court Justice and that the American public would be the winners when he was on the bench. If he recalls any different, it's because Stanford can get a bit addled when he's been drinking. And as I said, we did partake in a few cocktails that afternoon."

"It's going to be your word against the word of a highly respected Appellate court judge," the attorney stated. "Common sense would dictate . . ." Jim Bob interrupted with a scowl on his face.

"If common sense was lard most folk wouldn't be able to grease a pan," Jim Bob angrily replied. "Jury selection starts in three weeks. That gives you plenty of time to make sure we've got a damn fine jury. I don't chew my meat twice, so you best move on that."

STANFORD WINCHESTER WALKED PAST HIS SECRETARY Naomi's desk before halting and spinning in her direction.

"My, that was graceful," Naomi complemented her boss.

"Why thank you ma'am," Stanford said. "Kindly remind me again, when do we have oral argument in the Katrina victims class action appeal?"

"Middle of July, sir. In fact, the clerk's office just delivered a copy of the appellee's response brief. I put a copy on the left corner of your desk," Naomi replied.

"Excellent. I assume that Judges Sewell and Hammond also received a copy?

"Yes sir, I do believe so," Naomi stated. "And since you mentioned Judge Hammond, I just wanted to say that I couldn't be happier. It's time, yes sir, it surely is time."

"Naomi, I got no idea what you are talking about," Stanford said while looking at his secretary with a quizzical expression on his face.

"It's all the talk among the gals in the lunchroom," Naomi responded.

"And what would that be?" Stanford questioned.

"Well, you know, that you and Judge Hammond are dating," Naomi said with a wide smile.

"We are certainly not dating," Stanford said definitively. "Where ever did you hear such a thing?"

"Kathy, Judge Trebold's secretary saw you and Judge Hammond enjoying a cocktail and dancing together at French Tips, Juleps & Jazz the other day. She said y'all looked like you was having a grand time. We all just assumed you two was dating," Naomi related.

"Naomi Cutler, you've been working with me for over a decade now. You know what emphasis I put on making sure that we adhere to the facts around here. Circumstantial evidence is no proof of anything. So, let me lay out the simple facts for you and that rumormongering gaggle of hens down in the lunchroom," Stanford stated. "Judge Hammond and I are colleagues, nothing more. She happened to be walking to that establishment after work. Since it is on my way home, I accompanied her on the walk. We stopped to partake in a quick libation. The owner of the establishment, Posy Branch, was insistent on Judge Hammond and I dancing together. You see, Ms. Branch and I had the occasion to share a dance together at a White House dinner in my honor a couple of years ago when I was being vetted by the Senate Judiciary Committee. She was impressed with my small modicum of skill on the dance floor and wanted me to demonstrate that skill to Judge Hammond. It would have been rude and ungentlemanly of me to refuse. So, Judge Hammond and I had a single dance. We certainly are not dating. How would it look for the Chief Judge of a Courthouse to be dating another judge who is his junior? Dignity and responsible decorum disallow such a thing. Those are all of the facts. Please make sure that that wholly unsubstantiated rumor is quashed immediately."

"Sure, your honor," Naomi said skeptically with a grin. And then, as Stanford left her desk and walked into his office, he could hear Naomi softly say, "I think it's just wonderful."

"Women," Stanford mumbled to himself with exasperation and a shrug of his shoulders.

Stanford took a seat behind his desk and grasped the bound brief that Naomi left on his desk for him. He began to flip through the pages skimming the argument being made by the appellees in the Katrina matter. As he continued to read he shouted to his secretary, "Naomi, where is the appendix to this brief?" Naomi got up from her chair and stood in the judge's doorway.

"I left a copy of the response brief and the appendix to the brief with your law clerk, Brian. You never seem to want to bother with the appendix," Naomi replied.

"Well, yes that is generally true. But in this instance, I'd like to see the appendix. There is a reference in the brief to testimony in a transcript from the trial court that is supplied in the appendix that I'd like to read for myself. No hurry, but when you have a moment, could you kindly fetch it for me?" Stanford asked.

"Of course, your honor, I'll get it momentarily."

"Thank you, Naomi," Stanford said. He continued reading the brief. "A nicely crafted argument," he said to himself. "This is some fine writing."

CHAPTER 18

L ANDON HAMILTON PACED BACK AND FORTH in his office at the Re-Elect President Cochran campaign headquarters in Savannah. He ran his hand through his light brown hair, his hazel-colored eyes staring at the document on a clipboard.

"It's early June, we are still eight months from the Iowa caucus, so there is plenty of time to work on these numbers, but still . . ." Landon said to his aide Peter as he continued his pacing. "These are our own polling numbers, right?"

"Yup, that's the disturbing part," Peter replied with a shake of his head.

"Look it's Iowa," Landon said by way of explanation. "The Republican primary voters in Iowa are notoriously conservative and very Evangelical. It's no surprise that we are trailing. Heck, we didn't even win Iowa when the President ran for his first term. Yet, I didn't expect to find us trailing both Cletus Sawyer and Jebediah Wilson by double digits and be basically in a tie with Lamar Clarkson. We are talking about the incumbent President of the United States after all."

"Yes, but a sitting President who has royally pissed off the far-right wing of his party by striking a number of legislative bargains with the Democrats in the Senate," Peter added.

"True, but I think that what has really gotten the goat of the conservative Evangelicals is the fact that the President nominated a moderate jurist for the Supreme Court. It drives them crazy when they believe that *Roe v. Wade* could have been struck down if not for a more conservative pick for the Court," Landon surmised. "It's factually not true. We couldn't have moved the dial that far even if Stanford Winchester would have been confirmed."

"I understand that Winchester is going to be back in D.C. later this month to testify in the Jim Bob McCallum criminal trial," Peter stated.

"Yeah, I heard that as well," Landon agreed. "He's not going to get a White House dinner this time around I can assure you of that. His withdrawal of his name from the Supreme Court nomination still does not sit all that well with many at the White House. The First Lady, Sam Brainard, myself, among others are not fans of the Justice. Of course, part of the animosity on behalf of the First Lady was because she perceived Winchester to be the hand-picked candidate of Nathan Whitaker. She believed that Nathan foisted Winchester on the President. If you are seen as being affiliated in any way with Nathan Whitaker, you are dog meat in the eyes of the First Lady. A position that I am wholly in agreement with. The President needs to be protected from the overtures of that scoundrel Whitaker. Add to that, Jim Bob McCallum is no longer a supporter of the President which certainly hurts financially for the campaign to re-elect."

"Do we really want the political contributions of an alleged murderer anyway?" Peter questioned.

"First off, he's not been proven guilty of anything yet. And the scuttlebutt is that the prosecutor is freaking out because their case against him is so weak and circumstantial. But most importantly, the money of alleged murderers is still green and still folds really nicely. This is politics in America, Peter," Landon said with a sarcastic grin.

KATHERINE DOUGLAS STARED AT HER HUSBAND Senator Perry Douglas in disbelief.

"Truly Perry, you honestly think that there is no correlation between Robert's refusal to press charges against that homophobic hooligan and his unwillingness to have you bear the publicity about your own son's sexuality?" Katherine demanded.

"I said that I'm not sure if the two facts have a correlation in Robert's mind," Senator Douglas replied. "And besides, Robert is a grown man. He makes his own decisions. We can no longer tell him what to do or think."

"Yes, but what we can do, what you specifically can do is to tell your son how proud you are of him. How you have no issue about his sexuality becoming public, as long as Robert is fine with it. That you couldn't care one iota if Robert being gay loses you any votes with narrow-minded, bigoted voters. That your support and love for him is more important than any election. That is what you can do, Perry. And from the perspective of preserving your relationship with Robert, the sooner the better," Katherine challenged her husband.

"You're right. I'll give him a call and see if he wants to have dinner with his old man. It's just that he's never verbally come out to us, so I never wanted to insinuate myself into discussing his sex life. I always believed that it was his private business and if he wanted to share it with us, he would. But I guess after this unfortunate incident, the cat is now out of the bag," Perry said.

"The cat was never in the bag. You're a bright man, Perry. You profess to be a liberal on social issues. Yet, your obviously gay son lives his life out in the open right in front of you. Then when he is attacked and beaten for the sin of walking down a public street holding hands with his boyfriend, you act like this is all a new revelation about your son's sexuality. Well, it's not. Robert has been living openly as a gay man for almost a decade. So, don't act shocked now and defend your ignorance by claiming, 'gee, he never told me so.' You're smarter and more perceptive than that. Please don't insult Robert's intelligence by playing stupid," Katherine claimed harshly.

"I won't, I promise," Perry affirmed. "Henry and I occasionally had conversations about sexuality. We were both very old school on the topic. It's just the way we were raised. I never had conversations about sex with my father. You learned about sex in hygiene and biology classes in school or on the playground talking to the other guys. It wasn't something you ever talked to your parents about. It was that dirty little secret that wasn't brought up in polite company," Perry explained to his wife.

"I know, I get it. My mother and I didn't discuss sex much either. But times have changed and attempting to bury your head in the sand and pretend sexuality isn't prevalent or relevant to life is fool's play. Have an open and honest conversation with Robert about his sexuality. It's time. No, actually, it's past time, but he has to know that you are proud of him just the way he is. No election is worth causing your son to be ashamed or embarrassed about who and what he is," Katherine said with a loving smile.

"I couldn't agree more. I'll talk with Robert."

PRESIDENT COCHRAN AND HIS CHIEF OF STAFF walked around the White House grounds taking in some sunshine and fresh air. It was early

June in Washington and the rose bushes in the White House garden were in full bloom. However, at the moment, for the Cochran administration the bloom was coming off the rose.

"Did you get a call from Landon?" Sam Brainard asked the President.

"Oh yes. I understand that I'm toast in Iowa," Andrew Cochran responded with a half-hearted chuckle. "I'm basically in fourth place in a five-horse race. Thank God Carlton Smith has the personality of nondescript soft cheese."

"Well, and if that wasn't special enough, this morning on conservative talk radio, Pastor Jebediah Wilson was basically accusing you of devil worship in the White House," Sam said with a wicked smile.

"Oh, that is special," the President laughed. "Where in hell, pardon the pun, did this little nugget come from?"

"Apparently, it germinates from the allegations that the law clerk, Kate Wilson was killed by using a digitalis poison obtained from a Haitian voodoo queen in New Orleans. Since Nathan Whitaker is accused of Kate Wilson's murder, the correlation is that Nathan must have been practicing dark magic and devil worship in the White House. And, of course, if Nathan was involved in devil worship then one can readily assume that you were as well. Jebediah was quite convincing," Sam said.

"Why naturally," Andrew Cochran sarcastically agreed. "You know, Sam, I remember a time in the not so distant past when candidates may have stretched the truth a bit, but it wasn't commonplace to fabricate fantastic tales from whole cloth and preach them as the gospel truth."

"We refer to those days as the ancient past, Mr. President," Sam said shaking his head. "To some extent social media has made fact checking an arcane practice bordering on prehistoric. You just throw the electronic shit against the Facebook wall and see if it sticks."

"Speaking of sticking, any further information about whether our elusive Vice-President is going to stick with us or abandon ship anytime soon? Howard has been avoiding me lately like I have bubonic plague," the President stated with a chuckle.

"I've heard through some back channels that there seems to be some big money party contributors who are pressing for him to get into the Presidential race. No one from his office is acknowledging anything at this point. I have no word on whether and when the Vice-President would consider joining the primary campaign, but his potential political and monetary backing might be growing," Sam added.

"Time is wasting, isn't it?" the President plainly asked. "So, tell me, Sam, what should we do with our Vice-President while he forges for acorns in our forest?"

"I'm not sure that anything can be done at this moment, sir," Sam responded. "Rash moves done in haste are often regretted later."

"And I want to be President for four more years, why?" Andrew Cochran asked somewhat in jest though not completely.

"Because you're good at it. And someone needs to save the American people from the sheer lunacy of your primary opponents," Sam responded.

"OK, please keep reminding me of that fact, Sam. It's easy to forget at times," the President answered wearily. "Oh, and speaking of forgetting, I almost did. The First Lady informed me that she is giving a speech at a new art instillation in New York City a week from Friday. She is going to stay in the city over that weekend and visit with our daughter and her husband. I checked with Nancy and that Sunday I've got nothing on the books, so I'm going to take a mini-vacation and spend a day alone at Camp David. No staff, no press, no announcements, no you, just alone with the Secret Service boys. Let's keep it real low-key, alright?"

"Even if it's with dozens of Secret Service agents."

"Yeah, I'm noticing the increased presence. The other day, I was in front of the White House just stretching my legs for a few minutes, and there was a loud pop. I'm not going to lie; I jumped out of my skin for a brief moment. But within seconds, I was surrounded by agents. It's come down to a car backfiring on Pennsylvania Avenue is perceived as another assassination attempt and I am swarmed over by a bevy of security detail agents. It's not a good way to live, Sam."

A FEW MINUTES LATER, WITH SAM BACK in the West Wing, President Cochran motioned over to the head of his Secret Service detail, Billy James.

"Billy, I've got a favor to ask of you. This is strictly confidential and pretty much needs to be between just you and me. The First Lady cannot know, nor Sam, not even Nancy. I need you to make some arrangements for a short one day trip that I'll be taking to Camp David a week from Sunday. Do I have your confidence and assured secrecy?" President Cochran asked his Secret Service agent.

"Of course, Mr. President," Billy solemnly replied.

"Excellent."

CHAPTER 19

Posy Branch carefully arranged the large sign in the window of her establishment. She was about to start her new promotion of Karaoke Wednesday. So far, everything Posy had planned for her business had reaped great success.

In the back of the large room, Chiffon LaBelle was singing with the jazz band. Chiffon mournfully crooned along with the band.

"Southern trees bear a strange fruit. Blood on the leaves and blood at the root. Black bodies swingin' in the Southern breeze. Strange fruit hangin' from the poplar trees . . ."

As the song concluded, Posy said, "Oh Lordy Jesus, that is one sad and disturbing song. Who sang that?"

"Lady Day, uh, Billie Holiday," Chiffon replied. "It's called 'Strange Fruit.' My Grandma Lucinda taught me that song when I was about twelve years old. She wanted me to remember the ways of the world in the South. She told me, 'Ernest, sometimes you act so strange, Son. You best be aware of your history and take proper care. You gonna be challenged all of your days on this blessed earth. You got to fight for your rights 'cuz no one gonna give them to you easy.' And, she was so right in so many ways that she could not even imagine. In her own way, she knew I was going to be different than most boys. She was trying to prepare me for the struggles ahead of me. Even now, I have to battle for my sexual identity and respect every day. Nothing is given to you easy."

"That is the God honest truth," Posy agreed. "Honey, I've had to fight for respect all my life. I been called blonde bimbo so many times, shoot, sometimes I thought that was my name. God blessed me with some nice looks, and I sure ain't complainin'. Those looks got me a far piece in life. But no one ever took me serious. My ex-husband and his friends treated me like a dumb pet rock. Put Posy in the corner away from the smart folk. She only gonna embarrass you. They never believed that I could amount to much on my own. But, we gonna show them, ain't we Chiffon?"

"Oh hell, yes, we gonna show them all," Chiffon shouted in response. "We gonna turn this town upside down. They be sayin' look at them two smart, attractive and successful women making their mark on the Big Easy."

"We already doing it, girlfriend. We doin' it up good," Posy confirmed.

"Yeah, that the truth," Chiffon said before she hesitated for a moment. "Did Michael mention to you what happened the other day?" Chiffon asked.

"Nothing that I recall, why?" Posy asked.

"Well, it ain't nothing to worry about, but you ought to know," Chiffon started. "It was a couple of days ago around closing time. You had already left for the night, and Michael and I closed up. A couple of Cajun redneck boys was in here drinking and carrying on."

"Yeah, I remember them," Posy stated. "One had bright red hair, other one had that skin-head look."

"That's them. Been here a good long time, drinking and trying to pick up some girls. Them girls was having none of it. But them boys wasn't taking 'no' for an answer. So, like usual about 15 minutes before closing, we told them to drink up and they had to go. Well, they got real ornery. They was drunk and pissed off cuz them girls wasn't having none of their bullshit. So, they began yelling at me when I told them for a second time that they had to hit the road. Meanwhile, while they was cussing me out, the two girls they spent so much time talking to skedaddled out of there while they wasn't looking. When they realized that the girls had gone, they started to shove me and yelled, 'Look what you done did, you stupid nigger bitch! You chased our women away, now we want our money back!' I told them that ain't happening and informed them that I was going to call the police if they didn't leave right then and there. Well, they called me every name in the book. Michael who was in the back putting the money in the safe came out just in time. One of them had pulled out a knife and said, 'I'm gonna cut you, you crazy bitch.' Michael grabbed his baseball bat from behind the bar and began to swing. Them boys were in no condition to do battle with Michael, they was stumbling drunk. As they left the bar, they told me 'We gonna get you. We know what to do with uppity niggers like you.' Michael called the police, but by then them boys was long gone. Though we did describe them to the police officer."

"Oh, my word!" Posy exclaimed. "That's horrible. Did they hurt you?"

"No, not really. Just a couple of hard shoves, but really they didn't amount to nothing. Them boys was so drunk they could barely stand up straight," Chiffon replied.

"Well, we got to be careful. I'm gonna hire a bouncer to watch the door. I can't have them sort ruining the good times of our fine customers. And, I especially can't have anyone cussing out and threatening my sweet girl. That shit ain't gonna happen. Not in this here establishment!" Posy exclaimed.

CAROLYN BARNES AND SENATOR PERRY DOUGLAS stood together backstage at the Vic Theater in Chicago. The Senator was preparing to make a few remarks before a fundraising Rock the Vote concert in his honor.

"How is Robert doing?" Carolyn asked the Senator about his son.

"He's better. The facial injuries are healing well and he doesn't seem to have any lasting effects from his concussion," Perry Douglas stated. "But I'm afraid that I've failed him. He has no interest in pressing charges against his assailant, and I fear that a large part of that reason is that he doesn't want the press coverage. Especially the part about being gay and being attacked for holding hands with his boyfriend on a public street. He may be concerned that the fact that he is gay would affect my Presidential campaign."

"It's his decision, right? Why would you feel like you failed him?" Carolyn questioned Perry.

"Because I've not been a supportive father to my son," Perry explained. "We've never discussed his sexuality. He never brought it up verbally to Katherine and I. I was always all too willing to ignore the fact that he was living his life openly and proudly in front of me. He didn't have to say anything, I get that now. Yet, I never said anything either. I never acknowledged his lifestyle and choices. I never told him how proud I was of him. I never asked any questions about his boyfriend or their happiness together. I never showed any concern for his well-being as a gay man living in, at times, a repressive society. It's easy to talk the talk on the campaign trail as a so-called progressive liberal. Yet, here I am in a situation with my own son, where I have an opportunity to demonstrate progressive thoughts and actions, and more importantly love and support for my son, and I quietly cower in the corner unwilling to acknowledge the simple obvious truth. My son is gay. How can I preach acceptance to others when I cannot demonstrate it in my own home?"

"Unfortunately, I'm guilty of similar hypocrisy," Carolyn lamented. "Cam was so upset about being taken into custody for no good reason that he wanted to file a formal complaint against the officer, and look into potentially filing civil rights litigation, but I stopped him."

"Why?" Senator Douglas inquired. "And please don't tell me that it has anything to do with protecting me or the campaign from bad publicity."

"Well," Carolyn hesitated.

"Carolyn, oh please no," the Senator begged in response. "I will go on that stage and announce tonight that I am withdrawing from the race for the Democratic Party nomination for President of the United States, if I have one inkling that you would stifle your son's civil rights because of this campaign. It's not worth it. It's exactly the opposite of what we want to accomplish in this campaign. We want to expand everyone's civil rights opportunities in this country not constrict them. That is what we are working for, isn't it?"

"Yes, it is Senator," Carolyn replied.

"Well, it seems like we both need to understand that fact if we are to be better parents to our children and better politicians. If we do not preach a consistent message on the campaign trail and in our own homes, how can we expect anyone to believe us, either the American people or our own families?" Senator Douglas asked his campaign manager.

Carolyn sighed deeply and nodded her head in agreement. At that moment, the house lights went down and a solitary figure strode out to center stage and introduced the Tall Weeds to the large audience. The band then walked onto the stage and began to tune up their instruments. Dom DeMasso the lead guitar player of the band leaned forward and shouted into the microphone.

"Please join me in a rousing Chicago welcome for the man we are supporting this evening, the next President of the United States, your Senator, Perry Douglas!"

Perry looked at Carolyn and simply said, "Only the truth to be told, and here we go."

BESSIE COLLINS STOOD BEHIND THE COUNTER of her shop as Papa Levi took a broom to the wood floor.

"Seems like this here dust just seeps up through them floorboards," Papa Levi said as he busied himself with his sweeping.

"I done come to a conclusion about this business," Bessie announced. "I ain't gonna do any more séances here. I'll still do some tarot card and tea leaves readings but no more sessions with connecting with the spirits of dead folks."

"Why is that?" Papa Levi asked a bit surprised by the news. "You is very popular with folk seeking connection with their beloved departed. And we make good money doing so."

"It just ain't fitting for me to gyrate and moan and carry on during the séances. I'm a grown woman. Shouldn't be doing such things," Bessie unconvincingly responded.

"I see your lips moving and I hear the words coming out, but I done also hear them words being said by Lucius Collins. I ain't hearing Bessie Collins say them words," Papa Levi replied while staring directly at Bessie.

"He ain't wrong," Bessie stated defending the words of her husband.

"He also ain't here, Papa Levi said. "Lucius don't see the relief and happiness on folks faces after they finish a séance session with you. I do. He don't see the hope that customers have that they can carry on with life, even after losing someone close. I do. You give them peace of mind. Or at least you allow them to find it on their own. That's a profound service, Miss Bessie, it surely is. I'd think long and hard on wanting to get rid of that service for folk. But t'aint my business. I'm just here to help you much as I can. What you and Lucius thrash out ain't mine to say."

"Well, you done give me some pause, Papa Levi. I need to think on this some more. I surely do," Bessie replied with a sense of determination.

CHAPTER 20

IT WAS JUST A LITTLE AFTER 7:00 P.M. on a warm early June Wednesday evening and Stanford Winchester was seated at Arnaud's waiting for the arrival of his waiter and friend Lucius Collins.

"I am so sorry, Justice Winchester, I hope I ain't been keeping you waiting too long," Lucius profoundly apologized as he greeted Stanford.

"Ain't been nary a minute or two, Lucius. And you are always well worth the wait," Stanford replied.

"Let me go fetch you a nice Sazerac before I do anything else," Lucius offered.

"No arguments offered here," Stanford responded.

Lucius returned a few moments later with a cocktail crafted just the way Stanford enjoyed his Sazeracs.

"This here is a fine drink," Stanford offered after a long sip. "These warm temperatures and an exceptional cocktail are making me feel like a youthful man again."

"So I been hearing," Lucius smirked.

"And what does that mean, Mr. Collins?" Stanford playfully parried with Lucius.

"Well, only idle gossip," Lucius coyly replied.

"Oh, now you done did it," Stanford laughed in return. "You ain't walking away from this table until you let me in on this here gossip."

"Sir, a gentleman never indulges in women's silly chatter. Ain't no place for it amongst proper folk," Lucius said.

"Lucius, now you just trying to get my goat, ain't you?" Stanford chuckled while staring at his friend. "You best give."

"Well, if you insist," Lucius began. "Other night, Naomi and Virgil Cutler was here at the restaurant enjoying a lovely anniversary dinner together. Thirty years of blissful marriage. Ain't that just grand."

"Oh, I see where this is going," Stanford interrupted.

"While I was serving the happy couple, Naomi may have mentioned that someone at the Courthouse been having an extra bounce to their step. Someone been whistling tunes and smiling a lot. Naomi painted a picture of some spring lovin' making the Court a much happier place. Course, being the gentleman that I am, I couldn't possibly put names to such idle gossip. Just wouldn't be proper," Lucius stated, almost unable to contain his smile or his laughter.

"You no better than them other squawking hens at the Court," Stanford chortled. "I ain't dating Judge Hammond! There ain't nothing going on, other than the reckless invasion of privacy perpetrated by a bunch of legal secretaries with obviously not enough work to do, to keep their minds occupied with reality instead of made-up fantasy stories."

"Yes sir, whatever you say. The customer is always right," Lucius unconvincingly said to Stanford.

"What you getting at, Lucius? Don't you believe me?" Stanford quizzed.

"Well now, sir, I see your lips moving and I hear your words. But I also see how your heart almost bust out of your nicely tailored suit coat when you mentioned Judge Hammond's name. They is a sparkle in your eyes like fireworks on the Fourth of July at the Fairgrounds. I been knowing you for over 17 years now, and I haven't seen this side of you since before the unfortunate passing of Miss LeeAnn. Been 7 years since that sparkle was in your eyes, and your step got that special bounce. And you smiling from ear-to-ear. All I is saying, is that it surely is good to see it again, sir."

"Lucius, does it really show?" Stanford asked pensively.

"I ain't gonna lie to you. It sure do," Lucius responded. "You look like a man in love. Anyone who been there before knows the look. More importantly, he know that wonderful exciting and confusing feeling."

Stanford took another large sip of his cocktail. He nervously looked around the room like a young boy about to share a deep secret with a friend on the playground.

"She's a remarkable woman," Stanford whispered in hushed tones. "Intelligent, lovely, well spoken, a true Southern lady. I keep wondering what in God's word would she ever want with the old cantankerous likes of me?"

"Pretty much what you just described you see in her. Intelligent, distinguished, well-spoken, and a true Southern gentleman. Don't that sound like a perfect match?" Lucius asked Stanford.

"But tradition and decorum must be adhered to, don't you see?" Stanford asked, mostly not wanting to hear an answer. "I am the Chief Judge of the Fifth Circuit. Whitlee, I mean, Judge Hammond is a junior associate judge on the Court, appointed a little over a year ago. It would be highly improper for me to have a social relationship with Judge Hammond."

"All I know is that you got all the traits of a man in love," Lucius replied. "Life is too short. You can't be allowing true love to be left at the curb cuz you afraid of what may or may not look proper to other folk. Some time you just got to sweep decorum out the door and let happiness back in."

CAROLYN BARNES SAT ON HER COUCH in the living room of her home as she waited for her son Cameron to come out of his bedroom.

"What's up, Mom?" Cameron asked as he walked through the living room on his way to the kitchen.

"Sit down with your old mom for a minute Cam, I've got something I want to talk to you about," Carolyn asked her son.

"What did I do now?" Cam asked with an exasperated look on his face.

"Nothing, Darling. It's more of what I've done," Carolyn answered. "When I told you that we shouldn't file a complaint against the police officer who stopped you, I was wrong. And, if it comes to it, if you feel it is necessary to look into filing a civil rights lawsuit, we can pursue that as well."

"What's changed?" Cam asked a bit perplexed by his mom's change of heart.

"I was speaking with a friend, and I realized that I can't act as a liberal in my profession if I don't act like one in my private life. Your rights and your self-respect are paramount to me. I sincerely hope that I never forget that again," Carolyn stated as she reached out to take her teenaged son into her arms.

"No worries, Mom, I'm here to remind you," Cam grinned in return.

PERRY DOUGLAS STOOD OUTSIDE OF THE ENTRANCE to the restaurant entitled Wood, located in the Boystown neighborhood of Chicago. Turning a corner and coming into full view was the Senator's son, Robert.

"Thanks for meeting me in my neck of the woods," Robert said to his father, followed by a satisfied smirk, "Sorry, bad pun, but I couldn't help myself."

"Well, knock on wood that will be the last one," Perry kidded with his son. "Let's get inside and get a couple of cocktails in front of us."

"So, what's up Pops, what did you want to talk to me about?" Robert asked.

"Well, to get right to it, I guess I wanted to talk about my failure as your father," Perry Douglas matter-of-factly replied.

"Oh no, this isn't going to be a 'what did I do to cause you to be gay conversation', is it?" Robert asked with an uncomfortable worry.

"No, quite the opposite," Perry replied. "There, right there. You said that you were gay without hesitation. It came out wholly naturally as it should. You've been honest in how you've lived your life in front of your mother and me. I, on the other hand, for whatever reason I still can't pinpoint, felt like I needed that verbal confirmation from you. I was always waiting for the talk. Where you would come out to your mother and I by announcing it."

"Was there ever any doubt?" Robert asked his father with a quizzical look on his face. "I pretty much knew I was gay at the age of eight or nine."

"For me, yes, there was," Perry responded.

"Was that because you weren't paying attention to what I was doing and how I was acting, or was it that you did not want to pay attention?" Robert queried his father.

"Good question. Another one I don't know the answer to," Perry replied. "Probably a little of both. And I'm not proud to admit that. I could attempt to defend myself by pointing out that men of my generation did not talk outwardly about homosexuality. That this more accepting societal tolerance is new to me."

"Tolerance. That word is the crux of the problem, dad," Robert pointed out to his father. "One tolerates homosexuals like one tolerates the flu. That is until you take your medicine and it thankfully finally gets better. As long as you see gays as people one tolerates, we're not going to make much progress in this conversation."

"I'm sorry, a very bad choice of words," Perry quickly interjected.

"Says the seasoned politician running for president," Robert countered. "You are very careful about the words you choose. Just admit that tolerance was the correct word from your perspective."

"I am sorry, that is honestly not what I meant. I don't tolerate you. I love you, you are my son," Perry said as he looked into Robert's eyes.

"Would you love me more if I was straight?" Robert questioned.

"No, of course not."

"How do you know?" Robert asked.

"Because I can tell you that I love you as much today as I did when your mother put you in my arms a little over twenty-eight years ago minutes after you were born. I see you the same today as I did then. I see you with the love of a father towards his son. And I sure didn't know your sexual preferences then," Perry said as his voice slightly cracked.

"But you know it now, and you have no regrets and no concerns?" Robert asked.

"Not as long as you are happy. No." Perry responded.

"Then, I guess I'm not sure what this conversation is for?"

"It's for a father to sit down and have a few drinks and a meal with his son. It's for a father to tell that son how immensely proud he is of him. And it's to let his son know that his sexuality is immaterial when it comes to the love and support that father has for his son. The love and support that I have for you. Is that alright?" Perry asked Robert.

"Yeah, it's definitely alright," Robert answered with a smile.

BILLY JAMES, ONE OF PRESIDENT COCHRAN'S Secret Service agents, walked behind the President down the gravel path at Camp David. Billy leaned over and softly said to the President, "Waiting in the Aspen Lodge for the last twenty minutes, sir."

"Thank you, Billy. I've got it from here," Andrew Cochran replied as he took his bag from Billy and opened the door leading into the wooden lodge. Andrew looked around the dimly lit room until he noticed a figure sitting in a far corner of the room. The figure sprang to attention as the door opened and the President entered.

"Good morning Mr. President," the figure greeted Andrew Cochran.

"Good morning Nathan," Andrew Cochran replied.

Nathan Whitaker approached his friend, his President, unsure if he should extend his hand to shake the President's hand or encircle his best friend with his arms in a warm hug. As it turned out, neither was an option as the President turned away from Nathan and took a seat in a large upholstered chair. Andrew crossed his legs and his arms as Nathan quickly perceived the President's body language. A heavy uncomfortable tension filled the cavernous room.

"It is so good to see you, Mr. President," Nathan said with an uncomfortable smile.

"Have a seat Nathan," the President offered.

"The last time we were in this room we were drunk and high and singing our lungs out to Southern rock music," Nathan stated in an effort to lighten the mood.

"It seems like decades, though I suppose it was just a little over two years ago," Andrew Cochran responded. "A lot has happened since then, and unfortunately a lot of it hasn't been good."

"Mr. President, I am so sorry," Nathan began before he was quickly interrupted by the President.

"Nathan, let's forego with the formalities. It's just you and me, so just call me Andy. I did not have Billy ask you to join me here because I'm looking for apologies or frankly even explanations. I wanted to see you again, on the eve of your trial, to see if you are alright. Most of the people in my life want me to expunge you from my memory. To act like you never existed. Much to their chagrin, I cannot. You don't wipe forty years of your life away forever. It's not possible," Andrew Cochran stated.

"I'm so happy to hear you say that," Nathan said enthusiastically. "I wasn't sure if I'd ever see you again. I was ecstatic when Billy reached out to me to set up this meeting."

"Well, on that topic, you, Billy and I are the only three people on the planet who know about this meeting. I'd like to keep it that way," Andrew stated firmly.

"Of course, of course. I will never speak a word of this. I promise," Nathan swore.

"Good, thank you," Andrew responded. "I suppose if we're going to be here for a bit, we should make ourselves comfortable. I think that there is a pretty good bourbon stocked in the bar. Would you care to join me for a drink?"

"As long as I don't have to climb through the window of the professor's lounge at Vanderbilt to retrieve it, sure," Nathan replied. Andrew walked to the bar and poured two drinks. He handed one to Nathan and stated, "To better times."

"I'll certainly drink to that," Nathan said as the two old friends settled in for a long conversation. Andrew did not want to hear about the murder or any details about the trial.

Nathan attempted to explain his side of the story but was cut off by Andrew's interruptions or plain-spoken request of "let's change the topic, shall we?" Andrew did not want to dwell on the recent events, but preferred to talk about the distant past and their decades-long friendship. Interspersed between old college stories were polite conversations about people and politics.

"How is the First Lady?" Nathan asked.

"Sue Lynn is Sue Lynn. She's doing fine. She's in New York this weekend visiting with our daughter and her husband," Andrew replied.

"So, she doesn't know that you are meeting with me?"

"Oh, hell no!" Andrew exclaimed. "And it must stay that way. Your mere existence is not exactly serene dinner time small talk with Sue Lynn."

"I understand," Nathan said with his head bowed.

"I don't," Andrew shot back defiantly. "We were very close friends for forty years. We were brothers intricately involved in virtually all aspects of each other's lives. I'm not as cold and aloof as Sue Lynn is. I can't just turn my emotions off and on like tap water. Look, I'm not exactly sure what transpired. Your trial next week will begin to sort that out. And, if you are found to be guilty of the charges against you, so be it. But one way or the other, we are friends. Try as I, or others might, I can't change that fact, which is why we are sitting here today."

Nathan began to tear up. He was overcome with emotion. "I'm so sorry Andy, I'm so sorry," he repeated.

"Hey, I survived. My Presidency has survived. If you are innocent, and this is all an enormous misunderstanding, then I feel sorry for you," Andrew stated. "I just wanted to meet with you this afternoon, and let you know that I am thinking about you. That I still care about you."

"That is exactly what I have said in the letters that I sent to you," Nathan concurred.

"What letters?" Andrew asked.

"I wrote four or five letters to you over the last two years. I've asked my attorney to hand deliver them to the White House," Nathan explained.

"I never received them," Andrew said.

"Rupert Grassmonk, my defense attorney mentioned that they may never get to you. That they may have been kept from you by Sue Lynn, Sam or even Nancy," Nathan added.

"It wouldn't be Nancy, but I can certainly see Sue Lynn and Sam having a role in this," Andrew confirmed with an angry tone in his voice.

"Well, this visit is far better than any letters," Nathan said, putting a positive spin on things.

"Truly," Andrew agreed, as he stood up from his chair. "Probably time to get you back in the city, old chum. Billy will arrange for a driver to take you back to your home."

"Speaking of Billy, I've noticed on television that there seems to be an extended security detail," Nathan mentioned. "Are you alright? I was so upset when I heard about the attempt on your life at the National Prayer Breakfast."

"I'm fine, though I never thought that the same people who worked so hard to get me into the White House, just over two years later would be attempting to see me leaving it in a hearse," Andrew responded.

"Unfortunately, religious conservatives were never going to accept anything other than a strict pro-life appointee to the Court. It's pretty much all they care about," Nathan replied. "But I never thought it would come to this."

"We'll get by, but for now we better leave it at that," President Cochran answered.

"Thank you for this, Andy. It means the world to me," Nathan said, his voice cracking with emotion.

"Me too, me too," Andrew confirmed, as he reached out and took his old friend into his arms for a full and hearty hug. "Take care of yourself, Nathan. You spent so many years of your life attempting to take care of me. Good luck with your trial."

CHAPTER 21

P RESIDENT ANDREW COCHRAN LOOKED ACROSS the large conference room table and vigorously shook his head.

"Can either of you tell me why we should be spending a gorgeous late-June Sunday afternoon in this florescent lit hell instead of outdoors playing golf or doing virtually anything but this?" The President asked his Chief of Staff, Sam Brainard and his Campaign Manager, Landon Hamilton.

"Sir, we are less than three weeks from your first Republican debate and this is the first occasion where you've practiced at all for that event," Landon replied.

"Landon, this ain't my first rodeo," Andrew Cochran replied . "You might remember that I had debated prior to my two terms running for Governor of Georgia, and four years ago I suffered through twelve debates prior to the American people realizing that I had suffered enough and sympathetically voted me into office."

"Well, Mr. President, it's your call, sir. If you'd rather not practice for the debate, then . . ." Landon stated with a shrug as his voice trailed off.

"Christ, Landon! You're going to make a wonderful mother someday. You've got the guilt voice down cold," Andrew sarcastically replied. "Let's get on with this buffoonery so that I can watch the Braves game in a couple of hours."

"Fox News will be moderating this first debate," Sam informed the President.

"Oh great. So, the first question will either be: when did you stop beating the First Lady, or at what point did you decide to sell out your party and your moral values and compromise with the Democrats on the destruction of the Constitution?" The President smirked.

"I don't think that they care if you beat the First Lady," Sam chortled in response.

"That's probably true," the President replied. "From all of the television coverage they've been providing to Cletus Sawyer and Jedediah Wilson's bombastic claims that I am the Benedict Arnold of Republican Conservatism, I'm sure that they wouldn't mind lynching me from the fuselage of Air Force One right there in the Reagan Library. Plus, a couple of those Fox News anchors are still pissed with Sue Lynn for sitting them in the corner at a table with Posy Whitaker three years ago at her first White House luncheon."

"You know, one of them mentioned that fact to me a couple of weeks ago," Landon added.

"Oh, dear God, shoot me now!" Andrew Cochran exclaimed in frustration.

Posy Branch sat in the back office of French Tips, Juleps & Jazz with her business partner, Chantale Calypso. She ran her hand through her luxurious blonde hair waiting for Chantale to say something, anything.

"Honey, if you got something to say to me, just say it," Posy beseeched Chantale.

"I heard from my sister the other day. Our mother is not well. She has cancer and the doctors do not give her long. I need to sell this business so that I can move back to Haiti to spend time with my mother," Chantale stated with sadness in her voice.

"Sugar, I am so very sorry to hear about your mama. But, you don't have to sell," Posy countered. "Go back to Haiti, be with your mama. I understand. Chiffon and I can run things while you're gone. And then afterwards, you can come back and we can pick up where we left off."

"It is not so simple," Chantale replied. "I need the money to help pay for some of my mother's bills. I also want to go back and live in Haiti with the rest of my family."

"You sure you don't want to come back to New Orleans after you spend time with your mama and the rest of your family in Haiti?"

"Yes, I am sure," Chantale replied. "I want to go home. It is time."

"Well, we's doing real good here at the shop, but I don't have enough money to buy out your half of the business. At least, not yet. I'm probably gonna need to find another investor," Posy surmised. "But, don't you worry, we printin' money here. I'm sure I can find someone who wants a piece of this action."

"I don't understand. What action?" Chantale asked wholly confused.

"I got this. I got this," Posy excitedly said. "I got me a good idea. Everything's gonna be just fine. Chantale, you go take care of your mama. I'll get you your money. It's gonna be all peaches and cream."

"All I understand is you will get me money for the business?" Chantale asked shaking her head.

"Hell to the yes, Sugar Pie. Things gonna be sweet," Posy replied with a happy snort.

"I never understand this crazy woman," Chantale muttered to herself.

Papa Levi was counting up the register at the end of the day. He shook his head with a furrowed brow as he began to write the day's income into the ledger book that Bessie kept for the voodoo shops accounts.

"We ain't making nearly as much money as we did when you was doing séances and the such," Papa Levi informed Bessie.

"How much less?" Bessie inquired.

"Umm, looks to be about twenty-five percent less, give or take. Folk paid good money for them services and then they tip well too. Made them happy to know their loved ones was in a good place in the spirit world."

"But you see, Papa Levi, that right there is the problem. I be telling them what they wanted to hear, but I surely don't know. It was like I was lying to them to make them feel better," Bessie explained.

"Folk have themselves some moonshine to makes them feel better. Or have themselves a fine meal, to make them feel better. They done buy themselves some new clothes to make them feel better. So, iffin' they come to you and you tell them what they want to hear and they feel better, I ain't see no harm," Papa Levi challenged Bessie.

"I understand what you is sayin'. I surely do. But it just don't seem right to me. I ain't connecting with their dearly departed. I ain't taken over by the spirits. I just play acting. I just telling them what they want to hear. Just don't seem right, taking good money for that," Bessie responded.

"What if we bring a true mambo in to the shop to do the séances and the sacrifices?" Papa Levi asked. "A friend of your aunt, Queen Rita, is doing séances outside in Jackson Square. She helped the Queen when we do sacrifices down by Lake Pontchartrain. She's a mambo from Haiti.

Been so for many years. She don't pretend, she connects with the loa. She can help folks. Offer her services. Pretty sure she be willing to take 50% of what be the charge for her services and you'd get the rest."

"No dark magic! I won't cotton to it," Bessie stated emphatically.

"Don't need to be," Papa Levi replied shaking his head. "Her name is Esther. You want me to talk to her?"

"Let me think about it. Talk to Lucius about it," Bessie stated.

"Miss Bessie, you knows what Lucius gonna say. He ain't gonna like it. If you think it's a good idea, all you gonna get by telling Lucius is an argument," Papa Levi responded.

"You probably right," Bessie agreed. "Let me give it some proper thought and I'll let you know."

"More money never a bad thing," Papa Levi stated.

"True ," Bessie confirmed.

"Those boys are sweating right through their shirts," Rupert Grassmonk related to his client, Nathan Whitaker, in the comfort of his law office. "The prosecutors are losing their f-ing minds! We've got ourselves a fine, sympathetic jury. The judge granted our motion *in limine* striking the Winchester testimony from being admitted at your trial. Their key witness now is that law clerk, Ben Carroll. And I will poke so many holes in his story that that bucket won't carry water. Hell, it was nighttime, and he was over seventy yards away from you when he allegedly saw you going into the Ritz Carlton. First off, that boy doesn't know you from Adam. Only knows what he has seen on TV. And secondly, he wears contact lenses. He's no eagle-eyed sniper. I'm looking forward to getting that young man on the stand."

"Truly, things are looking good," Nathan concurred.

"The prosecutor was basically begging me to take a deal the day of jury selection because he knew his case was toast. Last thing a politically motivated district attorney with high ambitions wants on his record is a devastating loss in a high-profile criminal case," Rupert gloated.

"I don't want to get my hopes up too high, but we are certainly trending in the right direction," Nathan added.

"Don't look too cocky or confident when the jury is in the courtroom. Trust me, they're watching your every move. No outward smiling or any other signs of confidence. We have the jury we wanted, but juries can smell arrogance a mile away. They may like you now, but that can change in a minute if they perceive that you are overly confident in the proceedings. It's a fine line. You don't want to come across like a guilty man, but on the other hand, you don't want to seem too cocky either," Rupert cautioned his client.

"No worries," Nathan replied. "I've been running political campaigns for decades. I know what to feed the public. I'll display an air of confidence in my innocence without appearing assured of their sympathies. You have to earn a favorable public reaction, it is never to be taken for granted."

"I enjoy working with shrewd clients. Makes my job a whole lot easier," Rupert said with a sly grin.

JIM BOB MCCALLUM SAT ACROSS FROM HIS ATTORNEY in the opulent law office. He pushed his snakeskin cowboy boots against the edge of his attorney's desk.

"Jim Bob, with all due respect, that's a $15,000 vintage cocobolo wood desk," his attorney hesitantly stated.

Jim Bob slowly crossed his legs and dug his heels into the surface of the desk while lounging back in the equally expensive guest chair.

"And whose goddamn money pays for these lovely trinkets?" Jim Bob asked with a satisfied grin. "If I was you, I would be more concerned about making sure that my most important client gets exonerated from these bogus charges than being worried about a few scuff marks on your precious desk. Am I making myself clear?" Jim Bob asked while glaring across the expensive desk.

"Of course," the attorney quickly replied. "And I think that things are going well."

"We got ourselves a smart, well-selected jury?" Jim Bob asked with a grin slowly drawling through the words 'well selected.'

"Yes, I think we did very well with our *voir dire*," the attorney responded.

"And after?"

"Yes," the attorney softly replied averting his eyes.

"Then we are all set. I can have my good name and dignity restored and you can buy as many of these here desks as you can fit in your firm," Jim Bob confirmed.

"When does that snake in the grass, Stanford Winchester, testify? Jim Bob queried with a piqued rasp.

"Barring any major delays, in about 9 or 10 days, I believe," the attorney responded.

"Well, I'm looking forward to looking that Southern gentleman square in the eye," Jim Bob stated menacingly.

"We must be careful about appearances before the jury," the attorney warned.

"Jesus H. Christ, I ain't no damn fool!" Jim Bob spat in response. "Son, you don't make billions gambling in the business world if you sit there grinning like a toothless simpleton showing your cards. You don't need to preach to me about appearances."

"I'm sorry," the attorney meekly replied.

"I couldn't give a shit about sorry. Only words I care about hearing are not guilty."

Two days after meeting with his defense attorney, Nathan Whitaker stared at the screen of his ringing phone. The information about the caller was being blocked. "Unavailable". A sardonic smile crept across Nathan's lips as he answered his phone.

"Nathan Whitaker," the distorted male voice stated. Nathan did not hesitate.

"Look, you feckless fool, you have absolutely no clue what is going on, and I know for a fact that you are not speaking on behalf of the President. You are some moronic pissant that either works at the White House or for the campaign. Of that, I am sure. You were correct the last time you called when you said that I wasn't stupid. I'm not. I've got you figured out. You're trying to protect your turf. I get it. But, if you're calling me and threatening me because you are afraid that I will get back in the good graces of the President, that I will exert my influence, you're too late. I will crush you like the insignificant bug that you are. Am I making myself clear? Oh, by the way, this is where you hang up the phone and cower in the corner, hoping that I don't come after you with guns blazing. This game isn't on, you stupid fuck, it's over!"

Nathan hung up the phone and grinned with satisfaction, like the proverbial cat who just ate the canary.

CHAPTER 22

IT WAS THE LAST SUNDAY IN JUNE, and the Chicago Pride Parade was about to step off at the corners of Belmont and Halsted Street. This was not the first time that Senator Perry Douglas had marched in the annual parade. In years past, the politicians riding or walking in the parade usually occupied the front of the parade. Far distant from the floats of the Chicago area gay bars and establishments that had mostly naked good-looking young men and women gyrating to ear-splitting modern dance music. And in previous years, that is where Perry Douglas would march. However, this year would be different. Perry and his wife Katherine chose to march with the PFLAG parents and their children. PFLAG is an organization of parents who wholly support their gay, lesbian, bisexual, and transgender children. Perry and Katherine Douglas marched in the Pride Parade, flanking their son Robert, as the Douglas family all held hands and waved to the cheering crowds. And to make sure that his presence was duly noted a number of campaign staffers walked steps behind the Douglas family with a banner announcing, "Elect Senator Perry Douglas for President."

"You guys certainly didn't have to do this," Robert Douglas loudly stated to his parents as they walked down north Halsted Street in the Boystown neighborhood of Chicago.

"Yes, I did," Perry turned and said to his son. "I should have been here, along with you, years ago. I'm only sorry that it took an assault on my son to make me realize it."

"But is this good politics?" Robert inquired of his father.

"In this crowd, oh hell yes!" Perry enthusiastically exclaimed. "No other group gets louder and more sustained ovations from the crowd than the PFLAG parents. Well, with the possible exception of the precision twirling corp."

"I mean in general terms. Surely, you will be seen on national television holding hands with your gay son. How will that go over with the general electorate?" Robert queried.

"Well, the easy and truthful answer is that I don't give a rat's ass," Perry said with a smile. "I am a proud parent supporting my son, if some voters don't respect that fact that is more their problem than mine. That said, times are changing. Quickly. And one of the overwhelming reasons for that change is that gay people, like yourself, have announced to the people of this nation that they will no longer tolerate being closeted and oppressed. Civil rights are for everyone, not just men, or just whites, or just heterosexuals. I have fought for change during my time in the Senate, why would I hide my pride in my wonderful son from the public?"

"Good answer, Dad. You're catching on quickly," Robert said with a wide grin as he squeezed his father's hand a little tighter.

Perry Douglas could not contain his ear-to-ear smile.

POSY BRANCH AND CHIFFON LABELLE LEANED UP AGAINST the dark wooded bar at French Tips, Juleps & Jazz.

"Chantale done told you?" Posy asked Chiffon with a slow shake of her head.

"Yes, she surely did," Chiffon replied. "So sad to hear about her mama."

"Well, long term we gonna be just fine. But I don't have the money to buy out Chantale's share of the business right now. And girlfriend wants it all up front, she won't take some now and some later," Posy lamented.

"What about a business loan?" Chiffon inquired.

"That may or may not be an option. When I was younger, I made some poor financial decisions that messed up my credit. I ain't sure if I can get a loan. But, I'm going to look into it," Posy responded.

"If the appeal of my Katrina victims case holds up and doesn't get overturned by the Fifth Circuit, I should be getting a fair piece of money," Chiffon stated.

"Oh yeah," Posy said her voice filled with optimism. "You'd want to partner up with me in this business?"

"I would love to be your business partner," Chiffon quickly replied. "Problem is they don't have oral arguments in the appeal until mid-July."

"That's just a couple of weeks away. That would work out just perfect!" Posy exclaimed.

"No, Girl. It ain't like a trial court where you find out the outcome right when it's over. In an appellate court, you got to wait six months maybe more before you get a result. Then, I wouldn't get the money right away, it could take a little time after the decision of the court. We'd be talking that I might not see a dime until sometime after the first of next year," Chiffon explained.

"Shoot, that ain't gonna work. Though I love the idea of being partners with ya. I just need to find someone to loan me the money to buy out Chantale and then when you come into your money, we could just pay them back," Posy surmised.

"You know folks with that kinda money, cuz I surely don't," Chiffon stated with a grimace.

"I can't say right now that I surely do," Posy lamented while scratching her head.

Aaron Rose and Clay Grover waited at the stop light on Canal Street as they prepared to cross the street and into New Orleans Central Business District on their way to the law offices of Winslow Howard.

"Dear God, if it's this hot at the beginning of July what is it going to be like in the middle of August?" Aaron asked as he wiped the perspiration from his forehead.

"It's not the heat, it's the humidity," Clay offered.

"No. No. It's certainly an irritating, insufferable, and energy exhausting combination of both," Aaron replied. "Summers in Washington were no picnic, but this is absolutely debilitating heat and humidity. I'm sweating through my poplin suit coat."

"Just a couple more blocks to go," Clay encouraged. "Where's my husband who endured below zero temperatures and snow blizzard filled Chicago winters? Where's my weather warrior?"

"Rapidly melting," Aaron wearily offered in rebuttal. "Why do we have to walk everywhere?" Aaron asked while mopping his brow.

"Because it's a very walkable city, we live and work within a few miles of where we need to go. It's a great cardiac fitness exercise, and I'm not willing to pay $20 an hour for parking," Clay replied.

The guys finally arrived at their destination. A large high-rise office building that housed the law offices of their co-counsel who would be presenting the oral argument at the Katrina victims appeal before the Fifth Circuit.

"Oh my God!" Aaron exclaimed as he swept through the glass revolving doors that separated the outdoor muggy heat from the air-conditioned nirvana of the building's lobby. "This is heaven. And Belinda Carlisle was right, 'Heaven is a place on Earth.'"

"Sometimes you can be so gay," Clay laughed in mock scorn.

"THERE ARE THE WORDSMITHS WHO CRAFTED the argument that I have the pleasure to present," a tall and distinguished looking Winslow Howard stated as he extended his outstretched right hand to Clay and Aaron as they stood near the reception desk of the law firm.

"It's a true pleasure to finally meet you in person, after the many phone calls we've exchanged," Clay said while vigorously shaking Winslow's hand.

"Let's go to the conference room. I had one of our paralegals lay out all of the briefing and appendices for the appeal on the table. Is there something I can get you to drink?"

"Cold water with lots of ice would be perfect," Aaron blurted out quickly.

Clay nudged Aaron's shoulder as they walked steps behind Winslow toward the conference room. He had a slightly irritated smirk on his face.

"What!" Aaron softly protested. "I'm parched."

PRESIDENT ANDREW COCHRAN STOOD NEXT TO his rivals as they all waited to be introduced and walk to their assigned podiums where they would be participating in the first Republican Party debate of the Presidential election season. Meanwhile, Landon Hamilton, the President's campaign manager, nervously paced back and forth backstage as he watched the debate on a series of television monitors. The setting was the Reagan Presidential Library in California, in front of the suspended Air Force One that provided the backdrop to the debate. After cordial salutations amongst the candidates, the tenor of the debate quickly became confrontational. The debate moderator asked if the President had abandoned the base of the Republican Party during his first three years in office–a claim that had been made repeatedly by Cletus Sawyer.

"I have abandoned no one," Andrew Cochran began. "All I have done is to attempt to fairly represent all of the American people. The

Republican Party currently has about 30% of the American voting public that identifies as Republican. None of us on this stage can pretend that we can get elected if we only appeal to 30% of the voting public. I am the President of 100% of this country. My policy choices have been made to represent everyone in this country, not just the base of the Republican Party."

"Well, you certainly don't represent the base of the party, that is absolutely true," Cletus Sawyer argued. "You are the Benedict Arnold of Conservative Republicans," Cletus stated defiantly to loud and sustained applause from the gathered audience. "You nominated to the Supreme Court a man who has sided with the Democrats on the court as much if not more than he has with the staunch protectors of the Constitution such as Justice Allen Sallis. Justice Sallis continues the good fight despite not having the support of your hand-picked candidate who the Democratic Senate happily confirmed by a vast majority."

"And when has a President having a goodly majority of the Senate approving a President's appointments become a bad thing?" President Cochran countered. "We live in a democracy, where majority rules. It used to be that having majorities in the House and Senate supporting a President's agenda was a good thing, something that was admired. When did it become anathema to this party to develop consensus majority policies?"

"Mr. President," Cletus Sawyer drawled, "it is anathema to the true Conservatives of this grand old party to have their leader jettison every major policy position that he ran and won on during his election, in order to coddle to the liberal tenants of the Washington elite and the Democrats socialist agenda. Shame on you, Mr. President, shame on you!" Cletus ranted to a well-received standing ovation.

Two hours passed and things only got worse for the President. Jedediah Wilson basically accused the President of "cozying up to baby butchers and homosexual deviants." Additionally, he claimed that he had evidence that indicated that Andrew Cochran and his former Chief of Staff Nathan Whitaker performed satanic black magic rituals in the White House. A claim that the President outwardly scoffed and laughed at as "the delusional product of an unstable mind." Lamar Clarkson invoked images from the film "The Manchurian Candidate" in equating Andrew Cochran as a Democratic Party "plant" in the Republican Party, who was now carrying out their progressive agenda to destroy traditional American values. Only Carlton Smith, who at one point during the debate requested that more deference and respect be shown to the office of the President had anything remotely affirming to say about President Cochran. His attempt at bringing civility to a very uncivil public event was met with heckles from some in the audience.

"Well, I think that went pretty well," Andrew Cochran said sarcastically to his campaign manager, Landon Hamilton, shortly after the debate ended.

"It was better received outside the hall than in it, that's for sure," Landon said to the President as he examined snap data taken of voters watching and reacting to the debate on-line. "The good news is that Americans in general, thought you acted Presidential and agreed with your overall policy decisions and the tenor of your administration. After all, a 46% approval rating of a President with the American public, ain't so bad. However, among the Republican base, they hate your guts."

"Hmmm, how do we get the nomination of our party, when our base thinks I am a devil worshiper, and yet the public at large thinks I'm doing a decent job and that I'm not out to destroy the country?" The President clearly differentiated the problem of their campaign.

"That is a conundrum," Landon agreed.

Nathan Whitaker sat in his home watching the Presidential debate on television. He winced at every mention of his name. He shook his head when absurd accusations of White House Satanic rituals and homosexual influences were made by the President's challengers. He sighed deeply when he realized that it was his actions that put his best friend in the position of having to defend himself against the slings and arrows of Conservative outrage and manipulated and manufactured falsehoods. Yet, he pumped his fist when Andrew Cochran deftly defended himself and his record against the onslaught. He cheered when the President, rightfully and righteously ridiculed the preposterous lies and innuendos that cascaded his way from his opponent's self-claimed higher moral ground. He applauded when the President challenged some of the untenable policy positions of his rivals, demonstrating that he was the only one on the stage who possessed well-reasoned solutions to the nation's problems.

Nathan knew that his friend had suffered through a difficult evening. And he knew that a fair share of the blame for that difficult evening lay squarely on his shoulders. But in the end, the President came across as dignified and reasoned. Calm and assured amongst the bombast and snark. Nathan was proud of his President. He was proud of his best friend.

CHAPTER 23

STANFORD WINCHESTER STOOD IN HIS BEDROOM packing his suit-case for his trip to Washington to testify at the criminal trial of Jim Bob McCallum. Stanford knew that he was the key witness for the prosecution. After all, it had been his statements to the D.C. police about his conversation with Jim Bob at the Columns Hotel in the Garden District that led to Jim Bob's arrest. Several times since that conversation, a little over three years ago, Stanford had replayed over and over again in his head the exact words he recalled that Jim Bob had said to him. His entire world had changed on that fateful afternoon over a couple of Sazerac's. It was then that he realized that his nomination to the United States Supreme Court was nothing more than a calculated political arrangement and that the death of former Supreme Court Justice Albert Martin was a premeditated murder for the sole purpose of political expediency. Many nights he tossed and turned in his bed unable to sleep due to his perceived tangential and unassuming peripheral role in that heinous plot. He knew what to expect from Jim Bob's defense attorney. He knew that his recollection would be harshly questioned due to his age and the passage of time. That the validity of his remembrance of the facts would be subject to intense scrutiny. That his own sobriety at the time of the conversation would become fodder for accusations by the defense. Stanford had been an attorney and a trial court judge in his past. He was well aware of the arguments and personal attacks that awaited him. Yet, he would staunchly defend his truth, because he firmly believed it to be the truth of what transpired that languid April afternoon in the parlor of that New Orleans hotel.

Stanford glanced over at the framed photograph of his beloved wife LeeAnn, which sat on the nightstand next to his bed. Jim Bob McCallum was her cherished life-long friend. The Supreme Court nomination that Stanford had turned down upon hearing about Jim Bob's treacherous scheme was her dream for him. Over the matter of a few hours that afternoon, he had decided to turn his back on her dream for him and turn in to law enforcement her loving and supportive friend. The pangs of guilt over his decision still reverberated through his being as he stared at the photograph. Yet, Stanford knew that he had done the right thing, the only thing that his conscience and integrity would allow. He was prepared to live with that decision for the rest of his life. This trip back to Washington to testify at Jim Bob's criminal trial was the final culmination of that decision. Or so Stanford thought, as he closed and locked the suitcase positioned on his comfortable bed.

Bessie Collins sat on her bed staring out the window at the poplar trees in front of her home as she thought through her options. Only days before she had discovered her mother splayed across her kitchen floor for the second time in a month. Her mother Sandra's health had been deteriorating over the last two years. It had been almost three years since she was first diagnosed with Parkinson's disease. Living alone was clearly no longer an option for Bessie's mother. She thought about moving her in to her home to live with her and Lucius. And though Lucius never uttered a single word of protest over that possible option, Bessie knew that she could not provide the necessary care for Sandra while working full time at her shop. The best solution was an assisted living facility where an on-premises medical staff could attend to Sandra's increasing needs. Sandra had some money in her savings, but not necessarily enough to cover all expenses for an extended period of time. Bessie had been making good money at the voodoo shop until she decided to stop performing séances and other services. Bessie thought long and hard about Papa Levi's suggestion that she bring on Esther, her Aunt Rita's friend, who would provide those services at Bessie's shop.

Lucius entered the bedroom and sat on the bed next to his wife. "What you thinkin' bout?" Lucius asked as he reached over to take Bessie's hand in his.

"Mama and trying to figure out what's best for her needs," Bessie softly replied.

"I know sugar, things ain't gettin' much better. Sandra needs a whole lot more help than we can provide," Lucius acknowledged.

"Lucius, I been thinking about some things. So, hear me out before you go shaking your head and complaining," Bessie started. "I was making some real good money at the shop when I was doing them séances and such. But you was right when you said that I was just pretending and taking people's money without providing them with nothing more than play acting. But Papa Levi mentioned that a friend of my Auntie Rita is a Haitian mambo and she'd be willing to perform voodoo services for folks out of my shop. We would split the money 50-50."

"Bessie, I surely don't know about that. We already seen what kinda trouble come from all them voodoo practices," Lucius cautioned.

"Esther wouldn't practice dark magic like Auntie Rita did. I'd make her promise. But Papa Levi say she connects with the spirits and gives folks comfort. She is a true believer, so it wouldn't be play acting like I was doing. Folk be getting what they paid for. You got no idea how many customers come in and still asking for séances and other spiritual healing. I feel so bad when I got to tell them I can't do that for them no more. Plus, the extra money would come in so handy helping pay for mama's expenses," Bessie said with emphasis as she stated her case to Lucius.

"Bessie, you done know how I feel about all this voodoo. I don't think it's right. But it's your business, and I know it gives you satisfaction to run your own shop. You is my wife, and I love and support you. I've had my say, but I ain't gonna tell you what you can or can't do. All I'm saying is that you best give deep thought about what you is getting into," Lucius said with a shrug.

"I will Lucius, I do promise," Bessie said as she gave Lucius a kiss on the cheek.

CLAY GROVER STOOD OUTSIDE THE DOOR of his friend's apartment building in Washington, D.C. waiting for an answer to his repeated rings of the buzzer. After several more attempts, Ben finally responded.

"Hey man, come on up," Ben said through the apartment building's intercom system. Clay bounded up the two flights of stairs to find a soaking wet Ben dressed only in a dark blue towel standing in the doorway. His muscled torso glistened in the hallway lighting. Ben reached out and put his arms around Clay as he gave him a lengthy hug.

"Easy there, I'm a married man now and you're still wet," Clay teased his friend. "Been a while since I've been hugged by a nearly naked man that wasn't Aaron."

"Oh yeah, sorry," Ben apologized. "I thought I had time for a quick shower before you got here, but the cab must have made good time from the airport."

"Sure did," Clay confirmed. "I've got to admit, it's a little weird being back in the city. I haven't been back here since Senator Fitzsimmon's passing."

"Yeah, I know. How time flies, but nothing has changed all that much," Ben allowed.

"Speak for yourself," Clay smiled in response. "I'm an old married man now, practicing public service law in New Orleans. That's a far cry from being a promiscuous tramp and the Chief of Staff to one of the most revered members of the United States Senate."

"I meant the city, not you, silly," Ben chuckled in response.

"Oh yeah, that. Still looks the same on the ride in," Clay agreed. "Hey is Kramer Books on Connecticut still open?"

"Sure is, why?" Ben asked.

"I could sure go for one of their grilled buffalo cheeseburgers and I'd like to buy a book for the flight home," Clay stated.

"You've been here for less than 5 minutes and you're already thinking about food," Ben sighed.

"No, dear boy. I don't want to think about food; I want to go eat it," Clay countered.

"Can I get dressed first?" Ben laughingly quizzed his friend.

"Yeah, but hurry," Clay replied. "I'm hungry."

"Some things never change," Ben mumbled as he headed towards his bedroom to get dressed.

An hour later, Clay was picking at some of Ben's leftover French fries having already devoured his buffalo cheeseburger and all of his own fries.

"Finish them, they're all yours," Ben pronounced as he pushed his plate towards his friend.

"How are you feeling about testifying tomorrow in court? Clay asked between dunks of fries into ketchup.

"To be honest, I'm pretty nervous, which is why I am so grateful that you came up here to be with me," Ben confessed. "The prosecutor and I have gone over my testimony a couple of times, so I'm not too concerned about the direct examination. It's the cross-exam that has me a little freaked out."

"Just go back to your Harvard Law moot court days. You were probably drilled more on cross there then what you'll see tomorrow," Clay said encouragingly.

"Do you know who Rupert Grassmonk is?" Ben asked.

"Of course!" Clay exclaimed. "Oh crap, Grassmonk is doing the cross?"

"Yup, now you see why I'm nervous," Ben responded with an anxious grin.

"You tell the truth, plain and simple," Clay said. "He will question you about how close you were and the lighting that night, and how you could possibly know that it was Nathan Whitaker since you never met him in person? But you tell your story. Don't let him intimidate you."

"Yeah, you're right. I didn't do anything wrong. I just reported to the police exactly what I had witnessed," Ben assured himself while downing the remainder of his glass of beer. "But still, it's Rupert freakin' Grassmonk!" Ben gulped his words. Clay reached across the table and placed his hand over Ben's hand.

"No worries, my friend. No worries."

Whitlee Hammond walked into Stanford Winchester's office area knowing that Stanford was in Washington, D.C. to testify at a criminal trial.

"Good morning, Naomi," Whitlee sweetly greeted Naomi Cutler, Justice Winchester's long time secretary. "I was just wondering if you could tell me what time the oral argument for the Katrina class action appeal commences?"

"Surely, it's at 10:00am next Friday Judge Hammond, but it's on your Outlook calendar and I know that your secretary Wendy has the date posted on your desk calendar as well," Naomi replied.

"Oh of course, I'm just being a tad scatter-brained," Whitlee replied with a blush of her cheeks.

"Is there anything else that I can help you with?" Naomi asked sensing that the Judge had not come by Justice Winchester's office just to check on the time of oral argument.

"Well, I was wondering if Justice Winchester has a favorite spirit that he enjoys? He seems to like bourbon cocktails I've noticed," Whitlee asked. "He has been so kind to me and such a gentleman as we've prepared for this case, I'd like to buy him a bottle of something as a small token of my gratitude."

"I'm not sure exactly what brand he prefers. I've seen him drinking Colonel E.H. Taylor small batch bourbon and Maker's Mark 46," Naomi replied. "But I'm sure he'd much rather go to a bar or a restaurant in your delightful company and have a cocktail than to drink alone. Justice Winchester spends so much time alone, and he is such a gregarious social person. He hasn't gotten out much since his wife passed seven years ago. I don't think he has seen anyone since. It's such a shame, he has so much to offer in a relationship," Naomi added now in full meddlesome mode.

"Do you think it would be too forward of me to offer to take him to dinner after the oral argument hearing?" Whitlee inquired.

"No, not at all!" Naomi exclaimed as her cupid wings began to sprout from her back. "In fact, I know he'd be delighted, thrilled at the opportunity to get to know you better outside the confines of the courthouse."

"You really think so?" Whitlee happily asked. "The Justice seems to be such a stickler for proper decorum and Southern traditions and etiquette. In fact, I wondered if he would be a bit taken aback or even put off by being asked out for a social evening by a female colleague?"

"Put that thought right out of your head," Naomi insisted as she carefully took one of her love arrows out of its quiver and loaded it in her Cupid's bow. "I can safely say that Justice Winchester would be humbled and honored to be offered the opportunity to have a social evening out with someone he has such high regard and admiration of," Naomi concluded as she pointed and launched her match-making arrow at Whitlee Hammond.

"Well, if you really think that he wouldn't object, I will definitely ask him after he returns from Washington," Whitlee pronounced, followed by, "Thank you, Naomi, thank you for your helpful insights."

"It is surely my pleasure to be of assistance," Naomi stated with a huge satisfied smile crossing her lips.

Two days after her conversation with Lucius, Bessie Collins paced back and forth in the small back office of her shop as she waited for the arrival of Esther Francois. She had listened to what her husband Lucius had to say about bringing in a Haitian mambo to provide services to her clients, but she felt nothing was wrong with giving her clients what they wanted. And, of course, the extra money would come in handy with her mother's mounting medical expenses. The small bell over the front door of the shop announced the arrival of her aunt's friend, and perhaps, a new partner for her business.

"Ah, sweet Bessie, there you are," Esther said as she gazed at Bessie coming through the beaded curtain.

"Hello, you must be Esther," Bessie replied with a quizzical expression on her face. "Have we met before?"

"Ya, our paths have crossed twice before," Esther responded with a slight Creole-Haitian accent. Her dark skin was barely wrinkled for a woman in her mid-seventies. Esther wore an orange and green head dress that covered most of her long dark braids. Her deep-set eyes were almost black in color and seemingly stared right through you.

"I'm sorry I don't recall our meetings," Bessie replied.

"Once when you were a small girl, Queen Rita brought you to me so that I could read your aura," Esther began. "For a young girl, there were so many complexities. But most prevalent I saw red, which is vitality and energy. Also, green/blue the colors of one who is nurturing and caring, and blue/purple which indicates learning and spirituality."

"I don't remember that," Bessie said feeling a bit confused. "When was the second meeting?"

"When the Queen was placed in the mausoleum at St. Louis Cemetery, I was burning sage and cleansing the tomb. You were sobbing, my child. You did not see me for my face was covered with a death mask. But see you, I did," Esther stated.

"I'm sorry I don't remember seeing you before," Bessie said.

"No worries, no worries. You see me now," Esther repeated with a smile.

"Papa Levi tells me that you is doing readings and séances down in Jackson Square," Bessie said.

"Ya. The Queen had provided an old house for me to practice vodou as a mambo. But when she left this world for the next, I had to move on from that house. This is why I'd like to help you here. Provide services to your customers," Esther offered.

"One thing I sure do want to say is that I won't have no black magic in this shop," Bessie firmly stated.

"I understand. You should watch what I do. If there is something you are not sure of or do not want me to do, tell me. If we are to be partners, there must be trust. I want to earn your trust," Esther responded.

"Alright, that's a good place to start," Bessie agreed.

"The loa have brought us together. I know the spirits are pleased," Esther said as she looked upwards to the heavens. "We will make the Queen proud."

"I hope so," Bessie replied.

The White House cabinet meeting had concluded and Vice-President Howard Mason had pushed his chair away from the table in order to make a hasty retreat from the Cabinet room.

"Wait up a minute, Howard," President Cochran called to his Vice-President as he saw him head for the door. Howard Mason spun on his heels and faced the President. President Cochran walked over and placed his hand on Howard's shoulder and instructed him, "Walk with me, Howard. I haven't had a real conversation with you in a while now."

"Yes, Mr. President," Howard softly said.

"Howard, how have you been?" The President asked with a genuine smile.

"I'm fine, sir, just fine."

"Nothing bothering you? Nothing wrong? Anything you'd like to talk about?" Andrew Cochran asked.

"No, I'm fine," Howard Mason allowed.

"Did you see the Republican party debate?" Andrew Cochran asked.

"Yes sir, I thought it was scandalous the way the other nominees treated a sitting President," Howard replied.

"Well, thank you Howard, but I'm a big boy. I can handle a few political smear tactics," the President stated. "But I did see you being interviewed on the news a day later and let's just say your answers in response to some of the allegations proposed by my opponents as asked by the reporter were a bit tepid, at best. Do you have any doubts about what we are doing in this administration? About my fitness for office?" The President pointedly asked.

"No, sir. Nothing that I would air in public. Of course, we don't agree on every issue or policy but we come to things from different perspectives," Howard replied.

"Yes, of course. And I don't require a full-throated endorsement of everything that I propose. As you aptly pointed out, we have some differences in our political perspectives. We certainly don't need to be in lock-step on every detail. I just want to make sure that we are, at the least, rowing in the same boat," Andrew Cochran stated.

"Understood, sir," Howard Mason replied.

"You know, Howard, I hope that you don't view the Vice-Presidency as some sort of jail sentence. A penalty to be suffered through until your term is served. You can make out of it what you like. Some former Vice-President's embraced the role and had ample say in policy decisions. But yet others, were less enchanted with the position. If memory serves, I believe that one of FDR's Vice-President's, Cactus Jack Garner once infamously referred to the office of the Vice-President as being 'not worth a bucket of warm piss.' I'm sure you don't hold that same conclusion, now do you?" President Cochran asked with a wry smile and the wink of an eye. Howard Mason reared back slightly, surprised that the President would have mentioned Vice-President Garner of all people. But, he quickly gained his composure.

"Of course not. It is an honor to serve the President," Howard replied with a less than sincere smile of his own.

"Excellent, glad to hear it," Andrew Cochran responded. "I sincerely hope that you will come to me and we can talk about anything that is bothering you. Is that a deal?"

"Yes, it's a deal, sir," Howard quickly stated.

"Good. Don't be a stranger Howard," the President said as he moved forward leaving his Vice-President standing alone in the hallway.

CHAPTER 24

Posy Branch stood next to the bar at French Tips, Juleps & Jazz speaking with her bartender Michael. A tall, slender, pale man with short blonde hair and milky blue eyes walked into her establishment and glanced around the nail stations and bar area as if he were surveying a new home to purchase.

"May I help you, Sugar?" Posy asked the stranger.

"Are you the proprietor, Ms. Branch?" The stranger asked in a French-Creole accent.

"That would be me, but shoot everyone calls me Posy."

"My name is Olivier Bellevue. It is a pleasure to meet you Posy," the stranger stated.

"What can I do ya for?" Posy asked. "Would you like a manicure or a julep or both? Michael here makes one fine julep."

"I would like to be your business partner," Olivier stated bluntly.

"Excuse me?" Posy asked a bit taken aback by the forthrightness of his proposal. "Why do you think that I need a partner?"

"My dear Posy, I know that you ain't from around here, that you only been here for a short while. But there ain't no secrets in the Quarter's business community. We all know the time of day around here," Olivier stated. "Ain't it true that your current partner, Chantale Calypso is seeking to be bought out of her share of this fine establishment so that she can return to her homeland of Haiti to be with her dying mother?"

"How do you know that?" Posy asked with an irritated tenor to her voice.

"Same way that I know you don't have the money to buy her out right now," Olivier replied.

"Who are you?" Posy demanded. "I know your name, but mister I don't know you from Adam."

"Let's just say that I am a local competitor but also a big fan of yours," Olivier said with a sly smile. "I own and operate Nawlin's Nail Salon a couple of blocks from here on Dumaine Street. It used to be the most popular nail salon in the French Quarter until you showed up and created the hot new sensation in town."

"I'm going to ask you again, how do you know about Chantale's situation?" Posy questioned.

"Why, my dear, she told me. Chantale and I have been competitors in this area for years.

Long before you arrived and turned her dour waste of space nail barn into a fun and entertaining money maker. I saw her on the street the other day and she told me everything. She told me that she wanted out of the business and that she was becoming restless waiting for you to find a financial backer to assist you with a buyout of her share of French Tips. Chantale is willing to sell me her share of the business today. But I don't want to tread where I'm not welcome," Olivier explained.

"Why you want part of my nail salon if you got your own blocks away?" Posy skeptically asked.

"Precisely, my dear. I'm raising the white flag of surrender. Since you re-opened as French Tips, Juleps & Jazz in November my business has steadily lost its customer base. I'm looking at thirty to forty percent drops in income per month. I can't compete with your success. There isn't room in this area for both of us. I capitulate, Posy. You win. If you can't beat 'em, join 'em. Ain't that what they say? Now, I just want to sell off my property and use the money to reinvest in yours as your partner. It's just that simple, cher. There can only be one Queen of Nails, and it is you," Olivier stated his case.

"I ain't so sure," Posy replied. "My hostess Chiffon wants to be my partner."

"Then by all means, she should write Chantale a check and assume her place as your business associate," Olivier replied with a knowing smile. "Chantale doesn't care where the money comes from she just wants it and soon so that she can go back to Haiti."

"It ain't that easy," Posy responded.

"That is between you and Chantale. I'm here to make you an offer.

To present myself as a reliable and supportive partner. If you don't want me here, I will not force myself somewhere I'm not wanted," Olivier said.

"Look, I need to talk to Chantale. I need to figure some things out. Talk to Chiffon," Posy anxiously replied.

"Of course, of course. I'm not setting the timetable here, Chantale is. Talk to Chantale. I am merely presenting myself as an option to your financial dilemma. If both of you prefer not to pursue my offer, so be it. There is never any harm in making an entreaty," Olivier stated.

"Yeah, yeah. I got to talk to Chantale," Posy repeated.

"Excellent. Good day to you Posy. I sincerely hope we can make manicure magic together," Olivier said with a flourish as he sauntered out of the establishment back out into the street traffic of the French Market.

"Strange bird, that one," Posy related to Michael with a sneer.

AARON ROSE SAT ON AN OLD BIRCHWOOD ROCKING CHAIR on his front porch as he waited for Clay to arrive from the airport. He sipped at his sweet tea as he enjoyed watching folks lazily stroll down the street in front of his bright yellow shotgun home. It was a late Sunday afternoon in early July and the heat and humidity in New Orleans made everybody move a little slower, a little more deliberate. He gently rocked back and forth allowing the iced tea to refresh his senses while he inhaled the scent of fresh mint in his glass. Moments later, a taxicab pulled up to the curb and Clay Grover exited the vehicle. Clay smiled as he strode towards his house catching a glimpse of his husband rocking gently on their slightly askew wooden porch.

"What ya doing?" Clay asked as he approached the porch.

"You ain't from around here, is you?" Aaron asked in his best mimicked southern drawl.

"Why no sir, I ain't," Clay responded in his own authentic South Carolinian accent, quickly picking up on Aaron's playfulness.

"Sure is a hot one," Aaron stated as Clay stood at the base of the porch steps.

"Surely is. It's hotter than Hell's pepper patch," Clay replied exaggerating his accent even more.

"Well, I got me some nice cold sweet tea. Why don't ya sit for a spell and enjoy a refreshing beverage. Looks like you a travelin' man?" Aaron continued the banter.

"Thank you kindly, sir," Clay responded. "That is right neighborly of ya. I sure could use a cold drink. I am parched. As my mama Blanche

DuBois use to say, 'I've always depended on the kindness of strangers,'" Clay stated, stealing a line from Tennessee Williams, as he sat next to his husband in the second rocking chair on their porch and took a long sip of the iced tea.

Aaron couldn't hold back and just started laughing. "Really, you went there? 'Street Car Named Desire,'" he chortled in his normal voice.

"I sure did. Now, finish your tea because I'm about to rip off your white t-shirt and go all Stanley Kowalski on you," Clay stated seductively as he took Aaron by the hand and led him through the screen door into their home.

The sun had set and the moon graced the dark southern sky before Clay and Aaron reemerged from their bedroom and retook their places in their rocking chairs on the porch.

"You need to go away more often," Aaron said softly with a contented smile on his face while holding Clay's hand as the two rocked gently back and forth in unison.

"That was wonderful. What a marvelous way to come home," Clay agreed.

"So how did it go? How was Ben's testimony at trial?" Aaron inquired.

"Well, he was nervous as hell," Clay began. "I had no idea until the night before that he was going to be cross examined by one of the best defense attorneys in the country, Rupert Grassmonk. Given that dynamic, Ben did fine. Grassmonk cut into him pretty good about his ability to definitively say that it was Nathan Whitaker he saw going into the Ritz Carlton, but Ben held his own. He was so happy that I was there. I'm glad that I went to lend him moral support."

"You're a good friend, Clay Grover," Aaron said proudly.

"Well, Ben was pleased, and we had a couple of good meals and some nice conversation. All in all a good trip," Clay responded.

"So is Whitaker going to get off?" Aaron asked.

"Hard to say. But in talking about the case with Ben, he shared a number of comments the prosecutor had said to him. Sounds like a good portion of their case is based on circumstantial evidence and hearsay," Clay answered. "There is no smoking gun, so to speak, and no eye witnesses. It all seems rather nebulous for seeking a murder conviction, if you ask me."

"So why did the prosecutor seek a murder conviction if the case is that flimsy?" Aaron inquired.

"Politics, pure and simple, my dear. A Democratic district attorney is faced with the opportunity to take down the President's Chief of Staff and with him the fledgling Cochran Presidency. Please. He had no choice. It was a go for the throat political maneuver," Clay surmised.

"But it didn't take down Cochran's administration. In fact, his public approval rating isn't half bad," Aaron countered.

"Chalk that up to Cochran's ability to politically pivot. With Nathan Whitaker by his side, Cochran was prepared to go hard line conservative in their administration's philosophy. When the Whitaker scandal hit the White House, they realized that in order to survive they had to take a far more populist approach. They chose a moderate for the Supreme Court to replace Justice Winchester after he declined the nomination. Cochran reached out to Democrats in the Senate and got a number of infrastructure and social policy funding bills passed. His whole administration eschewed their hardline conservative dogma in favor of more centrist and pragmatic policies. It was a shrewd political calculation and it saved his presidency."

"And now he is being savaged by the far-right wing of his party. They're going all out to try to thwart Cochran from becoming the Republican Party nominee," Aaron replied.

"Yes, they are and that's a fight that has been brewing for quite a while in that party. But right now, the only thing I'm interested in savaging is my beautiful husband," Clay said with a coy wink.

"You're ready for round two?" Aaron asked.

"Oh, hell yes! Let's go, round two!" Clay said enthusiastically as he stood up from his rocking chair took Aaron by the hand and flashed a mischievous smile.

PERRY DOUGLAS SAT ON THE COUCH in the family room of his Chicago Lincoln Park home. A glass of white wine in his hand and his feet propped up on the coffee table in front of him.

"What do you think you're doing?" Katherine Douglas asked her husband with a stern look on her face.

"Getting ready to watch 'Game of Thrones' on HBO," Perry replied with a grin. "I hope the dragons are in this episode."

"What happens on Tuesday? Katherine harshly asked.

"Huh?" Perry replied with a quizzical look on his face.

"Perry Stephen Douglas, what are you participating in on Tuesday night in Des Moines?" Katherine queried her husband.

"Oh, the stupid debate," Perry replied with a sigh.

"Did you not promise Carolyn that you and I would work together on your answers to foreign policy questions this weekend? You've put it off all weekend long. Now it's Sunday night and you are more interested in watching fire-breathing dragons than preparing for the first Democratic Party Presidential Debate?" Katherine asked with an exasperated tone in her voice.

"Hmmm, when you put it that way, then yes. I think my priorities are in order. Watching dragons over debate points on Syrian rebels," Perry offered with a sly smile.

"Do you want to be President of this country?" Katherine challenged getting weary of her husband's cavalier behavior.

"Some days yes, some days not so much," Perry responded with sarcasm. "Look here my love, you and I doing flash card diplomacy quizzes will not aid my performance at the debate. I sit on the Senate Foreign Relations Committee, if I don't have my policy positions down cold by now I never will. Carolyn means well. She is doing her job and attempting to make sure that I am on my game come Tuesday night. But seriously, I've got this one. I'll either do fine or I'll crash and burn, but either way it's on me. It's my call. And right now, my call is that my lovely wife join me in enjoying a glass of wine and hopefully some dragon incinerated human barbecue."

"You've got the attention span and work ethic of a lazy eighteen-year-old," Katherine proclaimed with a slight smile.

"And the sex drive of one as well," Perry said as he reached out to Katherine and pulled her down onto the couch with his him. "I'll pour you a glass of wine, we'll watch some HBO and then I'll show you the eighteen-year-old sexual stud trapped in this middle-aged body."

"Well, it's not such a bad body after all," Katherine cooed as she snuggled into her husband's arms, sipped her wine, and prepared for dragon Armageddon.

PRESIDENT COCHRAN AND HIS WIFE SUE LYNN sat together in the White House residence watching the late Sunday night evening news. The story being covered was the outcome and analysis of the first Republican Party Presidential Debate.

"Where's the remote? We don't have to watch this," Sue Lynn said as she hunted around the coffee table for the television remote control.

"No, I want to see this," Andrew Cochran stated. "I don't need a mother, Sue Lynn. I want a wife. I don't need you attempting to protect me from bad news or anything that you deem a threat to my presidency."

"Where is this coming from?" Sue Lynn asked surprised as she looked at her husband.

"That doesn't matter. What matters is that I want you to stop treating me like some porcelain china doll that is too fragile to withstand any external pressure or trauma. I can accept criticism and blame from others without needing you to shield me from it. And I certainly don't need you intercepting letters from Nathan Whitaker because you're afraid I'll do something stupid to jeopardize my presidency."

"I'm getting the feeling that you've already done something stupid," Sue Lynn shot back with frustration.

"It's Sunday night. I'd just like to unwind a bit before I go to bed. I am in no mood for going to war with you over this. All I'm saying is please show me the respect any adult would demand from his or her spouse. You are not to pick and choose what correspondence I do or do not receive. Trust me, I will have this very same conversation with Sam and Nancy in the morning. We are done playing protect the President in an informational cocoon. I will decide who I speak with, who I associate with. I hope I've made myself clear, because if I have to have this conversation again, I will not be in such a tolerant mood. You'll excuse me, I'm off to bed. Alone tonight."

CHAPTER 25

Howard Mason sat on a sofa in the living room of his residence talking to his friend and longtime political advisor Mark Backus.

"He knows Mark, he knows," Howard said forthrightly to his friend.

"Howard, there really isn't anything to know," Mark replied. "I'm sure he has no idea of the few conversations that you and I have had together. He couldn't."

"Mark, he was toying with me. He talked about how some past Vice-Presidents have viewed their roles in administrations and he specifically brought up Cactus Jack Garner. Of all possible VP's, that is the one he chose to use to illustrate his point. Do you think that that is merely coincidence?" Howard asked a bit flustered.

"Yes, I do, and even if it isn't coincidence and he knows something, so what? You are free to disagree with the President. You are free to challenge his decisions or even his moral fabric. And you certainly are free to enter the race for the Presidency yourself. There is nothing going on here that is wrong or deceitful. This President, in particular, has given you ample reason to question the road he is taking this country down. He forms allegiances with liberal Democrats while he questions the trust of the Conservatives who helped get him elected in the first place," Mark stated strongly with a raised voice.

"Then what do you propose?" Howard pointedly asked. "Should I announce my intentions to seek the party's nomination for the Presidency in the near future? The first debate has already been held. How much longer can I practically wait if I want to have a real chance at winning the nomination?"

"Yes, actions will need to be taken soon. But perhaps, we wait just a bit longer for him to do something or say something that we can point to as the 'last straw' and why you are therefore compelled to enter the race," Mark advised. "He had an abysmal debate performance. Let the other nominees chew him up a little bit more and then you can pounce into the fray to finish him off. The others can do the dirty work, which clearly they have no problem in doing. This way, you stay above the nastiness of the personal political attacks. You remain the untarnished white knight that rides in to save the party from the Jedediah Wilsons and Cletus Sawyers. And of course, Andrew Cochran."

BESSIE COLLINS SAT QUIETLY IN THE BACK of the darkened small room of her voodoo shop as Esther Francois tilted her head towards the heavens and firmly grasped the hands of her two customers. Her body swayed back and forth as she verbally entreated the spirit of her customer's recently departed father to join them in the quiet room. Smoke billowed from the white sage smudge stick sitting on a side table near the small congregation. Suddenly, Esther's body became rigid and seemingly convulsed. Moments later a deep masculine voice began speaking through Esther, greeting "his" children and expressing his love. Bessie reared back in her chair, shocked by the transformation in Esther's voice. The session continued for twenty-five minutes with the children asking their father questions and Esther replying in the masculine voice. Abruptly, the small table jostled for a moment, Esther slumped into her chair as her normal voice returned. The customers profusely thanked Esther and Bessie and promised to return the following week.

"What just happened?" Bessie asked Esther once the customers had departed the shop.

"The spirits possessed me," Esther casually replied.

"But, that wasn't real. I mean you weren't actually possessed by their dead father?" Bessie questioned.

"Were they not convinced that they were speaking to their loved one? Did they not leave us feeling content with the knowledge that they believe their father is at peace in the spiritual world? Are they not filled with joy that they can continue a dialogue, complete unfinished emotional business with the parent they lost so suddenly and unexpectedly?" Esther asked.

"Well, yes, but . . ." Bessie replied before Esther interrupted.

"Who is to say what is real or not? It is real to them. They are at peace. What more does one need to seek truth?" Esther slowly asked.

"We search for certainty, but it is a task taken in vein. Spirits are real to me Bessie, even if they may not be to you. Seek your truth, but do not deny others the ability to seek theirs as well."

"I don't want to take people's money if we is just play acting," Bessie firmly stated.

"Did it look like I was play acting? Did it sound as if I was pretending to be something I'm not? Esther asked. "I do not play at spiritual enlightenment. This is not a game to me. So, if you would like me to continue providing a service to your customers, then I am happy to do so. But if you are uncomfortable with the service I provide, I will pack up my gris-gris and head back out to Jackson Square."

"No, no, I want you to stay," Bessie quickly interjected. "I want us to be partners and provide spiritual services to our customers."

"And what of tributes to the loa and sacrifices?" Esther asked.

"As long as it ain't involving dark magic, I suppose it would be alright," Bessie hesitantly replied.

"In a few days, I am doing a sacrifice down by Lake Pontchartrain for an old customer of Queen Rita's. Come watch," Esther offered.

Yes, I should see what goes on," Bessie responded.

"Papa Levi will get a chicken. I will tell you when," Esther stated. "Come with an open mind, Bessie."

"I will."

STANFORD WINCHESTER SAT ON THE WOODEN BENCH outside of the Washington D.C. courtroom waiting to be summoned to the witness stand by the prosecutor in the Jim Bob McCallum criminal trial. He had been prepped by the federal prosecutor the previous afternoon and he had also searched his memory to recall the exact events and language that transpired between him and Jim Bob that April afternoon a little more than three years ago. One of the assistants to the prosecutor came to fetch Stanford.

"Justice Winchester, it's time. They're ready for you now," the assistant stated barely above a whisper.

Stanford rose to his feet and slowly ambled into the courtroom. He did not glance over at the defense table as he made his way through the swinging gate that separated the gallery observers from the court's participants. As Stanford approached the witness stand, the trial judge gave Stanford a slight nod of respect. Stanford raised his hand and was sworn in by the courtroom bailiff. As he took his seat in the witness box, he glanced over to the jury and offered a faint smile. His eye then caught Jim Bob McCallum seated behind the defense table next to his attorney. Stanford could almost feel Jim Bob's unwavering stare drilling its way into his consciousness. The prosecutor approached the witness stand and he and Stanford went through the direct examination questioning that they had practiced the day before. Each well-framed question was responded to by a precise and simply phrased answer. Direct examination of Stanford Winchester, the chief witness for the prosecution, lasted for approximately ninety minutes. When the prosecutor concluded his questioning, the judge took a fifteen-minute recess. Upon return, Stanford would be cross-examined by Jim Bob McCallum's attorney. He had prepared himself well for the impending onslaught of questions and accusations. He was ready.

"JUSTICE WINCHESTER, DO YOU UNDERSTAND THE QUESTION?" Jim Bob McCallum's attorney questioned the prosecutor's chief witness.

"Yes, I do. I am attempting to visualize the exact words coming from Jim Bob's mouth. He said that Nathan Whitaker and he had merely arranged for Justice Martin to take an earlier train," Stanford Winchester answered the question.

"And this was in context with Justice Martin being in failing health?" the attorney asked.

"Yes. Jim Bob had just said that Justice Martin's departure ticket for leaving this world had already been punched, and that he and Nathan had only arranged for the Justice to take an earlier train," Stanford firmly stated.

"And from that nebulous wording you deduced that Jim Bob and Nathan had plotted and executed the death of Justice Martin? Is that what you're saying?" The attorney questioned the witness.

"Yes. It was clear as day what Jim Bob implied by his statement," Stanford professed.

"Why then doesn't it seem that clear to me, and certainly Jim Bob McCallum has a very different interpretation than yours? Could it be that you may be misremembering the statements that were made? That his meaning was misconstrued given the number of Sazeracs you imbibed that afternoon?"

"I only had one that afternoon with Jim Bob. I was clear-headed and fully in command of my faculties," Stanford emphatically stated.

"Lord knows a well-made Sazerac with a strong bourbon would have an effect on me especially on an empty stomach. You had not eaten that day prior to meeting with Jim Bob had you?" The attorney pressed his line of questioning.

"No, I had not eaten at that time of day," Stanford admitted.

"Then you drank an entire Sazerac on an empty stomach but yet you contend that it had no effect on your memory or perception?"

"That's correct," Stanford responded.

"Why that's an amazing feat, Justice Winchester. A full cocktail and it had no effect on your memory. Your recall of the precise language is without question. "That truly is amazing," the attorney reiterated to fully make his point.

The questioning continued as the afternoon wore on. Every word that Stanford Winchester recalled perfectly was challenged by the defense with ferocity and unwavering zeal. Stanford's sobriety was in question and the defense attorney pounced on every slip of a word or hesitation in Stanford's responses to his pointed questions. At times, Stanford's protestations about his sobriety were overly righteous and may have come across as less than authentic to the seated jury. Nonetheless, Stanford was unequivocal in his remembrance of what was said by Jim Bob McCallum that fateful afternoon at the Column's Hotel. But, the questions put forth to him were also compelling and tinged with truth. The jury was left with a puzzlement and a search for credibility and honesty. The defense had done an admirable job muddying those waters. No one understood that dilemma better than Stanford Winchester as he reluctantly strode down the two stairs of the witness box in that crowded Washington, D.C. courtroom in mid-July.

SENATOR PERRY DOUGLAS WAS READY for the first Democratic Party Presidential Primary debate. Or so he thought. It was a hot and muggy July evening in Des Moines, Iowa, and the air conditioning in the large auditorium was working at somewhat less than optimal effectiveness. Perry wiped the perspiration from his upper lip a few minutes before the candidates were to be announced by the moderator and take their places at their respective podiums.

"Anything we can do about the air conditioning?" Perry asked his campaign manager.

"Not in the next three hours, plus I'm told that Hellen Raymond enjoys it warm," Carolyn responded.

"Yes, but she doesn't look like she just stole something in this heat, I do," Perry countered.

"Nothing we can do about the a/c, so just look like you gave it back. Whatever you stole, figuratively give it back," Carolyn advised her candidate.

"You do understand how worthless your advice is to me?" Perry inquired.

"Of course, I do. I'm not an idiot. But it's the best I've got," Carolyn replied.

"Well, OK, that means a lot to me, coach," Perry said with a sarcastic grin. "Here we go."

TWO HOURS LATER, PERRY DOUGLAS WAS SWEATING like he had just finished running a marathon. He was heavily perspiring, and his throat was hoarse and raspy.

"That could have gone a bit better," Perry said to his campaign manager as he exited the stage after the first presidential debate on the Democratic side of the contest.

"Yeah, your response on what to do with Syrian refugees wasn't exactly spot on, and left you seeming weak on border control and immigration." Carolyn acknowledged.

"I wasn't about to go to the right of Hellen on immigration and Governor Stolts had the far-left lane on the issue under his control. There wasn't a lot of room to drive home a centrist position," Perry explained.

"Still," Carolyn said.

"Still," Perry Douglas repeated. "I'll do better next time around."

"That's reassuring to hear," Carolyn sarcastically quipped. Quickly followed by, "Hellen Raymond whipped your butt."

"She did. That is true. But that won't be the case going forward. I promise," Perry said wiping his brow.

"Beat down real good," Carolyn emphasized.

"I get it," Perry stated. "I get it."

CHAPTER 26

SAM BRAINARD TIP-TOED AROUND the President's debate performance at the weekly meeting about the campaign with the President.

"The public will quickly tire of all of this vitriol and enmity. It does nothing to solve the real problems of the American people and makes my opponents look petty and vindictive," President Cochran surmised.

"At the moment, Jedediah Wilson's claim that you and Nathan Whitaker were moral reprobates has him up by five points in the polls of Republican voters, with Cletus Sawyer just a point behind," Sam offered.

"For how long can a supposed man of God continue with this dogma of hatred and bigotry?" Andrew Cochran asked his campaign staff.

"As long as the polls show that it sells," Sam responded. "Jedediah Wilson may not be a politician but that is not to say that he is impolitic. He and his campaign staff know exactly what they are doing. They embrace innuendo and scandal because it sells. They will perpetually tie you to Nathan Whitaker because they see him as the rock that can take down this administration."

"Nathan has not been a part of this administration for almost three years. Our moderate and pragmatic domestic agenda has been the public's antidote to what some saw as his questionable behavior. When his trial is concluded he will be no more than a brief footnote to our Presidential tenure," Andrew stated definitively.

"But right now, his trial is drawing to a conclusion and his name is front and center in the daily news. Wilson and to a lesser degree Sawyer are playing that fact for all it's worth. If Nathan is found innocent, the evil cache with which they tie him to you will soon dissipate to some extent," Sam replied.

"There is no question on that score. Nathan will be found innocent. The prosecutor's case is wholly circumstantial. His name will be cleared and we can put all this behind us," the President insisted.

"Mr. President, respectfully sir, there will always be a degree of toxicity that accompanies Nathan Whitaker's name. Some people will always assume that he was guilty of the crimes he was alleged to have committed. He was just too careful and thorough in his premeditated actions to get caught," Sam countered.

"Damn it, Sam!" Andrew Cochran exclaimed. "I'm so sick of Sue Lynn and everyone else blaming everything on Nathan. I don't get a sniff of the White House without Nathan. I'm smart enough to know that, I don't understand why no one else will give him credit for that fact."

"Yes sir," Sam meekly responded.

"Meeting is over," President Cochran huffed as he quickly exited the room.

STANFORD WINCHESTER SAT ALONE IN HIS OFFICE at the Federal Fifth Circuit Courthouse in New Orleans. He knew that his words had been twisted and challenged enough by the defense attorney to establish reasonable doubt in the minds of McCallum's jury. Indulging in a cocktail with Jim Bob McCallum would prove to be the fact that gives pause to the jury wholly accepting his remembrance of the facts and therefore questioning his credibility. This fact alone stung Stanford as he sat quietly reflecting on his testimony.

"Judge Hammond is here to see you," Naomi Cutler, the judge's secretary softly said interrupting the contemplative silence.

"Hello Stanford, how are you? How was your trip to Washington?" Whitlee Hammond cheerfully greeted her colleague on the Court.

"I'm right as rain, thank you kindly for asking," Stanford replied with a hesitant smile. "How are you?"

"Why, I'm well," Whitlee replied as she took a seat in a chair in front of the large desk. "How did your testimony at trial go?" She asked.

"Hard to say, really. You know it isn't easy to predict what a jury pays a mind to in testimony. I told the God's honest truth of what transpired that day with Jim Bob McCallum and what he said to me. But as expected, the defense tried to muddy the waters. Tried to imply that I was too drunk that afternoon to faithfully recall what was said. Of course, there were the illusions of age affecting my memory and such, but the addled by alcohol gambit just stung me like a bee," Stanford said while slowly shaking his head as he spoke. "I asked Jim Bob for that meeting. I knew what I wanted to hear from him. I could have avoided all of these groundless innuendos if I had refused his offer of a cocktail or had a sweet tea instead. I should have known better. If Jim Bob gets away with the planned murder of a Supreme Court Justice because I couldn't refuse an alcoholic beverage, I will have to shoulder some of that blame."

"Nonsense!" Whitlee exclaimed. "Hindsight is 20/20. You are putting this all in context given what has transpired over the last three years. You had no idea what Jim Bob was going to say to you. You were friends having an afternoon drink."

"Thank you for defending me, but that ain't exactly right. I went there to confront Jim Bob. I was fairly sure that arrangements had been made that led to my nomination to the Supreme Court by the President. I just didn't know to what extent and precisely by whom. I should have been ready to hear anything and not done anything to compromise my position of clarity. I failed to act with behavioral restraint, as I should have. I am an officer of the Court, I acted irresponsibly, and Jim Bob took full advantage of the circumstances. He couched his words and stated things in a very obtuse manner. He offered me a drink which he knew I would partake in," Stanford allowed with a chagrined expression on his face.

"I'm sorry but I can't listen to you tearing yourself apart over accepting a cordial invitation of a cocktail from someone you had known for years. Stanford, you did nothing wrong. Nothing. If Jim Bob is acquitted it's because the prosecution never had a case that wasn't based on mostly circumstantial evidence. We were both trial court judges long enough to know what a skilled defense litigator can do to subvert or mire in doubt the facts of any case. A finer, more upstanding and dignified man does not exist. I will not listen to you doubt that for one minute," Whitlee said, her voice full of conviction.

"And how are you so sure?" Stanford asked with melancholy in his tone.

"Because I know you. I've worked side by side with you for well over a year. You don't lie, you don't fabricate stories. You are as honest and hard working as the day is long. I trust you implicitly and care for you immensely," Whitlee professed. Stanford sat quietly a bit stunned by Judge Hammond's revelation.

"Why Whitlee, I am without words. Your kindness and sincerity have silenced the rumblings of this old volcano," Stanford softly replied with a discernible blush in his cheeks. "Thank you for placing that faith in me, I am unworthy of such praise. I am unsure of how to repay you for your magnanimous support and kind words."

"Have dinner with me next Friday after we hear oral argument on the Katrina victims appeal," Whitlee unhesitatingly offered. "Let's have a nice meal together."

"As colleagues on the Court attending a dinner meeting?" Stanford questioned, attempting to frame a respectful way to describe a social arrangement between an Associate Judge and the Chief Judge of a federal judicial circuit court.

"If that is how you would like to view it, then yes," Whitlee pronounced.

"Excellent!" Stanford exclaimed, his demeanor now cheerful and his mind free of the preoccupation of his trial testimony performance.

"I look forward to it," Whitlee stated as she rose from the chair and turned to leave Stanford's office.

"Me too, Whitlee, me too," Stanford Winchester responded in a delighted chirp.

"You hear me? Cletus you there?" Jim Bob McCallum bellowed into the phone as he paced back and forth in front of the large floor to ceiling windows in his spacious corporate office in Baton Rouge. "Dagnabbit! What in blue blazes is going on with this damn phone?"

"Jim Bob, I can hear you just fine," Senator Cletus Sawyer replied.

"There ya is," Jim Bob reaffirmed. "I swear they make these crappy phones in China and they last for a couple of months if that," Jim Bob loudly complained. "Course, as you know, we now make some of the Lake Pontchartrain brands in China and they are some of the finest products made on God's green earth."

"What can I do you for?" Cletus Sawyer asked Jim Bob. "I'm on my way to a town hall meeting in Iowa City."

"That's right, you are running for President. Mostly on my dime, as you are well aware," Jim Bob smugly stated into the phone. "Now that my trial is coming to a close and my attorney ground up Stanford Winchester on the witness stand like so much cheap beef chuck meat, I just want to make sure that you are clear about my expectations."

"Frankly, Jim Bob, I am not quite sure I understand," Cletus Sawyer responded as he fidgeted in an upholstered chair on his campaign bus.

"Then let me make this clear for you, Senator," Jim Bob growled into the phone. "Once I am acquitted of all charges, I expect you to do your utmost to see that Mabel's name is rightfully associated with the new federal mental health research facility under construction in Baton Rouge. I want assurances that that facility will bear her name, and her name alone."

"I'm not sure I can do that. The Board of Directors of LSU, the Louisiana State government, and others all have a say in that decision, and from what I understand they rejected using Mabel's name after you were indicted on criminal charges. My sphere of influence on this matter is quite limited," Cletus replied.

"Your campaign funds are about to become quite limited as well," Jim Bob responded in a smarmy tone. "Look, you're an old dawg, Cletus. You know where the Alpo comes from. You know what you need to do to make sure that your food dish is amply filled. So, you best not be barking up the wrong tree. I love my hunting dogs. But if for one minute, you think that I won't put one down if he becomes too aggressive or don't know when to heel to my commands, then you don't understand me at all, Senator."

"Now, Jim Bob . . ." Cletus began to reply, but Jim Bob quickly interrupted.

"Cletus, the signal is breaking up. I can't hear you no more. You must be getting too far into the high corn. You are getting seriously close to being out of my sight and out of my mind," Jim Bob smirked as he hung up the phone.

NATHAN WHITAKER SLUMPED IN HIS EASY CHAIR at home, emotionally exhausted from yet another long day at court. He fiddled with the knot in his loosened tie, as he recounted the events of the past few days in his mind. Nathan felt confident that he would be acquitted of the murder charges brought against him by an overly zealous prosecutor. But after he is found 'not guilty,' then what? There was only one thing in this world that he truly wanted, and that was to once again be a part of Andrew Cochran's life. He wanted to turn back the clock and be at the side of his best friend. To counsel him, to protect him, to assist him and his admin-istration any way possible. The clandestine meeting at Camp David was an important and affirming first step, but it wasn't nearly enough. The idiotic threatening call he received only reinforced his belief that others around the President not only understood the bond between the two men but felt threatened by it. Nathan was resolute about obtaining his one goal, but first he had to completely remove the legal noose around his neck. Nathan grinned as he completely undid the knot in his dress tie and flung it across his living room.

CHAPTER 27

Dusk overtook the shores of Lake Pontchartrain as a small assemblage were illuminated by a crackling dry wood fire. Hushed chants, the clinking of timbales, and the beating of African hand drums presented an otherworldly atmosphere to the animal sacrifice to come. Bessie Collins stood slightly separated from the rest of the group, as she intently watched and listened to the gyrations and pleas to the world of the spirits. For now, Bessie was but a spectator of this Haitian ritual and practice. She had promised Esther Francois, that she would keep an open mind. She would observe and judge for herself if any human harm was being done in the name of sacrifices to the loa. Bessie stood in the humid twilight at the shores of the placid lake. Her eyes transfixed, her trepidations wholly intact.

Thirty minutes later, the ritual had concluded. The wood fire had been extinguished, and the bloody sickle knife laid in the sand a few feet from the headless chicken which was being drained of its blood by the forceful hands of Papa Levi. Esther shook loose her limbs as she attempted to recover from her trance like state.

"You see, it was a ritual like many religions observe. Nothing to be frightened of," Esther calmly reassured Bessie.

"I couldn't watch you cut the chicken's head off," Bessie confessed.

"No worries, child. I understand. It is but a means to an end. Trust me, far worse occurs nightly at restaurants and butcher shops all over the Big Easy. The sacrifice is to tell the loa that we are serious about our requests and honor their glory. The chicken meat will be tomorrow's lunch. The bones will be cleaned, bleached, and dried so that a tribute to the loa can be constructed," Esther stated.

"And what is the tribute for?" Bessie asked.

"Our client requires good fortune in a new business endeavor," Esther explained.

"Well, that sounds like it's alright. Can't see no harm, right?" Bessie stated in a questioning manner hoping for an acceptable answer.

"No harm at all," Esther replied. "The client will be pleased for the blessings of luck and prosperity."

"Ok, yes, if this is all it's about, I think it's alright. And we don't waste the chicken meat," Bessie reasoned.

"Nothing is wasted. The customer is happy and the money is good," Esther affirmed.

"No black magic, ever. You have to promise me," Bessie stated firmly.

"Ah, sweet Bessie. Have no fears, child. Esther is here now."

"You two ready to go?" Clay Grover called out to Aaron Rose and Emily Dubois, using the glass pane of his office door as a mirror as he adjusted his Duke blue-and-white-colored striped tie.

"Breaking out the school colors, huh?" Aaron chided his husband.

"You can never have too much luck can you?" Clay asked.

"You're sitting in the gallery. How far do you think that luck extends?" Aaron asked.

"You smarmy northern boys with your superior attitudes and indifference to customs, tradition, and seeking good fortune," Clay kidded in return. "Tell him Emily, tell him about the ways of the genteel South," Clay coaxed. Emily hesitated momentarily.

"We're all a bunch of moonshine addled, superstitious hillbillies that would rather stick pins in a doll than diligently prepare a well-conceived fact intensive oral argument," Emily said with a smile.

"Not exactly the rousing support of my Southern kindred spirit that I was looking for," Clay playfully admonished Emily.

"Oh, hell Clay, I had a grandma who played around in the occult just like you did. She would put a lucky rabbit's foot in my lunch box. She gave me amulets and other lucky charms throughout my life. I never bought into it for a minute. Intelligence and hard work will get you where you need to go, not some primal superstition or a lucky tie," Emily laughed.

"You two sure are a buzz kill," Clay responded.

"Alright let's go, we don't want to be late," Emily stated as she headed towards the door.

"Do your thing, lucky tie," Clay said as he pulled down on his Windsor knot one more time.

POSY BRANCH SAT ON A BAR STOOL next to her hostess, Chiffon LaBelle as both took a quick break while the afternoon business took a post-lunchtime dip.

"Sugar, there's something I got to tell ya," Posy said as she took Chiffon's large hand into hers.

"I know, I know," Chiffon said solemnly. "You got to take Olivier on as your partner."

"I tried to round up the money on my own but there just wasn't enough time. Chantale won't wait no more. If only you was coming into your money now. You know that I want to partner up with you girl-friend," Posy sincerely said to Chiffon.

"I surely do appreciate it," Chiffon replied. "There ain't no certainty that I'll be coming into any money if the Appeals Court overturns the trial court decision. So, I completely understand."

"I wish I could have found some way to make it work out. I reckon, we'll just have to make the best of it with Olivier. Though truth be told I ain't sure that I trust that man," Posy sighed.

"You got good instincts, Posy. Olivier is a snake in the grass. I use to get my nails done at his parlor for years. I seen the way he treats his nail girls. That boy disrespects them girls and treats them rough. He be tak-ing a percentage of their tips. Also, he be charging more on the weekends and holidays when tourists in town. Taking advantage of folk to make a quick buck. You best keep an eye on that one," Chiffon warned.

"Don't you worry girl, my eyes will be wide open. I moved to New Orleans to get away from men who wanted to control me and who thought I was just another stupid bimbo who could be pushed around. I ain't gonna allow Olivier to get away with nothin'. He got that cool manner. He think he can talk me into things. Well, Sister, that ain't gonna happen," Posy said forcefully. Chiffon nodded her head affirmatively as she glanced down at her watch.

"It be happenin' right now," Chiffon said. "Oral argument in my ap-peal case is taking place down at the Federal Courthouse. My attorney Caleb Butler and his crew are going to stop by French Tips after they done at court and fill me in on what happened. Though it be months before we know how them judges rule," Chiffon added.

"Well, you let me know when they show up. I'll have Michael fix them up some nice juleps on the house," Posy proclaimed. "Any friend of my girl Chiffon is a friend of mine."

"You is good people, Posy Branch. You surely is."

"Well, thank you Chiffon, I surely do appreciate them kind words," Posy said. "And you know I think the world of you as well, which is why we need to be extra careful. Michael was telling me that the two of you might have spotted them rough Cajun redneck boys casing the place the other night."

"Can't rightly say for sure. It was night and they was wearing ball caps so I couldn't tell if one was redheaded and the other skin-headed. But yeah, a couple of boys was standing out on the street for a while just looking to see what was what," Chiffon related.

"Did you call the police?" Posy inquired.

"Heck no. We can't be calling the police just cuz some boys are looking in from the street. They was too far away for us to know if it was the same ones. This is the Big Easy, Posy, iffin' we go calling the police on every unusual or suspicious character, we'd never be off the phone. Plus, it be like my grandma use to tell me, you can't be crying wolf all the time cuz when the real wolf done show, nobody come to help you," Chiffon responded.

"Yeah, I guess you're right. If being strange was a crime in this here city, there'd be no one on the streets, everyone would be in jail, including me and you!" Posy exclaimed with a loud snort. "I just want you to promise me that you'll be safe. Don't take no risks and watch out when you leave," Posy asked with great sincerity.

"Yes, mama, I promise," Chiffon replied with a wide grin.

The large appellate court room was filled with attorneys, observers, and the media. A boisterous vocal mélange filled the room as attorneys discussed strategy and the press jostled for position with court spectators in the gallery. Caleb Butler sat at the counsel table next to lead counsel for the appellees, Winslow Howard. Caleb turned and smiled at his associates sitting in the back of the courtroom. Clay gave a hearty thumbs up to his friend and colleague. Winslow Howard wiped the palms of his hands with a white handkerchief he had removed from his pocket.

"I've done dozens of oral arguments over the years, but I still get as nervous as a teenage boy on his first date before they begin," Winslow conceded to Caleb in a hushed whisper.

"I've seen you in action, you are remarkably skilled and mentally adroit," Caleb supportively replied.

"Thank you for that," Winslow quietly replied, as he watched the bailiff prepare to call the proceeding into order. "Time to try to kiss the girl."

The courtroom bailiff instructed the assemblage to rise as the three black robed jurists took their places at the bench. Chief Judge Stanford Winchester flanked by Judges Whitlee Hammond and Charles Sewell addressed the large gathering acknowledging the oversized crowd and pronounced interest in the very high-profile matter.

"Good afternoon," Judge Winchester began. "My word, we seldom have this kind of turnout for oral argument. Welcome to the United States Court of Appeals for the Fifth Federal Judicial Circuit. I am Chief Judge Stanford Winchester. For those of you who are new to the process, I'd like to briefly go over how we will proceed. Appellant's counsel will make opening statements and present the issues on appeal and argument in support. We will then hear from counsel for the appellees. Appellants will be granted the opportunity for a short rebuttal. Let me just say to counsel for both sides, that on behalf of myself and my colleagues, Judge Charles Sewell and Judge Whitlee Hammond, that we are more interested in a polite and pointed conversation with you rather than rigorous and contentious debate. Please attempt to succinctly answer the questions that we may ask instead of providing answers to questions you may have wished that we had asked. It will provide for a more informative and pleasant experience for all. With that said, may we please hear from counsel for the appellants?"

The counsel for the appellants walked to the podium facing the bench. He glanced at the digital timer that was placed just slightly to the left center of the podium which reflected the time that each side had assigned for their oral argument. After a short sip of water, he began, "May it please the Court . . ."

A little over an hour later, the proceedings had concluded. Both sides had presented their issues on appeal and arguments in support. Questions and banter from the Court were quickly analyzed by both sides in an effort to discern any predilections or concerns that each of the judges may have had with the issues presented and their arguments in support. In keeping with his stated intent, the questions to the counsel for both sides were reasoned and polite. Stanford Winchester did not believe in 'gotcha questions' or providing 'softballs' to the attorneys arguing before his panel. It was exceedingly hard for the participants to discern any of the judges' personal ideology or judicial preferences on the arguments presented. However, that didn't keep them from trying.

CHAPTER 28

"**D**ID YOU SEE JUDGE SEWELL'S REACTION to Winslow's response to his questions on the admissibility of testimony issue? He was nodding affirmatively with every point Winslow was making," Aaron enthusiastically stated to his colleagues as they sat at a table against the back wall of French Tips, Juleps & Jazz with their client Chiffon LaBelle.

"So, is that good?" Chiffon asked Aaron and the other attorneys who represented her in the appeal.

"That's very good, if you can believe and trust in the body language of judges during oral argument," Caleb Butler responded. "Sometimes you can read a judge and attempt to decipher the way he or she may decide a case based on the manner and type of questions they ask of counsel during argument. And then again, sometimes you can't."

"What about the other two judges?" Chiffon asked. "Could you tell what they was thinking?"

"Judge Hammond actively questioned both sides, but it was tough to get a good read on her. She seemed pretty impartial and asked each side some tough questions," Caleb surmised. "As to Justice Winchester, he is like a sphinx up there on the bench. He shows very little emotion and doesn't even physically move much. He is very stoic. I wouldn't want to play poker with him, he doesn't seem to have any tells."

"Did I hear someone mention Justice Winchester?" Posy Branch asked from across the room of her establishment. "That's my dance partner right there." Posy walked over to the table and warmly smiled and greeted her guests. Anybody need another julep? Michael is making a batch of pineapple ginger juleps. He's grating some fresh ginger root as we speak."

"That sounds fantastic," Clay said.

"Never seen my husband turn down an offer of food or drink. Ever." Aaron added.

"You two fine looking fellas hitched to one another?" Posy asked.

"Gonna be one year in September," Aaron acknowledged.

"Posy, the pitcher of pineapple ginger juleps is ready," Michael shouted from behind the large mahogany bar.

"Sugar, can you sashay your tight little behind over here with them juleps?" Posy called out. Michael walked over to the table and Chiffon introduced Michael to her legal team. Michael shook hands with everyone and smiled broadly. His gleaming white teeth sparkled in the bar lighting as did his naked shaved torso.

"Did you hear that these gorgeous boys is married?" Posy asked Michael. "I been trying to get this one to find a good man and settle down. You can't be a tramp forever," Posy said tilting her head in Michael's direction. Michael blushed as he shifted from one foot to the other.

"I tried to tramp around for quite a while," Clay confessed. "But then this beautiful, smart, loving man came into my life, and well that's all she wrote."

"See there, Sugar, we just got to find the right man for you," Posy said to Michael as he continued to blush and fidget in place.

"What about me, and finding me a man?" Chiffon interjected with a hearty laugh.

"You too, my sweet girl. I'm gonna start a dating service from my back office," Posy laughed and snorted. "But not right now. Michael, darlin', a couple of thirsty customers just walked in."

"It was very nice meeting you. I hope to see you all again. Duty calls," Michael politely smiled as he walked back to the bar.

"So Posy, you had mentioned something about Justice Winchester being your dance partner?" Caleb asked with an incredulous tone in his voice.

"Well, it was only once, but let me tell y'all, Stanford cuts a mean rug. He's a regular Fred Astaire," Posy acknowledged with a grin.

"Was that here at the bar?" Caleb followed up.

"Oh heck no. It was at one of them fancy White House dinners," Posy said very matter-of-factly.

"Excuse me?" Caleb responded nearly blowing pineapple ginger julep out of his nostrils. "The White House in Washington?"

"Yeah. It was a dinner in his honor when he was nominated by Andy for the Supreme Court," Posy related with a placid look on her face.

"Andy, as in President Cochran?" Aaron asked as the entire table sat in stunned disbelief at what they were hearing.

"Duh. Yeah. Andy and my no-good ex-husband were best friends. I went to a bunch of them fancy shindigs when I lived in Washington."

"And your ex-husband is?" Clay asked astounded by where the conversation was going.

"My ex is Nathan Whitaker, Andy's former Chief of Staff, before he decided to go around killing people," Posy said unflinchingly.

"Holy shit!" Aaron loudly exclaimed.

A COUPLE OF HOURS LATER THAT EVENING, Stanford Winchester and Whitlee Hammond sat together at Stanford's regular table in the main dining room of Arnaud's. A few moments later, Lucius Collins approached the couple grinning ear-to-ear.

"A very good evening to you. It's a distinct honor and a high privilege to be serving you this evening," Lucius graciously stated.

"Lucius, my dear old friend, I'd like to introduce you to my colleague, Judge Whitlee Hammond. Whitlee, this is Lucius Collins, the best waiter in the Crescent City," Stanford said by way of an introduction.

"Judge Hammond, it is wonderful to meet you. I've heard so many amazing things about you," Lucius fawned.

"Delighted to meet you as well," Whitlee Hammond replied. Whitlee looked at Stanford and asked, "Lucius is Bessie's husband?"

"Indeed, he is. Which makes him the luckiest man in all of New Orleans," Stanford responded with a chuckle.

"You know my Bessie?" Lucius asked.

"I've met her briefly once or twice at the courthouse while she was delivering a homemade pie to Stanford. Due to the extreme generosity of Justice Winchester, I was able to sample one of her pies. It was absolutely divine," Whitlee stated.

"Yes ma'am, that's my Bessie. No one can hold a candle to her pies," Lucius said beaming with pride.

"Lucius, Bessie and I have been friends for about eighteen years now," Stanford added. "You will not find two more kind-hearted, loving and loyal people on God's green earth."

Lucius smiled widely and slightly trembled, he was so proud to hear his friend describe Bessie and he in such glowing terms. "Thank you,

Justice Winchester. Thank you so very kindly for them lovely words," he choked out nearly moved to tears. After a brief hesitation to regain his composure, Lucius slightly fiddled with the white towel draped over his tuxedo jacketed sleeve.

"May I offer the fine gentleman and lovely lady a cocktail?" Lucius politely asked.

"Do birds have beaks?" Stanford asked with a smile.

"Oh yes sir, they surely do. They most surely do," Lucius smiled and laughed. "A Sazerac for Justice Winchester, and for Judge Hammond?"

"I probably shouldn't, but what do they say, when in Rome? I'll have a Sazerac as well, please," Whitlee giggled in response.

"Right away, it is my honor to serve you," Lucius said as he nodded and turned on his heels and swiftly moved towards the bar.

Two hours later while finishing their dessert of Strawberries Arnaud, Whitlee and Stanford watched as Lucius prepared Cafe Brulot for two. A deep rich coffee, lemon, cloves and cinnamon sticks were combined as Lucius peeled a fresh orange and carefully poured Orange Curacao and flamed brandy over the dangling orange peel into a pot. The theatrics of the preparation of the dessert coffee was only matched by the exquisite aroma and mellow exotic flavor.

"This is outstanding, pure heaven," Whitlee cooed as she sipped her coffee.

"I am so very pleased that you enjoy your coffee," Lucius said. "Is there anything else that I can get you at the moment?"

"We are good, thank you kindly, my dear friend," Stanford replied with a wink and a nod.

"This has been so lovely, I can't begin to thank you for sharing this experience with me," Whitlee sweetly said to Stanford. "We should do this more often."

"That would indeed be delightful, but of course, we wouldn't want to give people the wrong impression," Stanford responded.

"I certainly understand your position, Stanford, I do," Whitlee stated. "But life is short, and when you find someone that you wholly enjoy spending time with, I find it sad to think that that should be curtailed for the sake of appearances."

Moments later, Lucius returned to the table with the check.

"Lucius, my good man, here you go," Stanford stated as he handed his credit card to Lucius. "May I also ask you for the favor of calling for a town car? I'm going to escort Judge Hammond safely home."

"Most certainly. My utmost pleasure to do so," Lucius replied, as he walked away from the table.

"You don't have to do that Stanford," Whitlee said. "Plus, I thought we agreed that this dinner would be my treat?"

"I am many things, and some of those things are not very good. But if I am not a gentleman, I cannot live with myself. Please allow me to do this for you. I cannot tell you when I've had a more wonderful evening. This surely has been an extraordinary treat," Stanford said quite sincerely.

"Alright, but you must allow me to make it up to you another time soon," Whitlee responded.

"Motion granted, Judge Hammond, motion granted," Stanford replied with a smile.

The town car pulled up to Whitlee Hammond's home. Stanford exited the car and opened the door for Whitlee. He walked her to her door as she fished for her house keys in her purse.

"Thank you again for a lovely evening Stanford. It was absolutely perfect in every way,"

Whitlee softly said.

"It was my honor and pleasure," Stanford replied. As he was about to turn from her and walk back to the waiting car, Whitlee took him by the hand, moved closer to Stanford's body and gently and softly pressed her lips against his. Stanford's instinct to withdraw dissolved in a nanosecond, as he kissed Whitlee back. The sweet kiss lasted only a few seconds before they both said goodnight and Stanford departed. But for Stanford Winchester that kiss lasted a lifetime. A new and joyful lifetime.

A few miles away, Clay Grover and Aaron Rose were lying in their bed together discussing the events of a very busy and important day.

"I thought that the oral argument went very well. Winslow Howard was masterful," Clay summarized.

"He was making the arguments that you prepared," Aaron said with pride in his husband.

"The words aren't worth much in an oral argument setting unless they are presented and defended by a shrewd and extremely competent advocate," Clay added.

"It was hard to read the panel. I think we've got Judge Sewell on our side, which you might expect given that he is the sole Democrat on the panel. One might think that the two Republicans would side with the Republican administration accused of wronging the people who brought the class action. But then again you never know. I've got no idea where Justice Winchester will come down on this," Aaron said.

"Speaking of Winchester, I thought you were going to lose it when Posy Branch told us that she danced with Winchester. And then when she revealed to us that she was married to Nathan Whitaker, you did lose it," Clay laughed. "You all but fell out of your chair."

"C'mon, you were just as surprised as I was. We all were," Aaron replied.

"Jeez, they say it's a small world. That revelation made it the head of a pin-sized," Clay laughed. "Three years ago we were trying our best to stop Winchester from getting on the Supreme Court. We were dead set on defeating Andrew Cochran and Nathan Whitaker's nominee. This afternoon we're drinking juleps with the former Mrs. Whitaker. Go figure."

"She's a live wire, isn't she?" Aaron chortled.

"Sure is. Hard to picture her at refined and sedate White House functions," Clay responded.

"Oh, I'm sure she livened things up," Aaron said.

"Speaking of livening things up," Clay softly and seductively whispered as his hand went under the sheets and in the general direction of his husband's crotch.

"You're never going to get invited to a White House function acting like that," Aaron smiled as he appreciated Clay's manipulations.

"I'll take my chances," Clay moaned.

CHAPTER 29

NATHAN WHITAKER SAT QUIETLY IN THE PLUSH OFFICE of his attorney, Rupert Grassmonk. Two hours earlier, the jurors for his criminal trial were given instructions by the trial court judge. Nathan's fate now rested in the hands of twelve of his fellow citizens. He stared out the window looking at nothing in particular.

"You should probably go home and get some rest, Nathan," Rupert Grassmonk said to his client. "It could be a while before the jury comes back with a verdict."

"Don't sugar coat it, what do you think my chances are for an acquittal?" Nathan bluntly asked.

"Good. Very good," Rupert replied. "But you never know with juries. Do they really understand the difference between direct and circumstantial evidence? All of the precise jury instructions in the world can't guarantee a jury's ability to comprehend the difference. But your body language in the courtroom was excellent. There were several polite nods and smiles from some of the female jurors in your direction during the proceedings. You came across as a confident but not arrogant man. I like our chances."

"I want to thank you now, before we know the outcome, Rupert. I thought you were masterful throughout the trial but your closing argument was so compelling and spot on," Nathan praised his counsel. "You proved again why you are considered one of the best criminal defense attorneys in the country."

"Well, thank you Nathan. It's been an honor to represent you. It's not every day one is asked to represent the White House Chief of Staff."

Rupert and Nathan both reclined into their leather chairs. There was nothing more to do other than to wait.

"CAN YOU WAIT JUST ONE DAD-GUM MINUTE," Posy Branch said with an exasperated tone to her voice.

"It is done now. I signed the papers this morning. Olivier is now co-owner of French Tips," Chantale Calypso replied as she hurriedly gathered her personal possessions and placed them into a banker's box. "I have my check from him and will be leaving for Haiti tomorrow morning."

"That's all well and good, but you ain't gotta flee like you is leaving the scene of a crime. We been partners for nearly a year. Made some real good money together. Come sit and have a julep with me before you go," Posy asked her former partner.

"Yes, one drink," Chantale agreed.

"Mama ain't doing much better?" Posy asked with a look of concern.

"No. Just a matter of time now," Chantale somberly stated. "It is why I need to leave quickly. I want to have as much time to be with her before her time comes."

"I surely do understand. And I'll be sayin' a little prayer for her tonight. For you too," Posy added.

"I will miss you Posy. You are good people," Chantale stated softly with tears welling up in her eyes.

"You take care of yourself, Chantale Calypso. I'm gonna miss you calling me crazy all the time," Posy said with a sad smile.

AN HOUR LATER, OLIVIER BELLEVUE WALKED through the doors of his newly purchased stake in the establishment. He surveyed his surroundings like a king staring at his kingdom from a distant far off hilltop.

"There you is partner-of-mine," Posy said.

"Good afternoon Posy. I'm so very pleased that we could make this arrangement work out," Olivier responded.

"We'll get along just fine," Posy stated enthusiastically. "Olivier sounds so formal, mind if I just call you Olive?" Posy asked only half kiddingly.

"You most certainly may not. I am not some small salty soft and chewy globe," Olivier replied with utter dissatisfaction through pursed lips.

"Yeah, but you got a hard, black pit substituting for a heart, ain't ya?" Posy asked with a grin and a laughing snort. "Lighten up, Olivier, I'm just messin' with ya. You got to be able to laugh at yourself. Ain't you got a sense of humor?"

"Of course I do when someone says something funny. That just isn't the case here," Olivier grinned.

"You got some spice to ya, I like that," Posy said. "We gonna get down in the dirt and have us some fun."

"Oh, the dirt is gonna fly around here, that's for sure," Olivier responded with a knowing crooked smile.

MABEL MCCALLUM WAS SEATED in front of her bedroom dressing table as she vacantly stared into the ornate mirror. Her personal assistant and caregiver, Lucille, gently brushed her hair as Mabel occasionally softly let out a contented moan. Jim Bob McCallum entered the bedroom and observed from the corner of the room for a few brief moments.

"That's fine, thank you Lucille, I'll take it from here," Jim Bob said in a hushed voice as he took the hairbrush from Lucille and continued the gentle long strokes with the brush.

"Ain't that nice darling?" Jim Bob asked his wife. "I know how much you enjoy having your long lovely hair brushed and groomed. And if I may say, you're looking especially lovely today. Soon that ridiculous trial that I've had to suffer through will be over. In a few days my good name will be cleared and we can get back to our regular life together. Once I am acquitted, we will make sure that your name will forever be remembered in association with the new medical research center they're building in Baton Rouge. It's located just below that bluff that we use to kiss and cuddle at just off the LSU campus. How young we were then with nary a care in the world."

Mabel sat quietly, her eyes transfixed on her own image in the mirror. Jim Bob stopped his hair brushing momentarily, and Mabel made a small audible sound of protest. Jim Bob quickly resumed the rote brushing strokes.

"Just a few more days, and I'm gonna fix all of the wrongs that have been perpetrated against our family name. I promise you that, my sweet girl. You will receive all of the honor and prestige that rightly belongs to you. And we're gonna find new doctors and new treatments to help get you back to your old self. I will not rest until we've turned over every stone and taken all measures that are possible. I know in my heart that God will not allow a fine church-going woman like yourself to suffer. No. That surely won't happen. I will make sure of it."

Jim Bob continued the repetitious movement with the brush as a tear rolled down his weather worn cheek.

"COUNT IT ONE MORE TIME, PAPA LEVI," Bessie requested as she wrote the cash and credit card totals for the past week into her accounting ledger book. She watched carefully as he counted the money and she double checked the credit card receipts.

"Gots the same total," Papa Levi confirmed.

"This been the best week we done had in quite some time," Bessie cheerfully chirped. "I do have to confess that I wasn't convinced that bringing Esther into the shop was a good idea. But, the extra money we is bringing in sure is making me glad that we did."

"Glad you done made the right decision, Miss Bessie," Papa Levi agreed. "We almost doubling our weekly money. And Esther ain't even brung her Jackson Square regulars over to the shop yet. Once she get them folks in here, we gonna be in the high cotton."

"Let's not say too much to Lucius. He still ain't pleased about the whole deal with Esther. Thinks I'm just lookin' for trouble. No sense giving him anything to fret himself about," Bessie said.

"These lips ain't moving but to eat," Papa Levi replied.

"Alright then, we is in agreement. We keep on bringing in new business with Esther. Make sure that the customers are satisfied and happy. We keep our mouths shut when it comes to Lucius and we keep counting the money and smiling wide," Bessie said with a laugh.

"You done good Miss Bessie, real good."

"HALLELUJAH!" PRESIDENT ANDREW COCHRAN SHOUTED from a media room in the West Wing where he was carefully watching the television news report. His Chief of Staff, Sam Brainard came racing into the room to see what the commotion was all about.

"Mr. President, are you alright?" Sam anxiously asked.

"Couldn't be better, Sam, couldn't be better!" A very excited and happy Andrew Cochran exclaimed. "Nathan was acquitted of all charges. His name has been cleared. He's a free man!"

"That's wonderful news, sir. It truly is. But we need to be very careful about how we color our response of the acquittal to the press," Sam cautioned.

"Are you telling me that I can't be happy that my life-long friend has been exonerated from a series of politically motivated baseless charges? That I can't be seen as celebrating his freedom and new lease on life?" Andrew Cochran challenged his Chief of Staff with an irritated tone in his voice.

"All I am saying, Mr. President, is that we need to think about all of the ramifications of the White House's response and how your opponents will seek to twist and turn your words in the upcoming debates," Sam responded.

"Right now, Sam, I couldn't give a flying fuck about what those narrow-minded idiots will say," Andrew Cochran shot back with steely-eyed conviction. "I am elated that one of the few people in this world who I truly hold dear, my best friend, has received the best news possible. And I'm not going to allow you or anyone else to drag me down at this moment. I'll deal directly with my Press Secretary on a response. You don't need to be involved. Now, if you'll excuse me, I've got a phone call to make."

Minutes later, Nathan Whitaker excused himself from the celebratory scene outside of the courtroom as he quickly answered his cell phone.

"Hello, Mr. President," Nathan cheerfully said into his phone.

"I never doubted your innocence Nathan, not for one minute," Andrew Cochran greeted his friend.

"Thank you, Mr. President, you have no idea what that means to me," Nathan replied as tears of joy streamed down his cheeks.

"Congratulations! I couldn't be happier for you. I am sorry that you had to go through this whole ridiculous travesty of justice. You became the victim of a political witch hunt. They tried to take me down through you, but we are stronger than they could possibly imagine. My presidency survived and so did you, my friend," Andrew stated with indignation in his tone.

"Once again, thank you Mr. President," Nathan repeated. "But you've got to be careful about how you frame your response to my acquittal."

"Lands sake, Nathan! First Sam and now you," Andrew responded. "I don't give a flip about the political ramifications; I want the world to know that I could not be happier to see that justice was done. An innocent man who had been shamefully used as a pawn in a politically motivated farce and miscarriage of justice has been fully exonerated."

"I appreciate that sir, I truly do. But that isn't the most desirable approach to take immediately. Your response should be carefully crafted so as not to give your political opponents an opportunity to take advantage of the situation," Nathan replied.

"Once a Chief of Staff, always a Chief of Staff," Andrew said with a smirk. "You don't need to worry about me, my friend. And, you don't need to protect me. I've got a whole building full of people tasked with doing that job. Many of whom you hired. I want you to focus on yourself for a change. Take care of yourself, Nathan. We'll talk very soon. Again, congratulations. I couldn't be happier for you."

Nathan moved the phone away from his ear and placed it back in his pocket. He stood silently amongst a throng of jubilant friends and supporters, yet the only one he truly cared to celebrate with he had just spoken to on the phone.

CHAPTER 30

Six weeks passed and the calendar had flipped to September. Two Democratic Party primary debates had come and gone as well as three Republican Party primary debates. President Andrew Cochran still found himself trailing Jedediah Wilson and Senator Cletus Sawyer in polling of Republican voters. The Iowa Caucus was still five months away, but that didn't keep the Re-Elect President Cochran Campaign team from feeling the pressure to perform better in the upcoming debates.

Landon Hamilton, the President's Campaign Manager, nervously rocked back and forth in his chair as he scanned recent polling data on his iPad. "This isn't good," he mumbled to his polling consultant.

"No, it's not," the consultant agreed. "As it stands right now, the President will lose Iowa to Wilson, he might be able to pull out New Hampshire, but will then turn around and lose to Cletus Sawyer in South Carolina and most of the Deep South. We only see him carrying his home state of Georgia. He's got to pivot to the right, in order to appeal to the conservative base voters, but even at that, they probably won't believe that he is sincere. It will be looked at as pandering and a move of desperation."

"What's causing the most problems with the voters?" Landon inquired.

"The major issue is that the base feels like he sold them out. He campaigned for the Presidency as a rock-ribbed Conservative who was going to go to war with the Democrats after eight years of a liberal President and shrink the size of the Federal government. Instead, after the Winchester debacle and the scandal surrounding Nathan Whitaker, he chose a moderate to sit on the Supreme Court. Additionally, the base wanted him to fight tooth and nail with the Democrats. Instead, Andrew Cochran gave them compromise. There is no doubt that his drastic move to the center and his populist policies have garnered him support with Independents and even some Democrats. He would have a much better chance at winning a general election than any of his primary opponents. The problem is that he may never get to the general election because the base of the party will defeat him in the primaries. If he pivots back to the right now, that will most likely be seen as disingenuous."

"It amazes me that a complete nut job like Jedediah Wilson seems like a reasonable choice to Republican voters. His rhetoric is positively medieval," Landon stated.

"But we're not talking about Republican voters per se, we're talking about the right-wing base that turns up for primaries. It's a completely different animal," the consultant replied. "They eschew compromise for hardline unwavering dogma. Either you cater to them or you lose. It's that simple."

"Enough. You're giving me a migraine," Landon moaned in utter frustration.

CAROLYN BARNES SAT IN THE BACK OF THE CAMPAIGN BUS waiting for her candidate. She intently surveyed polling data as she waited. Moments later, she was joined by Perry Douglas, who was wiping his mouth with a paper napkin as he plopped down in a seat next to her.

"I am so sick of having to eat grilled corn on the cob and bacon on a stick," Perry complained. "I've got corn kernels wedged so far back in my molars, I can't even floss them out. When did campaigning for President become an eating contest?"

"You're in a good mood today," Carolyn sarcastically said in response.

"It's never ending. The ridiculous staged photo ops. Is this really how the greatest country in the world should be choosing their next President?" Perry harangued.

"Well, if we don't begin to see some changes in our polling numbers you won't have to worry because the next President won't be you," Carolyn bluntly replied.

"That bad?" Perry questioned.

"They're slightly better than last month, but Hellen Raymond is still ahead in Iowa polling by eight points," Carolyn sighed. "We need to do better at the next debate."

"That's next week, right? Centered on domestic and social justice policy?" Perry asked.

"Yes. Raymond is so right of center on social policy, she might as well be a Republican. We've got to go to her left and inspire our liberal base," Carolyn stated.

"That's not a problem. I have a long record of civil rights advocacy and promoting progressive social agendas. Last week, my son Robert asked me if he could come out on the road and campaign for me," Perry said.

"You sure you want to go there? Does Robert understand what he'd be getting himself into?" Carolyn questioned.

"I don't know. But he was rather insistent that he wanted to help. Of course, I'd explain to him all of the possible repercussions, not to mention the homophobic backlash. But he's a grown man. He understands the consequences."

"Let me talk to him," Carolyn suggested. "He might hear it as just so much dad-speak coming from an over-protective father. If I speak to him very forthrightly about what he'd be getting himself into, and he still wants to participate, then great. Robert is smart as a whip and highly articulate. He'd make a very good spokesperson for the campaign. But he's got to have a realistic perspective about the ugliness of the narrow-minded bigotry that he'd be confronted with."

"That's a good idea. Thank you Carolyn. You're right, he would think I'm just trying to protect him. It might be better coming from you. I'd enjoy having him on the campaign trail with me, but it's got to be his decision. And that decision needs to be a highly informed and thoughtful one," Perry said.

"I'm back in Chicago at the end of the week, I'll look him up then," Carolyn offered.

"Great, thanks again."

OLIVIER BELLEVUE SAT IN THE BACK OFFICE of French Tips, Juleps & Jazz pouring over the businesses Excel spreadsheet accounting ledgers on the computer. Posy Branch walked into the office and looked at him with a bewildered stare.

"What are you doing?" Posy asked her business partner.

"I'm going over the monthly receipts and expenditures," Olivier calmly replied.

"Chiffon handles the books for the business," Posy snapped back.

"Not anymore, I've relinquished her of those duties," Olivier responded.

"Why did you do that? Chiffon been handling the books since we started, and we been doing just fine. She got a real knack for numbers and ciphering," Posy stated with a vexed tone in her voice.

"Well, I'm your partner now, Posy, and as your partner I believe it is more appropriate for me to handle the financial accounts of our joint business enterprise. Chiffon is but a paid employee of ours. I'm sure she did an admirable job, but for now I'll take care of it," Olivier plainly countered.

"You should have said something to me before you took over the books," Posy demanded.

"Yes, you are right. I apologize, please forgive my minor indiscretion," Olivier apologized. "But going forward the finances for the business will be part of my responsibility while you handle customer relations and staffing issues."

"I ain't so sure I like that," Posy challenged.

"Would you like to handle the finances?" Olivier asked.

"Heck, I ain't so good with numbers," Posy admitted.

"Well, then it's settled. We'll both take care of what we are good at. I'll handle the finances because I am skilled at accounting, and you'll handle customer relations since you are such a wonderful people person," Olivier summarized.

"Still and all, you should have discussed it with me first," Posy sternly reiterated.

"You are quite right. Mea culpa," Olivier replied with a smug smile.

"If this is going to work, we got to talk to one another. Trust each other," Posy stated.

"I couldn't agree more," Olivier replied.

Thirty minutes later, after Posy left to run some errands, Olivier sat at the bar and spoke with the establishment's bartender, Michael.

"Over the last month or so that I've been here, I've noticed that Posy bosses you around a lot. Michael do this. Michael get me that. I find it a tad disrespectful," Olivier stated.

"It's alright. She don't mean nothing by it. It's just her way," Michael responded.

"Of course, that's between you and Posy, but I just find it somewhat rude and demeaning. She seems to belittle you at times. Perhaps, because you're a gay man and she doesn't fully respect gay men," Olivier posited.

"I don't think it's that, it's just how she acts when we are busy at times," Michael replied.

"Perhaps you're right. But I'm older than you, and as a proud gay man I have had to fight against being treated like an inferior all of my life. I started my own business years ago because I tired of being viewed as a second-class citizen by my former bosses," Olivier said while looking deeply into Michael's eyes. "As gay men in the business world we have to fight for our rights and our dignity. We are only as strong as the community bond we form together to fight against heterosexual homophobic tyranny. Don't you agree?" Olivier asked.

"I guess," Michael tepidly replied.

"Trust me on this, my dear Michael. Heterosexuals will never give us the respect that we deserve unless we join together and fight for it. It's the unfortunate way of the world, dear boy," Olivier firmly stated. "But now that I'm here, I promise that I will fight on your behalf. I won't let Posy push you around and demean you any longer. You deserve to be treated with dignity, and I will do my best to see that you get it. I've got your back."

"Ok, thanks," Michael responded.

Olivier got up from the bar and walked towards the back office. A contented smile creased his lips.

ESTHER FRANCOIS WALKED INTO BESSIE COLLIN'S VOODOO SHOP with a large smile on her face followed by two of Esther's Jackson Square clients. Esther was keeping her word and not only servicing Bessie's existing customers but also bringing in new customers to the shop.

"You see, my Bessie, new customers for your business," Esther announced proudly as she entered the shop. "Go in the back, I will be with you momentarily," Esther stated to her two clients, as she paused to speak with Bessie.

"What are they here for?" Bessie asked Esther.

"One is seeking a séance to communicate with her brother in the spiritual world, the other seeks a tarot card reading. Both will provide good money," Esther explained.

"OK, that sounds fine," Bessie replied as Esther went into the back room to be with her clients.

Bessie stayed in the front of the shop. She no longer thought it necessary to watch Esther when she was in a séance or doing a reading. Esther had gained her trust. And more importantly, the new money that Esther was bringing into the shop was helping Bessie provide for her mother's needs. It was a necessary arrangement Bessie kept telling herself as she busied herself cleaning the glass on the display cases.

"I HOPE YOU DON'T MIND THAT WE ARE HAVING a quiet night together instead of a large party," Aaron Rose said to his husband Clay Grover as they sat across from one another at a table in the Parlor room at Commander's Palace, located in New Orleans Garden District.

"Not at all. Why would I want to spend our first wedding anniversary with dozens of people when the only person I really want to be with is you," Clay smiled as he took Aaron's hand into his own.

"It seems like just a few days ago we were down here in the Big Easy, interviewing people for the Winchester Judiciary Committee hearings. We sat outside at Muriel's on the balcony and you talked about how interesting it might be living here. That was three years ago, and still it seems like yesterday to me," Aaron said.

"Yes, to some extent that trip started everything. It was during that trip that I realized how much I loved you. I suppose it's only fitting that since I fell in love with you here in New Orleans that this is where we were destined to be spending our lives together," Clay said.

"Do you ever miss Washington?" Aaron asked.

"Not for a minute," Clay quickly answered. "Do you?"

"A little sometimes, I guess," Aaron replied. "It's the excitement that I miss. The adrenaline rush that politics could give you when the Senators were in the middle of a floor fight or we were preparing for an important committee hearing. Don't get me wrong, I love what we are doing now helping our clients in the Ninth ward. It's just not the same. There's not the same gravitas or energy."

"I'll admit for the first three, four years in Washington, I lived off that energy and the degree of self-importance and satisfaction you get from being in the midst of the most powerful legislative body in the world. But, it takes a toll on you. It did on me. And then of course, when Senator Fitzsimmons died, all of the perceived power and influence you think you have fades away in seconds. I felt like no one in D.C. It took coming here and doing good work to make me feel whole again," Clay said somewhat wistfully.

"If we didn't get married and decide to move here together, do you think you would have moved down here by yourself?", Aaron asked Clay.

"I don't know. I'm so very happy that I didn't have to find that out. This city is wonderful. But I can't imagine living here and being as happy as I am at this very moment, if I wasn't sharing it with the man I love. I fall a little more in love with you every day that we are together Aaron.

You make everything else better because we are experiencing it together," Clay said sweetly and wholly sincerely.

"Happy Anniversary, Baby," Aaron said while raising his wine glass in a toast to his husband.

"Happy Anniversary, my love."

CHAPTER 31

JIM BOB MCCALLUM SAT QUIETLY IN A WAITING ROOM inside the office area occupied by the staff and aides to Senator Cletus Sawyer in the Hart Senate Office Building.

"Would you like some coffee or tea, Mr. McCallum?" Senator Sawyer's secretary offered their important guest. "The Senator was called away for a roll call vote on the Senate floor, he should be back in just a few more minutes."

"I am not accustomed to being kept waiting, wasting time," Jim Bob stated curtly.

"Yes sir, I completely understand. But it shouldn't be long now," the secretary explained. Several minutes later, Cletus Sawyer arrived at his Senate office flanked by a cadre of staff members. Senator Sawyer quickly noticed an irked Jim Bob McCallum fidgeting in his chair.

"I am so sorry to keep you waiting, Jim Bob, but the people's business doesn't always adhere to planned timetables," Cletus stated. "Please join me in my office, I hope my staff kept you comfortable."

"Cletus, I ain't here to sip on fancy French roast coffee from china cups, I'm here for results," Jim Bob said without a smile as he sat in the Senator's office as Cletus closed the door behind him.

"I am prepared to make yet another sizable contribution to your Presidential campaign, but I expect results," Jim Bob stated as he reached into his suit coat pocket and pulled out his check book.

"For Christ's sake, Jim Bob, put your check book away," Cletus admonished his major campaign contributor. "I can't accept money from you in this office. Hell, I got to go sit in a small cubicle in some office building a half mile from here just to make phone calls asking for political contributions."

"Cletus, I don't give a rat's ass what hoops this ridiculous system of campaign financing makes you jump through," Jim Bob snarled in response.

"I'll have someone from my campaign staff come to your hotel suite to accept your generous contribution," Cletus offered.

"Alright, but I'm only in Washington until tomorrow morning. So, you best get someone to me quick," Jim Bob stated. "Look here Cletus old boy, I don't want to bark at you. We are friends. I want to make sure we put a true Southern Conservative back into the White House. Andrew Cochran is a turncoat. He broke his word to our cause and to the American people who voted for him. He cannot serve a second term. And well, Jedediah Wilson is a loose cannon. There ain't no predicting where that boy will end up. He ain't a practical politician that one can rely upon."

"I wholly agree, Jim Bob, which is why I am running for the Presidency," Cletus responded.

"Yeah, about that, you need to step it up at the debates. You got to go for the jugular and show the American people you ain't a mealy-mouthed squish like Cochran," Jim Bob advised. "I got all sorts of connections who know a great many things. There are skeletons in Jedediah's closet. And I got information about Cochran that will make people pay attention. I can offer you all sorts of electoral assistance."

"Perhaps, we shouldn't be discussing this in my Senate office," Cletus said nervously while lowering his voice.

"That's all you need to know, Cletus. I can help you with contributions, a Super PAC, and information. But in return I need some promises that once you're President that you will right the wrongs that been done against me. I survived that sham of a trial. A well-accounted-for jury of my peers found me completely innocent of all the charges that that feckless Democratic prosecutor brought against me. Stanford Winchester was shown to be the inconsequential, doddering old drunken fool that he is. My name has been cleared. I expect that the damage that was done to my and Mabel's name by my scandalous prosecution will be righted by the next Republican President. Mabel must have the recognition she so rightfully deserves, starting with the naming of the Federal medical research center in Baton Rouge. You understand?"

"Truly, Jim Bob, this is not the time nor place for specifics," Cletus cautioned.

"All I need to know is whether you want my help, Mr. President?" Jim Bob slowly drawled with a sly grin.

"Of course, I do," Cletus responded.

"Excellent, Cletus, excellent. Let's get to work upscaling your pay grade, shall we?" Jim Bob said with a laugh as he slowly raised out of the office chair.

JUDGE'S STANFORD WINCHESTER, Whitlee Hammond, and Charles Sewell sat around a conference table in the Federal Courthouse in New Orleans. Before them were drafts of sections of their decision in the Fifth Circuit appeal matter that they had presided over in mid-July.

"The reason that I wanted us to meet together in person is to go over some of the discrepancies in the portions of our drafted opinion in the Katrina victims appeal matter," Stanford Winchester began. "We are unanimous in our decision and I think it would be helpful to go over a few of our concerns and discrepancies in coming to our decision. If we are a united front it should read as such, don't you agree?"

"Yes, of course," Charles Sewell replied. "It heartens me that we will be presenting a unanimous decision in such an important and landmark case. We all came to the same conclusion from slightly different contexts, so smoothing over our discrepancies for the final decision is an admirable and worthwhile pursuit."

"Speaking of the final decision, I'd like to deviate from our norm and read the final decision from the bench. Does anyone have any objections?" Stanford asked his colleagues.

"No, none. But is there a reason for presenting the decision from the bench?" Whitlee asked.

"Yes, a selfish reason. So, I'd be humbly honored and eternally grateful if you'd allow me license to issue our ruling from the bench of the Fifth Circuit," Stanford said glancing at both his fellow judges. "This will be my last decision rendered as Chief Judge of the Fifth Circuit. I plan to retire at the end of this year."

"But why?" Whitlee asked somewhat in shock by the announcement.

"The law has meant everything to me for most of my adult life. I have served our state and our nation the best I could from the bench. I am an old man now. And I have slowly learned over the past year or so, that there is more to life than just one's career. I'd like to spend the twilight of my life, in pursuits outside of the Courtroom. Life is too short to allow opportunities to slip by," Stanford Winchester said as he stared at Whitlee Hammond and gently smiled. Whitlee smiled in return with a knowing nod.

"By all means, Stanford, you should read the final decision from the bench," Charles confirmed. "I assume we will need an additional four or five weeks to get the final decision squared away and ready for presentation and publication."

"Yes, I think that is fair to say," Stanford added. "I was looking at the week before Thanksgiving. Somehow that seems fitting to me."

CAROLYN BARNES STOOD NEXT TO HER CANDIDATE'S SON, Robert Douglas, as he prepared to deliver a campaign speech at the University of Iowa. It was Robert's first time at public speaking, yet he looked cool and calm as he awaited his introduction.

"Are you ready for this?" Carolyn asked.

"Absolutely," Robert confidently answered.

"If there are any hecklers, just smile and stay with your speech. They are looking for confrontation, don't satisfy them by responding. It only emboldens them and others in the crowd who are there to disrupt you," Carolyn counseled. "You've got your dad's good looks, charm, and confidence, you're going to do great."

"Thanks, I'm not really very nervous. Should I be?" Robert asked.

"Nope, not at all. You're addressing a crowd of young people not all that much younger than yourself. They want to hear your story and also hear what you have to tell them about the Senator and what he plans to do for your generation. Speak from the heart, and you'll do just fine," Carolyn added.

Twenty minutes later, Robert's speech was over. He was backstage with Carolyn and his mother Katherine. Robert was grinning from ear-to-ear as he received a long and hearty ovation from the crowd.

"That was awesome!" Robert excitedly gushed. "When I mentioned that I was gay, I got a huge ovation from the crowd. Did you hear them start chanting my name? What an amazing adrenaline rush!"

"You're a natural," Carolyn enthused. "Your timing and delivery were spot on. You came across as natural and sincere. But keep in mind that this was a perfect crowd for you. Young college students who could relate to your story and who came to hear you speak because they mostly support your dad's policies."

"I had no idea that politics could be so much fun. What an incredible buzz," Robert giddily repeated.

"You did a wonderful job darling, I'm so proud of you. Your dad will be so very proud as well," Katherine told her son. "But one politician in the family is probably more than enough."

"Oh, trust me, Mom, I have no intention of leaving my job as an art gallery curator. I'm just happy to do what I can to help, Dad and his campaign. I felt that I owed him this after all of the support you guys have shown me over the last year."

Carolyn walked over to Robert and handed him her cell phone. "It's your dad, Robert," Carolyn happily announced.

"Hey Pops," Robert energetically greeted his father over the phone.

NATHAN WHITAKER SAT ALONE IN THE LIVING ROOM at his home. He flipped his cell phone over and over again in his right hand. Since his trial was over and he was a free man, he had plenty of time to spend with his thoughts. He had the freedom to do whatever he wanted with the rest of his life. The issue for that moment was what could or would he do? He had spent most of his adult life in politics working to ensure that his best friend, Andrew Cochran was a successful Governor and then President. He had very little time to enjoy the power and prestige of being White House Chief of Staff before his indictment and forced resignation. He had devoted his life to Andrew Cochran. He didn't have much experience doing anything else.

Nathan was a youthful fifty-nine years of age, he needed to begin a second act to his life. It was difficult for him to imagine what that might be. As much as he and his former wife Posy may have bickered in the past, at times, he still missed her energy and passion. Nathan was alone. A problematic state of affairs for a man who spent his life surrounded by interesting people who sought his approval and counsel. Perhaps a career as a K street lobbyist or political consultant, Nathan thought to himself. But in acquiring power and influence for his friend Andrew Cochran, Nathan had created a number of enemies. You can't rise to the pinnacle of political power without stepping on, or in his case, crushing some toes. Those enemies held grudges and would be far less inclined to help out Nathan since his dramatic fall from grace in the Cochran administration.

Since the end of his trial, Nathan intently followed the Presidential primaries on television and on the internet. He cringed as he watched his friend, the President, take volley after of volley of criticism and suffer humiliating and degrading name calling from his Republican party challengers. He fumed at what he perceived as a failed strategy by the President's campaign management. Nathan believed that the President needed to go on the offensive in his campaign. Instead, he witnessed Andrew in a defensive posture warding off the countless accusations of being a traitor to the Conservative movement, a movement that Nathan had helped cultivate and nurture leading to the President's election three years past.

Nathan continued to unconsciously flip his phone in his hand. He knew who he wanted to call.

CHAPTER 32

It was Halloween in New Orleans. For the staff at French Tips, Juleps & Jazz, it was another overflow crowd and a constant stream of money. Michael, the bartender moved swiftly from one end of the bar to the other attempting to keep up with the customers' drink orders. Chiffon LaBelle worked the room, keeping the patrons as happy as possible as they waited for any open tables or space at the bar. Meanwhile, the house band was shuffling through the Halloween prerequisites from "I Put A Spell on You", "Spooky" and "Superstition", to "Thriller." Posy Branch as well as her entire staff were attired in Halloween costumes. Posy and Chiffon were both dressed as witches, and Olivier Bellevue was bedecked as the devil. The band played a very respectable version of the Eagle's "Witchy Woman" as Posy moved effortlessly through the tight crowds on the dance floor. She turned and smiled and winked as she passed by the band on her way to the bar.

"Michael honey, we got thirsty people waiting on them drinks," Posy said to her bartender.

"Posy, I know I'm moving as quickly as I can," Michael replied with a grimace.

"I hear ya, Sugar, but this is the Big Easy. If folks can't get a drink in a timely fashion here, they will just mosey on down to the next bar," Posy added before walking back into the massive crowd in her establishment.

"Let me help you with juicing the fruit for the juleps," Olivier offered Michael as he took position behind the bar grabbing a fresh mango.

"Thanks that will help a lot," Michael said with a tired smile.

"As I told you a while ago, you and me got to stick together. Gay men gotta support one another," Olivier pronounced. "Just look at Posy and Chiffon strutting around like they're too good to be bothered helping out behind the bar. Posy is the owner, I get that to some extent. She's got to keep the crowd happy and staying put. But that tall cock in a frock, Chiffon, I don't get her role here at all. Well, other than being Posy's right-hand man or woman or whatever you wanna call it. Meanwhile, you get treated damn poorly and Chiffon ain't expected to do nary a thing to help out," Olivier vented.

"There's some truth to that," Michael acknowledged. "When we are busy like this, Chiffon should probably help a little more with bar duties. I've got one bar-back, Joe, and he can't keep up with washing the glasses and peeling the fruit and keeping the bar top wiped down properly."

"Chiffon doesn't pull her weight when times are crazy busy, like tonight. She just takes advantage of Posy's kind heart. But when it comes to the gay men here, that heart ain't always so kind."

"Sometimes it would be nice to have a little more help, but what can you do?" Michael asked.

"We work together to get some changes made, that's what we do," Olivier quickly responded. "I'm Posy's partner, you are her trump card. She can't afford to let the best bartender in the Quarter be unhappy and walk. She may be dumb, but she ain't that stupid. Chiffon is nothing but an employee. And one that doesn't help much and thinks too highly of herself. Certainly, there are better choices."

"Chiffon is a good person. Besides, that's Posy's decision," Michael stated.

"Yeah, but we can help her decide," Olivier said as he smiled and gently rubbed the back of Michael's tense neck. The devil was at work.

BESSIE COLLINS USUALLY CLOSED HER VOODOO SHOP at 7:00 p.m. every evening, but not on Halloween. Dozens of customers stood in line waiting to have a reading done or partake in a séance with Esther Francois. Papa Levi manned the cash register as amulets and gris gris were being quickly purchased by tourists seeking the perfect Halloween souvenir from New Orleans. Business had never been better, and Bessie was the kind and charming proprietor serving her growing client base. Esther was proving to be the perfect antidote for most of Bessie's financial worries.

Bessie was becoming more and more reliant on Esther's ability to increase the business's revenue. She was more trusting in Esther and less willing to question things. Things such as the package that was addressed specifically to Esther that had arrived earlier that day. It had come directly from Haiti. When Bessie asked what was in the package, Esther brushed off the inquiry claiming it was just a few potions.

"Nothing more than some plant extracts," Esther claimed as she hurriedly moved the package from Bessie's sight.

Bessie didn't want to rock the boat or cause tension with her profitable partner. The lines of customers were out the door, and the doors would stay open well past midnight on All Hallows' Eve. Spooks, witches, and zombies stood in line waiting for a session with Esther.

It was Halloween in the Crescent City and anything could happen. Aaron Rose and Clay Grover looked at each other and laughed. They were both dressed in intricate court jester costumes that they had purchased from a costume shop on Magazine Street.

"You look like a fool. Literally!" Aaron said to Clay as he moved his head from side to side making the small bells on the colorful ends of his jester hat ring with approval. "It's been ages since I've dressed up for Halloween."

"It's fun, isn't it? And we look so gay," Clay grinned in return.

"OK, Gay Clay, let's get down to Bourbon Pub and get the party started," Aaron replied.

Twenties minutes later the guys were inside Bourbon Pub having passed through crowds of costumed revelers. Much like during Mardi Gras, body paint often substituted for a costume or any semblance of actual clothing. With vodka sodas in hand, Aaron and Clay headed up the stairs to the packed dance floor and the balconies that ringed the establishment.

"This town knows how to have a good time," Clay stated.

"Yeah, but sometimes it doesn't know when to stop," Aaron responded.

"Why does the fun have to stop?" Clay questioned his husband.

"Because, that's life. It's not a big party all the time."

"Not sure I wholly agree with your argument, Counselor," Clay stated. "Life is short, you should enjoy yourself as much as you can."

"Spoken like a true hedonist," Aaron replied.

"Nothing wrong with that," Clay said as he took Aaron by the arm and led him back inside the bar. "Let's go dance for the pure joy of life," Clay demanded. To that, Aaron was a willing accomplice.

Four hours, and eight cocktails later, it was well after 1:00 a.m., and Aaron was wilting like a week-old cut tulip.

"I'm exhausted, I'm going to head home," Aaron stated wearily to Clay.

"Do you want me to go home with you?" Clay asked.

"Aren't you tired?" Aaron inquired in response.

"Not really, I'm wide awake," Clay replied

"Then stay. Have a good time. I can get home by myself. No sense in you going home if you're not ready," Aaron stated.

"Really, you don't mind?" Clay questioned.

"Not at all, I'll see you back at the house," Aaron said as they both went down to the street. Aaron gave Clay a kiss and left to go home. Clay went back inside the gay bar OZ, on the opposite side of Bourbon Street from Bourbon Pub. The go-go dancers were bumping and grinding on the bar tops, as their thongs bulged with dollar bills as well as the primary anatomical reason for the bulging.

Around 2:30 a.m., the upstairs bathroom was the center of lascivious and public sex. Clay watched and became aroused as several men engaged in various types of sexual behavior. One of the participants gestured over to Clay to join in the sexual festivities. Clay hesitated. He was torn by his latent promiscuity and his devotion to his husband. A long night turned early morning could become much longer and later as temptation attempted to crawl into Clay's alcohol addled head. Both heads.

CHAPTER 33

Two weeks later, it was mid-November and President Andrew Cochran was prepared for the fourth Republican Party Presidential Primary debate. By most accounts, the President had failed to separate himself from his primary competitors and had in fact been seen as losing some ground to Jedediah Wilson and Senator Cletus Sawyer. His campaign manager Landon Hamilton and some political consultants had advised the President to embrace the far-right orthodoxy of the Conservative base during the first three debates. That move to the Conservative right after three years of pursuing moderate values and compromised policies with the Democratic Congress would be seen as inauthentic and desperate, the President surmised. Andrew Cochran preferred to verbally pivot to a more populist and centrist rhetoric in order to claim the moderates within his party ranks, who were dissatisfied with the "all or nothing" approach of the vitriolic base of the party. The question was whether one could win without the base support of the party in a primary. President Andrew Cochran was about to put that theory to a test.

Unbeknownst to Landon or any other member of the President's campaign strategy team, Andrew Cochran decided on a change in his debate strategy with a move to more populist issues after a two-hour phone conversation with his former Chief of Staff, Nathan Whitaker. The call had taken place a couple of weeks earlier. What had started as a casual chat between old friends had taken on all of the characteristics of a lengthy political strategy consult. Nathan who had seen his friend fail in the prior debates, suggested a drastic change in course. Instead of offering yet another serving of base pandering rhetoric, Nathan suggested that the President eschew the Republican bases want of war with the Democrats in Congress in favor of a more conciliatory compromise with the Democrats to benefit the whole of American society. Moderation instead of dogmatic intransigence. Clearly, the President would be the only Republican in the primaries willing to express that point of view. It was a bold move, a drastic change of course. Instead of just defending his moderate policies, Andrew Cochran used his past compromise agenda to attack his opponents with the positive results. Americans had seen the economy improving with recent Congressional bills signed by the President. Even many Republicans noticed that compromise was not an evil plot resulting in destruction. It was an inspired and aggressive strategy that Nathan and Andrew contemplated and executed together. And, it worked.

The polling that took place immediately following the debate indicated that the President's more centrist and less strident view of politics appealed to the voters watching the debate. Andrew Cochran came across as something his rivals could not remotely duplicate. He looked and sounded "Presidential." The new Andrew Cochran led in the debate, instead of being yet another of a long line of unchanging voices in the Republican base echo chamber. He promised a continuation of his moderate policy positions over the last three years instead of the wholesale repudiation of those policies as championed by the Sawyer's and Wilson's of his party. Two hours after the conclusion of the debate, the story line as told by the television political punditry and social media was of the "Resurrection of the Cochran Presidency." The conclusive winner of the debate, the President's re-election trajectory was now headed in a positive direction. Once again, after three years of political banishment, Nathan Whitaker, at least informally, had the President's ear. And most certainly, his confidence as well.

Later that night, Landon Hamilton stared into the bathroom mirror in his hotel room. He understood what had happened, and that understanding hit him like a ton of bricks. The President, his candidate, had eschewed his advice and that of the other campaign advisors and had launched a brand new tactic. An aggressive attack defending moderation and compromise instead of the defensive posture and small gestures to the rabid base of the party who were looking for the appeasement that Landon had counseled. Landon knew that Andrew Cochran hadn't decided this change in his debate performance by himself. He correctly assumed the inspiration behind this new campaign strategy. And, more importantly, Landon knew that his days as the Presidential campaign manager were most likely numbered.

FOUR NIGHTS LATER, THE DEMOCRATIC NOMINEES for President were involved in their third debate of the primary season. The political polling had Senator Hellen Raymond about five points ahead of Senator Perry Douglas and fifteen points ahead of Governor Keith Stolts. After less than stellar performances in the first two debates, the Douglas for President campaign needed a game changer. The Iowa Caucus was a little over two months away. Buoyed by having his son, Robert, on the campaign trail with him, Perry Douglas felt reenergized and focused. Carolyn Barnes also saw a new vitality and fighting spirit in her candidate. The lethargy of the summer's campaign had slowly ramped up into an enlivened late fall election quest.

The smartphone screen held securely in the hand of Carolyn Barnes lit up like the night sky on the Fourth of July. A myriad of congratulatory emails, text messages and tweets flooded her inbox immediately following the debate's closing statements by each of the candidates. It had clearly been Perry Douglas' night and the elite circles of the Washington political milieu were acknowledging that very fact. Perry Douglas had spoken at length about his son during his closing statements. He promised that he would do his best to emulate what Abraham Lincoln did to end slavery in his efforts to once and for all end legalized discrimination against the LGBT community. When he announced that he was a proud PFLAG father, the youthful capacity college crowd at the University of New Hampshire erupted into sustained applause and loud cheers. The Douglas campaign now had a raison d'être to define it apart from its competitors. And Robert Douglas could not have been more proud of his father.

Katherine Douglas wrapped her arms around her husband's shoulders as he exited from the debate stage. She gave him a happily-received kiss on his lips.

"You were masterful tonight. On top of your game. Demonstrating to the American people what they would be getting with a President Douglas. And from the sustained applause in the auditorium and everyone's cellphones exploding with congratulations, it sounds like the message resonated."

"I can't lie to you, it took me a while to establish my step and find my voice in this campaign. But I think we can put that in the past now. We have a reason and purpose to our campaign that separates us from the other candidates. Now, let's go win this thing," Perry challenged.

"Absolutely."

Stanford Winchester stood stoically in his chambers while his secretary Naomi Cutler adjusted the collar of the judge's black robe so that it did not obscure his brilliant red and white striped bow tie. She then carefully picked some stray lint off of the judge's freshly laundered judicial garment.

"Thank you, Naomi, but I ain't being buried. Not quite yet," Stanford chuckled to his longtime assistant.

"No, you surely aren't. It will be many more years before that sad day. Good Lord, I pray not to see it. But this is the last decision that you will preside over in your long and illustrious career. There is a packed-to-the-gills courtroom out there, folks and media all up over themselves. So, what kind of secretary would folks think you have if I allowed you to go out there on this special day with your lovely bow tie hiding under your robe and lint stuck all over your robe?" Naomi challenged her boss.

"Point taken," Justice Winchester said as he spread his arms away from his body so that Naomi could arrange his shirt cuffs and smooth out the smallest of wrinkles on his robe. A slight sad smile crept across his lips as he realized that he would no longer have this wonderful woman, secretary, advisor, confidant, and friend taking care of his every need and ensuring he looked his best taking his seat on the appellate court bench that he so loved and revered.

Stanford stood with his fellow jurists, Whitlee Hammond and Charles Sewell, as they waited inside of the door leading to the Fifth Circuit Appellate Courtroom. They stood in anticipation of hearing the courtroom bailiff call the Court to order. Once the door opened, Stanford Winchester followed his colleagues to the bench taking his accustomed seat in the middle. He glanced around the courtroom taking it all in.

After greeting the courtroom participants and guests, Stanford Winchester took a sip of water, cleared his voice, and began to read the decision rendered by the Appellate panel. Stanford read the case summary, the facts and procedural history, and then the discussion of the decision and the legal precedent cited in support of the conclusions that the panel had reached. And then finally, Stanford spoke the words that everyone in the courtroom had waited months to hear, "Judgment affirmed. Judge Whitlee Hammond and Judge Charles Sewell concur."

The courtroom exploded with loud banter and cheers. The district court decision had been upheld. The Katrina victims reward would stand and the plaintiffs would receive their hard-fought monetary restitution for their suffering and loss. The Federal government agencies had been found to be negligent in their response to the crisis in New Orleans. Justice Winchester understood the enormity of the situation. He allowed the gallery to celebrate for an extended period of time. Once the courtroom began to settle down, Stanford gaveled the proceedings back to order.

"It has been my great honor to serve as Chief Judge of the United States Court of Appeals for the Fifth Circuit. I have known no greater challenge and no greater joy than to serve the American people from my seat on this bench. I have been truly blessed. However, my time has come to step down. I will be retiring from the bench at the end of this year. I humbly thank my fellow jurists for the opportunity to be a small part of a revered judicial body. May God bless each and every one of you and may God bless these United States of America."

The participants and spectators in the Court stood and gave a rousing ovation to Justice Winchester, who politely nodded his head and smiled. Stanford and his two fellow jurists stood and exited the Courtroom. As soon as they were out of public sight, Whitlee wrapped her arms around Stanford's shoulders and began to gently sob.

"Oh, this is far from the end, my dear," Stanford whispered to comfort her. "This is only the beginning."

CHIFFON LABELLE SAT IN THE BACK of the crowded courtroom and wept tears of joy. Caleb Butler rocked his client gently in his arms as she became overwhelmed by the circumstances. It had been over a decade since she had lost her lover, her dog, her house, and most of her worldly possessions to the devastating waters of Hurricane Katrina and the subsequent levee break. A lot of suffering, regret, and loss had consumed Chiffon over the years. She had shed many tears of confusion, blame, and anger. It was so much different to be awash in tears of happiness and joy. Her long legal battle was justified. She would be receiving her due restitution and respect.

ONE HOUR LATER THE BAND AT FRENCH TIPS, Juleps & Jazz was playing a funky version of Kool & The Gangs song, "Celebration." Aaron

Rose and Chiffon LaBelle shook their groove thing as the party had just begun. At a table in the back of the large room, Caleb Butler could only shake his head and smile as he spoke to his associates Clay Grover and Emily DuBois.

"I'm not surprised that Judge Sewell was on our side, but the fact that two Republican judges including the staunchly conservative Stanford Winchester would basically side with Katrina victims against the Republican administrations on both the state and federal levels, I have to admit does shock me a bit," Caleb stated between sips of his mango julep.

"You see, that's the problem, right there," Emily challenged Caleb's assessment. "Y'all want to pigeonhole Justice Winchester as this inflexible firebrand Conservative who only sees things through an ideological prism. That couldn't be farther from the truth. I clerked for him for two years. We had many conversations about how he interprets the law. He told me countless times, 'Emily follow the facts. Trust in the Constitution. If they take you down what many might deem as a progressive road so be it,'" Emily stated. "Justice Winchester demanded a fair interpretation of the law over loyalty to his party's political positions. He often railed against what he saw as moneyed establishment Republican ideologues usurping the Tea Party and its followers to vote in elections against their own personal interests."

"Three years ago, I would have said that you were naive and not viewing the world realistically," Clay responded. "That your affection and loyalty for Justice Winchester was coloring your perception. Now, I'm not so sure. I do believe that the preponderance of facts were on our side, yet, I wouldn't have been completely shocked if the panel would have ruled in favor of the appellants. The decision was very well written and compelling."

"It was mostly Justice Winchester's hand that was involved in writing that decision," Emily confirmed. "I know his style and verbiage, and I'd say a good 75 percent of that decision was written by Justice Winchester."

Moments later, Aaron and Chiffon rejoined the group at their table. A smiling Chiffon fanned herself after working up a good sweat on the dance floor.

"That boy can dance," Chiffon stated loudly to Clay while gesturing in Aaron's direction. "The way that boy can move on the dance floor, moving them hips and shaking what his mama gave him, you must be one happy man, Clay Grover."

"True dat, Sister Chiffon. Now you is hard preachin' on a Sunday morning," Clay confirmed with a hearty laugh.

"Do you think the appellants will file an *en banc* motion for hearing before the entire Circuit or file a writ of certiorari and petition the Supreme Court?" Aaron asked Caleb while blushing and attempting to quickly change the topic.

"I don't think so. They seemed to be resigned with the outcome, and especially after it was a unanimous decision. We'll know for certain in sixty days, but for all intents and purposes, it's over," Caleb replied. "I'd think that Chiffon should receive her damages award in January or so."

"That surely does sound good to me," Chiffon said with a smile. "But honestly, and, Caleb you know this better than anyone, you was with me from the jump. The money is nice, but all I really wanted was an acknowledgement that my government had turned its back and dragged its feet instead of coming quick to help me and all the folks of the Ninth ward. If it was the wealthy parts of Miami instead, FEMA and all them would have been there moving heaven and earth to help in a few hours instead of days and weeks. We was treated like a third world country. In some cases, worse. I've been waiting for ten years for an apology. For someone in the government to acknowledge that we was wronged, that we was mistreated. Today, I got my acknowledgment. It can't bring back the dead or lessen the suffering. But it surely makes me proud to be an American again."

"Me too, Chiffon," Caleb added. "Me too."

CHAPTER 34

IT WAS THE WEDNESDAY BEFORE THANKSGIVING and Aaron Rose and Clay Grover stood at the curb at O'Hare Airport in Chicago looking for a silver Lexus SUV.

"He knows we're at the arrivals level, right?" Clay asked Aaron, as they waited to be picked up by Aaron's father at the airport.

"Duh!" Aaron replied with a sneer. "My father's not an idiot. He knows where we are. But traffic is backed up to the Kennedy expressway. We're not the only one's flying on the day before Thanksgiving."

"So, tell me again, where are we going on Saturday afternoon?" Clay asked.

"It's a large sports bar in Lincoln Park called Joe's. It's a fundraiser for Senator Douglas' Presidential campaign. The Senator will be giving a short speech. There's a couple of bands that will be performing. Plus, some of my old buddies on his staff will be there. I'm excited to see everyone again. It should be fun," Aaron gleefully replied.

"Will Brett and Carol be there?" Clay asked.

"Yup."

"Excellent, they're good people. I knew them before I knew you," Clay stated.

"Been with the Senator for over ten years now," Aaron replied. "I think his son Robert will be there as well. I haven't seen him in years, but I understand that he's been a real help on the campaign trail. Especially talking to college crowds and courting the LGBTQ vote."

"Nice. I look forward to chatting him up," Clay responded.

"There he is, there's my dad's SUV!" Aaron exclaimed while grabbing his suitcase and waving wildly.

"Thank God."

STANFORD WINCHESTER STOOD IN THE KITCHEN of Whitlee Hammond's lovely home in the Garden District as he watched her prepare a delicious Thanksgiving dinner for two.

"Are you sure there's nothing that I can help with?" Stanford asked as Whitlee took a vegetable casserole dish out of the oven.

"Well, you can open that bottle of pinot noir that you kindly brought and let it breathe a bit," Whitlee replied with a sweet smile.

"Truly, Whitlee, you shouldn't have gone through all of this trouble for the likes of me," Stanford faintly protested.

"Nonsense. I've owed you a dinner for months now, and you absolutely refuse to allow me to pay for anything when we are out in public. The only way that I could repay my debt was by making you dinner myself. And even at that, you brought two amazing bottles of wine that cost far more than all the ingredients for a Thanksgiving dinner. Besides, I love to cook, and I don't get much opportunity to do it up right. Living alone, I tend to eat more takeout or make a simple chicken breast and some vegetables than prepare a four-course meal from scratch. This has been great fun for me," Whitlee responded.

"It certainly smells delicious, though I am having a wonderful time just standing in a kitchen and chatting with a lovely woman," Stanford stated sincerely.

"Are you having any second thoughts about stepping down from the bench at the end of the year?" Whitlee asked while basting the turkey.

"Nope, none," Stanford bluntly replied. "I have to admit that in the past, being on the Court has been a lifesaver for me. After LeeAnn died, if I didn't have my work to focus on, I would have slipped into such a deep dark depression, I'm not sure I would have ever gotten out of it. And, almost three years ago after the debacle that became my nomination to the Supreme Court, if I didn't have the Fifth Circuit to return to I would have been lost. Then a year after that fiasco you were appointed to the Fifth Circuit bench and everything changed for me. You brought a new energy and positivity into my life. I feel younger and more invigorated today than I have for decades. Of course, I will miss the law. But there is more to life than one's career. And, I have had a long and satisfying career on the bench. Sometimes, you just need a change in your life. I'm happy for a change."

"Good, I'm glad to hear it," Whitlee replied. "Any ideas about what you want to do with the second chapter of your life?"

"Much more like a short epilogue than a second chapter," Stanford mused. "I've got a few ideas, yes. I've looked into teaching a couple of classes at Tulane Law School during their winter semester. I'm also going to see if I have the discipline to write a book. After decades of dealing with facts and rules, I'd like to try my hand at fiction. Make some things up from whole cloth. You know, one of those courtroom dramas or such that has no connection to the real practice of law."

"That sounds wonderful. I'm sure you'd do very well at both. You have so much to offer new law students. They could learn a lot from such a distinguished jurist," Whitlee stated.

Moments later, Whitlee opened the oven door and leaned over as she began to remove the turkey from the oven.

"Allow me to help with that, it's heavy," Stanford offered as he took the oven mitts from Whitlee and lifted the turkey and roasting pan from the oven rack. "If I was a younger man, I'd look into a civil rights practice like the one my former clerk Emily has joined with Caleb Butler. Serving the people who need representation without the overwhelming drive for nothing more than partner profits at a large law firm. Don't get me wrong, I've done very well in my life. I was fortunate enough to be born into a family of means. I never wanted for anything. But I also didn't spend my entire life in the myopic pursuit of the almighty dollar. My actions were not wholly driven by the desire to accumulate more wealth and buy more things. It is a true shame that some practicing law these days look more towards the salary involved instead of the pure love of the law."

"Perhaps, you can impart that knowledge to the eager young minds at Tulane Law," Whitlee stated.

"Yes, I look forward to that," Stanford agreed.

"But for now, dinner is ready. Would you like to carve the turkey?"

"Oh, my yes, indeed. What a great honor," Stanford said with a very satisfied smile.

Nathan Whitaker scrolled down his contacts list on his smartphone. The phone rang repeatedly before going into voice mail. Nathan quickly decided that he would leave a voice mail message.

"Good afternoon Mr. President, this is Nathan Whitaker. I just wanted to call and wish you, the First Lady, and your entire family a very

Happy Thanksgiving. May God bless you and your family with happiness and joy on this splendid day. Also, I just wanted to tell you that I thought your performance at the last Presidential debate was masterful. It was a true joy to watch. I wish you continued success, sir, and hope to be able to talk again soon in the near future. Once again, Happy Thanksgiving, Mr. President."

With that Nathan ended his call. He smiled briefly. But, it was more of a sad, discontented grimace than an actual smile of happiness. Nathan's life had changed so drastically over the past three years. He had gone from a position of ultimate power and prestige to a rather directionless state of mere existence. He used to spend hours each day in the company of his best friend, who was the most powerful man in the world. Now, his contact with his lifelong companion was limited to very infrequent phone calls. Nathan not only felt lost but also a great loss. For more than forty years, Andrew Cochran was the center of his world. Now, Nathan existed only in a very far-off galaxy.

Nathan went back to his living room with his solitary plate of takeout turkey and gravy. He watched the Dallas Cowboys Thanksgiving Day football game, alone.

IT WAS THE SATURDAY AFTER THANKSGIVING and Clay was surveying the buffet table at the Douglas for President fund raising event at Joe's Bar in Chicago.

"I always know where to look for you at a crowded event," Aaron Rose said to Clay while he put his arm around his husband's shoulder. "Are you having a good time?"

"Yeah, I was just dancing with Carol to the Dave Matthews cover band. We were 'tripping billies.' It's so great to see her again," Clay replied. "How about you?"

"Yes, it is nice to see some of the staff members I spent so much time with, and of course, I had a nice conversation with the Senator. Have you talked to him yet? He was asking about you," Aaron said.

"No. He's so busy shaking hands and talking with dignitaries and campaign contributors that I didn't want to disturb him," Clay answered.

"You should seek him out before he leaves. He specifically told me that he wanted to speak with you," Aaron stated.

"Me?" Clay asked a bit shocked. "He wants to talk with me?"

"Probably just wants to make sure that you're treating me well. He kind of sees me as a second son," Aaron boasted. "I think he's leaving soon. Carolyn told me they have another event this evening. You should seek him out. I'm gonna go hang out with his son Robert for a while."

"Senator Douglas, it's a pleasure to see you again, sir," Clay said as he shook hands with Perry Douglas. "This is a wonderful event."

"Clay, I'm so very pleased that you and Aaron could make it. I haven't seen either of you since your wedding day a year ago September."

"Yes sir, and thank you so much for the generous gift. I watched the last debate, you were great. A good deal of your civil rights advocacy reminded me of Senator Fitzsimmons," Clay said with a smile.

"Well, there's a good reason for that, Clay. Let's be generous and just say that I 'borrowed' a good deal of that rhetoric from Henry. He was the master, I was merely his willing pupil. I've got to tell you, Clay, there is not a day that goes by when I don't think about Henry. I miss him so," Perry said with a wistful smile.

"I do as well, Senator," Clay replied.

"And that is why I wanted to talk with you," Perry Douglas said as he drew closer to Clay. "Look, I'm going to be frank. We are still two months away from the first primary vote being cast. Most polls have me trailing Hellen Raymond. So, what I'm about to say can certainly be categorized as putting the cart before the horse. But, please hear me out. I spent years watching you take charge of Henry's office and staff. With you in charge everything functioned like clockwork. Henry held you in such high esteem, and rightfully so. As do I. You understood how to make things work in Washington, not an easy task. Henry trusted you completely, which is vital in the snake pit in which at times we need to function. You were supremely loyal and highly competent in your role as Henry's Chief of Staff. Which is why I'd like you to at least give some thought about working for me as my White House Chief of Staff, if I am lucky enough to persuade the American people into making me their next President."

Clay stood in stunned silence. He had only had a couple of beers that afternoon, yet he was quite sure that he must have been drunk. He wasn't sure what to say.

"I know this must have come out of left field from your facial expression," Perry kidded Clay.

"Senator, I'm not sure what ballpark I'm in or what sport I'm playing," Clay responded with a blank expression.

"I just wanted to put that out there for you to think about. Clearly, I don't need an answer anytime soon. Heck, I could be back home licking my wounds before the South Carolina primary. But, please consider it. I'm only asking because I am absolutely certain that you would be my best choice. I can never be the man Henry Fitzsimmons was. So, it would be my honor to have his Chief of Staff aiding me at the White House," Perry sincerely stated as he took hold of Clay's shoulder.

"Senator Douglas, you do me a great honor, sir. I am humbled that you would ask me," Clay answered, still a bit unnerved by the unexpected event.

"Just think about it Clay. We'll touch base in a couple of months and see where we are in the polls and our standing in the primaries. Until that time, let's keep this just between you and me, ok?" Perry asked.

"Yes sir, of course, Senator," Clay responded.

"Good, very good. It was great seeing you and Aaron again. I see Carolyn waving me over. It must be time to move on to the next rubber chicken dinner. I must go. Take care. We'll talk again soon," Perry said as he shook Clay's hand and walked towards the door of the bar.

A few minutes later, Aaron spotted Clay standing alone motionless at the side of the cavernous room.

"There you are," Aaron greeted Clay as he approached him smiling. "I saw that the Senator left a couple of minutes ago. Did you have an opportunity to talk to him before he departed?"

"Oh yeah," Clay audibly sighed.

CHAPTER 35

It was the midst of the holiday season and things were bustling at French Tips, Juleps & Jazz. Posy Branch had decided to take a short weekend trip to see her mother in Savannah before Christmas. Olivier Bellevue was in charge of the establishment and Chiffon LaBelle was having none of it.

"Look here Olivier, if you think that you can boss me around just cuz Posy is gone for a couple of days, child, you got another thing coming," Chiffon barked at Olivier.

"You better understand that I'm your boss. You are nothing but a hired employee. I don't care what kind of money you're coming into with your lawsuit, you will never be a partner in this business," Olivier ranted in return.

"Well, we'll see what Posy has to say about that. This is her place not yours. She come up with the idea. She put her money and energy into it. She drove you and your nasty little nail salon out of business. She done all this. You was just lucky enough to be in the right place at the right time when Chantale needed to go home to be with her mama. Posy hired me and she the only one who can fire me," Chiffon huffed.

"When I tell you to do something, you'll do it," Olivier demanded.

"I'm gonna do my job, like I been doing for over a year now. Ain't no one complaining about what I been doing but you. And Honey, you ain't shit in my book," Chiffon fired back.

"No Girlfriend, you're wrong. Michael complains about how you don't pitch in when times are busy. Ain't that right, Michael? Olivier asked while turning towards Michael who was busying himself behind the bar.

"Leave me out of this," Michael quickly responded as he turned away from the ongoing fray.

"He does say it, he just doesn't want to hurt your feelings," Olivier added.

"I'm a gonna do my job, you do whatever it is that you do," Chiffon stated. "But I'm telling you straight up, stay outta my face, Olivier. You ain't the boss of me."

Twenty minutes later, Chiffon was in the back office while Olivier continued chatting with Michael.

"Posy is an idiot," Olivier pronounced. "Before I became her partner, I use to think that she was a smart and talented businesswoman. She came to the Big Easy and turned Chantale's failing nail salon into an immensely popular money-making venture. But once you get to know her, it's clear she's just another blonde bimbo who spread her legs for the right man and got lucky."

"I really don't want to talk about this," Michael nervously responded.

"We've got an opportunity here," Olivier stated. "It'll be like taking candy from a baby. Posy's too stupid to know what's going on. We just need to get rid of that big offensive she-man Chiffon. We can run this place Michael and make lots of money together. You and me. Just think about it."

PRESIDENT COCHRAN EXITED THE BACK OF THE WHITE HOUSE as he walked with his Secret Service detail towards the readied helicopter to take him to Baltimore for an economic conference.

"Pete, where's Billy James? Is he on vacation or ill? I haven't seen him in the last week or so," Andrew Cochran asked of one of the Secret Service agents assigned to protect the President.

"I'm sorry Mr. President, I thought you knew," Pete replied.

"Knew what, Pete? Is Billy alright? Did something happen to him?" The President questioned with a look of concern on his face.

"I assume that he's alright, sir," Pete answered. "Billy James suddenly and unexpectedly resigned from the agency about two weeks ago."

"Why? Was it for family or medical reasons?"

"I'm not sure, Mr. President. My understanding is that Billy received a very lucrative job position as Vice President of Personnel and Security for a large private corporation in the South. Billy is from Mississippi, so he'd be closer to his family home," Pete replied.

"Do you know the name of the corporation?"

"No sir, I do not," Pete responded.

"I'm sorry that I didn't get a chance to say goodbye and thank Billy for his service. He had been with me since my inauguration day. Please do me a favor, Pete, and find out what company Billy went to. I'd like to pen him a thank you note and send it to him," Andrew Cochran requested.

"Of course, Mr. President. I'll make sure that I get that information to you as soon as possible."

"Thanks Pete. We better get going. My guess is that they're not going to start this meeting without me."

As soon as the President's helicopter, Marine One, touched down in Baltimore, Pete had the information that the President had requested.

"Mr. President, I have the name of the company where Billy James is now employed. It's on this sheet of paper and I've made sure that it has been conveyed to your secretary Nancy, sir," Pete stated as he handed the President the folded paper.

"Thanks much, Pete," Andrew Cochran replied with a smile as he unfolded the paper and stared at the information in disbelief.

"William R. James, Vice President of Personnel and Global Security, Lake Pontchartrain Brands, Inc., Baton Rouge, Louisiana."

IT WAS TWO DAYS UNTIL THE FINAL Democratic Party Presidential Primary debate before the end of the calendar year. It would also be the candidates' last chance to appeal to the caucus voters prior to Election Day for the Iowa Caucus. Carolyn Barnes approached her candidate as he sat at the back of the campaign bus preparing his closing remarks for the debate.

"What's up, Sunshine?" Perry Douglas greeted his campaign manager.

"Why, you're in an especially good mood," Carolyn replied.

"I'm energized, Carolyn. I've hit my stride. We're closing the gap on Helen Raymond. I'm just two points down according to the *Des Moines Register's* latest polling," Perry enthused.

"Perry, I didn't want to say anything until after the debate, but our security detail insisted that I talk to you immediately," Carolyn stated in a very serious tone. "It has to do with Robert out on the campaign trail."

"Oh, dear God, what is it?" Perry questioned with great concern.

"As you know, this afternoon Robert was making a campaign speech at the student union at the University of South Carolina in Columbia. It was a good-sized crowd and he was very well received," Carolyn explained. "After he completed his speech, Robert took a few questions from the audience and indulged in friendly conversation with the students as he normally does. The topic of the South Carolina football team came up. Clearly, Robert does not follow college football."

"No, not at all. He abhors most sports. Why what happened?" Perry asked.

"You do know the name of their football team don't you?" Carolyn inquired.

"Oh no!" Perry exclaimed.

"Oh yes," Carolyn replied. "When Robert was informed by one of the students that the name of the football team was the Gamecocks, he had a little fun with it. The security detail informs me that a somewhat inebriated frat boy did not take kindly to Robert innocently poking fun at the team name."

"Yeah, I could see my son having a field day with that. What happened?" Perry questioned while shaking his head.

"According to the report that I received, the frat boy shouted something to the effect of, 'Get off the stage. You damn cock sucker!' Robert turned toward him and sweetly smiled and replied, 'Yes I am, which probably puts me in the same good company as your mother.' A few other choice words were exchanged."

"No, he didn't," Perry stated his head now buried in his hands.

"Well, the irate frat boy charged the stage screaming, 'I'm gonna kill you!' at Robert. Robert was never in any real danger. Security was able to apprehend the young man before he could get anywhere near Robert. But security takes any threat extremely seriously, which of course they should, and wanted me to alert you to this incident immediately," Carolyn related to Perry.

"I guess I'm not completely surprised. Robert has a sharp wit and can be wildly sarcastic when he wants to be. Let's pull him from any further campaign events until I have a chance to sit down and talk to him about appropriate responses to hecklers. He's doing a great job with the college crowds, but I'm not going to take any chances with my son's health and well-being. Mental or physical. Please tell me that there were no media cameras in attendance," Perry begged.

"No, just a few college newspaper correspondents covering the event, not even the local press."

"Good," Perry said as he exhaled.

"You're showing your age, Senator," Carolyn responded. "Name me one college student that doesn't have a smartphone. The whole thing was captured by several of the students who were in attendance, and the video is already trending on Twitter."

"Let me see," Perry requested. Carolyn scrolled through her smartphone and pulled up a video of the incident. Perry Douglas watched intently with a grin on his face.

"Look at that smarmy Cheshire cat grin on Robert's face as he verbally spanked that frat boy. Of course, that is totally inappropriate and we can't have that on the campaign trail. But that's my boy! He's always had a mouth on him since he was around six years old," Perry stated with just a modicum of parental pride.

CHAPTER 36

STANFORD WINCHESTER STOOD INSIDE HIS OFFICE at the Federal Court Building in New Orleans. He took some of his personal effects and carefully placed them into a banker's box. Every photograph or certification or plaque honoring an aspect of his service over his many years on the bench all had certain memories attached to the items.

"Justice Winchester, what do you think you're doing?" Naomi Cutler asked with a touch of pique in her voice. "Did I not say that I would take care of packing up all your belongings?"

"Yes, you did, Naomi and I do appreciate it. But some things I wanted to handle myself, if you don't mind," Stanford Winchester sweetly replied.

"Course, I don't mind," Naomi responded. "But I know who you are and what you do. You start with a few things, come 2:00am you still sliding photograph frames into newspaper. They ain't no end to you once you get started."

"I guess I do do that, don't I?" Stanford asked not having thought about his work patterns before.

"What's so precious that you want to pack it yourself?" Naomi inquired.

"Well, one is a photograph of me and LeeAnn sitting up on the appellate bench the day I was made Chief Judge of the Circuit. The other is a photograph of me and you taken the first day you came to work for me. Look at that smiling young face of yours. I look as old and withered as I do now," Stanford said with a gentle smile.

"Stop now! You ain't aged a day. You are as distinguished looking as ever. A fine-looking mature gentleman," Naomi protested.

"Oh, how I am going to miss your little white lies that you tell to make me feel better," Stanford stated. "I am going to miss that cheerful smile every morning and . . ." Stanford stopped as he began to choke up with emotion. Naomi looked at her boss, her dear friend, with tears rolling down his cheeks. There was no levee strong enough to contain the torrent of her tears as she moved into Stanford's strong squeezing embrace and began to sob. They both cried together in a long intense hug. Moments later, Stanford ended their embrace and handed a clean folded handkerchief to Naomi.

"I'm sorry I didn't mean to get all teary on you Justice Winchester," Naomi apologized as she took the handkerchief from Stanford.

"First off," Stanford began. "Never apologize for showing your emotions. I could not seek a greater indicator of our shared love and respect for each other, so thank you for sharing that with me. Secondly, in 13 days, at the stroke of midnight on December 31st, I will no longer be a judge. I will be just another retiree. I insist that my friends call me by my Christian name. So, starting right now, may I ask my dear friend Naomi Cutler to stop calling me Justice Winchester?"

"Yes, you may Stanford, you most certainly may," Naomi stated with a grin as she wiped away her last tears.

Several minutes later, Whitlee Hammond showed up in Stanford Winchester's office doorway.

"Got a minute?" Whitlee cheerfully asked Stanford.

"Yes, of course," Stanford said clearly and distinctly.

"I just wanted to let you know that I am going home to Austin over Christmas to see my family. I was wondering if you had plans over Christmas, and if you'd like to come along?" Whitlee asked.

"Oh, Whitlee, that is a lovely gesture, thank you. I routinely go to my brother Malcolm's house and spend time with his family. It's truly one of a very few times during the year that I get to see them," Stanford responded.

"Of course, Christmas should be spent with family. I fully understand," Whitlee replied.

"However, if you are back before New Year's Eve, I would be delighted if you would be my guest for dinner on New Year's Eve?" Stanford asked.

"I'll be returning to New Orleans on December 29th, so yes, I'd love to join you for dinner on New Year's Eve," Whitlee beamed.

"Excellent, then it's a date," Stanford stated with a contented smile.

CHIFFON LABELLE AND POSY BRANCH busily placed small floral arrangements on the tables that had been reserved for Caleb Butler's party. Caleb was throwing a Christmas party at French Tips, Juleps & Jazz, for his twenty-five Katrina victim clients and his legal staff.

"The place looks right pretty," Chiffon said as she placed the last arrangement on a table and surveyed the holiday decorations adorning the large establishment.

"It does look nice," Posy agreed.

"As nice as we may make the place look, we still got that cancer, Olivier, inside us," Chiffon softly muttered.

"I know. But nothing is forever," Posy responded.

"Posy, the nail gals been saying Olivier been bad mouthing you for a while now. Saying how dumb you is, and how unfair you been treating everyone," Chiffon confided to her boss and her friend.

"Ain't nothing but words," Posy replied. "Folks ain't stupid they know what he's doing. I know what he is doing."

"How long you gonna let him get away with this?" Chiffon asked.

"Long as I have to," Posy answered. "You still doing what we talked about?"

"I surely am, and you was right all along," Chiffon stated.

"Keep doing what you doing, girl. When the time is right . . ." Posy whispered.

CALEB BUTLER HELD A JULEP GLASS high in the air as he toasted his clients for their perseverance and dedication during the long ordeal that was the Hurricane Katrina class action lawsuit. All of the work and frustration would culminate in a sizable monetary damages award for each of his clients.

"So, when do you think my girl Chiffon will see her money?" Posy asked Caleb in the midst of the raucous celebration.

"I would think around mid-January," Caleb told Posy and a very happy Chiffon.

"You have some ideas of what you're going to do with the money?" Caleb asked Chiffon.

"I'm gonna get me a mortgage on a nice small house here in the Quarter with a little backyard for a dog or two. Then I'm gonna finish up my gender change surgery. I also got a few other ideas," Chiffon replied while looking at Posy and giving her a wink of an eye.

"Well, good luck to you," Caleb said. "You've certainly earned some good things in life after all you've been through."

"Amen to that," Posy wholeheartedly agreed.

Clay Grover fidgeted in his chair as he sat next to Aaron Rose at a table in the back of French Tips.

"What's wrong honey? Aren't you having a good time?" Aaron asked his husband. "You're usually the life of the party."

"I'm fine," Clay replied.

"I'm not so sure," Aaron countered. "We've been here for over an hour, there is a wonderful buffet spread just feet from our table, yet you haven't had anything to eat."

"Just not hungry," Clay said with a shrug of his shoulders.

"Now I know something's wrong," Aaron kidded in return.

"I'm good, really. Just have a lot on my mind," Clay replied.

"Anything you care to share with your loving and concerned husband?" Aaron encouraged.

Clay hesitated as he looked around the room and observed the festivities going on around him. "C'mon, let's have some fun. Dance with me," Clay asked Aaron.

"Sure," Aaron agreed. "But was there something you wanted to tell me?"

"Just that I love you so very much," Clay said as he took Aaron by the hand and led him to the dance floor.

"I just wanted to wish you a very Merry Christmas, Nathan," President Cochran said into his phone.

"Thank you, Andy, that means so very much to me," Nathan Whitaker replied to his lifelong friend. "How are Sue Lynn and your children?"

"They're all fine. We're heading to Savanah for Christmas Eve and Christmas day. It's been so long since we celebrated the holidays in our home. It's been since right before my inauguration three years ago," Andrew Cochran lamented.

"Yes, I remember. Posy and I were there to share Christmas day with your family," Nathan added.

"How is Posy? Do you keep in touch at all?"

"Not really. Our divorce wasn't terribly amicable. But then again, neither was a goodly portion of our marriage," Nathan related. "Last I heard she was living in New Orleans and running a nail salon near the French Market. I've been told that she's doing quite well for herself."

"Well, good for her. Posy is a beautiful and interesting woman," Andrew stated.

"Oh, she was interesting to put it mildly," Nathan concurred. "We had our share of fights, and at times, Posy could make life a bit more colorful than I would have liked while I was Chief of Staff, but I'm glad she is having success in her life. At her core, Posy's a good person, with a good heart."

"Look Nathan, there is something that I thought I should tell you," Andrew Cochran stated, his tone becoming serious as he changed conversation topics.

"What's up Andy?" Nathan asked.

"Do you remember Billy James?"

"Sure, from your Secret Service detail."

"Yes, exactly. I found out not long ago that he left the Secret Service and took a lucrative position as head of personnel and security for a large private corporation," Andrew said.

"Well, you can't blame him for trading in his government experience for a better paying position in the private sector," Nathan responded.

"He's with Lake Pontchartrain Brands in Baton Rouge," Andrew bluntly said. An extended silence lingered on the other end of the phone.

"Nathan, you there?" Andrew finally asked.

"Yes, I'm here. Sorry, I was just trying to filter through the possible ramifications," Nathan finally replied. "Jim Bob McCallum is now financing a good portion of Cletus Sawyer's presidential campaign, so clearly Jim Bob thinks he can use Billy against you. What would he know that could potentially cause harm to your campaign?"

"The only thing that I can think of is the couple of times that you and I were at Camp David. The hunting trip early in my administration, and our meeting a few months ago," Andrew summarized. "Anything having to do with any policy related conversations that he may have overheard he is expressly forbidden from discussing."

"Then it's got to be about our relationship. Undoubtedly, Jim Bob and therefore, Cletus is going to attempt to make hay tying you to me. He will question your judgment and ethical standing when it comes to who you associate with," Nathan said.

"You're a free man. You were fully acquitted of all charges. There would be no substance to his claims," Andrew argued.

"Cletus and Jim Bob will not allow facts to get in the way of their effort to smear your integrity. They don't care about the truth, only the illusion that they can paint for the Republican base voters. They will attempt to portray me as a moral reprobate and excoriate you for associating with me," Nathan added.

"Well, they can bring it on. Billy saw or heard nothing other than two old friends together. Let them try to color that into something that it's not and we can beat them at their own game," Andrew defiantly stated.

"We?" Nathan hesitantly asked.

"Of course, we. You're going to help me take them down in this primary election, aren't you?" Andrew asked his friend.

"Most certainly," Nathan happily replied.

"Excellent, Nathan," Andrew said with vigor. "Oh, and there is one other thing that I wanted to talk to you about. In addition to the likes of Cletus Sawyer and Jedediah Wilson, I think I may soon have a primary challenger from inside the White House."

"Howard Fucking Mason!" Nathan responded with disgust in his voice. "I never trusted that bastard from the beginning, but we needed Ohio and fortunately he was able to narrowly deliver it for us."

"It's not a certainty yet, but all indicators are that Howard sees an opportunity here and believes that I am too weak to withstand the onslaught I'm getting from the far right of our party," Andrew conceded.

"Of course, he sees some cracks in the ship of state and is aware that you are trailing in the polls and taking on some water, so he is scurrying to jump off what he perceives to be the sinking ship, just like any self-preserving rat would," Nathan replied with venom.

"If and when things become clearer that he is headed toward challenging me for the nomination, should I just ask for his resignation?" Andrew asked his old friend and trusted advisor.

"Nope. Andy, I think that you should do the exact opposite. I would suggest going out of your way to praise the work and loyalty of the Vice-President. Make it appear to the press, at least, that you consider the Vice-President to be a good and loyal member of the administration, and that you look forward to working alongside him for another four years after your re-election. Paint the picture of a united administration willing to fight for what's best for the American people. Loyalty and trust should be your clarion call. Then, if and when he decides to announce his candidacy for the Republican Party nomination for President, he's the one who appears to be a traitor to the cause. He'll look small and self-centered. He'll look like nothing more than what he truly is a political opportunist. There are still several members of the press who support your presidency who would leap at the opportunity to write that story," Nathan stated with satisfaction.

"You might be onto something, old chum," Andrew pronounced.

"No one likes the husband who leaves the faithful and loving wife. He will, of course, paint a very different picture, yet that may just seem like self-motivated excuses and a justification for his own uncontrollable ambition instead of valid reasons for challenging his 'political partner.'"

"Shrewd, indeed. Thank you, Nathan. I'll talk to you again very soon. Oh, and of course, Merry Christmas!"

"Merry Christmas, Andy."

CHAPTER 37

The crowded main dining room at Arnaud's buzzed with excitement, conversation, and laughter. It was New Year's Eve and the customers were ready for an excellent meal and some good jazz music to bring in the New Year. Seated at Stanford Winchester's usual table were Calvin and Lucille Putnam, Stanford, Whitlee Hammond, and Bessie Collins. Bessie's husband Lucius was working as a waiter that evening, and Stanford had asked Bessie to join his group so that she could be with Lucius as the clock ticked toward a new year. A year that would be quite new and different for Stanford. At the stroke of midnight, he would officially be retired from the federal bench. For the first time in decades, he would no longer be a state or federal judge. He would be 'Citizen Winchester', and for one specific reason among others, he was relishing his new status. The jazz band played as Stanford surveyed the joyful room and then scanned his eyes around his table of invited guests. The Putnams had been New Year's Eve guests of Stanford's for many years. Lucille and his beloved wife LeeAnn were famous friends. Calvin, Stanford had known since before his days on the Louisiana Supreme Court. Adding Whitlee Hammond and Bessie Collins to the festivities made the end of one year and the beginning of the next just that much more special.

"A gracious good evening and a very Happy New Year to this distinguished table," Lucius Collins stated as he approached the table. Bessie stood up for a moment and gave her husband a hug and a kiss on the cheek.

"My word, don't you look mighty fine," Lucius said to Bessie as she rose from her seat.

Bessie was in a lovely black cocktail dress with her hair done in small intricate braids. "God done blessed me, ain't no doubt about that."

"You go on Lucius," Bessie said as she blushed deeply.

Stanford also took his turn to stand and wrap his arms around Lucius, something he seldom did in public. "Happy New Year, my dear friend," Stanford softly whispered into Lucius' ear. Lucius was a bit taken aback by the public display of affection from Stanford. He smiled in return as a small tear formed in the corner of his eye. He quickly gained his composure.

"I have never been more delighted to wait on a table in all my long years of service here at Arnaud's," Lucius sincerely professed. "May I offer this esteemed table some cocktails to begin this festive and special evening?"

"Do birds have beaks?" Stanford joked.

"Oh yes sir, they most certainly do, they most certainly do!" Lucius responded with a hearty laugh.

After cocktails and dinner, Stanford and his guests lingered over coffee, dessert, and brandy. As is his wont, Stanford danced with every woman at his table at least once. But, Stanford saved his dance at midnight for Whitlee. He took her into his arms and held her close as the couple moved gracefully around the small dance floor.

"What a lovely evening, I am so happy that you invited me to be a part of it," Whitlee cooed as she snuggled next to Stanford.

"Well, it's after midnight, you know what that means?" Stanford asked with a knowing grin.

"Of course, we are entering a New Year," Whitlee replied.

"Yes truly, and also I am no longer Chief Judge of the Fifth Circuit. So, I'd like to take this opportunity to ask if I may court you, Ms. Hammond?" Stanford asked smiling while holding his date in his arms.

"My gracious, Stanford, you didn't need to wait until now to ask me to date you," Whitlee answered with a short giggle.

"But I did. I most certainly did," Stanford replied. "You see, Whitlee, I am a willing victim to tradition, and a righteous guardian of professional and social decorum. I understand that these are lost values in today's society, yet they mean a lot to me. In good conscience I could not properly court you while we were working together at the Court and I was in a senior position. It would not have been the proper thing to do. Therefore, I waited until this moment to ask you if we may date going forward."

"Please don't tell me that you gave up your position on the bench just to date me?" Whitlee asked, almost begging for Stanford to say no.

"There were many reasons, including my own personal feeling that I had accomplished everything that I could accomplish on the bench. It was time to step down," Stanford admitted. "When you were appointed to the Court almost two years ago, things began to change for me. For over six long years I had been wallowing in self-pity over the passing of my wife LeeAnn. I never imagined that I could ever fall in love again. Then I got to know you and realized that there is more to life than just one's career. I became aware once again that happiness was attainable. That love was not just something for the young. I love you, Whitlee. I knew it from the day we first met. I want to prove to you that I am worthy of your love," Stanford whispered into Whitlee's ear as they concluded their dance. Stanford twirled Whitlee one last time before taking her back into his arms. They both smiled at each other locked in an embrace that would start the beginning of a new year. And a new love.

Jim Bob and Mabel McCallum sat together on a large sofa in their mansion located in the heart of New Orleans' Garden District. Jim Bob held his wife in his arms as they watched an old Bing Crosby musical on television on New Year's Eve. Jim Bob stroked his wife's head as she let out a contented moan. Full sentences were no longer available to Mabel. A very few words and audible contented sighs were the only forms of conversation that were left after the ravages of her disease.

"We're going to get everything worked out, Mabel," Jim Bob assured his wife. "Now that the trial is behind me and I am free to do what I like with my money and influence, we are going to right all of the wrongs perpetrated against our family. You, my love, will have a lasting tribute built in your honor. I have contacted a number of doctors in Europe who we will bring here to try another experimental therapy. I will move heaven and earth to get you better again, my dear. Those who caused us so much grief and pain will pay for their sins. God is righteous, their trespasses will not be forgiven."

Jim Bob reached over and grasped a nearby water glass. He moved it to Mabel's lips and she took a small sip. He then took a tissue and wiped her mouth as they both reclined back onto the large sofa. It was the start of a new year for the McCallums, but Jim Bob could only look fondly at the past. He was well aware of the future.

Aaron Rose and Clay Grover reclined on their couch in front of their fireplace. The television in the corner blared music from a musical guest at the televised Times Square ball drop and celebration of the New Year. They toasted each other with champagne as they snuggled together.

"You sure you don't want to go to the Quarter and be around the celebrating crowds of people?" Aaron asked. "There's still plenty of time, if you wanted to go."

"Nope, I'm content just sitting here with you. Keep it real low key," Clay replied.

"Low key is not usually your thing," Aaron responded.

"That's not entirely true. There are plenty of times that I want it to be just the two of us."

"Yeah, but not on major holidays," Aaron countered. "And that's fine. I like going out and having a good time. We're too young to act like an old married couple who has given up on being social and enjoying life."

"Very true. We still go out to dinner and to bars, dancing, drinking and acting a fool once in a while," Clay replied.

"When was the last time you acted like a fool?" Aaron teased his husband.

"You'd be surprised," Clay muttered mostly to himself.

"What was that?" Aaron questioned.

"Look, this probably is not the time or the place, but there are a couple of things that have been eating at me that I have to get off my chest or I'm going to explode," Clay asserted with a serious look etched across his handsome face.

"Ok," Aaron softly stated, a bit concerned.

"Remember on Halloween, you went home early and I stayed out. Well, I was drunk. That was a fact. Also, I had smoked some weed a guy offered me on the balcony of Oz. When I went to the bathroom, there were a number of guys involved in various sex acts. I watched for a while. I was aroused, I can't deny it. One cute guy waved me over to join in. I didn't. Aaron, I swear it. I didn't do anything, but deep down I really wanted to. What kind of a husband does that make me?" Clay asked while staring into Aaron's beautiful green eyes.

"A human one," Aaron matter-of-factly responded. "We all get tempted from time to time. It's only natural. The real test is how you respond to the temptation not that you were tempted. If it was me, I probably would have stood there and watched for a while as well. We've got a stack of porn DVDs in a box under the bed because it's fun and arousing to watch other people have sex. Honey, that's nothing to be ashamed of."

"And the fact that I wanted to join in doesn't bother you?"

"Well, maybe just a little, but the fact of the matter is that you didn't. That's what matters. You cared enough about me and our relationship not to indulge in promiscuous sex. I know you Clay, I know how you were before we got married. The fact that you didn't participate only indicates how far you've come and how much our marriage must mean to you," Aaron replied as he took Clay's hand into his. "Now what's the other thing you said you needed to get off your chest?"

"I'm violating a trust by telling you this one, but I feel horrible not sharing it with you," Clay began. "It was right after Thanksgiving when we were still in Chicago."

"My, you're covering all of the holidays," Aaron kiddingly smirked.

"It was at Senator Douglas' campaign fund raiser. I had a conversation with the Senator after you told me that he wanted to speak to me. Well, he asked me if I would at least consider being his White House Chief of Staff if he wins the Presidency."

"What?" Aaron nearly shouted in utter shock. "What?" He repeated.

"Aaron, I had no clue. It came as a complete surprise to me. The Senator mentioned that he used to watch me operate as Senator Fitzsimmons' Chief of Staff, and how he admired how I kept the Senator's office in order and running well. He was very complimentary."

"What did you say?" Aaron challenged.

"What could I say? I told him that I would give it some thought. I didn't outwardly reject the offer nor did I express any great interest," Clay replied. "Senator Douglas did ask me to keep this between me and him for the time being, but I have been feeling so guilty not sharing this with you."

"Wow! That is truly amazing," Aaron said shaking his head.

"I can't tell if you're pissed off or happy," Clay said trying to read Aaron's emotions.

"Why would I be pissed off?" Aaron asked completely perplexed. "One of a handful of people in this country who has a chance to be the next President of the United States asked my husband to consider being one of the most powerful and important men in the world, and I wouldn't be thrilled? Are you fucking kidding me? That's great news!" Aaron enthused as he wrapped his arms around Clay. "Why would you think that I wouldn't be filled with joy over the news?"

"I don't know. I mean, you worked for him all of those years as one of his top aides. Perhaps you might be a little jealous," Clay answered.

"I wasn't his Chief of Staff. I don't know the first thing about being a Chief of Staff. You do. And you did it exceedingly well for years for one of the most revered and powerful Senators in Congress."

"I also didn't know how you would feel about going back to Washington," Clay added.

"I love it here. I love the work we do. I love our clients. I love Caleb and Emily and everyone else at the office. I love our little slightly slanted bright yellow shotgun house. But an opportunity like this? People dream and fight for a possibility like this. Have you given it much thought?" Aaron asked.

"Of course, almost daily. But a single vote has not been cast yet. Why get my hopes up for something that is so uncertain?" Clay responded.

"Because it's so freakin' awesome!" Aaron shouted with glee. "I'm going to get another bottle of champagne. We got some celebrating to do," Aaron exclaimed. And then as Aaron turned back from entering the kitchen and looked at Clay, he added with a devilish grin, "Oh, and you better be prepared to do more than just being a sexual spectator tonight."

"No worries," Clay responded with a huge smile.

CHAPTER 38

IT WAS THE MIDDLE OF JANUARY. It was gray and chilly in New Orleans. It was cold and blustery in Washington. And a layer of newly fallen snow blanketed the bustling streets of Chicago. Senator Perry Douglas and his campaign manager Carolyn Barnes walked north bound down Dearborn Street, from the Kluczynski Federal building, where the Senator's Chicago office was located, towards his campaign headquarters on East Randolph Street. An aide and a couple of Secret Service agents trailed slightly behind them.

"The first new snow of the New Year is lovely in Chicago, don't you think?" Carolyn asked her candidate.

"Yes, it is. For the first few hours until the downtown traffic and pollution turns it crusty and gray," Perry replied.

"Spoken like a true realist," Carolyn stated.

"Speaking of reality, how are the latest Iowa polling numbers?" Perry asked.

"We are in a dead heat with Hellen Raymond. The numbers have been steadily going up a point or two a week since the last debate. Clearly, the good people of Iowa like the new Perry Douglas. Robert has been really connecting with the college-aged voters. He's become a real asset to your campaign. He's also become somewhat of an internet celebrity. The video of him from the confrontation with the frat boy in South Carolina is still being re-tweeted on a regular basis. It's gone viral. We also have the support of most of the LGBTQ groups who were sitting on the sideline or slightly leaning towards Governor Stolts until Robert became involved in your campaign," Carolyn reported.

"And what of the security concerns and any further threats?" Perry questioned.

"The overwhelming response that Robert's been getting on social media is very positive. But, of course, there are a few detractors and threats. Our security detail vets all threats thoroughly and most are nothing more than silly macho vibrato."

"Still, if there is anything remotely serious in those threats, I want Robert pulled off the campaign trail," Perry emphasized. "We had a good chat at Christmas about toning down the rhetoric and not going after hecklers. Robert understands, but the boy, at times, has a wickedly sharp tongue and his mother's defensive reflexes."

"I didn't know that Katherine had defensive reflexes," Carolyn stated. "She's always so sweet and charming around me."

"Oh please! If I ever give the indication that I am challenging something she said and feeling too full of myself, that woman will cut me down like a brand-new chain saw through a young sapling tree. Fast, pointed and ruthless comes the caustic wit and over the top sarcasm. Her tongue can be a stiletto surrounded by those sparkling white teeth of hers," Perry responded with a smirk. "Robert has his mother's temperament and ability to cleverly criticize and demean, while all the while looking you in the eye and smiling. At times, you don't even realize that you've been verbally eviscerated until you look down and figuratively see your entrails spilling out onto the tile floor."

"Good to know, for the next cocktail party were both at," Carolyn grinned.

"They may be Sweeney Todd and Mrs. Lovett, but they are mine, and I want them protected above all else," Perry reiterated.

"Understood," Carolyn affirmed.

LANDON HAMILTON WAS TRANSFIXED AS HE STUDIED the polling data on his iPad. A few feet away, President Cochran checked a few of his notes as he prepared himself for the last Republican Presidential Primary debate before the Iowa voters would take to the polls in less than three weeks' time.

"Just a couple more minutes Mr. President," Landon informed his boss.

"Cletus is going to come after me tonight on my relationship with Nathan Whitaker,"

Andrew Cochran informed his campaign manager.

"The topic of the debate is foreign policy, how on earth will he be able to slip that in?" Landon asked a bit surprised by the President's analysis of his opponent.

"Who knows?" President Cochran replied. "I'm sure he will attempt to tie it into an argument that I don't possess the moral capacity to be commander-in-chief."

"Why would you even conceive that he would come at you tonight with that line of attack?" Landon inquired.

"A former member of my Secret Service detail, Billy James, is now working for Cletus' main campaign contributor. Undoubtedly, he will take what little information Billy provided to him and attempt to twist and contort the truth about my relationship with Nathan," Andrew Cochran responded.

"Sir, you didn't mention this before, we could have prepared for it," Landon stated a bit frustrated. "If you're right about this line of attack, just state that you haven't seen or talked to Nathan Whitaker in three years and the past is relegated to the past."

"I've got this Landon. I'm not going to lie. I'm prepared, I've got the truth on my side," the President asserted.

"It's time, Mr. President. Good luck," Landon said. As the President walked onto the debate stage, Landon's shoulders slumped and his head bowed. His fears had been confirmed. He was no longer, in fact, running the President's re-election campaign.

Ninety minutes into the two-hour debate, Senator Cletus Sawyer in response to a question about his judgment and temperament as President in possible foreign relations crises, attempted to turn the moderator's question into an attack on the President's behavior.

"Well, what I can tell you is that the American people would not need to wonder about the moral and ethical leadership of a President Sawyer's administration," Cletus Sawyer began. "The American people could rest assured that I have the moral authority and a true belief in God's plan to make the right decisions at 3am in the morning. I know for a fact that the same cannot be said about Andrew Cochran. Heck fire, we don't even know whose bed he would be in when that call of crisis would come. It has come to light that President Cochran had his disgraced former Chief of Staff, Nathan Whitaker covertly smuggled into Camp David, while the criminal Whitaker was standing trial for murder. In previous debates the right Reverend Wilson has pointed to possible satanic worship at the White House and questionable sexual activity of these two close 'friends.'

The old saying is where there is smoke there is fire. The status and nature of the relationship between President Cochran and Nathan Whitaker is shrouded in smoke. Marijuana smoke from what I'm told by an extremely reliable source. The American people deserve to know what is going on with their President and his lascivious behavior with another man."

"Mr. President, you have three minutes to respond to Senator Sawyer's comments," the debate moderator stated.

"I don't believe that Senator Sawyer's baseless accusations and crass innuendos deserve a reply. They debase this entire proceeding. They cheapen the political process. Debating concrete ideas and approaches for solving this country's foreign policy concerns is one thing. Indulging in smear tactics and reckless speculation only points to the small mindedness of very small men. Senator Sawyer's wild musings are fueled by comments from a former member of my Secret Service detail. That person has been given a lucrative job by one of Senator Sawyer's major campaign benefactors. It is true that I had a private meeting at Camp David with my former Chief of Staff and longtime friend Nathan Whitaker. The purpose of that meeting was so I could personally give Nathan Whitaker my support and friendship in his most difficult days. Is that not what friends do for one another? Anything aside from that is simply not true. It does not even meet the standard of pure speculation. It is nothing more than the salacious lies from a warped and desperate mind. I am running on my record over the last three years as President. I know that some do not appreciate that I choose to govern with an open mind to new ideas and a tolerance for compromise to solve the myriad of problems this great nation faces in an ever-changing geopolitical world. I understand that some view my governance over the last three years as a seismic shift in my GOP loyalties. So be it. I am not President of the GOP, I am President of all of the United States. I will not eschew my duties to serve all of the American people to placate political ideologues and policy purists. If that is what you want there are others who will deliver on those myopic party tenants. I gave moral support to an old friend at a time of great need. If that is the charge, then I am most certainly guilty. Nothing else transpired during that meeting. You can believe what you want to believe. But if you want a President who will continue to strive to solve our nation's problems and protect our people as I have for the past three years, then the American people have no better friend that they can always rely on than Andrew Cochran. I am here to support all of you without exception," Andrew Cochran eloquently and persuasively responded, to wild cheers and applause from the debate audience.

One hour later, backstage at the site of the debate, Landon Hamilton was reading off the snapshot polling data taken during the course of the debate.

"When you responded to Sawyer's comments, Mr. President, your approval rating was in the ninetieth percentile. The numbers for trustworthiness and integrity were off the charts. Sawyer's numbers plunged after he made his assault on your character. That tactic backfired completely!" Landon exclaimed, attempting to hide his inner disappointment.

"Thanks Landon, that's good news," Andrew Cochran replied with a slight smile. "But if you'll excuse me, I have a phone call to make to an old friend."

Landon shrugged as the President walked into another room to make his private phone call to Nathan Whitaker. At that moment, Landon understood what it felt like to be 'crushed like a bug.'

CHIFFON LABELLE SEEMINGLY PRANCED THROUGH THE DOORS of French Tips, Juleps & Jazz with a huge smile beaming from her candy red lips.

"Girl, look at you!" Posy Branch proclaimed. "You look as happy as a flea on a fat dog."

"That surely is the God's honest truth," Chiffon responded. "My damages award check from the class action suit done come this morning. I just picked it up from Caleb Butler's office. And there is a goodly number of zeros and commas I'm here to tell ya."

"That is wonderful news," Posy said with a big grin.

"So, now what we gonna do?" Chiffon asked in a hushed voice as her eyes scanned around the large room.

"We got everything put together. It's just a matter of time. But first thing is you got to get that check into your bank account. We gonna bide our time just a little longer, and then we'll make our move," Posy said.

"Hallelujah! God surely is good!" Chiffon said while she looked towards the heavens.

"GOD IS GREAT, AND HE WILL soon have his requisite revenge," the note from a 4chan chat line read. FBI Director James Turner reviewed a lengthy series of electronic conversations from the members of the radical right group, 'Killers for Christ.' This was yet another example of disturbing chatter on the website about the need to take deadly action against President Cochran. The Director reread and attempted to understand a specific line of the conversation that read, "Like Odysseus springing from the Trojan Horse, we will smite the immorality of this heathen traitor within our midst. He will never see it coming because his downfall will come from his own encampment."

Past threats against the President from this radical group had become common and regular. But none of the prior threats had any content about an attack coming from within. This was a new and disturbing line of dialogue. And, it greatly troubled Director Turner during the beginning of a new election year.

CHAPTER 39

IT WAS THE FIRST TUESDAY IN FEBRUARY, the Iowa Caucus. The candidates from both major parties had combed the state for almost a year. It was a sun-filled day, the temperatures were in the mid-thirties, and the voters of Iowa were showing up at caucus locations all over the state in record numbers. At the Douglas for President campaign office in Iowa City, staffers and volunteers were busily arranging transportation for their senior citizen voters to get to the polls. Carolyn Barnes sat in a hotel suite with her candidate, Senator Perry Douglas, as she let out a long and loud sigh.

"Stress getting to you?" Perry asked his campaign manager.

"As my son Cameron would say, 'mos def,'" Carolyn replied with a faint smile.

"It looks like it's going to be a nail-biter. You and Senator Raymond are in a virtual dead heat. The latest polling percentages are well within the margin of error. It could be a very long night," Carolyn said with a weary shake of her head.

"Well, we've done everything that we could. I am so proud of how we've run our campaign. We have stuck to the issues and stayed away from the disgusting name calling that is going on with the Republicans. I'm no huge fan of Andrew Cochran, but the lack of respect he is getting from his own party is appalling. He is, after all, the sitting President of the United States. He deserves better than to have his morality challenged by the fringe lunatics running against him," Perry Douglas stated.

"I've been in politics for over twenty years. Just when you think you've seen the tide ebb at its lowest, along comes another regressive wave pushing away from the shores of political sanity and proper civil campaign decorum," Carolyn allowed.

"Ah yes," Perry wistfully sighed. "My dear friend and mentor, Henry Fitzsimmons, use to say that these days 'politics has gotten dirtier than two ticks mud-wrestling in an outhouse'. I loved that one. And mind you, Henry wasn't above getting into the fray. In fact, at times he sought out confrontation when he felt he was in the right. However, Henry was always a gentleman even in his most contentious moments. That type of civility is becoming a lost art in political discourse. We are left with mud-slinging and worthless debasing prattle substituting for debating issue-oriented differences."

"Not for our campaign it hasn't," Carolyn proudly affirmed.

"As the kids would say 'true dat'," Perry Douglas uttered with a laugh.

Back at the White House, Landon Hamilton was still officially doing his job and keeping President Cochran apprised of the polling number data.

"It's going to be tight, sir," Landon explained to the President. "Jedediah Wilson is getting a boost from the Iowa Evangelical voters, but our numbers are right there. It's going to be neck and neck."

"What about Cletus?" Andrew Cochran asked.

"Sinking like a rock," Landon replied with a satisfied smug smile. "His personal attack on you at the debate put a real hole in his numbers. He has been dropping ever since. Seems like the good people of Iowa do not cotton to such scurrilous attacks on their sitting President."

"Then why am I still battling with Jedediah Wilson in the polls?" The President inquired.

"I think there are two things at play with Wilson," Landon surmised. "First, Wilson's comments about you lately have been much more couched, less obvious. He saw his numbers drop when he brought up the whole satanic worship voodoo angle several months ago. Since then, he has let others make those groundless accusations and has avoided a full frontal assault on your morality and behavior. And second, and most obvious is that there are a lot of Republican Evangelical voters in Iowa. A lot. He is a prominent televangelist from a major church in Arkansas. He's just going to get a high percentage of those voters regardless of their respect for you as President."

"And what of Lamar Clarkson and Carlton Smith?" Andrew Cochran asked.

"Single digits for both of them. They've never really been a factor right from the get-go. Cletus Sawyer always had more money and a better organization so he took most of the vote for the Southern politicians not named Cochran. Which will leave it as a three horse race going forward," Landon explained.

"Aren't you forgetting someone?" The President coyly asked.

"It's hard to be part of a race if you're not running," Landon surmised.

"Howard Mason may be on the sidelines for now, but he is watching very carefully. He is biding his time and waiting for me to stumble and fall," Andrew Cochran added.

"Then he could be waiting for quite a long time," Landon stated with a smirk.

MUCH LATER THAT EVENING, all of the Iowa caucus polling places had certified their vote counts. The results from the Republican contest for President were as follows: Jedediah Wilson with roughly 34 percent of the ballots cast, President Andrew Cochran with 33 percent, Cletus Sawyer with 24 percent, Lamar Clarkson with 6 percent, and Carlton Smith with 2 percent.

On the Democratic side of the Presidential race it was Perry Douglas with approximately 42 percent, Hellen Raymond with 40 percent, and Keith Stolts with 14 percent of the votes cast by the Iowa caucus participants. As Landon Hamilton had aptly predicted, Lamar Clarkson and Carlton Smith withdrew from the Presidential primary battle the next morning, as did Keith Stolts. Three candidates remained on the Republican side and two for the Democrats. The month of February had just begun. However, the race for the White House was in full stride.

POSY BRANCH STRODE WITH PURPOSE into the back office of French Tips where her business partner Olivier Bellevue was seated behind a desk with his feet precariously pressed against the edge of the old worn desktop and the chair slightly teetering on its back legs.

"You keep that up and you're going to fall on your ass," Posy warned.

"Nope, not me," Olivier confidently responded.

"We'll see," Posy muttered.

"What's up?" He asked.

"I need to talk to you about a few things," Posy stated. "First off, I'm going to hire another bar back with some bartending experience to help Michael. Second, I'm going to install a new tampon dispenser in the women's restroom. That old one gets stuck far too often. Girls be yelling at me that they put their money in but they ain't getting nothing in return. Finally, I want you gone. Now."

"Yeah right," Olivier scoffed.

"Olivier, you are just like a used tampon as far as I'm concerned. I no longer got any use for you."

"You stupid bitch, I'm not going anywhere," Olivier countered.

"Yes, you are," Posy reiterated. "Y'all," Posy called out and moments later she was joined in the back office by Chiffon and Michael who was holding the baseball bat that he kept behind the bar to handle unruly customers. "We can do this real easy and civil like or we can bring the authorities in. Your choice. You see Olivier, since you decided to take over the business accounting for French Tips, Chiffon been keeping her own separate version of the books. She been double checking all the receipts and cash. Apparently, your books and hers don't match up at all. In fact, there seems to be thousands of dollars unaccounted for in your books. Plus, Michael and all the nail gals been telling me how you been bad mouthing me behind my back. How you been trying to turn them against me. Only problem there, is that none of them like you one little bit. We is all friends here. You are the unwelcome one, and we are about to get rid of you. I been taking a back seat to men like you all my life. That's ending right here and now."

"You can't prove anything. Just my word against that Amazon freak!" Olivier defiantly demanded.

"Well, that ain't exactly right," Posy said with a knowing smirk. "You see, right before Chantale left, I had a couple of security cameras installed back here in the office. Chantale, she had cameras in the front of the salon but she never thought it necessary to have cameras here in the back, which I'm guessing you knew. Any who, my mama always preached to me, safety first. And since, this is where we count the money daily and do the books, and have our safe, it only made sense to install security cameras where the money is. Don't you agree? They's right up there, hidden real good," Posy stated as she pointed to the small inconspicuous cameras in the back and front of the office. "All of this is to say that we got months of tape showing you putting a goodly portion of the business's cash on hand into your wallet. Funny how a couple hundred a day adds up. So, here is what I propose. Chiffon just happens to have her check book with her. She can write you a check for the entire amount of money that you paid to buy out Chantale's share of the business. We won't even make you pay us back for the money you done stole all this time. You can consider that as your parting gift. Take the check and sign this agreement declaring that you are givin' up your share of the business. Caleb Butler drew this up for us. It's so nice to have friends who is lawyers, dontcha think? Oh, and his notary public is sitting at the bar right now having one of Michaels' special peach and ginger juleps. She can notarize the signed document to make it all official and such. Or, the alternative is that Michael here is going to call his good friend who is a sergeant for the New Orleans police department. And we gonna invite him over and we can all have a visit together and watch some video tape. Choice is yours Olivier, but either way you gots to go."

"You aren't going to get away with this, you crazy cunt!" Olivier ranted as he sprung to his feet. His face flushed with anger and his hand balled up into a tight fist. Michael quickly stepped towards Olivier, his glistening muscles flexed as he squeezed the baseball bat in his hands ready to swing at a moment's notice. Posy lifted her cellphone so that she could dial.

"Michael, sugar, what is the name of your friend at N.O.P.D?" Posy sweetly asked.

"Sergeant Norris Coaltree," Michael responded. "Just ask the duty officer for him."

Moments passed as Olivier stared with sheer contempt at Posy as she began to dial.

"Alright, I'll sign," Olivier yelled as he sat back down in the chair. Chiffon began to write a check and Michael motioned for the notary public to join them in the office with copies of the sales agreement and transfer of rights.

Ten minutes later, multiple copies of the legal documents were signed and notarized and Chiffon handed her check for the purchase price for a share of the business to Olivier.

"Nice doing business with you," Chiffon cooed at Olivier.

"You're gonna pay for this," Olivier shouted as he stood and headed towards the office door.

"Thanks for shouting, Olivier, the security cameras also have small microphones. I'm guessing that Sergeant Coaltree would be able to hear that nice and loud," Posy added. "I sincerely hope that you don't give us any reason to share the tape of this with him. But once again, that is your choice."

Olivier stormed out of the building. He walked down the nearby streets of the French Quarter in a fit of rage. He passed a home that had a couple of poplar trees and a Southern oak in its front yard instead of the more traditional New Orleans style garden. He stopped briefly and stared at the large trees. He then continued to walk on cursing up a storm and acting demonstrably angry causing passersby to cross the street in fear of his irrational behavior.

Meanwhile, the jazz band at French Tips, Juleps & Jazz, played, "When The Saints Go Marching In" while Posy and her new business partner, Chiffon LaBelle danced with Michael in the middle of the large floor, as they sang along with the band and laughed together.

LESS THAN A MILE AWAY, WHITLEE HAMMOND gently rocked back and forth in one of the two wicker rocking chairs on the second floor balcony of Stanford Winchester's Royal Street home. It was a cool night so Stanford offered Whitlee a wrap to place around her shoulders.

"You sure it's not too cool for you out here?" Stanford asked.

"Oh no, I'm perfectly fine," Whitlee replied. "It's so pretty up here, and I love listening to the street sounds coming from Bourbon Street."

"Yes, there's always sound and bustle when you live in the Quarter," Stanford stated. "You know I lived in the Garden District for years. When I moved to this house it took me a while to get use to the street sounds. It's so tranquil at night in the Garden District. But now, when I'm away from home, I miss the constant buzz that you get living in the Quarter."

"I completely understand. I find it energizing, life affirming, if you will," Whitlee added.

"Precisely, life affirming," Stanford agreed. "And speaking of life, I know that my days are numbered. So, I must tell you Whitlee, that the last several weeks that we have been dating have been the best thing that has happened to me in many years. I am once again happy. Truly happy. And as you so aptly put it, I am energized again. This is a long way of saying that I can't imagine my life without you." Stanford stood up in front of Whitlee's chair and then dropped to one knee. "I know that we have been dating for less than two months, but I also know that my mind is made up. I hope yours is as well. Whitlee Hammond, would you do me the great honor and provide me the life-affirming joy of being my wife?" Stanford sweetly asked as he took Whitlee's hand into his.

"Of course, I will," Whitlee softly replied as she wrapped her arms around Stanford's shoulders as tears streamed from her eyes. The couple then kissed lovingly, passionately.

"I apologize that I don't have a ring to present to you, but tomorrow morning we will take a stroll down Royal Street and you can pick out something lovely at the jewelers," Stanford said with a smile. "We can also discuss when you'd like to marry."

"How about June?" Whitlee asked. "I always thought I'd like to be a June bride."

"Then June it is," Stanford agreed. "Come on, let's go celebrate. Let's take a walk down to Fritzel's and have some champagne and perhaps have a dance or two," Stanford suggested.

"That sounds lovely," Whitlee gleefully replied.

Stanford and Whitlee walked out of Stanford's house toward his front gate. As Stanford opened the wrought iron gate for Whitlee to pass through, on the street just outside of the gate was a small hand-crafted object. Whitlee stooped over and picked it up to examine the intricate interwoven structure.

"What is this?" She asked. "I've seen a few scattered throughout the French Quarter. Usually they've been crushed underfoot by the crowds in the Quarter, this one seems very much intact."

"That's right, you probably don't have these in Austin," Stanford responded with a grin. "It's a voodoo symbol. They are as common in parts of the Quarter as discarded strings of Mardi Gras beads."

"What is this made of?" Whitlee asked as she studied the small object.

"Dried and bleached chicken bones and usually hemp," Stanford stated.

"What are they for?" Whitlee inquired as she handed the structure to Stanford.

"Nonsense and superstition if you ask me," Stanford responded with a grin. Stanford cast the object to the side of the street. He then inter-locked arms with his bride-to-be as they strolled down the street headed towards Fritzel's for some champagne to toast their love and lives together. In the distance, a street band played a familiar jazz standard as the French Quarter, as it always does, celebrated this cherished thing that we call life.

CHAPTER 40

The large maple trees of New Hampshire produce about 90,000 gallons of maple syrup each year. As the frozen sap in the maple trees begins to thaw it moves and builds up pressure within the tree. When the internal pressures reaches a certain point, sap will flow freely from any fresh wound in the tree. Freezing nights and warm sunny days create the pressure needed for a good sap harvest. In mid-February the New Hampshire maple producers wound their sugar maples by drilling a small hole in the trunk of the tree. They insert a spout and attach plastic tubing to that spout as the tree drips its crystal clear sap into a bucket. While the mighty maples of New Hampshire bleed for the processing of maple syrup, so too do the politicians seeking the most prestigious elected office in the world attempt to tap into the political consciousness of the New Hampshire electorate. This is the hope and the folly of the Republican and Democratic candidates running for President of the United States. It was mid-February and they were all in search of the most 'saps.'

Senator Perry Douglas was fresh off a narrow victory in the Democratic Party Iowa Caucus. He had gained the flow of political momentum. If he could tap into his inner arborist and channel the progressive and social policies of his friend and mentor, the late Senator Henry Fitzsimmons, perhaps he could be well on his way to winning the Democratic nomination for President.

Robert Douglas was making yet another speaking appearance at the University of New Hampshire on behalf of his Presidential candidate father. Smart, articulate, and affable, Robert began his campaign remarks much like he had done several times in the past few months with a few kind-hearted jokes about his famous father. But this time, the personal comments and witty banter were interrupted by the popping sounds of bursting campaign balloons. At least that was what most thought until the campaign security detail assigned to Robert raced to his side as he laid prone on the elevated stage staring up into the florescent lights of the large auditorium. His blood flowed freely from the fresh wounds. The sounds of screams of shock and panic filled the air.

"Robert! Robert!" Perry Douglas cried out. His arms flailed as his brow dripped with panicked sweat.

"Perry, Perry, wake up!" Katherine Douglas demanded of her husband as he continued to thrash in their hotel suite bed. Moments later, Perry Douglas bolted upright and breathed heavily as he soaked in his own perspiration.

"Was it that same dream?" Katherine softly asked as her husband's breathing began to moderate and he began to regain his composure.

"Yes," Perry sighed, as the comforting sense of awakened reality renounced the wild panic of his reoccurring nightmare state. "Yes," he wearily repeated.

CHIFFON LaBELLE WALKED SWIFTLY DOWN THE DARK BACKSTREETS of the French Quarter after a long day at work. She had just closed French Tips, Juleps & Jazz, the nail salon/nightclub/bar that she had recently become part owner of with her friend and business partner, Posy Branch. It was after 2:00am, and the seemingly perpetually busy streets of the Quarter were generally quiet and mostly empty for a change. Chiffon walked past a house with large trees in its front yard. A rarity for the French Quarter, where well-groomed gardens were typical. Chiffon took a moment to admire the majesty of well-groomed healthy trees existing steps away from bars, restaurants, and t-shirt shops. She thought of having a home in the French Quarter, now that she had won her monetary award from the Hurricane Katrina victims lawsuit. She thought that she might have enough money for a down payment. Her life was now flush with new possibilities. Though her next move to a new life was to complete the hormonal therapy and sexual identity surgery that would fulfill her transformation from her former self as Ernest Johnson to her new identity as a fully realized woman. It had been a long time coming, but she was excited for the change and a new life to come. Chiffon picked up her striding pace. She was on the move. She was going home.

STANFORD WINCHESTER AND WHITLEE HAMMOND were in the process of building a life together. Where they would call home was not an issue of debate. Whitlee had not only fallen in love with Stanford but also with his home on Royal Street in the French Quarter. One month into his retirement from the Federal bench, Stanford was beginning to enjoy life at a simpler and slower pace. He began to enjoy and embrace his leisure time. He looked forward to his June wedding and spending the rest of his life with the woman he loved. Besides, Mardi Gras was just a week away and for the first time in his adult life he could take in the parades and the pageantry without the concerns of judicial duties and obligations. It was shaping up to be a very good year for Stanford Winchester.

BESSIE COLLINS WORKED ON HER SMALL BUSINESS accounting ledgers as she heard Papa Levi call out to her from the front of the shop.

"Fed Ex man here, Miss Bessie, want me to sign for these here packages?"

"Sure, go on, I'll be out in just a minute," Bessie replied.

"This box from New Mexico," Papa Levi announced.

"That one must have the dreamcatchers I ordered. I can't keep them on the shelves, they's so popular," Bessie said with a happy giggle.

"This small box is addressed to 'Esther Francois', looks to be sent from Haiti," Papa Levi noted. "Probably something from her kin folk, I reckon."

"Then I wonder why Esther didn't just have it sent to her home?" Bessie asked. "Speaking of, I haven't seen Esther for going on two days now, you know where she is?"

"Last she told me, she was meeting with one of her old Jackson Square clients. Had some business to attend to. She did ask me to fetch her a chicken the other day for a sacrifice she be doing down by Lake Pontchartrain tomorrow night," Papa Levi stated.

"You know what it for?" Bessie questioned with a furrowed brow.

"I surely don't, Miss Bessie. She got some of her old crew to work the sacrifice with her. Done told me that she wouldn't need my help for that one," Papa Levi related.

"Well, go leave that package for her in the back next to her chair. She'll get it when she get it," Bessie said while untangling some of the dreamcatchers contained in the box she opened.

THE POLLS IN NEW HAMPSHIRE HAD BEEN CLOSED for almost three hours and though a small percentage of the vote still needed to be counted the final results were apparent. On the Republican side of the primary contest, Cletus Sawyer had roughly 32 percent of the vote tallied, followed by President Andrew Cochran with 30 percent, and Jedediah Wilson with 27 percent. Two contests into the primary season and the incumbent President of the United States was still without a primary contest victory.

Meanwhile, on the Democratic side of the ledger, Perry Douglas had garnered 48 percent of the vote with Hellen Raymond gaining 44 percent of the vote. Senator Perry Douglas had accomplished his second win in as many contests. Each race was very close, but a victory is still a victory and the Douglas campaign and its supporters could not have asked for a better start to the Presidential race for the White House.

AARON ROSE AND CLAY GROVER SAT NEXT TO EACH OTHER on the couch in their quaint yellow shotgun home watching the New Hampshire election results on television.

"Well, are you getting excited yet, Mr. White House Chief of Staff?" Aaron asked his husband.

"Whoa now, there's a long way to go," Clay cautioned. "And I certainly didn't say that I would take the job."

"Why the hell not?" Aaron challenged.

"Because I'm not 100 percent sure that I want to get back into politics again. I'm quite content sitting on this couch, snuggling up to you and drinking some wine," Clay replied.

"We are talking about White House Chief of Staff, right?" Aaron countered with a bewildered expression on his face. "You would be one of a very few people involved in making high level policy decisions that would set the course for this country's future."

"Yes, my love, I understand the functions of the job, I'm just not sure that I want that kind of responsibility; that I'm prepared or talented enough to assume that type of monumental responsibility," Clay responded just above a whisper.

"I'm perfectly fine if you decide that you don't want the job, but I don't want to hear you doubt whether you can handle the job. You are smart, articulate, and you have a big heart and the decisions you would make would be coming from the right place. Your judgment is impeccable. After all, you decided to marry me, didn't you?" Aaron asked with a sweet smile on his handsome face.

"Yes, I did, and it was the best decision that I've ever made," Clay confirmed. "We are a long way from the finish line. The recent polls show

Senator Douglas trailing Senator Raymond by double-digits in South Carolina. They are basically tied in Nevada polling, and then there is Super Tuesday. Momentum can change drastically in a week. There's no need now to debate something that may never come to fruition. So instead of getting all worked up about something so nebulous, I'd rather sit here with you, wholly contented with drinking some more wine and eating some more cheddar popcorn."

"You see there, just proving my point, what sage decision making," Aaron chuckled while burrowing himself under Clay's enveloping right arm.

THE KLIEG LIGHTS BATHED THE PODIUM in a sea of artificial brightness as President Cochran stood behind several microphones. "I just want to take a moment to congratulate Senator Sawyer on his hard-fought victory in New Hampshire. For the second week in a row my campaign has come close to victory, but as the old saying goes, 'Close only counts in horseshoes and hand grenades.' We will continue to fight the good fight and try to do better. But even though we continue our electoral quest, my first and foremost priority is to serve the American people as their President. Together with my exemplary and loyal Vice-President, Howard Mason, we will continue to do the people's work, striving to help every one of our nation's citizens achieve their American dream. Vice-President Mason has been by my side each and every day these past three years as we work in lockstep to attempt to give the people of this country what they want and deserve from their government. I look forward to continuing our work together as a united team if the good people of this nation decide that we should both serve a second term. To that end, it's onward to South Carolina and beyond. We both thank you for your support. God bless you all, and God bless these United States of America."

"DID YOU SEE WHAT THAT BASTARD JUST DID?" Vice-President Mason nearly yelled into the telephone.

"Look, it's not the end of the world, Howard," the Vice-Presidents' chief advisor Mark Backus counseled.

"Mark, he tied the rope of his sinking ship around my god-damn neck!" Howard exclaimed. "I knew that he knew that I was considering challenging him in the primaries. That asshole hasn't publicly said a single good thing about me in three years. Now, I'm his 'exemplary and loyal Vice-President'? Fuck him!"

"Calm down Howard. No one has come close to taking a foothold on this election. Clearly, the Republican primary voters aren't enraptured with Andrew Cochran anymore. They have given both of his opponents victories while he lags behind," Mark pointed out to his old friend.

"So, now what? How do I get the albatross of his failed Presidency off of my back?" Howard questioned.

"Let me think about it overnight. I'll get back to you tomorrow. In the interim, don't do or say anything rash. Our goal is still the same. The primary voters will flock to your side after you announce your intentions. This is but a minor bump in the road to the Presidency, Howard," Mark assured.

"I hope so Mark, I sure hope so."

THE VERY COLD NEW HAMPSHIRE PRIMARY night gave way to a more temperate and gloriously sunny New England morning. The maple syrup literally poured into the plastic buckets from newly opened wounds. There was no denying the fact that the sap was running.

CHAPTER 41

Two days later, Senator Perry Douglas was talking to a tree. The Senator stood before the enormous Angel Oak tree located on Johns Island, South Carolina.

"Hello Henry, it's been a while since we've spoken. I just wanted to catch you up on what's been going on," Perry Douglas began as he softly spoke in the presence of that magnificent old tree.

"I've been spending a good deal of time in your home state lately, and you were absolutely right, it is home to some of the kindest, warmest and most loving people you will ever find in this wonderful country of ours. I love the food and I truly love the people of this state, but I just don't think that the feeling is mutual. I'm just a little too liberal and a little too Northern for their tastes. And, I get it, it's fine, though I'd rather not be losing to Hellen Raymond by almost twenty points. But she is the local girl from North Carolina, and as you always use to tell me, 'Southerners stick together.' But the good news is that I won Iowa and New Hampshire, not by a lot, but still two very nice victories. If I can escape South Carolina without getting completely blown out, I'd consider that a moral victory. Of course, Katherine sends her love. That woman is as solid as this tree. She is the one that keeps everything together while I'm out here foraging for votes. Oh, and my boy Robert is on the campaign trail helping me with the youth vote. He's a natural when it comes to talking to crowds, much like you were. So at ease and personable. I only wish that I could be as comfortable in my own skin as he is. A while back he was right here at the University of South Carolina giving a speech at a get-out-the-vote rally. He was quite amused at discovering that the football team's name was the 'Gamecocks.' Needless to say, he had some fun with the name, which led to a verbal altercation with one of the students. A frat boy who was a bit overserved took offense. Robert dressed him down with such wit and sarcasm, you would have enjoyed it. It sort of reminded me of how you could take down one of our Senate colleagues with your stiletto wit in such a charming and innocuous way."

Perry Douglas paused as he moved closer to the tree and deeply sighed.

"I miss you each and every day, my dear friend. I hope you don't mind, but I asked Clay Grover if he would consider being my Chief of Staff if I am fortunate enough to persuade the good people of this country to elect me as their President. He and Aaron make such a fine couple. I see a little of you in Clay. You did such a fine job grooming him, I can only hope to replicate just a modicum of your unique mentorship. Well Henry, it's time to go my friend. We will talk soon. I've got a rally in Charleston in an hour or so."

Five days later, the primary voters of the Palmetto State had made their wishes known. In the Democratic primary, Senator Hellen Raymond scored an easy and predictable victory amassing 56 percent of the vote. Perry Douglas finished a very distant second with 40 percent of the ballots cast.

The Republican primary was much closer. The winner was Jedediah Wilson who garnered 33 percent of the vote, followed by Andrew Cochran with 31 percent and Cletus Sawyer with 30 percent of the vote. For the third primary contest in a row, the incumbent President of the United States failed to achieve a victory. The press and social media exploded with accounts of a failing Presidency.

The morning after the South Carolina primary, Vice-President Howard Mason requested and received an audience with President Cochran.

"Good morning Howard," the President cheerfully addressed his Vice-President.

"Good morning sir, but is it really?" Howard Mason asked.

"Why of course it is. The sun is bright on this mid-February day. It's a very long race, Howard, I'm still jogging. I've finished second three times in a row losing by only a couple of percentage points every time. A little more focus and effort on our part and we can turn this thing around," Andrew Cochran said encouragingly.

"Yes, well that is actually the crux of why I wanted to see you," Howard Mason stated as he pulled a white manila envelope from his suit coat inner breast pocket.

"Put that away Howard, you are not resigning today," the President said with a gentle smile.

Howard stared at the President with an incredulous expression on his face, while meekly uttering, "But."

"I'm not saying that you cannot join the primary fray. In fact, throw your hat into the ring today, the more the merrier," Andrew Cochran cheerfully stated. "All I'm asking is that you give it a week and think about it. You don't need to resign the Vice-Presidency in order to challenge me for the Republican Party nomination in the primaries. A principled battle for the nomination does not need to be uncivil, unless of course, that is the route you prefer to choose. So, just think about it, will you? Wait until after the Nevada caucus. If at that time, you still choose to resign, bring along that letter and a good bottle of bourbon and we will toast each other and wish each other well. In the meantime, that gives me a little time to think about your possible successor."

"I don't know what to say?" Howard muttered.

"Say yes, Howard, say yes to at least a little wiggle room for both of us," Andrew requested.

"Alright, yes. I'll give it some thought Mr. President. One week's time," Howard responded.

"Yes, excellent, one week's time," the President stated. As Howard Mason turned to leave the Oval Office, President Cochran added with a chuckle, "And if you still want to resign at that time, don't forget to bring the good bourbon."

"Yes sir."

The very next morning, Vice-President Howard Mason held a hastily-prepared press conference where he formally announced his intention to seek the Republican Party's nomination for President of the United States. When asked by the press corps if he intended to resign his office and whether he felt that he could adequately serve a President whom he was now opposing, he simply responded, "I am not resigning from President Cochran's administration at this time but may choose to do so at a later date depending on intervening circumstances."

"Well ain't that a kick in the head," Senator Perry Douglas said to his campaign manager Carolyn Barnes as they watched the Vice-President's press conference from the Senator's hotel suite high above the Las Vegas strip.

"People used to say that 'Democrats fall in love while Republicans fall in line,' guess you can get rid of that old adage," Carolyn responded with a short high-pitched hoot.

"Did you see that coming? Were there any rumblings that I was unaware of?" Perry asked with a curious grin.

"I had heard a couple of rumors, but I passed them off as just that, rumors," Carolyn allowed. "Cochran and Mason were never close, nor did they even seem to like each other very much. But, then again, JFK and LBJ couldn't stand each other. It was always a marriage of convenience and necessity, but I never imagined that Mason would jump ship and challenge his own President."

"Strange times indeed. The Republican Party is turning into a free-for-all," Perry stated. "But enough about them, let's talk about me. What's the latest polling?"

"There isn't much in the way of polling. Caucus states are odd to begin with and Nevada is the oddest of the odd. We've done some internal polling but not much in the way of national polls. Given that, it's a toss-up, we think. Maybe a slight advantage to Senator Raymond," Carolyn allowed.

"I'll take that. Sure she can claim some momentum with two wins in a row, but I think we can hold our own on Super Tuesday two weeks hence and then see where things go," Perry acknowledged.

"Yup, that's the strategy," Carolyn said with a nod. "One other thing Senator, Robert is itching to get back on the campaign trail. He calls me almost daily asking about his next appearance. Should I continue to be vague in response to his inquiries?"

"I know, I know. He's bugging his mother as well asking why he hasn't been allowed to do a speaking engagement since right before New Hampshire. I'm just not ready yet. It was just a dream, I know, and generally I'm not a superstitious person, but still . . ." Perry stated as his voice trailed off.

It was not until the early morning after the Nevada caucus that the final vote results became certified. The Nevada Democratic Caucus voters presented Senator Hellen Raymond with a narrow victory over

Senator Perry Douglas by a 2 percent margin, 47 percent to 45 percent. In the Republican contest for the Presidential nomination, Jedediah Wilson had 32 percent of the vote, followed by 30 percent for Andrew Cochran, 19 percent for Cletus Sawyer, and a very respectable 18 percent for Howard Mason, given that the Vice-President had announced his candidacy only a handful of days before the caucus. Jedediah Wilson had won 3 of the first 4 Republican primaries or caucuses. Similarly, President Cochran continued his string of four consecutive second place finishes.

THERE WAS A LULL IN THE CUSTOMER TRAFFIC at French Tips, Juleps & Jazz on that Tuesday late afternoon. Michael cleaned up the bar area and began peeling fresh fruit for his famous juleps. Posy sat at the bar reviewing some new marketing material for the establishment.

"Posy, what do you think about the election, given that you were once friends with President Cochran?" Michael inquired of his boss. "Who do you support?"

"I ain't exactly political, and nothing against Andy, he always treated me well, but I'd probably go for the gal from North Carolina. About time we have a woman running things. Sure can't screw things up any more than the men already have," Posy laughed. "Speaking of women running things, where's my gal Chiffon?"

"She's in the back doing the books," Michael replied. Posy walked to the back room, peaking her head through the open door.

"Hey girl! Can you close tonight with Michael?" Posy asked.

"Sure. You got a date or something?" Chiffon asked her friend.

"No, Darling. Promised my mama I'd spend a night chatting with her and catching-up and all on the phone. You know, just a couple of hours of girl talk," Posy responded with a smile. "Gonna open me up a nice bottle of wine and kick back with mama on the line."

"Sounds nice. You go on, Michael and I got this," Chiffon replied.

APPROXIMATELY 1000 MILES NORTH AND EAST of New Orleans in Washington, D.C. a man received a text message that simply read, "Time has come today. Time."

CHAPTER 42

IT WAS A RELATIVELY SLOW NIGHT at French Tips, Juleps & Jazz. By closing time, the place was empty, a rarity. Chiffon LaBelle locked the safe and the back room. Michael checked around the bar one last time just prior to activating the alarm system for the establishment. Chiffon and Michael walked out into the relative quiet of the French Market area.

"I'm going to head over to Bourbon Pub for a nightcap, care to join me?" Michael asked.

"No, thanks, Sugar, I'm going to walk home and call it a night," Chiffon replied.

"Do you want me to walk with you? I can always come back," Michael offered.

"No, Baby, I'm fine, you go have some fun. I'll see you in the morning."

"Good night, be safe," Michael interjected.

"Always baby, always." The two friends and co-workers hugged and then each went their separate ways.

THE FOLLOWING MORNING IN WASHINGTON, D.C., Vice-President Howard Mason was waiting outside of the Oval Office for his scheduled appointment with President Cochran. In his hands he held a wooden box and a white envelope.

"You can go in now, Mr. Vice-President," Nancy, the President's secretary instructed.

"Good morning, Mr. President," Howard Mason stated.

"Good morning, Howard," the President chirped in return. "Congratulations on a very admirable showing in Nevada last night. Given the fact that you had announced your intentions to pursue the party's nomination just days earlier, you did quite well. I'm sure that bodes very well for the future. Well, I see that your holding a wooden box and an envelope in your hand, I guess we know what that means."

"Yes sir. Thank you for affording me additional time to consider my decision, but after careful thought and reflection, I do believe that it would be in the best interest of both of us, the party and the country, if I tender my letter of resignation," Howard said clearly and without hesitation.

"Well, I've got to admit, that saddens me Howard. I think that we could have made it work, but I fully understand and appreciate your position," Andrew Cochran responded.

"Here sir, is my letter of resignation, as well as a pretty good bottle of bourbon," Howard stated.

"With regret, I will accept your letter, but I was just kidding about the bourbon. Please keep it and enjoy it yourself," the President replied with a sincere smile.

"No sir, the bourbon was part of the bargain. It would do me great honor if you would accept it as a token of our three years of shared efforts on behalf of our beloved country," Howard insisted.

"If you're going to put it that way, then, yes, I graciously accept your generous offer."

Howard handed the wooden box to the President. Andrew Cochran opened the box containing the bottle of aged bourbon.

"Elijah Craig single barrel bourbon aged for 21 years. This is exquisite stuff. Thank you so much Howard. Would you like a little taste?" Andrew Cochran offered.

"No, thank you sir, it's a little early in the day for me," Howard replied.

"Me, too," Andrew Cochran agreed. "Besides, I've got a meeting in ten minutes with our U.N. Ambassador, probably not a good idea to go into the meeting smelling of bourbon. Why don't you stop by later today and we will have a toast together?"

"Possibly sir, thank you. At the moment, time is scarce and I have a campaign to plan," Howard stated with a slight grin.

"Yes, you do. It's been a pleasure working with you," Andrew Cochran said as he extended his hand to his Vice-President. The two men engaged in a hearty handshake.

"Goodbye, Mr. President," Howard said as he began to turn to leave the Oval Office.

"Good luck to you, Howard. I'll see you at the next debate."

SEVERAL HOURS LATER, IN THE LATE afternoon, the President's secretary Nancy heard a loud thud and a crashing sound coming from the Oval Office. She knocked on the door. "Mr. President?" She called out. Moments later, the Secret Service agents raced into the office and cradled the President in their arms. Within a few minutes, the President was being carefully laid onto a gurney and was being administered to by a White House physician. Swiftly the President was taken from the office as his vital signs were closely being monitored and he was being administered oxygen through a mask. Broken crystal glass shards were scattered across the President's desk. The opened bottle of bourbon sat at the side of his desk.

CLAY GROVER AND AARON ROSE WERE walking home together in New Orleans after having completed a good day of work at their law office.

"My phone is exploding with text messages," Aaron said as he fished his iPhone out of his pants pocket. "Oh my God! Oh my God!" Aaron exclaimed.

"What is it?" Clay asked, his voice filled with concern.

"President Cochran has been taken to a Washington, D.C. hospital, he is in critical condition," Aaron yelped.

The couple were within steps of a tavern where the televisions behind the bar were blaring the news story. Others came in from the street and stared at the television news stories in horror and utter dismay. Some people began to openly sob as they watched the frantic reports. The facts were slow to surface. Some reported accounts were quickly debunked and retracted. Other confirmed facts began to take hold and became part of the dialogue of what may have transpired. Before long, it was revealed that in all likelihood President Cochran had been poisoned. And the poisoning was caused by a derivation of the toxic substance digitalis. Aaron and Clay stared at each other unable to utter a sound.

A FEW MILES AWAY, BESSIE COLLINS WAS in her kitchen preparing dinner for her husband Lucius. Lucius frantically bounded through their front door yelling for his wife.

"Bessie! Bessie!" Lucius exclaimed. "Turn on the television!"

"For goodness sake why? Bessie asked. "You be acting like a wild man."

"They trying to kill the President!" Lucius shouted.

Bessie quickly took hold of the remote control and turned up the volume. Her pretty face contorted as she listened to the details in the news report. Tears began streaming down her eyes. Once she had heard enough, she grabbed her shawl and went running out of the house. She ran as fast as she could down the street towards Jackson Square. Lucius tried his best to keep up with his wife, huffing and puffing as he trailed her pace. There, at a small folding table at the edge of the square, sat Esther Francois. She was doing a tarot card reading for a client. Bessie ran directly towards the table and accidentally knocked the customer off of his metal folding chair. Bessie stood in front of Esther with tears streaming down her cheeks and her lungs burning from her sprint.

"Esther!" She screamed. "Esther, what you done did? What you did?" Bessie cried out in anguish and disgust, as she fell to her knees and yelped and cried like a wounded dog.

AS THE EVENING PROGRESSED MORE AND more details became apparent. Aaron and Clay had made their way to their home. They sat motionless together, their eyes transfixed on the television screen. Aaron had his laptop at his side, and he would occasionally turn from the television to surf the internet to see if he could uncover any other details that were not being presented by the network news broadcasts.

The facts known at that time were that President Cochran had ingested digitalis poison that was contained in a bottle of bourbon. The bottle of bourbon had been given to him earlier that day by Vice-President Howard Mason along with his letter of resignation. With the President in critical condition and unconscious, the Constitution required that the Vice-President temporarily assume the duties and responsibilities of the Presidency. Yet, at the same time, the Vice-President was being questioned by the FBI as a potential suspect. The Speaker of the House of Representatives was quickly escorted to the White House by the Secret Service. And, the country teetered on the brink of a Constitutional crisis.

"It had to be a set-up," Clay insisted. "Howard Mason would not have knowingly handed the President a bottle of poisoned liquor the same day he was resigning his Vice-Presidency, and just days after he announced that he was challenging the incumbent President for the Republican Party nomination. It makes absolutely no sense."

"I agree," Aaron added. "Howard Mason is many things, but he is not stupid and I doubt very much that he is a murderer. Someone set him up to take the fall. There is no other reasonable explanation. Since he had tendered his letter of resignation to the President earlier in the day and it was accepted, does that mean that the Speaker of the House is now in charge of the government?"

"I don't know, I would think so. But, honestly I have no idea what the process is when a Vice-President resigns? Is it effective immediately or is it contingent on the naming of a replacement?" Clay asked.

"Who would have had the motivation to attempt to murder the President and frame the Vice-President for the crime? Who had that kind of access? This isn't like the Evangelical minister shooting attempt last year, this is an inside job. But who?" Aaron ruminated.

"Someone who has an interest in Cletus Sawyer or Jedediah Wilson becoming the Republican nominee and possibly the next President?" Clay posited.

After several moments of thought, Aaron looked at Clay with utter disbelief. "No! It couldn't be. No!" Aaron exclaimed.

ONE DAY LATER, POSY BRANCH AND MICHAEL sat a French Quarter police station. Their friend and co-worker Chiffon LaBelle had not shown up for work that day. Every effort they made to call her went unanswered. Late in the afternoon they went to her home and knocked and rang the bell without a response.

A police officer approached them with a world-weary expression on his face.

"I'm so sorry to tell you that we have some very bad news that I need to share with you. Earlier this morning, we found the body of a black pre-operative transsexual woman in the Quarter. There was no identification found on the body. All of her possessions had been removed. We ran some preliminary DNA tests and referenced dental and medical records, and I'm sorry to say that we believe it to be your missing friend, Chiffon LaBelle."

"No! It ain't her! No, it's not my Chiffon, you are wrong," Posy shouted, her entire body trembling.

"I'm so very sorry, Ms. Branch, but the description and medical records are a match," the officer softly stated.

Posy let out a blood curdling scream as she began to sob uncontrollably. Michael took her into his arms attempting to comfort his friend as tears rolled down his cheeks.

"How did she die?" Michael questioned between his own sobs and gasps for air.

"She was found this morning hung by the neck from a large poplar tree not far from the French Market. She had been severely beaten before being hung," the office said barely above a whisper.

"No! No! No!" Posy shouted and moaned. The life went out of her pretty blue eyes as she wailed until she could barely breathe. "It was Olivier Bellevue. He did this, he did this to my beautiful girl!" Posy screamed.

"He used to work with all of us. He threatened us when he left," Michael added.

"We'll look into that. I'll get some more information when you're able to help us," the officer said, while gently patting Michael on the shoulder. Posy cried relentlessly while clutching Michael until she passed out from sheer exhaustion.

"We're gonna be fine. We got to be for Chiffon," Michael whispered as he clutched his dear friend close to his chest and rocked her gently in his trembling arms.

But nothing would ever be the same. It couldn't be. Unforgivably heinous crimes, cannot stand without penalty. Some things require retribution.

The brutal winter winds moaned through the limbs of the leafless cherry trees surrounding the Tidal Basin in Washington, D.C. While the weeping willow trees that had been planted since the wholesale devastation of Hurricane Katrina in New Orleans City Park bowed and shed some leaves to February's heavy gusts.

THE END

Photo by Molly Johnson

Mr. Catalano resides in Chicago, IL. He has obtained a Bachelor of Arts and Master of Arts degrees in Political Science. He has melded his life-long fascination and love of politics with numerous years of working in the legal profession, into this love, that of writing fiction.